NEVER SAY NEVER

The Ladies Who Brunch Book One

HARLOW JAMES

Paperback ISBN: 9798410017886
Special Edition Paperback ISBN: 9798369601471

Cover Designer: Abigail Davies, Pink Elephant Designs
Editor: Jeanine Harrell, Indie Edits with Jeanine

"If you can't get someone off your mind, maybe they're supposed to be there. Remember: the mind can recognize what the heart is trying to deny."

Unknown

Contents

Prologue

Charlotte

One Month before High School Graduation

The crunch of the gravel under my sneakers echoes out into the night. Normally, I wouldn't venture out here this late, but I needed to get out of my house before I blew up like a hand grenade.

I can't listen to my mother go on and on about prom and graduation any more. I don't care about those things as much as she does, but she just can't seem to get that through her head.

Like a beacon calling me home, the sight of the lights dancing on the water draws me closer, like a breath of fresh air and a semblance of peace.

Allen, the old security guard who mans the gate at night, gives me a polite nod as I walk up to him. We have a mutual understanding— I'm allowed to come and go as I please as long as I bring him a Snickers bar each night I pay the park a visit.

"You got your payment?" he asks as I step up to his station.

"Always, Allen. You know I'd never let you down," I say as I shove my hand in my purse, locate the Snickers bar, and politely hand it over.

"Dependable as always, Charlotte." He licks his lips as he tears open the wrapper. "But just to forewarn you, you aren't alone this evening."

"No?"

"Nope. Someone else wanted to get lost tonight too."

I twist my head to look out over the small park on the edge of a lake, a historical landmark in town that closes to the public each night at eight. But since my bribery skills are up to par, Allen lets me in here whenever I want.

I love being here after hours when it's completely empty. It allows me to remember a simpler time when being a kid was all about what games you were going to play, how fast you could run, and the excitement that came when you buckled in for a ride that you knew would make your stomach flip.

Now life is about making decisions regarding my future and putting up with my mother and her incessant nagging for just a few more months until I can move out to California for college.

I can't fucking wait.

"Well, if I cross paths with this other person, listen out for my scream, will you?"

Allen chuckles. "I don't think he'll do you much harm. Have a good night." With a tip of his hat and a bite of his candy bar, Allen waves me off as I trek further into the park, the gravel ending beneath my shoes as I hit the grass and make my way for the best part of this little slice of heaven—the carousel.

Only one row of lights is on along the top as I walk near, but that's actually what I prefer. The dim lighting casts a soft glow around the ride, just enough to be able to see, but not too bright that you can't see the water in the distance or your eyes sting from the iridescence.

I open the metal gate, the hinges squeaking as I do, before walking around the carousel to locate my favorite horse, Maribel. Stepping onto the platform, I take a seat on the full sleigh bench right behind her.

"It's been a while, Maribel," I say, placing my bag next to me on the bench and then reaching for my notebook, eager to get a few journal entries in. The journal covered in sunflowers stares back at me, full of words and secrets I don't dare utter out loud.

As I flip open to a fresh page, I write down the date and get to work, sorting through my feelings and the events of the night that got me here. But I only get two sentences down before a voice startles me to my right.

"Charlotte Montgomery."

Twisting to the side, I find Damien Shaw, the boy I hate more than drivers who don't use their turn signals, leaning over the metal fence that encircles the carousel, his arms dangling over the bars as he props himself up.

"Ugh. What are you doing here?" I ask, turning my attention back to my notebook and finishing my thought that he interrupted.

"I might ask you the same question."

"Not that it's any of your business, but I actually come here quite often."

"Really? Because so do I." That catches my attention.

Looking back over at his slimy smile, piercing blue eyes, and his head covered in a backward ball cap, I glare in his direction. "Since when?"

"Since the beginning of senior year," he says, removing his hat to scratch his head only to put it back in place once he's done.

"Are you stalking me, then?" I shut my notebook.

He huffs out a laugh. "Hell no. I guess I've just been lucky enough never to cross paths with you until now. Seems my luck ran out tonight."

"Apparently mine did too. Now if you don't mind, I came out here to be alone, so…" I wave him off, but he just stands there as his face falls.

"Yeah, well, you're not the only one who wants to be alone, alright?"

As I lean back on the bench, clutching my notebook to my chest, I think about how many entries in here are centered on the boy standing in front of me—my nemesis, the one person I love beating more than anything even though just the sight of him makes my blood boil.

Have you ever had a person in your life you could classify as a frenemy? Someone you have to play nice with, tolerate, and act like you like them—but deep down, you both try to outdo the other and feel deep joy when you succeed? Well, that's Damien for me.

I'm not sure when our little competition began, but as far back as I can remember, Damien and I have competed to be the best at anything and everything in school. To make matters worse, our parents are best friends, so we have to see each other all the time.

And he always acts like we're such good friends in front of them, when in reality, the boy has perfected each and every way to get under my skin.

"What on earth could you possibly need to get away from?" I scoff, opening up my notebook once more when I realize I don't really care why he's here and the quicker we get this conversation over with, the better.

"Nothing I'm sure perfect little Charlotte Montgomery could understand. I bet you can do no wrong in your parents' eyes."

That comment has my pulse flaring. "You have no idea what my life is like, Damien." He has no clue what my mother says every day that makes me feel less than, how an A on every test or paper never feels like enough, and that constantly worrying about my physical appearance is making me consider skipping breakfast all together now.

"Ditto, Charlotte," he spits back, instantly defensive and standing up from his perch against the metal fence.

"So why don't you try to explain it to me, huh? Or is the poor little rich boy just pouting because he didn't get into UCLA like he wanted?"

Damien smirks with a cocky grin. "Seems USC knew what they'd be missing out on if they didn't take me though, huh? Bet you can't say the same," he counters, knowing that getting into USC was my dream and I was unsuccessful in securing that. On the flip side though, Damien wanted to get into UCLA and I was able to, so we both got what the other person wanted—yet another reason for this hatred between us to continue.

"God, I can't wait until we graduate and I can leave you and this crummy town behind," I grumble as my hands shake from the adrenaline running through me.

"I know it'll be hard not to want to keep tabs on me, Charlotte, but please, try to restrain yourself."

"Eat a bag of testicles, Damien."

"No need to get technical, Char. I'm familiar with the parts of the male anatomy."

"I just wanted to be clear. If I said balls, you might try to eat a football or something." I shrugged. "Who knows why on earth USC would let you in…"

"The admissions committee at UCLA must have been drunk when they read your personal statement. That's the only explanation as to why they'd let *you* in."

"God, I'm so happy I'll *never* have to see you again."

"Don't worry, Char. I'm sure I'll still haunt you in your dreams."

"Those would be nightmares, Damien."

"Well, don't worry. I'm sure you'll be able to find someone out in California to dry your tears and tuck you in at night."

"Promise me something, Damien," I say, leaning over slightly on the bench. "When we get to Los Angeles, pretend like I never existed. I don't want you to think of me, seek me out, or wonder if I'm doing better than you. Because I will—that's a fact. And the moment we leave this town, you don't exist anymore."

He rolls his eyes. "Piece of cake, Char. I'm tired of having to worry about you anyway." He tosses a candy wrapper into a trashcan nearby and begins to walk away. "Here's to never seeing you again."

"Bye, Damien!" I call out as he walks away and I turn back to my notebook on my lap. Fuming and even more desperate to count down the days until I leave, I open up my page and continue writing, vowing to the paper and myself that I would never think about Damien Shaw again.

But you know what they say…

Never say never.

Chapter 1

Charlotte

Present Day

"**P**edestrians have the right of way!"

I glare at the driver of the car that almost took me out in the crosswalk, throwing up the bird for good measure. Stone-faced and looking annoyed that he had to slam on the brakes to avoid hitting me, the driver waits until I'm just past the hood of his sports car before peeling out in the intersection and resuming his reckless driving.

"Jesus Christ. It's a Sunday. Where on earth could you be speeding off to?" I grumble to myself as my feet find the safety of the sidewalk and then I continue on my trek to Frankie's to meet my girls. Although, this is California, so everyone is always in a goddamn hurry to get places, myself usually included.

But it's a Sunday morning in Los Angeles, the scorching sun already shining brightly and beating down on my skin, and today is the one day I allow myself to rest. For the beginning of May, the heat is making its presence known, but soon the temperatures will drop again, playing tricks on the natives—teasing us with the warm weather, snatching it back, and then hitting us for real with a vengeance once summer officially starts.

I love summer though. And I love California. But boy, do you pay the price for the good weather. However, it's exactly where I wanted to be after leaving South Carolina for college on the other side of the country and deciding to stay here after graduation.

The vibration of my cell phone pulls me from my thoughts, and my mother's name flashing across the screen has me debating whether I should even answer the call.

I love my mother. I do. But most of our conversations these days consist of friendly reminders from her about my nonexistent love life. Add on updates of people from back home getting married and having kids, and what the latest trip is that her and my dad are taking, and I feel reprimanded in a backhanded way for choosing to establish myself in my career and avoid incessant dating in the pursuit of a man.

Just another reminder of how I'll never measure up to her expectations.

Growing up it was all about my social status and what I was wearing. Now it's about any man that she thinks would make a good husband. The woman even made a dating profile for me so she could sort through potential matches. I delete every one she sends me.

"Good morning, Mom," I say once I pick up the call. I know that avoiding this conversation will only mean dodging multiple attempts for her to reach me throughout the day. I'd rather get the chastising over with this morning so I can enjoy the rest of my day off without dreading our conversation.

"Charlotte, honey. How are you?" The southern twang in my mother's voice always brings a sense of comfort, even though she has the kill-them-with-kindness technique nailed down flawlessly behind her cheery drawl. The saying "you kill more flies with honey than vinegar" was invented to describe the way a southern woman can take you down a few notches with just her words alone and a tight-lipped smile.

"Great. I'm on my way to meet the girls right now for brunch."

"Oh, how are they? I must say, you four always look like you're having the best time in your pictures on Facebook," she replies sweetly. "Too bad you're all still single." *And there's the first jab.*

"What do you need this morning, Mom?" I ask, avoiding feeding into her disappointment with my relationship status as I enjoy the small reprieve of shade from the trees lining the sidewalk as I continue toward brunch.

"It's been a week since we've spoken. Forgive me for wanting to check up on my only daughter." This is also her way of reminding me that I'm the only way she'll ever have grandchildren.

My parents tried for years to have another kid after me, but were never successful. Secondary infertility—as it's called—is a real thing, something she also likes to remind me of now that I'm over the age of thirty. Each year that passes lessens my chances of having children— as if I need her friendly reminders each time we speak.

"I'm good, Mom. Busy. Work has been crazy."

Being a senior advertising editor for *Revision Magazine* is every career aspiration I could have dreamed of. I work for one of the most profitable magazines for women in the country and get final say on all advertising that goes in each issue. I make more than enough money to support myself and am damn good at my job.

But apparently that's not what my focus should be on at my age.

"Charlotte, honey…how are you ever going to find a husband if you keep working the way that you do?"

Pinching the bridge of my nose, I keep walking, grateful that

Frankie's is only one block away now so I'll have an excuse to get off the phone with her. "I don't *need* a husband, Mom."

"I know, I know. You've always been independent and headstrong. But don't you want a man to take care of you? Someone to grow old with like me and your father have? Don't you want to have children and give us grandchildren?"

"I don't need a man to take care of me, Mom. This is the twenty-first century. Women can be just as successful if not more than a man can, and I do very well for myself. And not every woman wants children." I actually do someday, but I know plenty of women who are choosing not to have kids these days and there is absolutely nothing wrong with that. Society might think differently though—and by society, I mean my mother.

"You know, if you don't find someone soon, you'll never get to celebrate a thirtieth wedding anniversary like me and your father, Charlotte. I'm just worried about you."

And there it is—the glaring reminder that my life is practically over because every day I remain single is a day I won't get to live in wedded bliss like my parents. However, if you do the math—I'm thirty and that's how many years they've been married, so can we say shotgun wedding, everyone?

"How is the planning going for that, by the way?" I ask, hoping to steer her attention away from me and this dreaded topic that gets more stifling every time I pick up her phone calls.

"Oh, so stressful. I know it will all be worth it once we get there, but coordinating everything from thousands of miles away is wearing on me. Your father is actually taking me to Napa next weekend to help take my mind off it so we can hopefully relax."

Oh, to live my parents' life and be able to take a trip to unwind from the stress of planning another trip.

"Sounds like just what you need," I reply sweetly through clenched teeth. Just as I arrive at Frankie's, my mother drops another bomb on me.

"We actually have a layover in Los Angeles, so we thought it would be the perfect time to see you, Charlotte. I miss my girl."

A sigh leaves my lips and my shoulders fall from her words. "I miss you too, Mom." Hey, I know my mother can annoy the shit out of me, and clearly doesn't understand healthy boundaries on some topics, but she's still my mom. And I can't remember the last time I saw my dad other than on Facetime.

"So, do you think you can make some time for your parents on Friday? Take off for a few hours and have lunch with us? Take us to one of those hip new restaurants in L.A. that all the celebrities go to."

I snort at her one-sided view of Los Angeles. Yes, there are a ton of famous people that live here, but more often than not, southern California is just full of normal people trying to live their lives as best they can while basking in the sunshine and drowning in debt from the cost of living here.

"I think I could make some time for you."

"Perfect. So…"

"Listen, Mom? I just got to the restaurant, and the girls are waiting for me inside. We'll talk more on Friday, okay?"

"Of course, dear. Tell the girls I said hello. I can't wait to see them next month for the renewal."

"They're looking forward to seeing you too. Love you, Mom."

"Love you, Charlotte. And make sure anytime you leave the house you have your makeup on, sweetie. You never know when you might run into *the one*."

I roll my eyes as I end the call, cursing under my breath while I open the door to Frankie's Diner, grateful that our brunch always includes bottomless mimosas. Lord knows I need a few after that conversation.

The smell of greasy food hits my nostrils as I step in and see two of my best friends waiting at our usual table. Penelope will be fashionably late as always, most likely due to whatever social event she was out at late last night.

As I walk up to the table, Noelle stands from her seat to greet me. "You look like you need a drink more than I do."

As I intercept her hug, I give her a squeeze and then lean back so she can read my face. "I just got off the phone with my mother."

"Oh, Jesus. Yup, we definitely need champagne." She puts her hand in the air to get Frankie's attention, the old man who owns the establishment and treats us like the queens we are. "Frankie! We're ready for the booze!"

"Be right there, hun!" he calls back as Noelle takes her seat again and I move around her to greet Amelia.

"Hey, babe." I kiss her on the cheek as she stands and pushes her glasses up her nose, her curly blonde hair tickling my nose as I lean in to give her a hug as well.

"Charlotte. You look stressed," she says when we part and I take a seat across from her, settling into the cushioned chair.

"When am I not stressed? Sundays are supposed to be relaxing, but my mother made sure to ruin that idea before I've even had breakfast." I reach for one of the menus behind the corral of condiments, debating if I should try something new this morning. I'm usually a creature of habit, but emotional eating is my forte, and I definitely deserve some carbs after the week I've had.

"What did she say this time?" Noelle asks just as Frankie comes by with a tray of glasses, a carafe of orange juice, and two bottles of champagne.

"Frankie, Frankie, Frankie. You are my favorite man on the planet." I reach for the champagne and take a swig right out of the bottle.

"Charlotte has had a bad morning, if you can't tell," Amelia explains as I fight the bubbles from going up my nose. Luckily, I manage to maintain my composure as I take down the liquid and set the bottle on the table.

"My sweet Charlotte," he says in his Greek accent. "How can I make your day better?" I smile up at our friend, his bald head shining under the fluorescent lights above us, his bushy eyebrows drawn together.

"Just keep the mimosas coming, Frankie." I reach for his hand, squeezing it for good measure.

"Of course. I'll come back when Penelope arrives."

We watch him take off and then Noelle starts filling our glasses with the perfect mixture of champagne and orange juice—eighty percent booze, twenty percent juice.

"Okay, so back to your mom…"

"What else would she say to put me in a mood?"

Noelle sighs and Amelia shakes her head. "Still pressuring you to find a husband, huh?"

"I swear, it's like my parents can't be proud of anything I've accomplished because I'm not married and popping out babies on top of it. Back in high school, the pressure was to be the perfect daughter —get good grades, dress the part so we looked like the perfect family, and rank in the top five of my graduating class. But now as an adult? I think I'd rather go back to those expectations than the ones she's holding me to now."

"Your dad feels this way too?" Amelia asks, taking a sip from her glass once Noelle slides one to each of us.

"Honestly, he just goes along with what my mom says. It's probably the reason they've been married this long—she gets to do whatever she wants and he just lets her."

Noelle chuckles. "Honestly, that sounds boring. I mean, ideally you think if a man lets you get away with bloody murder, you'd be happy.

But I want someone who's going to challenge me and fight back. It's no fun to be right if no one argues otherwise."

I tilt my glass toward her, clinking them together. "Amen. And that along with the fact that most men have an issue with a woman who is just as successful and powerful as they are, it's no wonder I'm still single. It's like my success is a threat to their manhood, or something."

"Good morning, bitches!" Penelope strides up to us looking way too dressed up for a Sunday morning brunch. Noelle, Amelia, and I are dressed down in sundresses or leggings and a flowy top—but Penelope strides up to us in a strapless black dress that clings tightly to her body and four-inch heels. Her hair is piled up on her head though, as if she didn't brush it and just threw it up on her way out the door.

On second thought…

"Are you doing the walk of shame?" I ask her as she takes turns kissing us all on the cheek.

"No, because there is no shame in my walk at all," she states proudly, plopping down into the seat next to me and reaching for her drink. After she drains half the glass, she sets it down and continues. "Why should any woman, or person, for that matter be ashamed for getting laid the night before?"

"They shouldn't. Please forgive me," I apologize happily.

"Can I counter that question with why you insist on calling us bitches?" Amelia interjects.

"Have you ever come across a female dog that's been threatened? Or someone who is clearly displeased? They're ruthless, defensive, and not afraid to bark and protect themselves or their young. Now, you three aren't my offspring, obviously…" She tilts her head. "But I know that if anyone threatened any of us, we'd all be there to defend one another." Her smile widens as Amelia shakes her head back at her. "So, don't take it the wrong way, Amelia Be Delia…it's truly a term of endearment for you all…" And then she smirks before ending with, "Bitches."

Noelle snorts, I chuckle, and Amelia sighs, relenting to the fact that Penelope did what she always does—shuts any naysayer down. "Why do I even bother asking anymore?"

"Because that's who you are, my friend." She reaches across the table and bops Amelia on the nose. "And don't ever change."

"So who was the lucky guy?" I ask just as I see Frankie head in our direction.

Penelope shrugs. "Just some bouncer at the club for last night's event. He checked off all of my boxes, and definitely knew how to press my buttons…the right ones that is, if you catch my drift." She bounces her eyebrows as Frankie arrives at the table.

"Penelope," he greets her. "So fancy for brunch today."

"I always try to look good for you, Frankie," she says, flashing him a wink.

"None of you ladies have to try hard to do that." See? This is why this man is the best. Too bad he's twenty-five years too old and married. "So are we having the usual today?"

"I'm gonna have the blueberry pancakes today," I reply, switching it up from my usual egg white omelet. A girl's gotta live a little and carbs do solve problems, despite what some people might tell you.

"Veggie omelet with hash browns," Noelle says.

"Oatmeal and a side of fruit." Amelia answers before placing her menu back in place behind the condiment corral.

"And for the lovely Miss Penelope?" Frankie asks, smiling down at her. It's a good thing his wife is cool as hell because I know the flirtation is harmless from Penelope, but I'm not so sure about Frankie.

"Strawberry waffle. Extra whipped cream, please." She flashes him a wink and then Frankie reciprocates before walking back behind the counter. "So what were you all talking about before I got here?"

"Charlotte's mom," Noelle replies.

"Oh, dear. What did good ol' Savannah have to say this morning?" I go to answer, but Penelope cuts me off. "Let me guess…still pushing you to find a husband?"

"It's like you know my life, or something," I mock before taking down another sip of my mimosa.

"Girl, you know I love your mom…but her harping on you about this annoys the shit out of me and makes me want to channel my inner bitch to defend you. It's 2022—women are no longer living their lives in pursuit of a husband and there is nothing fucking wrong with that."

"I completely agree, but my mother can't understand that."

"I just don't understand why this is so important? Why does a woman have to have a husband to be happy?" She glances around the table at us as we all ponder her question.

"She doesn't, but it doesn't mean we can't have one and be happy too," Noelle replies.

I glance over at Noelle, not sure where her mind is at—because if there's one of us that I know for a fact that wants that life, it's her.

Noelle, Amelia, Penelope and I all met in college at UCLA. We had a freshman English class together and have been inseparable ever since. Penelope was in a sorority, so she tagged us along to the parties and gave us the more classic college experience without the drama of actually being in the sisterhood. But no matter what life threw at us, we tackled it together. Now in our early thirties, we're all well-established in our careers and financially independent—qualities that any woman should be damn proud of. However, now it's all of society's archaic demands that we feel breathing down our necks. Well—society and our parents, in my case.

Noelle works as a literary agent for a big name publisher downtown. She gets off on finding the next big romance author, searching through hundreds of queries just to find that diamond in the rough.

And I guess after reading about fictional happily ever afters for a living, you become obsessed with finding your own.

"You don't have to have one to be happy," Noelle clarifies. "But I do know that I don't want to die alone."

"You won't. You'll have us," Penelope counters. "We're going to be those badass old ladies at the retirement center fucking shit up and running the place when the time comes."

"Sorry, Penelope, but your lack of a penis is a big problem." Noelle sighs and we all laugh. "And *wanting* a husband and *needing* a husband to be happy are two very different things, so I do see your point. Choosing to have a man in my life is different from just having one because someone tells me that's what I'm supposed to do."

"Exactly," I chime in, pointing a finger at Penelope. "It's not that I don't want to get married one day, but I'm not going to settle on the first guy I cross paths with just so I'm not alone anymore."

"And you don't need a man to experience sexual pleasure," Amelia adds, the quiet one of our group but definitely not the least outspoken. "Most women can get themselves off better than their partner can. Believe me…"

Penelope grins from ear to ear. "I always love when you remind us that you sell dildos for a living, my little Amelia Be Delia. So please, elaborate further…"

Amelia rolls her eyes as she takes a drink of her mimosa.

Amelia practices as a sexual therapist, helping couples with their physical and emotional relationships, and has developed a line of prod-ucts they can purchase to aid them along their journey, as well as helping single women be more confident sexually, particularly after experiencing trauma. Thus, she obviously sells toys, but she's used her sexual psychology degree and minor in business quite well since we graduated. However, it always still shocks us how she makes her living given how well we know her and how she can be perceived as the shy, quiet type.

Although, you know what they say—it's always the quiet ones that are freaks in the sheets.

"I don't just sell dildos, Penelope," Amelia chastises just as Frankie arrives with our food. Her cheeks light up like Rudolph's nose while Penelope laughs at her reaction. "I help people achieve the best sex of their lives."

"Anything else I can get for you lovely ladies?"

My eyes scour the table. "Maybe another bottle of champagne?"

"You got it." He walks away as we all get ready to devour our food.

"I know, Amelia. I just like giving you shit. But this reminds me, I think my Rabbit died, so I'm going to need a replacement soon."

Amelia takes a bite of her oatmeal and replies without even looking up from her bowl. "I'll send you an invoice."

Then Penelope turns back to me. "Well, just know that if your mother says something to me while we're in Hawaii next month, I'm not holding my tongue," she says around a mouthful of her waffle. "Lord knows I have to watch what I say around enough people working in PR that I'm bound to slip up at one point and she may just be the not so innocent victim."

My parents decided to do an anniversary/vow renewal in Hawaii next month and invited anyone who wanted to come, which included my three best friends. No way were they going to pass up the opportunity for a vacation, and to offer me the support to deal with my mother reminding me over and over that I'm still single.

I will be there for almost an entire week though as there are multiple events with family and friends of the family leading up to the ceremony, so the girls will be flying out after me.

My parents come from old money, which basically means they're royalty down in the south. Think of my childhood as countless country club outings, debutante balls, and pressure to live up to the Montgomery name.

And lord knows I played into that role far too well. Of course, beating out one person in particular from our circle in certain circumstances helped fuel that fire for me.

"She means well. I get that she just wants me to be happy, but her definition of happy and mine are completely different. She and my dad will be in L.A. on Friday for a layover on their way to Napa, by the way. That was her reason for calling me. They want to visit, so I'll be subjected to her ridicule in person for a change…always something I look forward to." Rolling my eyes, I slide another bite of my blueberry pancakes in my mouth, knowing I made the right decision with this sugar-laden breakfast this morning. "She'll probably criticize my hair color and my clothes on top of that since we'll be face to face. You know how my L.A. style is so outlandish for a southern girl."

"Oh, we haven't been to Napa yet on a girls' trip," Noelle acknowledges, bypassing my complaints completely. "I think we definitely need to make that happen."

"You had me at Merlot," Penelope jokes, which makes us all laugh around our food.

We finish up brunch while catching up on our weeks. Sunday brunch is a meeting we keep with one another as much as possible. My girls are my family out here, the people I know will always have my back and that I can count on the most.

Every woman needs a group of women to surround herself with that make her feel confident enough to be exactly who she is. I found my tribe at eighteen, and now we're all stuck together until one of us kicks the bucket. Penelope jokes that she already has our cemetery plots picked out and paid for, but at this point, I wouldn't put it past her.

I left brunch yesterday feeling lighter and confident again in where I'm at in my life, but then Monday morning rolled around and my job had my head pounding before noon. My boss, the editor-in-chief, came in and told me that the board wants all of the advertising for the year fulfilled before the end of June, meaning we have to be prepared for six months from now, which in the publishing world can be a difficult task when trends and hot topics change daily, especially now thanks to social media.

But I told her we'd get it done and I instantly called for an emergency meeting with my team. After a brainstorming session, I sent everyone out with their list of contacts and got to work on my own set of duties. Lunch time rolled around and my grumbling stomach couldn't be ignored any longer, so I decided to go down the block to a local sandwich and salad shop to get some fresh air before a long afternoon ahead.

"Hi, what can we get for you today?" The college-aged kid behind the counter greets me as I stare up at the menu, flashbacks of working a similar job infiltrating my mind as he waits for my decision.

"I'll have the Greek salad today, no onion please, extra feta cheese, and with grilled chicken." Put feta cheese on anything and I'll eat it. Put extra, and I'll love you forever.

He enters my order, I pay, and then take my stand with the number on top and find a spot outside so I can enjoy the warm weather while I wait for my food. Large tan umbrellas shade me from the sun, but I slip my heels off and peek my toes out from under the shadow above me to help warm up my feet.

As I wait for my food, I check my emails on my phone, replying to a handful I had to ignore while in my meeting this morning. But a figure inside the shop catches my attention as I slide my eyes in that direction.

And then my stomach drops.

Damien Shaw.

My childhood nemesis and the one person I swore I would never see again once I left for college is standing just inside the same place I just vacated.

Funny how reminders of a life in South Carolina can follow you to southern California and reappear when you least expect them.

I sink down slightly in my chair, blanketing my hair across my face, attempting to conceal myself as I take this opportunity to scope out my previous competition in, well, everything.

You see, Damien and I weren't friends. And we weren't enemies. We were *rivals*, hell bent on outdoing the other in any and all aspects while growing up. Best score on a math test? That was a competition. Best performance in the school play? I beat him on that one almost every time. Captain of the sports team? He clenched football while I soared in soccer.

And the thing that irritated me more than anything is that he would act like we were best friends in front of our families, so everyone thought he was just the sweetest young man on the planet.

But I knew better. I knew the real Damien Shaw. And he was a dick.

Still looks like one too, although I will say he has definitely grown up and learned how to fill out a suit in the time since I last saw him.

Twelve years? Has it really been twelve years since high school graduation when I vowed to never be near him again unless I absolutely had to?

As our last interaction plays back in my mind, my current situation forces me back to reality just as one of the employees comes by with my salad.

"Thank you." I make quick work of pouring the dressing over the top and stirring the contents while continuing to sneak a peek at Damien, who's still standing in line inside, talking to another man in a suit that I have no clue the identity of, but their conversation seems intense.

Damien was always tall, but like I said before, he's filled out, packing on probably thirty pounds of muscle compared to when I saw him last. His dark brown hair is freshly cut, short on the sides and slightly longer on top, messily styled so he looks just professional enough but also casual and put together. And he has a short, trimmed beard–a new addition that he never sported back then but is unfortunately working well for him.

He's wearing a dark gray suit that looks tailored to his body, or it's just a really good designer label—hard to tell from where I'm sitting. Standing with his hands in his pockets, the sides of his coat are pushed out just enough to tell that he didn't gain a beer belly in college and instead has a slim waist that the belt on his slacks hangs just perfectly on.

Damn. I would have loved nothing more than to see that he let himself go a little.

On the contrary, it seems to me that Damien takes very good care of himself, even more apparent as he turns toward the counter and I get a glance at his backside, his trousers stretched tight across his ass and thighs.

My God. Did Damien always have an ass you could bounce a quarter off? Or is that new too?

Charlotte…are you salivating after Damien Shaw's ass right now?

Ugh…what is wrong with me? Although seriously…look at it!

I shake off the thought and start to inhale my salad, realizing now that he may see me depending on where he and his friend decide to sit. I don't want him to see me. I don't want to even fathom what our first encounter in twelve years would be like, especially while I'm sitting all alone eating my lunch, a detail I'm sure he'd be happy to point out.

Deciding that it's better to leave before he spots me, I snap the lid back on my salad, grab my iced tea, and quickly clean up my table, depositing my trash in the nearby trashcan before exiting the courtyard through the side gate.

As I walk back to my office with my food and drink in tow, reeling from that blast from my past, another detail hits me that I didn't even think about until I saw him today; Damien's parents are friends with mine, and will most likely be at their vow renewal next month, which could only mean one thing—Damien will probably be there too.

Chapter 2

Damien

Knock, knock. "You busy?" I lift my eyes from my computer to see Jeffrey, my right-hand man here at work, leaning halfway into my office.

"Not really. What's up?" Closing down my browser, I lean back in my chair and clasp my hands over my chest.

"Word around the office is that Dave has some big news to deliver at the meeting today, something about a high-profile client that he wants to land more than anything."

That has my ears perking up. "Is that so?"

"And you know who he's going to be banking on to nab it?"

"Us, my man. It has to be us."

"Damn straight." Jeffrey stands tall again, buttoning up his jacket. "I can smell that promotion, Damien. We're so fucking close."

"Don't I know it, bro. Don't I know it." Standing from my desk, I follow suit and button up my coat, eager to get a seat in the conference room before all the good spots fill up.

This little bit of information just turned my fucking morning around after that phone call with my mother. Nothing like the sweet reminders of my former life in South Carolina and impending events to attend to put me in a bad mood. Migraines should have names like hurricanes in my opinion, so you know who to give credit to for bringing them on.

But then Jeffrey—sweet, brother-from-another-mother, Jeffrey— just turned my fucking day around with this exciting development in the office.

Striding into the conference room, I notice there are only a few associates filling the seats, so Jeffrey and I grab our spots near the front of the table and wait for the rest of our colleagues to join in. By the time Dave walks in the door, the room is filled with anticipation.

"Good morning," he says, greeting us as he stands at the head of the table, his hands tucked into the pockets of his beige slacks. Dave has been here since he graduated from college and has worked his way up to a senior account director, which is where I want to be. Goldstein Advertising has grown exponentially in the five years since I've started working here, and they're looking for new account directors to expand the business even further and open up new departments.

And I want one of those positions, with Jeffrey by my side as my account manager.

"Good morning." We all reciprocate the greeting.

"I'm sure you're all wondering why I've called this meeting today when it wasn't on the calendar. But it's a good reason we've all gath- ered here today. A very good reason."

Rubbing my hands together under the table, I wait for him to drop the carrot that's metaphorically dangling in front of my mouth right now.

"We have quite the opportunity presented to us today, landing an account with an up and coming product line that is promising big changes in consumer habits."

Is it a sports drink? Car manufacturer? Toilet paper company? You know how crazy people can get about toilet paper.

He takes a deep breath and then delivers the news. "Remedy, a women's health line centered around menstrual health and products, is looking for their next advertisement campaign, and we want to be the people they choose to help them in this next wave of business."

Insert screeching brake sounds

Say what? A women's health line? Menstrual health? You mean —periods?

Several sets of eyes scour the room, but all of the women in the chairs sit up taller in their seats while Jeffrey and I look at each other like someone just told us that Tom Brady was *actually* going to retire.

"This is a huge opportunity. Companies like this that offer the entire scope of women's needs have so much growth potential in the market, and that is why we want to secure this account. I already have a team in mind that I think can bring us success on this front." And even though I know this is nowhere near my forte, I'm still shocked when my name doesn't fall off Dave's lips. "Elizabeth, Kerissa, and Ashley, I know you three can come up with something stunning to present to the client next month. We have plenty of time to develop the best idea going forward, and I'm expecting magic, people."

I feel my brow furrow, still confused as fuck over what just happened as Dave says a few more things unrelated to the announcement he just dropped on us, and then the meeting is adjourned. But Jeffrey and I don't even bother moving from our seats, staring off into the empty room once everyone has left until he finally breaks through the silence.

"Well, there goes our shot at a promotion." He slowly stands from his chair, exhaling heavily.

"What do you mean?"

"What do you mean, what do I mean?" Throwing his hands up in the air, he studies me as if I've grown two heads. "I mean, Dave already gave the account to the girls, so what are we gonna do?"

I stand from my chair, renewed purpose beginning to flood through my veins. I don't know the first thing about periods or women's health, but damn it—I'm good at my job and I deserve this promotion. And so does Jeffrey. "We're gonna go into his office and ask for a chance to make a pitch as well."

Jeffrey scoffs, laughing under his breath until he realizes I'm serious. "Are you fucking joking right now?"

"Does it look like I'm joking?"

"No, and that's what's scaring me."

"Jeffrey, you and I deserve this. We've worked our asses off and have nabbed high-profile clients that Dave was never able to secure himself."

"But we're talking about periods, Damien. Blood and hormones and…" He trails off and shudders at the thought.

"I know. It's not ideal, but maybe this is also our chance to prove that we can sell anything, man. And I do happen to know a thing or two about women."

Jeffrey scoffs. "Making a woman come and dealing with her period are two very different things, my friend."

"Then we're just gonna have to do some research and learn. Hell, it took me a while to figure out just how well to push a woman's buttons, if you know what I mean," I say with a proud smirk. "But once I realized every woman is different, it became a challenge to see how quickly I could solve the puzzle. This is our chance to solve the most challenging puzzle yet." I slap him on the shoulder before I turn for the door with the intent to walk straight into Dave's office and fight for our chance at winning this account, not wanting to waste another second.

Jeffrey scurries after me, catching up to me in the hallway. "Where are you going?"

"Dave's office."

"Now? You don't want time to prepare?"

I shake my head. "Nope. I want him to know we're serious at this very moment. Go in guns blazing, show him our dedication to winning this account for him before he stands firm in his decision to give it to the girls."

Jeffrey blows out a breath. "I hope you know what you're doing."

"Not at all. But that's part of the fun." I shoot him a wink just as we arrive outside of Dave's office. I knock on the door that is ajar, waiting for him to acknowledge us.

"Come in."

As I push open the door, Dave comes into view, standing behind his desk, staring down at papers strewn all over the surface. But when he looks up, his brow rises with surprise. "Damien. Jeffrey. How can I help you, gentleman?"

"Do you have a moment to speak with us?"

"Yes, of course. Anything for two of my top guys." He takes a seat behind his desk, but then glances at his watch. "However, I do have another meeting in ten minutes that I need to get to."

"No problem. This won't take long." Jeffrey follows me deeper into Dave's office, shutting the door behind us. "Dave...we'd like a chance to win the Remedy account for you."

Dave's brows rise even further. "Really?"

"Yes." I stand tall, clasping my hands in front of me.

Dave gives us a quizzical look before sighing out loud. "Look, Damien. You and Jeffrey are good. Hell, you're two of my top Junior

Ad Executives. You guys can sell a sports drink or car to just about anyone. But this Remedy account…it's different."

"We know."

"A woman is just better programmed to sell a product to another woman, especially pertaining to a situation that a man has no experience with." He shrugs. "I'm sorry."

"I hear you, Dave…but…"

"Besides, the female psyche isn't something I reckon you have that much experience with, is it, boys?"

"What do you mean?" I ask, wondering where he's going with this line of thinking.

Dave grins as he clasps his hands together behind his head. "I was like you two once upon a time—young, unattached, enjoying women for one night only, and then moving on without a second thought. But now I'm married, and it's different. Being with the same woman changes you."

"So you think we can't sell this to women because we don't have girlfriends? Or wives?"

"I mean, that's part of it. Being in a relationship means knowing more about a woman than you've ever learned before. Believe me, after watching my wife deal with her period, I have a totally different perception of her life as a woman. And not just that, but the preconceived notions she battles every day, the stereotypes and unrealistic expectations put on her to do everything and be everything, the way she questions her identity all of the time. It makes me glad I have a penis, you know?"

"I'm very grateful for my dick," Jeffrey chimes in, and I fight like hell not to roll my eyes at him.

Being a woman can't be that bad. And selling products to women? Hell, if it's something they obviously need to live their lives, how hard can it be? Throw some pink packaging on it, make it sparkle with some glitter, and they'll be flying off the shelves.

You don't need to know a woman's mind to be able to sell her something. But if Dave thinks I do, then perhaps he needs to think I agree with his way of thinking.

I don't like to lose, and I sure as hell know that we can win this account if we're just given the chance. And this is my chance to finally stick it to my dad, show him that I am working my way to the top where he thinks I should be, but in a career I chose.

Dear God, please don't smite me for what I'm about to say. "Well, I guess it's a good thing that I'm actually dating someone now."

Jeffrey coughs as if he's choking on his spit, but I stand there, keeping my eyes fixated on Dave so he doesn't think I'm bluffing. I can feel the sweat running down my spine as I await Dave's reaction. My poker face is pretty decent, but this is not the type of lie I'm used to telling.

"Really? You're dating someone?"

"It's new." *Yeah, brand fucking new, as in I didn't even know about this fictional relationship until just right now.*

"Well, when did this happen?"

"About a month ago. It's someone I knew from back home. We reconnected and realized there were unresolved feelings there." *Just keep digging your hole, Damien.* "And I totally understand what you mean about knowing more about a woman once she's a part of your everyday life. It has changed my view on a lot." Jeffrey pokes me in the shoulder, trying to gain my attention, but I swat him away, continuing to focus on Dave.

Dave's smile is infectious as he stands from his chair and walks around his desk toward us. "Well, this does change things. I didn't realize you were in a relationship, Damien."

"Yeah. It's getting pretty serious too." *Stop talking, Damien. Stop fucking talking.*

"I'd love to meet her. And maybe she can give you some insight that might help you come up with a campaign." He continues to smile at us both while my heart fights to break out of the straight jacket it's trapped in inside of my chest.

"I know she can. So does this mean you'll give us a shot at the account?"

With a narrowed gaze but his lips still smiling, he nods his head. "Yeah, what the hell. Let's see what you two are made of."

I reach out to shake his hand, fighting the urge to jump up and down for joy. "You won't regret this, Dave."

"I hope not. Make us look good, gentleman."

"Shall we tell the girls they have competition, or will you?" I'd love nothing more than to burst their bubbles, but I also know we have our work cut out for us, so there's not much time to gloat.

"I'll let them know. They won't be happy, but I think having more than one idea to choose from could actually be a good thing. And hell, we could always merge the two ideas if they both show merit." He nods, agreeing with himself. "Yes, this is a good idea. Thanks for coming to talk to me, boys."

"Thank you for the opportunity, Dave. We won't let you down." I spin on my heels, pulling a perplexed Jeffrey behind me, exiting Dave's office and power walking down the hallway until we're both secured behind my office door and I let out the breath I was holding. "Fucking hell."

"Damien! What the fuck?" Jeffrey whisper-shouts as I start pacing the room. "What the hell were you thinking?"

"I was thinking that it's bullshit that our relationship status determined whether we got a shot at this account or not," I bark out.

"But you lied and said you're dating someone. What the hell is Dave gonna do when he finds out this woman doesn't exist?"

"He's not going to because you're not going to tell him…"

A knock on my door interrupts our conversation. Jeffrey's closer, so he opens the barricade, revealing Dave standing on the other side of the door.

"What's up, Dave? Did you need something?"

"Actually, I came to invite you to the executive dinner next weekend, Damien. It's usually a bunch of directors, the members of the board, and their wives or girlfriends. Couples only. And since now I know you're seeing someone, I'd love for you to tag along."

My heart is pounding. "Dinner?"

"Yeah. It's always a good time. And it would be a great networking opportunity for you…give you a glimpse at what could be a possibility in your future." He winks.

Clearing my throat as sweat drips down my butt crack, I flash him the biggest smile I can muster. "We'll be there. Thanks for the invite."

"My pleasure. Now get to work, boys." With a mock salute, he exits my office, and Jeffrey closes my door once again.

"I'm fucked." Pulling on my hair, I begin pacing again.

"Yeah, you are. What the fuck were you thinking, Damien?"

"I don't know, okay?" I say, throwing my hands up in the air, but then irritation sets in. "I just think it's bullshit that we weren't given the same opportunity because we don't have vaginas."

"Kind of like reverse sexual discrimination?" he asks.

"I guess." I shrug, and then reach for my bottle of water on my desk, unscrewing the top and draining what's left inside.

"Well, what are you going to do? Now you have to find a woman to play your girlfriend, and bring her to this dinner."

"I know, I know." Glancing at the time, my stomach growls just as the thought of lunch enters my mind. "I can't think on an empty stomach, though. Let's get some food and then I'll figure out what the hell we're going to do."

"We? This was your idea, moron. Why am I involved?"

Stalking across the room, I get close to his face, his eyes widening as I prepare my pep talk. "Because this is your promotion too. We fucking deserve this, Jeffrey. And I hate to lose. Losing is not an option."

"You didn't say a name, right?" Jeffrey asks as we stand in line at The Chop Shop, a custom salad and sandwich bar down the street from our office. They have a meatball sandwich that would even make Joey from *Friends* cry. It's what I order every time.

"No, I made sure of that." At least part of my brain was thinking when I started babbling about my make-believe girlfriend.

"That's good." He blows out a breath. "So, where are you gonna find a girl?"

"Woman. I need a fucking *woman*. Someone that Dave would believe would date me, and is smart enough to play along with this charade and not make me look like a dimwit." I'm not trying to toot my own horn, but I take pride in pulling in attractive women consistently. There's a certain look I go for, and Dave has been out with us on one too many occasions to know that I have a type—shorter than me, but long legs that look great in heels, dark hair, and an ass—the woman has to have an ass.

"What if you call up a woman you've already been with? Ask her to do you a favor?"

"That would require me knowing their phone numbers, and that's information I avoid at all costs." Yeah, I'm not the monogamous type. Shoot me, but at least I'm honest about it. The women I choose to spend a night with are told way ahead of time what the terms and conditions are of our interactions.

And my policy has worked swimmingly up until now.

I wish I had an ex-girlfriend I could call upon for a favor, someone that still liked me enough after the relationship was over to agree to some shenanigans like what I've gotten myself into. Sadly, the longest relationship I've ever had was my long-standing competition against Charlotte Montgomery, my childhood nemesis, and royal pain in my ass.

Speaking of asses, the woman walking outside to the courtyard right now has an impeccable one.

Jeffrey snaps my fingers in front of my face. "Dude. Focus."

"I'm trying." I shake him off, glancing back to the menu, settling on the meatball sub that will bring me copious amounts of joy right now after this horrid day so far. "Do I put out an ad?"

"For a fake girlfriend? Do people do that?"

I shrug. "Fuck if I know. Tinder?"

"That's only going to get you laid," he admonishes. And I know it would help me relax right now, but that's not going to solve my problem. "Match.com?"

"I'm not looking to get married, fucker. I'm looking for someone to pretend to be my girlfriend for like, a month…maybe two, tops. Just long enough to appease Dave, win this account, and prove that we can sell anything. I don't want to lead someone on. No, whoever I find to agree to this has to know exactly what the stakes are—pretend to be head-over-heels for me in front of my boss, and perhaps tell me a little about her period to help us with this pitch."

Jeffrey shudders. "Please, no period talk before we eat."

I chuckle. "Agreed."

We place our orders and as I turn around, déjà vu punches me in the gut.

Charlotte Montgomery? Is that really her?

I squint in her direction, watching her shovel salad in her mouth like if she doesn't eat it fast enough, it will disappear. I wonder for just a moment if my eyes are playing tricks on me since I can only make out the side of her face, but the upturn of her nose is what caught my attention.

I always thought that little characteristic of hers gave her character that other girls lacked.

When she brushes her hair from her face, exposing her neck and causing her to turn her head, I confirm what my gut already knew.

Charlotte Montgomery is here, just a few feet away from me, and I can't help but laugh at the irony of her appearance given the subject of the phone call with my mother this morning.

You see, there is nothing like the mention of this particular brunette to instantly put me in a sour mood, especially when I've spent the last twelve years pretending like the woman never existed. When we both left for college, I felt like I could breathe knowing I no longer would feel compelled to compete against her in everything, even though I knew she would also be in southern California for school. But Los Angeles is a huge city, home to almost four million people. I knew the chances of us running into each other were slim to none, so I didn't think otherwise once we said our goodbyes after high school and started our own lives.

The truth is, our rivalry has roots that I'm not proud of. But damn, did I love making metaphorical steam come out of her ears. I loved watching her clench her teeth together when I beat her at anything, and the girl had sarcasm nailed down to a science at a very young age.

Fighting with her was my favorite source of entertainment growing up, which reminds me just how long it's been since I've seen her—and the fact that I'll be seeing her sooner than either of us would have hoped.

Pretending like Charlotte never existed has been a soothing balm to my soul. But seeing her right now only serves to remind me that she does exist, and so do her parents, who just so happen to be best friends with my parents. So when Mr. and Mrs. Montgomery decided to celebrate their thirtieth wedding anniversary in Hawaii with their closest friends and family, guess who were the number one guests on the list? And guess who was second?

If you aren't saying me right now, you're not fucking paying attention.

The idea of seeing Charlotte again after all this time had my chest tight and tension building in my neck since I got off the phone with my mother this morning. And now with her directly in front of me, a new wave of nausea has spiked, but then a light bulb clicks on.

"What are you staring at?" Jeffrey slides directly in front of me, blocking my view of Charlotte sitting outside.

"Nothing. But I think I have an idea."

His entire face perks up and then spins his head on his neck, surveying the customers around us. "Really? What? Who?"

"Let me make sure that she's even an option before I get your hopes up. But if she's up to it, then I'll definitely keep you in the loop."

He huffs out his displeasure like a toddler. "I don't see why you can't tell me."

"Because convincing her to go along with this will be more difficult than shaving my balls."

Jeffrey winces. "Damn. Doesn't it fucking hurt when you nick one just right?" He hisses, and then cups his junk.

"It makes me wonder if having a vagina might be easier."

And then he laughs. "Fuck no. I'll cut my balls every day rather than deal with that."

"Same, dude. Same."

By the time our food is ready and I turn back around to see if Charlotte is still there, her table is empty. Jeffrey and I push through the door that leads to the courtyard where she was just sitting, and I search the area, but it's as if she evaporated into thin air. And it makes me wonder if I was truly just seeing things, that my mind conjured her up since the mention of her name earlier today.

But once I turn my head to the right, I catch her striding down the sidewalk, elongated legs in sexy as fuck heels, her dark brown hair cascading down her back in loose curls, a white satin top and black pencil skirt hugging her body, and an ass that any man would appreciate.

Fuck me. Charlotte Montgomery has an ass, and that should have been my first warning that what I was about to do was not a good idea.

With desperation looming over me like a black cloud after yesterday, I relent to the fact my options are slim given the predicament I dug myself into. When I got home last night, I did a little social media stalking and discovered quite a bit of information about Charlotte and what she's been up to in the last twelve years, hoping it would help set the stage for my idiotic plan.

Senior Advertising Editor at *Revision Magazine*. UCLA graduate with her BA in Advertising and her MA in Business. Four girlfriends that seem to be in almost every picture she posts to social media, which isn't a ton. Maybe one or two a month, or at least that's what I can see publicly on her profile. We're not friends, so who knows what she posts on a daily basis. Dear God, I hope she's not one of the women that posts a shit-ton of selfies, or pictures of every meal she eats.

I might just have to find someone else if that's the case.

Unfortunately, Charlotte is one of my only options, and I wouldn't have even considered her in the first place if I hadn't seen her yesterday. It was as if hearing her name conjured up her presence, but perhaps it was a little kismet timing as well. I did tell Dave that my girlfriend was someone I reconnected with from my past, so there's no better person to fit that bill than Charlotte.

As I sit at my desk, stewing over my plan to put this scheme in motion, my mother calls me.

"Hey, Mom."

"Damien. How are you, Son? Gosh, I miss you."

"I miss you too, Mom." Spinning around in my chair, I turn so I can stare at the buildings through the small window in my office, envisioning my mother sitting on the couch with a cup of tea in her hand. "Did you finish that book I sent you?"

"I did. And now I'm ready for my next one."

Her enthusiasm makes me smile. "I'll get one to your house in just a few days."

When I moved out to California for college, my mother and I made a pact to send each other books back and forth. I've always been an avid reader, a love that my mom instilled in me from a young age. I got into thrillers and historical biographies as I got older, so my mother suggested that I recommend a book to her that I thought she'd love. So once I did, she returned the favor, and we've been doing this back and forth since then.

"So how's work? Anything exciting coming up?"

I cleared my throat. "Actually, I'm going to be working on a pitch for a very high profile client in the next month or so."

"Really? What's the product?"

"Uh, it's for Remedy," I say, slightly nervous for her reaction.

"Wait…the feminine products company?"

"That's the one."

"Oh, honey! That's amazing. Congrats! Who would have thought that my son would be selling tampons one day?" She laughs and I can't help but reciprocate.

"Thanks. I know it's not my norm, but I wanted the challenge, and it might help me get that promotion I've been after."

"Well, that will certainly be music to your father's ears," she says, and a spike of irritation runs through me.

"It's none of his business," I counter, far more surly than I mean to be with my mother.

"Damien…"

"No. Please don't involve Dad in my business, okay? Besides, who knows if my campaign will win, so there's no need to get him riled up for nothing."

She sighs. "I just wish you two could see eye to eye…"

"It's just better this way, Mom." I spin back around to face my computer, eager to get off the phone now. As soon as my father is brought up, my body goes into fight response. Old habits die hard. "But look, I've got a meeting in a few minutes, so I should probably be going."

"Oh. No worries. I understand. I am so proud of you though, sweetie. I know you'll do great."

"That means a lot, Mom."

"And I'm so glad I get to see you next month for the Montgomery's anniversary party."

That twinge of concern builds up again for that encounter, but I push it right back down. "I'm glad I get to see you too."

"Talk to you later this week?"

"Absolutely. Love you, Mom."

"Love you too, Damien," she replies, and then the line goes dead.

I heave out a sigh of relief, and then shake off the conversation with her. Anytime she brings up my dad, it raises my blood pressure.

But I have far more important things to worry about at this moment—like getting Charlotte to agree to be my fake girlfriend.

With the intent of reconnecting first before asking her for a favor, I decide to take a long lunch today to head to her office. I have no idea if she'll be available, but perhaps I can at least secure an appointment with her for later this week if she blows me off. I might have to bribe her secretary to keep my name off her schedule so I can keep the element of surprise, but we'll cross that bridge if we get to it.

Revision Magazine's main office is three blocks away from Goldstein Advertising, where I work. Go figure. The woman has been within a one-mile radius of me for years, I never knew, and we never managed to cross paths. See? Los Angeles is plenty big for the two of us.

But now I need Charlotte in my space. At least for the next two months. I just hope to God she doesn't try to kill me the second we lay eyes on each other.

Straightening my jacket and taking a deep breath of courage, I open the doors to her building and head straight for the elevators, looking up the location of her office on the directory framed on the wall of the elevator car I'm in. I hit the button for the twentieth floor, and then wait anxiously to arrive at my destination.

When the elevator dings, I step off and am instantly assaulted by shades of white and pink everywhere. It looks like the inside of a Victoria's Secret, minus the lingerie and headless models, which in my opinion are the best part.

The reception desk at the front with a glass wall behind it, displaying the name of the magazine blocks my entrance to any of the halls, so I straighten my tie, make sure my hair is in place, and get ready to charm my way back to my target.

"Good afternoon. Welcome to *Revision*. How can I help you?" The receptionist behind the counter greets me.

"Hi there." *Smirk, wink, and smirk again.* "I'm here to surprise an old friend."

"Oh, that's wonderful." The cheery blonde jostles her mouse to wake up the computer in front of her. "And who might that be?"

"Charlotte Montgomery."

The blonde winces. "I'm sorry, but Miss Montgomery is a very busy lady and her schedule is quite full. I can speak with her secretary and see if we can make you an appointment?"

Now it's time to turn on the charm.

I lean forward, bracing my forearms on the counter, getting as close to the woman as possible so she can sense my sincerity, but not too close that she thinks I'm actually interested in her. "I'm sure you can do me this tiny favor, right? I mean, I haven't seen Charlotte since we were kids. When I found out she works just a few blocks away from me, I had to come by and say hello. It's not every day that two people who grew up together on the opposite side of the country end up working only three blocks away from each other, am I right?"

"Oh my gosh. That's incredible," she squeals.

"Exactly. And I know she's going to be just as excited to see me as I am to see her." *I hope she doesn't have any sharp objects in her office though, on second thought.*

Shaking her head, she relents. "Okay. I can't let this reunion pass you two by. Go on ahead. Her office is down the hallway on your right, last door on the left."

"You're a peach." Another wink, and then I stand up again and straighten my suit out. "Thank you, Emily," I say as I glance at her name plate on the counter by the computer.

"Of course. I hope you two reminisce for hours."

"Oh, I'm sure we'll have plenty to discuss."

With a pep in my step and satisfaction running through me, I head in the direction Emily told me to go, anxious to get this initial meeting over with. As I turn down the hallway, I catch glimpses of several offices, all with frosted glass windows so the outlines of people are visible, but no details can be determined.

The door to Charlotte's office is open, so I step inside to see a large room, complete with a small kitchenette to my right, a few couches around a coffee table to my left, and a desk in the center of the room, with a closed door behind it.

As I walk up to the desk, I realize this is where her secretary sits, since the name plate in front of me obviously doesn't show hers. Grateful for one less person to have to go through to get to the girl, I step around the desk and head for the frosted glass door that closes off Charlotte's office from this room.

Blowing out a nervous breath, I raise my hand and knock on the door, awaiting an acknowledgment from the other side.

"Come in," a voice calls back, a voice that just hearing again has my veins pumping blood through my body at a faster rate.

I twist the knob and push open the door, fully expecting to see Charlotte sitting behind her desk like a queen on her throne, ready to smite any peasants that step foot in front of her. But that's not what I see at all.

The chair behind her desk is empty, but I know she's in here. I heard her voice.

And that's when my eyes veer to the left to find Charlotte face down on a massage table, with a sheet covering her lower half, and nothing else.

Jesus fucking Christ.

Seriously?

"Running late today?" she asks, pulling me from the panic attack I'm having as my feet remain frozen in place.

What should I say? She clearly thinks I'm the massage therapist here for her massage.

"Let's get going, please. I have a meeting in an hour and don't want to be late." She snaps her fingers in the air, but keeps her head down in the hole for her face.

Not sure what to do without giving myself away, I decide to deepen my voice at a poor attempt at disguise and just go along with this charade, slowly closing the door behind me. "Uh, yeah. Sorry about that. I had trouble finding the place."

"Wait? You're not Sonya," she says, lifting her head up slightly, preparing to come face to face with me. But I don't want her to see me. Not like this.

Then what the fuck are you going to do, Damien?

I guess I'm giving her a massage, subconscious.

Practically running across the room, I press my hand to the back of her head, holding her in place.

"What the…"

"Just relax. Don't move. This is *your* time. Seeing me will ruin the illusion of the ambiance." *What am I even saying?*

She sighs. "Okay, I guess you're right. I really need this. Let's get going, shall we?"

"Absolutely."

I've never given a massage in my life, but how hard can it be?

I look to my side and notice a table with oils and lotions on top, and a few hot towels in a warmer. Damn, it must be nice to have these types of perks at your job. Perhaps I need to talk to Dave about in-office massages for all of the employees. Maybe after I earn this promotion.

"Is it okay for me to use these oils?"

"That's what they're there for. I always supply the products I like so Sonya doesn't have to take the price of them out of her commission."

"Well, that's thoughtful of you." Huh. Didn't expect something like that from Charlotte given she's receiving a massage in the middle of the day at her place of employment. If that doesn't scream high maintenance, I don't know what does.

"Sonya is a godsend when it comes to my sciatic pain, and the lower back issues I've been having. So I hope you're up for the challenge."

"I'm always up for a challenge," I reply, forgetting to mask my voice for a moment since that competitive edge I always get around her slams right back into me, just like old times.

"Are you going to start?" she asks, slightly annoyed, yet reminding me of what I have to follow through now that I committed to this.

"Oh. Yes, of course." I reach for the oil, but then think twice about removing my jacket and rolling up my sleeves before I begin. The last thing I need is to go back to the office covered in oil stains that probably won't come out of this suit. At least I'll smell good though.

After I shuck my jacket and roll up my sleeves of my white button-down to my elbows, I squirt some oil in my hands, lather them up, and gently press my palms to Charlotte's back, trying to recall every feeling and memory of getting a massage I've ever had in my life— which hasn't been that many, unfortunately.

"Here." She lifts up slightly, moving her long hair to the side, exposing her neck. And as she does and I get even more of a glimpse of her silky skin, it finally hits me—*I'm fucking massaging Charlotte Montgomery.*

Hell *has* to have frozen over for this woman to allow me to touch her.

Newsflash, she doesn't actually know it's you, fucker.

Battling my internal dialogue, I slowly start to move my hands up and down her back, making a trail that starts at the base of her spine and then moving my hands out along her shoulder blades as I work my way up, pressing deeply to loosen up her muscles. A sunflower tattoo covers one of her shoulder blades, instantly bringing forth memories of a younger version of her walking down the halls of our school with her backpack covered in the same flower.

I focus back on kneading her muscles, and she definitely feels stiff.

Yeah, seems like other things are getting stiff now too.

She's so soft and this oil smells fucking amazing, like peaches and cream, with a hint of mint.

As I brush my knuckles over her neck to the base of her skull where it meets her spine, she lets out a moan, and through no fault of my own, my dick fucking twitches.

What the actual fuck?

"That feels so good. You can go harder if you like."

Tipping my head back, I stare at the ceiling, clenching my jaw in agony as her words stir up other settings where those words coming out of her mouth would be music to my ears.

But that's the last thing I should be thinking about. Hell, that's not something I've *ever* thought about Charlotte up until this moment.

This is *not* how this reunion was supposed to go.

But I'm knee deep in this predicament, so I might as well give one-hundred percent. I'm no quitter, and I'm not starting now. Besides, it will be worth every ounce of shock on Charlotte's face if she ever finds out about this.

With renewed purpose and delight in pulling this off without her knowing, I get to work and rub the woman down, seeing just how many moans I can get to escape from her lips.

"Are you new to this?" she asks, halfway through the hour.

"Actually, yeah. Today is my first day." Not a lie, technically.

"Well, you're doing amazing. I'll make sure to give you a glowing review."

"I appreciate that." A good 'grade' from Charlotte Montgomery? Oh, this is going to make her face turn beet red. I can't fucking wait.

"Would you mind moving down to my sciatic now?" she asks, reaching behind her and shoving the sheet south, exposing her ass to me.

And fuck me sideways—seeing it in person after admiring it the other day is making my slacks tent up faster than a clown coming out of a Jack-in-the-Box.

Her black, silk thong is perfectly situated between luscious mounds of flesh, the kind that a man like me loves to smack just so I can see it turn red from my hand. And it's not just her ass that is perfect—no, her entire bottom half has filled out into womanly curves that only a grown man can appreciate.

No offense to the naturally skinny women, but this man here loves some meat to grab onto. I want a woman that has some weight to her, that embraces her body and isn't afraid to let me see all of it—stretch marks, cellulite, and everything in between. It's those curves and that meat that make me lose my fucking mind.

And Charlotte's body—well, at least her backside—fits the bill for what turns me on the most.

Glancing down, I realize my dick is completely unaware that we're supposed to be flying under the radar, so I'm forced to push my hips back slightly as I hover over her so she doesn't feel my third arm poking her too, if you catch my drift.

When I first touch her ass, I have to fight my own moan from leaving my lips. Her muscles are toned, but not overly so, and her skin is smooth and blemish free—it's a sight I'll never forget as long as I live.

Jesus, now I'm thinking about envisioning her butt as I jerk off later. God, help me, please.

"Yes, right there."

You're fucking killing me here, woman.

"Harder."

Christ.

"Deeper."

I have never come in my pants before, not even as a teenager, and I am not about to do it now as a thirty-year-old man. But if she doesn't knock it the hell off, this just might be my first time.

"That's it. Right there."

"Are you fucking kidding me?" I mouth out to no one but myself.

Clenching my jaw down tighter than a screw that won't come loose, I put some muscle behind my hands, and give Charlotte the deep and tough massage that she wants.

When the alarm goes off on the table next to the oil, I breathe out a sigh of relief that this torture is now over. However, I did not accomplish one measly detail of what I wanted to do today by coming over here.

"That was amazing. Thank you..."

"Jeffrey," I finish for her, assuming she was looking for my name. *Jeffrey could have been a massage therapist in another life. It's possible.*

"Jeffrey. That was perfect." She moves to push herself up again, but I shove her head back in the hole.

"No, don't move," I say, panicked, but then relax my voice. "Lay there for a minute and let your body relax. You're going to be dizzy when you rise." That part I know is actually true after a massage. "And please wait until you hear me leave to sit up to preserve your modesty." *Although I just saw way too much of your naked body, I wouldn't mind seeing the front side too.*

"Oh. Okay. Well, thank you."

"You're welcome, Charlotte."

Without making too much noise, I reach for my jacket and hightail it out of her office, gently shutting her door behind me before leaning up against the glass. Closing my eyes, I exhale with relief, grateful that

I'm alone when I look back into the room just outside Charlotte's office and see no one else here.

"Fucking hell."

Before Charlotte can come out and see me, I take off the way I came, past Emily at the front desk before she can ask questions, and straight into the elevator that brought me up to this incident that could only serve as an indication of the web of lies I'm slowly getting myself caught in.

But damn—what a way to be lured in…

Chapter 3

Charlotte

When the door shuts to my office, I brace myself for the fuzziness I know is going to crash into me as soon as I sit up, so I move slowly to a seated position as I pull the sheet around my body so I don't fall off the table.

That massage—that was not the typical massage I get from Sonya.

There was something different about the way Jeffrey touched me, the path his fingers took as they danced across my skin, the hesitation in his voice as he pressed his palms into my back, but then the confidence I felt in his touch once he grew more comfortable. Perhaps he was just nervous since it was his first day, but what concerns me even more, is the reaction *I* had to his massage.

It's been a while since a man has touched me, and even though the massage was not meant to be sexual, his touch had desire flowing through my veins and straight down to the juncture between my legs. The unnecessary reminder of how long it's been since I had sex was all

I could think about as the awareness of a man massaging me remained steadfast in my brain.

I tried hard to hide the way he was making my body feel, but at one point, all I wanted was for him to inflict some pain so I could focus on that and not on how amazing it truly felt. So I told him to press harder, massage deeper, and then all I could think about is how saying those words out loud made me sound like Monica from *Friends* getting a massage, moaning sex noises even though that's exactly what I was trying to avoid.

With a glance at the clock, I shake myself out of the haze I'm in knowing I have to get to my meeting and now I'm running behind. Once I'm dressed again, I open the door to find Helen back at her desk, sipping on her drink from her lunch.

"Did you get any work done?" she asks me as I walk past her desk.

"No, I had my massage."

Helen's face scrunches up with confusion. "What do you mean? Sonya called earlier and left a message while I was out. Apparently, she had an emergency and couldn't make it."

"I know. They sent a replacement."

Her brow furrows further. "Are you sure? She said she'd make it up to you next time since they didn't have someone to cover her."

I shrug, even though my intuition is telling me something is off here, but I don't have time to dig into this further right now. I'm going to be late. "Well, I guess they found someone. And he was great. I told him I'd make sure to leave a glowing review with the company."

Helen relaxes once she hears the cheeriness in my voice. "Oh, a male massage therapist? Was he good with his hands?"

"Um, yeah. He was." *Stop thinking about it, Charlotte. Your skin is all tingly again.*

"Maybe I need to get regular massages."

"You know I love mine. They always make me feel more relaxed."

"I bet they do," Helen replies suggestively. And all I can do is shake my head at her. "Okay then. Off to your meeting?"

"Yup. See you in a little bit."

I walk out of my office and down to the conference room where all the senior executives were called to go over the finances for the end of the quarter. And even though I try really hard, my thoughts carelessly drift back to my massage from earlier, and what I wouldn't give for it to have been a happy ending instead.

"Have you ever been turned on by a massage?" I say out loud, right after our drinks are delivered. It's Wednesday night and a new restaurant in town opened this week, so naturally, Penelope got us a reservation from her many connections.

"What were you having massaged?" Noelle asks as Penelope snickers.

I roll my eyes but answer the question anyway. "It was my normal weekly massage, but Sonya wasn't available so they sent a man in her place. And he was..." I stare off into space, revisiting that hour on Monday for the hundredth time.

"Was he hot?" Amelia asks. "It's normal to find a member of the opposite sex attractive, even if they are your massage therapist."

"That's the thing. I never saw him. He came in, insisted I didn't lift my head from the table and got to work once he got a little more comfortable. And then the more he touched me..."

"Did you get a happy ending?" Penelope asks before taking a sip of her martini.

"God, no. But I definitely was revved up and ready to go by the end." I smack my forehead. "Jeez, you guys. I've been fantasizing about a faceless massage therapist for the past forty-eight hours. I need to get laid. It's been so long."

"How long?"

I think back as far as I can, but Penelope interjects before I can answer. "If you have to think about it for that long, it's been *too* long, my friend."

"I know. And it's not like I haven't taken care of myself, you know? But sometimes you just need an actual dick."

"Hear, hear."

"I have some new models of toys you can take a look at if you're looking for something new," Amelia chimes in.

"Thanks, but there's that feeling that a toy can't give you. I think that's what I'm missing."

"I get what you're saying," Noelle speaks. "Being with a man isn't just about his dick sometimes. It's about feeling wanted, touched in places other than your pretty kitty, right?"

"Exactly." I point across the table at her. "And the last time I experienced that was with Tom."

"Oh, three-position Tom," Penelope sings. "Do you think he's learned anything new since he was with you?"

"Probably not. The man was such a creature of habit in his entire life that it filtered into the bedroom. I knew exactly what he was going to do before he even did it. Sex was always the same, which doesn't help my need for something filthy and raunchy right about now."

Penelope nods. "Sometimes a woman just needs to be fucked, and fucked well. Hair pulling, ass smacking, dirty talking sex."

"To dirty, raunchy, sex!" Noelle cheers as we all lift our drinks to clink our glasses together.

I lift my glass to my lips just as a figure to my right catches my eye. And then I almost spit out my cocktail. "Oh my God," I whisper, setting my drink down and then turning my body away from that direction.

"What?" Amelia asks as the three of them start perusing the room.

"Don't look over there."

"Why?"

"Because I don't want to draw his attention over here."

"Who?"

But it's too late. The deep timbre of his voice sends a chill down my spine, a reaction that is completely unnatural around him. But hell, it's been twelve years. Perhaps my body forgot that we hate this man. "Charlotte Montgomery. Long time, no see."

I twist in my chair to find Damien Shaw staring down at me, his hands deep in the pockets of his navy blue slacks, and his matching jacket hanging open revealing a solid white dress shirt with the top two buttons undone. That same cocky grin I remember from growing up is stitched across his lips, and his hair is perfectly styled, making him look sharp and professional.

I hate that he looks like Robbie Amell's doppelganger with a beard, and my body definitely agrees with enthusiasm.

"Damien Shaw. Wow. God must have known that my day was already shitty, so he decided to rub salt in the wound by making you appear."

He chuckles and then smiles even harder, revealing perfect white teeth and drawing my attention to his lips. "I knew you were still in L.A., but what a coincidence that I run into you now and here of all places." He glances around the room and then back down to me. "Although I'm not surprised that the Senior Advertising Executive of *Revision Magazine* is dining at this establishment."

"So you've been stalking me all of these years? That's really sad that you felt like you needed to keep tabs on me."

"Yeah, just wanted to make sure you're still coming in second place."

"If memory serves me correctly, you came in second more often than I did."

"Sorry, Charlotte. The only time I come second is after the woman I'm with comes first."

Noelle clears her throat, breaking the stare-down I'm having with Damien, drawing my attention back to my friends. "Care to introduce us?"

"I suppose. Girls, this is Damien Shaw, the definition of a narcissistic man-child, and someone I grew up with back home."

"I can see your ability to throw out insults hasn't wavered. Good to know," he replies before moving to shake each one of my friends' hands as they give him their names in return. "Nice to meet you, ladies."

Penelope's eyes dance up and down Damien's body, and the spike of jealousy that sparks in my chest comes out of left field. *What the fuck was that?*

"The pleasure is all ours, Damien," she croons. "So you and Charlotte know each other from South Carolina?"

"Oh yeah. Charlotte and I were thick as thieves, weren't we, Char?"

"The only thieving going on was me stealing your pride every time I beat you at something."

Damien tsks. "Now, now, Char. Don't make me bring up stories and embarrass you in front of your friends."

Noelle raises her hand like a fucking kindergartner. "I want to hear some stories."

Penelope joins in with her hand in the air. "Me too! Me too!"

I smack both of their hands down before glaring in their direction. "Perhaps another time." And then I turn to Damien again. "Well, this has been lovely, but our food will be here soon, and surely you have some other person to terrorize."

Damien laughs and then tilts his head to the side. "You look good, Charlotte," he says with sincerity that has me narrowing my eyes at him and my heart rate escalating. "Time has been good to you, indeed."

"Uh… thank you." I can feel my cheeks getting hot, but I won't dare let him see that I'm reacting to him.

"I guess we'll have more time to catch up in Hawaii next month, won't we?"

A rock lodges itself in my throat. "Unfortunately, yes."

He looks around the table, making eye contact with each of my friends. "It was great to meet you, ladies. See you around, Char." And then he walks away, giving me yet another glimpse of his ass that I appreciated far too much the other day.

A heavy sigh leaves my lips as I pick up my drink and drain the rest of it, practically slamming it on the table before searching the room for our waiter to order another.

"So, uh…are you gonna explain who that was? Or are we just going to ignore the fact that the man that just stood here at our table was hella fine?" Penelope asks as I close my eyes and take a deep breath.

"That was Damien Shaw."

"Yeah, we got that much information," Amelia sarcastically replies.

"We were rivals growing up."

"Like how?"

"Everything with that man was a competition, and he loved beating me almost as much as I loved beating him."

Noelle's eyebrows shoot up. "You do have one hell of a competitive side. But why on earth did you never tell us about him?"

"Because when I moved out here for college, I vowed to keep him out of this new chapter of my life. I focused so much of my time and energy competing against him as a child that I feel like my priorities were completely misplaced. And I knew he was coming out here for college too, but I knew the chances of us running into each other were slim. So I hopped on a plane and pretended like he never existed. Until Monday…when I saw him again for the first time."

"You saw him on Monday?" Amelia asks.

"Yeah, at The Chop Shop. I left before he could see me though. But running into him here tonight is…"

"Coincidental?"

"Yeah, to say the least."

Penelope goes to speak just as the waiter comes by and drops off our food, so she waits for him to leave. The cuisine here is a mix of Mexican and Asian flavors, and just seeing the food in front of me is making my mouth water. Once he makes sure we have everything we need she starts again. "What was he saying about Hawaii? He's going to be there?" she asks as she breaks off a piece of her quesadilla and shoves it in her mouth.

And all I can do is sigh while pinching the bridge of my nose. "Unfortunately, yes. His parents are best friends with my parents, so it comes as no surprise that he was invited."

"Don't your parents know you two hate each other then?" Noelle asks, chewing a bite of her rice. "Why would they invite him?"

"Ha. No. On the contrary, they thought we were best friends. Damien always acted like the perfect little angel in front of our parents, even though he was nothing but a little twerp when they weren't around."

"Twerp. Now there's a word that doesn't get used enough," Penelope laughs. "We need to bring that one back."

"I'll do my best to use it as much as possible."

"Do you think he's dating someone?" Noelle questions.

"The hell if I know, and the hell if I care. Why do you ask?"

"Because that means he might bring someone to Hawaii. It might make things awkward."

"Why would it make things awkward?"

"Because the sexual tension between the two of you is so thick, you need an extra-large condom to slide over that dick," Penelope says without ever looking up from her plate.

And I choke on my saliva. "Jesus, Penelope. And no way. I would never. Besides, that man's penis has probably been removed due to one too many infections."

Amelia chooses this time to share her observations. "On the contrary, he actually had quite a nice bulge in his slacks. I'd say he's a solid seven inches hard."

"What the fuck, Amelia? You were checking out his dick?"

She just shrugs casually as she chews. "It's just something I do, given my line of work."

"Well, this night took an interesting turn," Noelle quips before turning back to me. "Look Charlotte, just breathe. The man is attractive, I give him that. But other than seeing him occasionally around the city and in Hawaii next month, is it really that big of a deal that you ran into him?"

I shake my head. "No. It's just odd, given the timing of everything. And after that weird massage on Monday, and the phone call with my mom this morning…"

"Wait…Mommy called again?" Penelope asks.

"Oh yeah. And get this shit. She told me I need to find a date for Hawaii now since she kind of told all of my parents' friends that I'm seeing someone."

"What on earth?" Penelope shouts.

"Yup." I lean back in my chair, my appetite completely gone at this point. Which sucks, because I really like food and was really looking forward to this meal about twenty minutes ago. "So now I have this pressure to find someone to take, and you know how hard that is."

Noelle nods. "You're preaching to the choir, sister. I can't find a normal man on this side of Hollywood Boulevard. Good luck finding one that you feel comfortable introducing to your family, and all of their friends."

"Exactly. Ugh, you guys. Why must everything happen all at once?"

"Because that's the rule of three," Amelia says. "Now that you've had your third strike, you should be good for a while."

"Let's hope so. Between the pressure at work, pressure from my mom, and now running into Damien, I'm not sure how much more I can take."

Penelope snaps at the waiter walking by. "We need four more martinis over here, please. And keep them coming."

"If you don't leave now, you're going to be late for that lunch with your parents." Helen stands in the doorway to my office, giving me her motherly glare. She may be twenty years older than me and my assistant, but the woman still scares me a little bit.

I continue staring at my computer screen, reading the article in front of me. "I'm aware. That's why I haven't left yet. I can just claim I lost track of time with work and miss it altogether."

"Charlotte Montgomery, go have lunch with your parents. There will come a day when they will no longer be around, and then you'll kick yourself for not seeing them every chance you could."

I glance up to see Helen's face soften. Given her age and her comment, I can only assume her parents are no longer around. "Fine. You're right."

"Yes, I am. It's a gift."

With a small laugh, I close out of the file I was reading, grab my purse, and walk past Helen so I can exit the building. "Please have a fresh cup of coffee and some Excedrin waiting for me when I return. I'm almost positive I'm going to need it."

Helen gives me a mock salute. "Yes, ma'am."

Smiling to myself, I head for the elevator and check my appearance in the shiny metal doors while I wait to be taken down to the ground level. When my mother confirmed our lunch plans this week, I made sure to pick a restaurant that I knew she would be happy with and was also close enough that I wouldn't have to drive to get there. Traffic and finding a place to park in Los Angeles could qualify as its own version of The Hunger Games.

I arrive at Water Grill Restaurant about ten minutes before my parents are scheduled to arrive, so the hostess takes me back to our table and I settle in, checking emails on my phone while I wait. The smell of fresh seafood assaults my senses, and the open room is buzzing with chatter and business. There's a reason this place is busy on a Friday afternoon for lunch, and the menu is raved about all over social media.

My nerves spike as I wait for my parents to arrive. Mostly I'm excited to see them, but the other part of me knows that being subjected to my mother's meddling ways in person is a whole different ball game than when I'm speaking to her on the phone.

"Damn. We cross paths again."

I look up to see Damien towering over me, dressed in a classic black suit that makes his eyes pop even more. His cocky presence holds me captive before I snap back to reality.

"I think this is God's way of telling me to dine at home." *Seriously, how on earth can this man not exist for this long, and then start popping up everywhere I go?*

"I take it you're not happy to see me."

"Uh, that would be a no." I glance around the busy restaurant. "What are you doing here, Damien? Did you know I would be here or something?"

Sliding into the seat across from me, he crosses his leg over the other, resting his ankle on his knee. "Not at all. This was just luck."

"Luck is a strong word."

Damien's eyes travel all over me, and I swear I can feel his gaze draw a map all over my skin. "Who are you having lunch with?"

"That's none of your concern."

"Oh, come on, Char. We were friends once…"

"Ha. No, we weren't. I think we were better at making each other's lives a living hell than being anything close to friends."

"You're gonna sit there and pretend you're not at least a little bit happy to see me?" he asks, holding up his finger and thumb with a little bit of space between them while smiling like he's pleased with himself for making me irritated.

"I'd rather be getting a pap smear than be talking to you," I fire back.

"Ouch. That doesn't sound fun."

"And neither is this conversation. Now, if you'll excuse me…"

"Damien? Is that you?" I look up to find my mother and father standing behind Damien in his seat, the utter shock and awe on my mother's face more annoying than the man sitting in front of me. And my heart drops down into my stomach.

But Damien stands, buttoning up his jacket before intercepting my mother for a hug. "It is. My word, Mrs. Montgomery…you look more beautiful than I remember." *Ugh, kiss ass.*

"Oh, you are too sweet, Damien," my mother replies as they hug and then he releases her. She cups the side of his face. "You are so grown up. It just doesn't seem possible."

"Yes, well, I'm afraid that's what happens. Turning thirty kind of made me accept it myself."

"I know. I told Charlotte that she needs to start using night cream if she isn't already, or she'll never find a husband."

I roll my eyes as Damien looks back at me, a questioning smile on his face. "Well, I happen to think she's even more beautiful now than she was when we were growing up."

My God. He's laying it on thick, isn't he?

"Of course, she's beautiful. But the older she gets, the more I'm worried she'll end up alone. She'll have her job, but no one to keep her warm at night, right, Charlotte?"

I'm clenching my jaw so tight that I might crack a tooth.

"There's nothing wrong with a woman being dedicated to her career," Damien adds, catching me off guard. "I think it's impressive. And Charlotte is a knock-out in the looks department, so there's no need to worry there, Mrs. Montgomery. I mean, that is the reason why we're dating now, isn't it, sweet pea?" he asks as he turns to me and I feel my eyes bug out.

Um…what the fuck did he just say?

"What? You two are dating?" My mother screeches, pulling people's attention to us all across the restaurant.

But I'm frozen in my seat, my jaw dropped open as I try to process what the hell is happening.

"Oh, Char…you didn't tell your parents about us?"

I'm going to murder him. Yup. I think poison will do.

"Damien," I grate out, moving to stand. But he walks over to me, blocking me from my parents as his body gets dangerously close to mine.

"Just go along with it," he whispers. "I'll explain later."

"I'm going to kill you," I spit back.

"In that case, I prefer to be cremated." Then he spins back around to face my parents, and places his arm around my waist, drawing him into me. "I'm so sorry Mr. and Mrs. Montgomery that you had to find out this way, but I guess Charlotte wasn't ready to tell everyone just yet. We've been keeping things quiet as we sort through our feelings, but your daughter and I reconnected, and I couldn't help but give in to the feelings I think I've had for her all along," he says as he stares down at me, a look of pure adoration in his eyes.

He always was a good actor, and it seems he's only perfected his role as a big fat liar in our time apart.

"Charlotte? Is this true?"

I momentarily debate whether I should reveal Damien's scheme to my parents right here and now, and expose him once and for all as the slimy guy he's always been. But then I realize that this may work out in my favor. If my mom thinks I'm dating Damien, then maybe she'll back off a bit with her ridicule. Perhaps bringing him to Hawaii as my date will satisfy the lie she told that I was dating someone to begin with, without the task of finding someone else in a sea of millions of men that I don't know. And finally, it's not like Damien and I will let this get more complicated than it needs to be because deep down, we can't stand each other. This little ruse can last as long as I need to get some reprieve from my mom, especially once my parents return back to South Carolina. They'll never know it was all fake until I decide when it ends for good.

However, one question still remains—*why on earth did Damien say we're dating to begin with? What the hell is he getting out of this?*

I know we can discuss that later, so I put that question on the back burner, and dive headfirst into the shit show I'm currently living through. And then I do something I never thought I would. I admit to dating Damien Shaw out loud, choking down the bile in my throat as the words leave my lips. "Yes, mom. It's true."

She jumps up and down in front of us, squealing even louder than before. "Oh my God, you two! I'm so happy!"

"I can tell, Mom," I whisper, as my eyes bounce up and down with each jump she makes. I reach out to her, trying to get her to stop. "But you need to calm down. People are staring."

"Oh, let them stare. My daughter is dating someone and not just anyone, but someone we wholeheartedly approve of, isn't that right, Cal?"

My father just smiles as he watches my mother lose her shit with excitement. "I feel like there's no better man for you, sweetheart."

Seriously, Dad? Are you that naïve?

"That means a lot, Cal. Truly." Damien reaches out to shake my father's hand again.

"Is Damien joining us for lunch? Is that why he's here?" my mother asks enthusiastically.

But Damien actually uses his brain for once since he started opening his mouth earlier. "Unfortunately, no. I have another meeting I'm here for. But when I saw my girl across the restaurant, I couldn't *not* come over and say hello." He places a kiss to my temple, and I want to scream. But my entire body breaks out in goosebumps. Apparently, my nerves are confused about what to feel toward him right now.

My mother clasps her hands together over her chest. "Oh my goodness. That is just so sweet." And then she shakes her head in disbelief. "I just can't believe that of all the people for you to date, Charlotte, you end up with the boy from back home."

I have to fight the urge to laugh. "You and me both, Mom." And then I turn to Damien. "You'd better get going so you're not late, *honey.*"

"You're right, *sweet pea*." He leans down to kiss my cheek, but whispers in my ear at the same time. "I'll call you later so we can talk about this."

"You don't have my number," I whisper back.

"Yes, I do. I got it from my mother."

"You're sick and twisted. I have no idea what's going on right now."

"Don't worry. I'll explain." With another kiss on my cheek, he stands fully again, says goodbye to my parents, and then takes off in the other direction of the restaurant toward another room that is more closed off than the one we're standing in, blocking him from our view. Which is good for him, seeing as how I could murder him with my eyes right now if he sat in my line of sight.

As I watch him walk away, my entire body alive from his touch and the adrenaline running through me from our lie, I spin around to see my parents have finally taken a seat but were watching us the entire time.

"Charlotte. I'm speechless."

"Ha. You and me both, Mom," I say as I finally sit back down in my chair.

"Why didn't you tell us?"

What can I say that won't give us away, or invite more questions that I don't know the answers to? Damien obviously had a reason for this little charade, and until I know exactly what's going on, I need to be as vague as possible. "I don't know. I mean, it's Damien. It's new. I just wasn't sure how you'd feel about the entire thing."

"Why wouldn't we approve?"

I shrug, trying to play the innocent daughter. "I don't know. But I'm still processing it, so can we leave it be for the time being, and just catch up?"

"I think that's a great idea," my father interjects, winking at me from behind his menu.

But my mother sighs in protest. "Learning about your love life is catching up, Charlotte."

"For once, can we have a conversation that doesn't pertain to my love life, Mom? I'm begging you."

"Fine," she relents, and I'm grateful that at least I have some time to avoid discussing the giant elephant in the room.

"Why don't you tell me about Napa? And Hawaii? And all of the things you have planned while you're there? Or what's going on back home?" I ask, veering the conversation to a more neutral topic that I know will keep my mother gabbing for hours.

"Oh. There's just so much going on, Charlotte. First..." she starts speaking at lightning speed, and I try to listen. I do.

But in the back of my mind, I'm wondering how in the hell I just ended up in a fake relationship with Damien Shaw. What the ever-loving-fuck just happened?

Chapter 4

Damien

"What the fuck took you so long, bro? Did you fall in the toilet?"

I arrive at the table that Jeffrey has been waiting at for the past twenty minutes or so, shaking but feeling victorious. "No, fucker. I never made it to the bathroom."

"Then what the fuck have you been doing?"

I can't help the curl of my lips, pleased with how Charlotte fell right into my lap and my plan. "I was finding myself a fake girlfriend."

Jeffrey's mouth drops open. "What? How?"

Taking my seat, I unbutton my jacket and take a deep breath, trying to get my heart rate back down. "Dude, it's a long story, but fate was on my side."

"Spill before the waiter comes back to take our order."

So I do. I tell him about seeing Charlotte on Monday, about

running into her Wednesday night at the new restaurant in town and then seeing her again just now with her parents.

"So her parents gave you the opening?"

"Basically. Her mom kept making comments about how she's going to be single forever and shit. It was the perfect opportunity to get her mother to shut up and convince her to go along with my plan."

"So she agreed?"

"Not exactly, but I'm going to call her later so we can meet up and go over the details."

Jeffrey leans back in his chair, shaking his head and smiling in awe. "I can't believe it. You really pulled this off."

"Did you really doubt me?" I ask, reaching for my glass of water and draining half the liquid. Apparently lying through my teeth makes me thirsty.

"I mean, for a moment, yeah. I thought maybe you were going insane coming up with this idea. But now…well, hell, now I want to know how this all plays out."

"I hate to lose, Jeffrey. And this is one instance where I can feel the win before the competition has ever begun."

"Come on, Charlotte," I mumble as I glance at my watch for the tenth time in the past minute. I'm sitting in a corner booth at Crank, a local bar known for its business-minded clientele. A bunch of us from the office frequent this place for happy hour, and it's always full of men and women in suits, kicking their shoes off after a long day at the office and sitting back with a cold drink in hand.

I figured buying Charlotte a drink would help butter her up and convince her to go along with this charade, so I suggested meeting here when I texted her after our run-in at lunch. I've had her phone number for years when my mother gave it to me, suggesting I contact her and see how she was doing. But that was at least five years ago, so I was grateful that the number was correct and I wouldn't have to ask my mom for her information again, inviting a ton of questions.

I know Charlotte already agreed to this by playing into the act I put on in front of her parents, but knowing her, I'm sure she'd love nothing more than to tell me to kiss her ass and leave me hanging now that she's had time for reality to set in.

The funny thing is, I'd kiss her ass all day long. When the fuck did Charlotte turn into a sexy woman? Was she always attractive and I could just never look past the fact that she was my competition? Or did that voluptuous body, that I've already seen too much of, come out from hiding in the time we've been absent from each other's lives?

Fifteen minutes past our arranged meeting time, the door opens and Charlotte steps through it wearing the same bright red dress from earlier that hits just below her knees and highlights her hourglass figure. Her hips swing from side to side as she walks in and then stops to search the room, looking for me in the sea of people. And even though I know I should alert her to my location, I take just another moment to admire her before things get intense.

Her long, dark brown hair is down in curls still, half of it pulled back away from her face. Her dress is sleeveless, highlighting her toned arms and perfectly sized chest. And she's got on black shiny heels that her toes peek out of, making her seem taller than I know she really is and conjuring up inappropriate images of those heels wrapped around my back in my mind.

But her eyes—they're piercing, analyzing the room, seeking me out just before she swings them in my direction and we lock gazes.

Fire and ice burn from her eyes as she narrows her gaze, takes a deep breath, and then stalks toward me, approaching me with such determination that a part of me wants to cower away.

But I'd die before I let her know that. Charlotte cannot know that she affects me, and secondly—why the fuck is that even happening in the first place? I've never backed down from her before.

But you've also never needed her help before.

Focus on the task, Damien. You just need her to play a part for your job. We know you both can act, so this should be easy.

Keyword and hope being—should.

I want to make a comment about how she's late, but I'd better not poke the bear before I ask for my favor. "Charlotte," I greet her as I stand and move to kiss her on the cheek. But she plants her palm in my face, stopping me before I reach her.

"There will be no more of that."

"Let's just put that on the list of things to discuss tonight, shall we?" I say, standing up again and then gesturing for her to slide into the other side of the booth.

"Oh, I think we have plenty to discuss."

"Let's get you a drink first." I lift my hand to get the waitress's attention and she comes over speedily. "My date would like a drink, please."

"Of course. What can I get for you?"

"Martini, please. Three olives."

"Coming right up." She walks away, leaving us alone again.

"Martini, huh? I guess I always thought you'd be more of a wine drinker." I spin my glass of beer around just to keep my hands busy as I try to ease into the topic of the evening.

"I like most alcohol, but I feel like gin is definitely going to help me get through this conversation the best."

"Well, I appreciate you meeting with me."

"Start talking, Damien," she demands, crossing her arms over her chest. "Please tell me why you told my parents that we're dating." With a lift of her brow, I hear her tap her shoe on the floor beneath us.

Sighing, I lean forward and brace my forearms on the table. The waitress comes over with Charlotte's drink, placing it in front of her, but she doesn't even reach for it yet. She just continues to glare at me. "I need you to pretend to be my girlfriend."

"Why?"

"Because I kind of told my boss that I have one, and he didn't believe me." Sure, we'll go with that for right now.

She scoffs and finally reaches for her drink. I watch the curl of her lips around the rim of her glass but fight the distraction as best as I can. "Well, that was stupid."

"Hey, I'm not saying it was smart, but I'm up for a promotion, and having a girlfriend will help me get it."

"Since when do you lie and cheat to win?" And then her eyes widen. "Oh my God! Is that how you beat me in high school? I always knew I was smarter than you in Calculus. The fact that you got better grades than me on those tests was bullshit."

Smirking across the table at her, I cross my arms over my chest. "Sorry, babe, but I never had to cheat in school. I was just better at math than you were."

She rolls her eyes. "Well, now I don't believe you."

"You don't have to. This is completely different."

"Really? Because to me, it feels the same." She leans forward in her seat. "It's been twelve years since we've seen each other, Damien, and all of a sudden I see you three times in one week."

"Wait? Three?" My heart is pounding as I think of where we've run into each other. The only two times we're both aware of are at the restaurants, the first with her friends, and the second with her parents. So does that mean that she knows about her massage?

"Yeah. I saw you on Monday at The Chop Shop, and I honestly thought at first I was seeing things. But then it kept happening, which makes me think you've been following me."

"It was coincidental, I assure you." Internally, I release the breath I was holding, but then realize that she must have seen me that day as well. "So is that why you ran away? So we wouldn't have to speak to each other?"

"Contrary to what you might think and how you obviously operate, I have a job that I had to get back to, a job that I worked my ass off to get without lying to get it."

"Hey, I take my job seriously too, hence why I cared enough to lie."

"Why do you need a girlfriend though? I'm not following."

I take a sip of my beer, thinking about how much detail I want to give her. So I settle on a vague truth. "There's a new account that we're trying to land, and I know that if I do, that promotion is mine. It's for a women's product though, and my boss didn't seem to think I could come up with a good enough pitch since I'm out of touch with what women really want."

"Because you're an asshole?" she teases.

"No, because I don't really date."

"Ah. Why doesn't that surprise me…"

With a cocky grin, I reply, "I have too much to offer to keep it all for one woman, Charlotte."

"Too much syphilis? Newsflash, Damien. Women don't want that."

Damn, the girl can still bust my balls, and I'm not hating the smug purse of her lips while she does it. "We're getting off topic."

"Yes, please tell me how this is supposed to work? I'm a busy woman and don't have time to play a part in your low-budget play."

"I heard. You spend so much time on your job that you still don't have a husband, isn't that right?"

"Excuse me?"

"Whether you want to admit it or not, I think part of you agreed to my little charade in front of your parents just to get your mother off your back…am I right?" She doesn't say anything. Just continues to glare across the table at me. "That's what I thought."

"So what's your point?"

Clasping my hands around my beer, I stare her down. "My point is, both of us can benefit from this little arrangement, Charlotte. You get your mother off your back, we'll go to Hawaii and play the couple in love, and then fake a break up later when we see fit. Meanwhile, I get to show my boss that I'm in touch with my feminine side and clinch the promotion that I know I deserve."

Her face is contorted in a way that I can't read, like she's seeing my point but doesn't want to. "What all would I need to do to keep up my end of the bargain?"

"What do you mean?"

"Like, how in-depth do I need to play this part? I have a life and can't be at your beck and call all the time. I'm not going to show up at your office unannounced every day so your boss can see me, or wear a shirt that says, 'Damien is my man.' I have some self-respect."

"We can go back to the shirt later," I joke. "But to answer your question, the first order of business would be a dinner next week with some work associates. It's a big deal. I've never been invited because I'm not part of a couple, and almost all of the members of the board will be there, so it's a great opportunity to impress them."

"Where do you work?"

"Goldstein Advertising," I reply.

Her eyebrows shoot up. "Wow. We actually work with them quite a bit."

"I know, but you've probably never crossed paths with me since you're selling to women, and I don't really do that."

"So why not wait for another account? Why not do what you know you're good at instead of going through all of this?"

And that has me smiling. "Oh, come on, Charlotte. You should understand more than anyone how I love a challenge."

She rears back in her seat as her brow furrows, like my words confused her or something. But then she shakes it off and takes another sip of her drink. "I guess I understand."

"This is about proving myself and getting a chance that wasn't given to me because I don't have a vagina."

"You sure about that?" she mocks.

"You want me to whip out my dick and show it to you right now?" I fire back.

She huffs out a laugh. "No. That's not necessary. And while we're on the subject of your dick, there will be no instances whatsoever where that thing will come anywhere near me, got it?"

"So you're agreeing to this?"

She sighs in defeat. "Sadly, yes. But for my own reasons."

"Your mom seems like she's very concerned about you becoming an old maid."

"Yeah, she is. Which is preposterous. I'm only thirty, you know? But she keeps reminding me that if I don't find someone soon, I'll never be able to celebrate a thirtieth wedding anniversary like her and my dad."

"That is pretty incredible…I mean, if that's your goal in life."

She laughs. "Yeah, I can see that you obviously have no desire to go there."

"That's not true," I say more defensively than I intended, but I run with it. "Marriage isn't something completely off the table for me. I just haven't found somebody yet who's ever made me want to consider it."

She points a finger across the table at me. "And that's the point your boss was trying to make. Being with a woman, or a significant other to be more general, will make you change your outlook on things. And you clearly have a one-track mind."

"Well, you obviously haven't found your prince charming."

"Yup," she answers dryly, taking another sip of her drink. "And I do want someone someday, but I'll be damned if I settle to appease my mother and these ridiculous societal expectations put upon women."

God, when she gets fired up, my body keeps having this weird reaction—like I wonder how passionate she gets in other situations.

Focus, Damien. "Okay, so you'll do this then?"

"I have no idea why I'm even agreeing to this because it's you— and me—but what the hell? I don't feel like I have anything to lose at this point. And it prevents me from having to find someone on my own."

I place my hand over my chest. "Damn, you make me feel so warm and fuzzy, sweet pea."

"Hey! While you mention it, please for the love of God, stop calling me sweet pea."

I throw my head back in laughter. "Why? What's wrong with sweet pea?"

"I hate pet names. They are so impersonal and some just make me cringe." She shivers in her seat.

"Okay. Fine. No sweet pea." *Yeah, I'm still going to fucking call her that now that I know she hates it.*

She heaves out a sigh, leaning back in her side of the booth. "I can't believe I just agreed to fake date Damien Shaw."

"Charlotte Montgomery, I'm going to be the best fake boyfriend I can be."

She cackles and then drains the rest of her drink. "That's the only way you'd ever be my boyfriend, Damien—by both of us pretending that this is real—because there's no way in hell that you and I would be together in reality."

Surprisingly, her words cut, stabbing me in the chest. But I shake it off. I don't need Charlotte to like me. But I do need her to *act* like she does. And if that means that I might have to butter her up a bit in the process, then so be it. Again, I never back down from a challenge.

Chapter 5

Charlotte

"You're here early," Noelle greets me at our table at Frankie's. It's Sunday morning and the first time I'm seeing the girls since I had my drink with Damien Friday night. After I agreed to his proposition, I told him I was tired and needed to go home—which wasn't a lie. But mostly I just needed to get away from him, away from his cologne and that smirk, and those light blue eyes that kept eating me up as I sat across from him in the booth.

"Couldn't sleep. Thought I'd get a head start on drinking," I say as I raise my mimosa up from the table.

"Everything okay?"

"Um…well…"

Noelle places her hand over mine that's lying flat on the table. "Charlotte…"

"Let's just wait until the other girls get here so I can tell you all at once."

"You're not pregnant, are you?"

"Oh, God no. It's nothing that drastic."

She blows out a breath of relief. "Okay. Not that that's a bad thing, per se. But sorry, my mind just went there really quick."

"I totally get it. The curse of being a woman. We conjure up the most dramatic scenarios in our heads like that." I snap my fingers at her.

"Good morning," Amelia says cheerily as she arrives and gives us both a hug.

I watch her take her seat next to Noelle. "You seem like you're in a good mood today."

"I am. One of the couples I'm working with had a breakthrough last night." She beams as she pours her glass of champagne.

"That's wonderful, Amelia."

"These two were in deep trouble when they came to me, girls. And knowing that I helped them…" She inhales deeply and then blows out the air as her eyes well with tears. "It makes me feel like I'm doing what I was meant to do."

Noelle and I both congratulate her again just as Penelope shows up wearing a long black maxi dress and her hair down straight. No matter how many times I see her, I'll never get over how much she looks like Cindy Crawford, height and all. "What's up, bitches?"

"You look well-rested today. No wild parties last night?"

"Nope, that's the weekend after next, and you girls are coming with me. There's a new club opening downtown and I got us a VIP booth for the night, naturally." She flicks her hair over her shoulder. "I actually stayed in last night and tried reading one of those books you're always pushing on me, Noelle. But sadly, I fell asleep about fifteen minutes in," she says as she takes her seat next to me.

"Did you not like it?"

"No, it was good. But this is why I can't ever finish a book you give me, girl. No matter how entranced I am in the story, I can't seem to keep my eyes open."

"That's just a product of getting old, my friend," I tease her.

"Well, I refuse to accept that. Although, the other night I slept on my arm wrong and it's been killing me ever since." Penelope stretches her arm out to the side.

"I felt my back spasm on me the other day when I bent over to throw away a piece of trash," Amelia adds.

"I choked on a piece of chicken the other day while I was home alone you guys, and I seriously thought that was how I was going to die," Noelle says as we all just stare at each other.

"Well, I agreed to be Damien's fake girlfriend so he can impress his boss and my mom will stop bothering me about finding a man," I spit out, figuring since everyone else was throwing out the conundrums in their life, I might as well add mine.

Noelle starts choking, Amelia stares across the table at me, and Penelope starts clapping slowly. "Charlotte wins with the biggest problem in our lives currently."

"Start talking, Charlotte. Amelia, fill up our glasses, and Penelope, tell Frankie we will all have our regular orders," Noelle commands, and my three best friends get to work as I sit in my chair, grateful to have friends like them and finally being able to process this out loud.

Once everyone settles back in, I start explaining how Damien and I came to this agreement—lunch with my parents, meeting for drinks, and then the small tasks that he asked me to do as his love interest.

"You really think this is a good idea?" Noelle asks as we all start eating our food.

"I mean, no. But at the same time, he had a point. You should have seen my mother, you guys. She's always loved Damien, and would have probably picked him out of a catalog for me herself."

"And what is he getting out of this again?"

"Being able to impress his boss." I shrug. "He didn't tell me what product he's trying to sell, but clearly his boss didn't think he was in touch with his feminine side enough to be up to the task, so he lied about being in a relationship."

Penelope snickers. "You know, you could have some fun with this."

"What do you mean?"

"I mean, give him a true glimpse of what it's like to be with a woman, make his life a living hell a little bit, you know? Get really emotional on him, text him at all hours of the day, start leaving shit at his place. You could pull a *How to Lose a Guy in Ten Days* on him."

I ponder her suggestion as I take another bite of my spinach, feta, and egg white omelet. I swear, I'll eat anything with feta cheese. "That might be fun, actually."

"Yes, or it could make things turn sour really quickly," Amelia challenges. "Given your history with him, I don't know if trying to get a reaction out of him would be a good idea. This is already complicated enough, especially given the sexual tension between you two."

"I know you think it's there, but I assure you, nothing is going to happen." *Then why is your vagina throbbing at the thought of him in his suit the other night, huh, Charlotte?*

"Honey, if it doesn't, I will streak naked up and down Hollywood Boulevard," Penelope says. "And even though I'd have no shame in doing that, I'm pretty sure I'll never have to deliver on that promise. I can't believe you don't see what the rest of us do."

"I mean, is Damien attractive? Yes. But that doesn't mean I would ever let myself go there, especially now." I clutch my head between my hands, staring down at the table. "My head is swimming, you guys. In a matter of a week, this man comes back into my life and now he's my fake boyfriend. How did this happen?"

"I, for one, am grateful for the source of entertainment," Noelle mumbles around a bite of her food while smiling. "It's been a while since something exciting has happened to one of us."

"Glad I can bring some drama into the group."

"It's not drama, and part of me understands why you agreed. I'm just worried you made a rash decision and aren't thinking everything through," Amelia corrects me.

"I honestly don't know if this was a good idea or not, you guys. But hell, it's worth a shot. My mother keeps texting me and asking me questions about Damien, which I've been avoiding until we talk again. But now I don't have to worry about finding a stranger to come to Hawaii with me and sharing a room with a man I don't know." And then it hits me. "Oh my God. I'm going to have to share a room with Damien."

"What? Why?" Noelle asks.

But Penelope answers for me. "Because if they're a couple, why would they stay in separate rooms, girl? Come on. You read romance novels for a living. I'd expect you to keep up with all of the details better than this."

Noelle huffs. "Not every author I work with writes romance, Penelope. And sorry, but this champagne is going to my head. It would have clicked in a second."

"It's going to be okay. Hopefully by then, you two will feel more comfortable around each other and you'll have boundaries in place. Please, Charlotte, make sure you set up boundaries with him so things don't get fuzzy," Amelia pleads.

"Boundaries?"

"Yes, like how he's allowed to touch you, what you're willing to share about your fake relationship out loud so he doesn't inadvertently embarrass you, and make sure you two agree on how and when this will end."

"Boundaries." I nod. "Okay, I can do that."

"Also make sure you agree on a safe word when he ties you up when you two start fucking," Penelope snickers.

"Come on you guys," Noelle interjects. "If Charlotte says nothing is going to happen, then let's support her in that decision. She's one of the smartest, most determined women I know. And although I don't think this is the smartest decision you've ever made, you know we are here to support you no matter what." Reaching across the table, she takes my hand in hers.

"Thanks for the bout of confidence."

"You've got this, Charlotte. And once you get laid and get to experience hate sex for the first time, please make sure to call me and give me all the details." Penelope winks at me as I reach for my mimosa and down the rest of it. At this rate, I'm afraid I might develop a drinking problem from the chaos that is wreaking havoc in my life right now.

But I can handle this. Noelle is right. It's Damien—I put up with his annoying habits and sarcasm for years. What're a few weeks if we both get something out of it?

I'm not sure how or why this happened, but there's no turning back now. I'm officially dating my nemesis, and no matter what my friends say, I have no intention of seeing or touching his dick.

Striding down the sidewalk, I take another sip of my iced coffee in my hand as horns honk in the background through the streets of downtown L.A. As much as I can, I try to walk to and from lunch to offset the calories I take in each day, and having lunch outside of my office is important to me so that I get to soak in the California sunshine. I learned early on in my job from other senior executives that if I didn't take time for myself each day, I would end up resenting my job, and that's the last thing I want to do.

I love my job.

Working for a woman's magazine has allowed me to give a voice to the everyday issues women deal with—from society, from ourselves, and from men. We celebrate women who are making waves in business, following their dreams, and living in each and every phase of their lives. Furthermore, we provide a place to present fact over fiction and hard-hitting topics of discussion that are hot in the market right now.

My job has made me feel more confident in who I am and what I want, but I wish that my lack of a man in my life didn't make me question that. It's funny how as a woman, you can feel like you have everything together in one aspect of your life, and yet still feel that you're failing in another. And then there's days where you feel like nothing you're doing is good enough, despite everything you've been able to accomplish so far. That feeling—it's the one hold my mother has over me, and now because of Damien, I'm intent on taking it back. The only person that should have the power to make me feel inferior is myself, even though I have nothing to feel inferior about. Being a woman is really tough sometimes because of that voice in our heads that never shuts up. Sometimes she's our biggest cheerleader, and other times she's our worst enemy.

And I know it sounds hypocritical that I'm using Damien and lying to my mom to deal with this problem, but sometimes people need a little smoke and mirrors so they can leave you alone. My mother wants to believe what she sees, so I'm giving her something to appease her while appeasing myself in the process. Sounds like a win-win to me.

As I walk down the sidewalk, I take a turn I normally wouldn't because I'm headed somewhere I've never been before. I see the sign for Goldstein Advertising up on my left, the tall building stretching up into the sky with glassy windows reflecting the sunlight. Now that I know that Damien works here, my mind is conjuring up many ideas about who he is compared to the version of him that I knew.

If the man was willing to lie for his job, he must be feeling some sort of pressure. Apparently, he's not coming in first place around here all the time as well, and deep down, I love that—because at that moment Friday night where he admitted to making up a fake girlfriend to get ahead—he seemed human to me for the first time. Not just this guy that I hated with every fiber of my being years ago, but a person who struggles just like everyone else with inferiority.

Knowing that the dinner with his boss is this Friday, he sent me a text Sunday afternoon, asking if I would be willing to stop by his office sometime this week to make an impromptu visit and show my face, laying the foundation of our relationship.

When I was in high school, I played the lead role in every play I could. I know that understanding the other characters in the show is just as important as knowing my own role. So with the intent to do a little research and hold up my end of this deal, I open the door to the lobby of Damien's building and take the elevator to the level where I know the show must begin.

Stepping out onto the tile floor, I see the Goldstein logo hanging proudly on the wall to my left and a receptionist desk directly in front of me, very similar to how Revision looks when you arrive on our floor. White floors and black décor give the place a classy look without looking too gaudy. It's stylish and a good first impression to potential clients.

With purpose, I walk to the main receptionist and wait for her to acknowledge me since I can see she's on the phone.

"Hi, there. How can I help you?"

"I'm here to see Damien Shaw."

She narrows her eyes at me. "Do you have an appointment?"

"No, but I'm his girlfriend and I'm here to surprise him." *Good job, Charlotte. You were able to say those words without the threat of puking.*

"Damien has a girlfriend?" she asked, clearly astonished, further supporting his claims about his boss not believing him to be the dating type because apparently others feel the same way.

"Yeah, I locked him down a few months ago. It wasn't easy, but it's always rewarding when you can be the one to tame a guy, am I right?"

Public service announcement, ladies: Don't ever go after a guy with the intent to be the exception for him. You are not the one that gets to decide that. He is. And if you keep pursuing him and he doesn't want to commit, you're the only person who looks like an idiot in that situation for going after a man that clearly doesn't want to be the guy you need him to be.

"Ugh, yes. I hate when they can't figure out that you are the answer to all of their problems, you know?" she asks, smacking her gum. The girl has to be twenty-two, fresh out of college. Ah, to be young and completely naïve about men still.

No thank you.

"Well, Damien and I actually knew each other as kids. He's definitely grown up a bit since then because believe me, he never would have had a chance with me back then." I wink at her, but deep down, I wonder if anything I've said about Damien is true. From what I've seen so far, Damien still seems to be the boy with something to prove. But honestly, don't we all have something to prove to someone?

"Gah! I love that. Childhood sweethearts." She clasps her hands against her chest.

"Something like that. So can you tell me where to go? I've never actually been here, but I just couldn't go another minute without seeing him." *Oh, wait…there's the bile I was waiting for earlier.*

"Of course." She pushes back in her chair and then stands. "Go straight ahead until you hit the second hall on your left. Turn down that one and then he's the third door on the right."

"Thank you so much." I grab my coffee and the coffee I grabbed for Damien and head in the direction she said. As I walk through the floor, I can feel eyes all over me, curiosity filtering out into the air. It may also be because I wore my Calvin Klein dark gray dress that I always feel like a million bucks in. The confidence a certain article of clothing does for a woman is something you can't put a price on, especially when you're walking into a nerve-wracking situation.

Taking in a shaky breath, I arrive at Damien's office and knock on the door, listening to a muffled conversation on the other side. But when he answers the door, the view of him standing there in his dark gray suit with the L.A. skyline behind him has saliva pooling in my mouth in an instant.

Every time I see him, my body reacts stronger than the last time. There is something about a man in a suit that makes my vagina wake up and summon every hormone in my body. Although, given how long it's been since I've been with a man, it has to be purely coincidental that Damien is making that happen—right?

"Hi," I say a little more breathlessly than I intended.

"Charlotte." The smile on his face is bigger than I've ever seen it, which makes me wonder if it's genuine or not. But then my eyes shift behind him where I see two other men rise from their spots on the couch and begin to approach me. "What a surprise, babe. What are you doing here?" Damien asks enthusiastically, signaling with his voice that this is a time to get into character.

"Well, I was in the neighborhood and stopped at that coffee shop we love, so I decided to bring you a little afternoon pick-me-up."

"Aw, thanks, sweet pea." He winks as he takes the coffee from me and then leans into my ear.

"I should have slipped something in your drink," I whisper as I wrap an arm around his neck at the same time his hand falls to my waist.

"How do I know that you didn't?" he mumbles back in a low whisper.

"Guess you'll have to take a sip and find out."

When Damien releases me, I smile sweetly up at him before directing my attention to his associates. "I'm so sorry. I hope I wasn't interrupting anything."

"We were actually just about done, but I'm glad that we were running a little behind so I had the chance to meet you." The shortest of the three of them moves toward me with his hand outstretched. "I'm Dave, Damien's boss."

"Oh, hello. I've heard so much about you," I lie.

"All good things, I hope," he teases as he casts a glance at Damien and then back to me. "Although I can't say the same about you. Seems Damien has been keeping you a secret."

"Oh, well, that was my idea actually. We sort of have a history and I was adamant about figuring out where this was going before telling people." I reach up and pinch his cheek. "Good to know he followed directions."

"Believe me, the last thing I want to do is piss you off, sweet pea."

I clench my teeth at him while Dave laughs at us from the side. "Sounds about right. If your woman is happy, everything else will fall into place, Damien. Don't ever forget that."

"I'm learning that fact very quickly."

"I wish I had more time to chat, but duty calls. Charlotte, it was lovely to meet you," Dave says, reaching for my hand once more. "I look forward to Friday when I can introduce you to my wife, and you can tell me more about how Damien locked down a beautiful woman such as you."

"Oh, he was very analytical in his pursuit of me, I assure you."

Dave chuckles. "When a man sees something he wants, he'll always go after it. Nice work today, gentleman. I'll see you later."

The three of us watch Dave leave and the other man who hasn't introduced himself yet shuts the door behind him, blowing out a breath as he leans his back against it. "Holy shit. I was holding my breath the entire time."

"Relax, Jeffrey. I told you Charlotte wouldn't let us down," Damien replies, setting the coffee down on his desk after he walks away from me.

"Jeffrey? I had a massage therapist named Jeffrey last week. You don't happen to moonlight as one in your spare time, do you?"

Jeffrey's eyes grow big as he slides his gaze over to Damien and then back to me. "Nope. Never rubbed anyone down in my life."

Damien clears his throat. "No, Jeffrey here is my right-hand man and the other half of my team up for the promotion that we want," he says while shuffling papers around his desk. "He also knows about our arrangement, Charlotte, so no need to put on a show anymore."

"Good to know. Nice to meet you, Jeffrey." I turn back to Damien. "Now back to the important stuff. What did I tell you about sweet pea?"

"You *are* scary." Jeffrey pulls my attention back to him.

"Excuse me?"

"Damien said you have a death glare that could kill someone in their sleep," he replies.

I shoot a glare over at Damien. "You don't have to be asleep in order for it to work."

"You don't scare me, woman," Damien says without looking up at me.

"Is that so?" I take a step toward him. "You know, I agreed to this, but you never know what may come out of my mouth, Damien. You might want to watch what you're telling people about me."

That catches his attention. He lifts his eyes up to mine but then he drops them down my entire body with a slow speed that makes me feel frozen in place. And I hate that the way he's looking at me makes me wish Jeffrey wasn't in the room right now. I don't know what would happen, but in my mind, it's definitely not rated PG and it involves me on top of his desk.

Jesus, it really has been too long.

"I'm aware, which is why we need to meet up one night this week to go over our story."

"What?"

"Dinner. My place. We need to be on the same page, know the details of our relationship like the back of our hands so our story adds up. Like the fact that I don't drink coffee, but rather, tea." *What the fuck? Is he British now?* He glances at the cup I brought him then back to me. "The last thing I want to do is make a slip in front of Dave and make him suspicious."

"What kind of monster doesn't drink coffee?"

Jeffrey snickers as Damien rolls his eyes. "The kind that doesn't like the taste of it. I tried to, but it's just not for me."

"Well, that's unfortunate. Coffee is amazing. I can't function without it."

"It is unfortunate but particular to me. And that's something that my *girlfriend* should know. So, like I said, we need to coordinate our story. I'm sure there are details about you that I should be aware of as well."

"What if I'm busy?"

He sighs, standing to full height. "Then move some things around. This was part of the agreement, Charlotte. You do this for me, and I'll keep your mom off your back, and play my part in Hawaii. Come on… don't make this harder than it needs to be."

The part of me that is used to fighting Damien about everything wants to continue the battle for control. But the rational part of my brain knows that he's right. We need to be on the same page.

"Fine. I can fit you in Thursday night. Tomorrow I have a hair appointment, and Wednesday night I have other plans." Damien doesn't need to know about my waxing appointment, I'm sure.

"Thursday will work."

"What about our plans to work on the pitch?" Jeffrey interjects, almost heartbrokenly.

"We'll work on it a bit before Charlotte comes over. Once she gets there, I'll just kick you out," Damien replies.

Jeffrey scoffs. "I see how it is. You get a fake girlfriend and I'm already the second choice." He fans his face dramatically. "I thought it was bros before hoes forever, man?"

"Don't worry, Jeffrey. Damien will not be getting any hoe treatment from me, so if you two are into that sort of thing, he's still your man."

Damien shakes his head, pinching the bridge of his nose. Clearly, he's irritated right now, and apparently, Jeffrey and I aren't making the situation any better. "I swear, this all better be worth it."

"It will be. Just think about the perks, the raise, the bigger office that will all come out of this if we win." Jeffrey walks over to Damien, slapping a hand on his shoulder.

But Damien just stares across the room at me, a furrow on his brow and a hint of embarrassment on his face too. "There's a lot to gain, but a lot to lose too."

Feeling flustered and annoyed at the same time, I take Damien's vague words as my cue to leave. "Well, I have work to do as well, gentleman, so I'd better be going." Turning on my heel, I head for the door, but Damien calls out after me.

"Charlotte, wait." I spin around to see him stalk toward me, the command in his posture overbearing and intimidating as he approaches me. When he arrives just a few inches from where I'm standing, I have to crane my neck back to stare up into his light blue eyes, eyes that seem to be hiding so many feelings behind them. Perhaps this little ruse is putting even more pressure on him than he thought.

"Thank you for stopping by. I know it made an impression with Dave and will help with Friday night."

"You're welcome."

"I'll see you Thursday then, right?"

I simply nod before turning around and opening the door. "See you later, beautiful," he calls after me, causing me to turn around to see his face. And for a moment I wonder if he really meant those words, or he just said them aloud because other people might hear him.

It shouldn't matter either way, but on my walk back to my office, uneasiness rests in my stomach when I realize that I truly wanted to know the answer.

Chapter 6

Damien

"Who was that?"

I look up from my desk to see Elizabeth, one of the other creative marketing managers, standing in the doorway of my office.

"Who are you talking about?"

"The woman that was just in your office. Forgive me, but I don't think I've ever seen a woman up here with you two." She slides her eyes over to Jeffrey and then back to me. "For a good reason."

"That was my girlfriend, Elizabeth, not that it's any of your business," I answer, my heart pounding from just having to announce that out loud.

I thought having Charlotte come into the office was a good idea, but I'm shocked by how rattled having her here has made me feel. It was like she stepped into my territory and made all of these old tendencies come alive again—especially when I think about why we started competing in the first place.

I shake that thought from my mind and then turn my attention back to Elizabeth.

"You—you have a girlfriend?"

"Yes..."

"Since when?"

"Uh, about a month and a half ago?" I say, making a note to let Charlotte know during our meeting that's what I'm telling people around the office.

Elizabeth narrows her eyes at me. "Interesting."

"Did you need something, Elizabeth?"

Jeffrey still stands frozen in place, watching this entire conversation play out. It's no wonder he's single. He can't handle a woman that has bigger balls than he does.

"Well, I came by to wish you luck on your pitch."

My brow rises. "Is that so?"

"Yeah, Dave told me you two wanted in on the account," she explains, moving further into the room. "Can't say I wasn't surprised, but when Dave assured me you had something to offer to the table, I wanted to come over here and make sure you knew what you were getting yourself into."

"I'm fully prepared to give the best pitch I can."

"Is your girlfriend gonna help you?" she draws out, lifting her hand to play with the collar of her blouse. And I don't fall for the trap in the slightest.

Elizabeth has always had a thing for me, but I've never dipped my pen in the company ink. And besides, Elizabeth is blonde. My eyes have only ever drifted toward brunettes. Funny how that hasn't really been a blip on my radar until recently.

"That's none of your concern."

"Well, you know…" Her hand moves her blouse open further as she leans over my desk now, trying to give me a front-row seat to her cleavage. But my eyes stay firmly planted on hers. "We could always work together if you guys get stuck."

"Is that right?"

She nods slowly, biting her bottom lip. "There might be some late nights that will need to happen, but maybe Dave has this pitch all wrong. Maybe joining male and female powers will give us all the brainpower needed to land the client instead of pegging us against each other."

"I personally love a good pegging," Jeffrey says before realizing what he implied, his eyes going wide. "I mean, shit…that's not what I meant. I meant I like competition, not pegging. I'm not into that, not that there's anything wrong with that if you are…"

"Jeffrey, shut up," Elizabeth spits at him before turning back to me. "What do you say, Damien?"

Fighting the urge to laugh, I lean back in my chair and clasp my hands over my chest. "As delightful as that sounds, I think we'll pass, Elizabeth."

She scoffs. "You're serious? You really think you can land this account when you aren't female?"

"I don't need to have a vagina to sell products to people with vaginas."

Her back straightens, and then she's glaring down at me. "Well, you're certainly cocky enough to think you're going to win."

"Oh, I have plenty of confidence in us." *And cock to back up the cockiness, but I don't say that out loud.*

With a roll of her eyes, she marches away from my desk and back toward the door. "I can't wait to beat you guys. You have no idea what you're getting yourselves into."

"I appreciate your tenacity, but you'll be crying in your Cheerios when we beat you."

"I don't eat Cheerios, you fool. Way too many carbs." And then she stalks off, slamming her heels on the tile as she marches back to her office and out of my sight.

"Why are all of the scary women coming in here today?" Jeffrey asks, breaking the silence. "The next thing I know, my mom is going to walk through that door."

"Doesn't she live in Missouri?" I ask, spinning in my chair to face him.

He nods. "Yeah, but I haven't returned her phone call in a week, and knowing her, it wouldn't surprise me if she'd hop on a plane just to tell me off in person before asking me if I'm okay."

Glancing back at the door, I sigh. "Women are downright terrifying sometimes, aren't they?"

Jeffrey nods. "I'm still waiting for my balls to come back down from when Charlotte was in here."

Charlotte.

God, she looked gorgeous when she came in here today. Her dress was sexy, but not in an unprofessional way. Her hair looked stunning, long and shiny under the lights in the ceiling, and her eyes had nothing but a slight shimmer on the lid and thick dark lashes to frame them.

These are all things I shouldn't be noticing about her, of course, especially because finding her attractive not only goes against every natural instinct I've been taught to feel about her, but it's making my head swim with how my attraction might affect my end goal here.

I just need to keep her hating me, and everything will be alright.

"You ready to call it a day on the report?" Jeffrey asks, pulling me back to the present.

"Oh. Uh, yeah. I have a few things I need to take care of before I leave, anyway."

He salutes me and then heads for the door. "Sounds good. See you tomorrow, man."

"Yeah, see ya."

"And I'll bring over the supplies on Thursday for our brainstorming session."

"Sounds good. Thanks."

As I spin around and stare out the windows, I take a deep breath and remind myself that this will all be worth it. It has to be. No reward is possible without a minor risk.

"What on earth were you thinking?" I stare down at my dining room table covered in feminine products. Boxes of tampons, packages of pads, panty liners, menstrual cups, feminine sprays, and women's underwear are scattered all over the surface. The dipshit bought women's underwear. *insert facepalm

"There were way too many options. Like, how the fuck does a woman make a choice on what to use? And how was I supposed to know what to buy, Damien?" He gestures to the table. "At least now we can look at everything and make an educated decision."

I shake my head, staring down at the floor. "All we needed was a few things, Jeffrey. Just a few. Tell me, how much money did you spend?"

Jeffrey huffs and then licks his lips. "Get this, man. Almost three hundred dollars!"

"What?" I shout. "That's preposterous."

He nods. "I know. This shit is not cheap, my friend. And to think, women have to buy these things each month, *have to*. Some options are cheaper than others, but the top-selling brand was the most expensive one."

"And it all just goes in the trash, or gets flushed down the toilet."

Shocked, I stare down at the products again. I think we are in way over our heads here. How on earth are you supposed to sell this shit to women? Why do they pick one brand over the other? Is it always about cost? Comfort? The fucking packaging?

Jeffrey grabs one of the menstrual cups and opens it up. "What is this?"

"Do you not know how to read? It's a menstrual cup."

He rips open the package and holds it up to the light. "It looks like a shot glass."

"I'd hate to be around and watch someone confuse the two, that's for damn sure."

Nodding in agreement, he sets it down and then grabs one of the tampons sitting on the table and opens it up.

"What are you doing?"

"Research." He rips open the plastic and pulls out a plastic tube that is shiny and pink. "Jesus. What is this?"

"It's a tampon, dipshit."

A small plastic tube slides down from the main tube. "Whoa." Then he pushes the small tube back up and the cotton piece expels from the top. "Fuck!"

"This is entirely too disturbing to watch."

"This is crazy, man," he says just as I reach for a tampon of my own, needing to experience this for myself—for research purposes obviously. But then the buzzer for my apartment interrupts my thoughts.

"Can you get that, man? It's probably the food for when Charlotte gets here."

"Sure." Jeffrey drops the pieces to his tampon on the table and then moves behind me as my mind starts to spin and I open the package, extracting the tampon from within. But the voice behind me is not one I was banking on hearing just yet.

"What the hell did I just walk into?"

Spinning around, I see a wide-eyed Charlotte staring at me as her eyes bounce back and forth between the table, me, and Jeffrey.

"It's, uh, not what you think."

"I'm sorry. What do I think? I think it looks to me that either you two are men who experience man periods—which means they are, in fact, a real thing—or, you bought all of these supplies for me since you knew I was on my period and might need an item or two."

Jeffery squirms to my side, his lips twisting up with disgust. But I don't want this to look worse than it already does.

Thinking on my feet is one of my many talents, so my brain lands on a rebuttal faster than she expects. "What if we bought all of this to donate to a woman's shelter, huh?"

Charlotte's eyebrows rise. "Well, then I would say that's pretty awesome since those places are always running short on items like these, especially underwear." She moves to the table and grabs one of the thongs that Jeffrey bought, holding it up to the light. "Although, just so you know, I'm sure women in a shelter wouldn't care about panty lines, but at least you have good taste."

"I bought those more for me," Jeffrey spits out, sticking his foot in his mouth yet again.

"Oh really, Jeffrey? You like a little butt floss?" Charlotte teases him, and I can't help it, I fucking laugh.

"No! Fuck!" He reaches up and pulls on his hair. "I just meant that I liked them, like if a woman were to wear them, I'd think they're hot."

"Well, they are pretty," Charlotte says, admiring the red silk. "I actually have a pair of these. But just so you know, thongs aren't really period friendly."

"How so?"

"You really want me to go on?" she asks just as the buzzer sounds again. Jeffrey moves to the door again, and even though I know Charlotte could give me some insight on the matter we're discussing, this was not the topic I intended to talk about this evening.

"Maybe another time. Jeffrey here was just about to leave, and I'm going to put this stuff away."

"Sure, sure. Kick me out." Jeffrey walks into my kitchen holding a cardboard box full of brown paper bags. He sets the box on the counter and then moves to help me collect the items and put them into the second bedroom in my place. "We didn't even get to test any of this out." And then he turns to Charlotte. "Say, Charlotte. How do those tampons fit in—you?"

"What do you mean?"

Holding several boxes, he begins to attempt to balance them in his arms. "I mean, do you…how do you…does it hurt when you stick them in your, you know." He widens his eyes.

Charlotte grins. "Jeffrey, you do know that tampons are way smaller than a penis, and those fit in my…you know." And then she starts laughing, covering her mouth. "Oh, unless you're sized more like a tampon…" She winces. "Then, I'm sorry for assuming."

"What? No!" he shouts, but I just push him toward the room.

"Stop talking while you're ahead, man."

"I don't have a small penis though!"

"I really don't want to know how you were planning on testing out any of this," Charlotte adds as we walk away from her, her face contorted as she moves over to the food.

"We'll be right back," I call over my shoulder, heading for the spare room. Jeffrey follows me inside. "What the fuck, man?"

"What did I do? I was just trying to get more information from a woman, you know…the people we're supposed to be selling this shit to."

Frustrated beyond belief, I set the items on the bed haphazardly. "You know what? I can't even get into this right now."

"It's okay. We've got time, Damien," he says, clasping me on the shoulder. "Take care of things with Charlotte tonight and we can reconvene tomorrow at the office."

"Yeah. Okay."

"But if you get a chance to pick her brain about periods, don't waste the opportunity." He winks and then walks back out of the room as I follow him.

Charlotte is opening up the bags of food as we make our way back into the room. "What did you get?"

"Some pasta and salads from Tony's down the street," I reply.

Her face lights up. "Spaghetti and meatballs and the antipasto salad?"

I nod, surprised that she knew what I'd order. "Yeah, actually."

"That's the best dish there. I'm impressed. I didn't think you'd order one of my favorite meals."

"Well, it just so happens to be my favorite too."

Her face falls, surprised at our commonality as well. "Oh."

Jeffrey clears his throat. "Well, I'm going to be going. You two have fun and try not to kill each other, alright?"

"I make no promises," Charlotte replies, lifting the containers of food from the bags and placing them on the counter, inhaling the mouthwatering aroma as my mouth begins to salivate too. Fuck, I'm really hungry.

Jeffery chuckles and then moves for the door. "And just so we're clear, my penis is definitely bigger than a tampon. See ya tomorrow, Damien."

Shaking my head at him, I hold the door open for him. "Have a good night, man." And then he's gone, leaving me alone with the woman I never thought I'd ever be buying dinner for.

Now that Jeffrey is out of the room and all of the feminine products are far from my mind, I finally get a moment to take Charlotte in.

She's wearing black capris made of some type of stretchy fabric, high-lighting her curves and that ass of hers I can't seem to get out of my mind. A light pink tank top hugs her torso, and her long hair that I prefer down is thrown up in a ponytail that swings with each of her movements.

Her look is such a contrast to the business persona I've only seen her in so far, but part of it reminds me of what she was like before we left for college—the girl next door that I grew up with and secretly admired—not in the attractive sense, but for the simple fact that her confidence seemed to be unwavering. Seems she's still packing pride underneath that tough shell.

But I'd die before I let her know that.

"Jeffrey sure is interesting."

"You have no idea."

I hear her chuckle and then she turns to the food again. "Do you have plates?" she asks as she pops open the lids of the boxes.

"No. I don't own any of those," I answer dryly.

Her eyes lift to mine. "Was that supposed to be sarcastic?"

"I don't know. What kind of question is that? *Do I have plates?* What do you think I do, eat my food off the counter?"

She rolls her eyes. "I don't know, Damien. You've always seemed to be a little less refined than most to me and you're a bachelor. For all I know, you only survive on takeout and eat cereal for dinner most nights."

That comment has me smiling. "Actually, you're not quite off base. Cooking is not my forte, and I feel that cereal can be eaten at all hours of the day without any repercussions."

"Just give me a plate, please," she says, holding her palm out. I reach up into the cupboard next to my stove, taking out two plates for us, but Charlotte's outburst has me freezing in my movements. "Holy shit. Is that a tea kettle?"

Slowly, I turn around to face her, taking in the shit-eating grin on her mouth. "Yes…"

And then she puts her hand over her mouth to stifle her laugh. "Oh my God. You have a tea kettle."

"I told you. I don't like coffee."

"But this is…"

"What?" I ask, setting the plates on the counter and then crossing my arms over my chest. "What's so funny about this?"

"I'm sorry." She shakes her head while reining in her giggles. "I just never imagined you being the type of guy to own a tea kettle. I'm seeing you in an entirely different light right now."

"For your information, this tea kettle is top of the line from William Sonoma and was a gift from my mom when I moved into this place," I state proudly, hellbent on making Charlotte eat her words for giving me shit. "I can customize the temperature and brew strength on each pot, and it tells me how long it's been since the tea has been brewed so I don't drink bitter tea. It's also dishwasher safe and programmable like a coffee pot." I turn back around, grab the plates, and move to the counter to dish out the food.

"Wow. Okay, that's actually kind of cool." She gets closer to my tea kettle to check it out. I keep my back to her as I scoop out the food onto the plates, but her words catch me off-guard "I'm sorry. It's just…" She takes a deep breath and then lets it out. "This is something I was not anticipating about you."

"Well, even more reason why we should actually get to know each other better. The last time we saw each other, we were self-centered teenagers and our hatred for one another overruled any common sense. We're adults now, and I don't know about you, but I am not the same person I was back then."

I feel her hand connect with my forearm, the heat of her touch zinging across my skin. My body slips into a frenzy, remembering how it felt touching her on that massage table, the way the electricity that coursed through my hands and into her body was a surprising reaction I was not anticipating. And my question is, does she feel that too when we touch?

"You're right. I'll try to keep an open mind."

"Thank you," I relent. "And if you're on your best behavior, maybe I'll make you a pot of tea and show you what that bad boy is capable of."

She laughs, the sound so jovial and light that it gives me a glimpse of her I don't think I've ever seen around me—carefree Charlotte. I wonder if she's ever felt like she could just relax around me before? I sure as hell have never felt that way around her.

But here's to trying new things in the spirit of going after what we both want.

"Come on. We can eat on the couch." I grab the plates and head for my living room, placing them both on the coffee table stationed between the couch and my recliner, another gift from my mother.

My apartment isn't huge and fancy, but it's a lot for a bachelor like me, and a place I'm proud of because I earned it on my own. It's comfortable and home for now until I can afford something a little more refined for my taste, a house that this new promotion would help me acquire.

"I have some wine if you're interested," I offer as I stand and see Charlotte headed toward me, the sway of her hips purely hypnotizing.

"That sounds great. Red or white is fine by me."

"Okay." I go back into the kitchen, pouring us both a glass of chardonnay, and then join her once again in my living room.

"Thank you. Your place is nice, Damien," she says before taking a sip of her wine, glancing around the room.

"Thanks. The rent is more than I'd like, but it has laundry facilities and a gym. Can't really beat that."

"It's a lot neater than I thought it'd be too."

"What are you trying to say? You think I'm a slob?" I tease.

"Not necessarily. I just know most men don't care to clean up after themselves." She grabs her plate and dives into her food with hunger, and it's fucking sexy. "God, all this salad is missing is feta cheese."

Jesus…the way she eats is sexy, Damien?

"Feta cheese?"

"Yes. I love it. If anything has feta cheese, I'll eat it." And then I watch her shove raw onions in the salad to the side. "Now raw onion on the other hand can go to hell."

"Feta cheese and no raw onion. I'm going to store that information away for later." I reach for my plate and begin eating too. "And to piggyback off your last comment, I guess without my mom to clean up after me, I've learned to do it myself."

She snorts. "You always were a momma's boy."

"Again, you saw the tea kettle she bought me."

She takes a deep breath and sets her fork down on her plate. "Okay. So I guess it's time we discuss what I came here to, right?"

I nod in agreement. "Yeah. We need to make sure our relationship details match up. Dave will notice, and he's not the only one."

"What do you mean?"

"One of my colleagues came by after you left Tuesday asking about you. Your presence stirred up quite the gossip mill around the office."

"Really?"

I bob my head up and down again. "I told you. I don't date. This is why people are going to be skeptical and I need this to be believable."

"Okay. So, how long have we been seeing each other?"

"I told one of my colleagues the other day that it's been six weeks."

"That's it? That doesn't seem long…"

"No, but any longer and I think it would invite even more questions why you haven't been talked about. And, a bunch of us went out for drinks about two months ago and I definitely didn't leave the bar alone. So if the timelines overlapped, that wouldn't look good for me or you."

Her eyes veer to the side, away from me. Shit, I probably shouldn't discuss my past hook-ups around her. It's not that I'm ashamed, but I don't want to make her uncomfortable. Besides, I barely remember that woman. It's not like she meant anything.

But you sure as hell remember what Charlotte looked like naked, don't you, Damien?

Well, at least her backside.

"Okay, six weeks," she agrees, diving back into her food but avoiding my gaze. "And how did we reconnect? Does anyone know that we knew each other before?"

"Yes, actually. When I came up with this lie, I told Dave I was with someone I knew from back home. It just so happened that I saw you later that day and I thought the timing couldn't have been more perfect."

She huffs. "Lucky for you."

"Hey, don't forget you're getting something out of this too."

She sighs. "Yeah, I know. My mom called the other day asking about you…"

"Really?"

"Yup. I told her we were hanging out tonight, which wasn't a lie. But if she only knew…"

"Why do you care so much about what she thinks?" I ask, understanding that feeling more than she may realize. If I really told her about my dad and how he played a role in our little competition growing up, she'd probably accuse me of lying.

"I don't. Not really." She leans forward to place her plate on the coffee table before curling her legs underneath her on the couch, clutching her glass of wine in both hands. "It's just exhausting having to constantly defend myself, you know? Just because I'm single doesn't mean I haven't accomplished anything in life. I've worked my ass off to get where I am in my career, but that just never seems to be good enough for her. Every time I feel confident about where I am, one conversation with her can derail my entire mood. And I don't know that she does it on purpose, but it's stifling."

"I get it. I do."

"Really? How?" she asks, but before I can answer, her phone rings. "Sorry. Hold on." She leaps from the couch and walks over to her purse, giving me the perfect glimpse of her backside. Fuck, her ass is exquisite. "Oh, shit. It's my mom," she says, spinning around to face me, clutching her phone to her chest.

"Okay…"

"She's trying to Facetime me."

My mind instantly sparks with an idea. "Let me answer it."

"What? No!"

"Why not? She knows we're hanging out together. That's probably why she called."

"But…"

"This will work to our advantage, lay some groundwork for Hawaii. Remember, we have to sell this to your parents, Char. Your mom is going to want breadcrumbs. I know her."

Charlotte bites on her bottom lip, and the sight has my dick stirring. *I wonder if she does that during sex?* "Okay, fine. Just…be vague."

"Got it." She hands me the phone and I swipe to answer the call before it ends. "Hello, Mrs. Montgomery."

"Damien? Is that you?"

"Yes, ma'am. In the flesh."

"Where's Charlotte?"

"She's in the bathroom. I told her you were calling and she said to answer. How are you? You're looking beautiful as always." That grants me a blinding smile.

"Oh, Damien. You are just so sweet. Some things never change, I guess, huh?" she says as Charlotte rolls her eyes behind the phone that is currently facing me.

"Well, some things do change, Mrs. M., like the fact that Charlotte finally gave me a chance after all these years." I wink over at Charlotte as she shakes her head.

"I know. I still can't believe it, but I feel as though this was all meant to be." She brings her hands under her chin, and I swear, I can see hearts in her eyes. "I secretly always wondered if there were feelings between you two."

"Seems as though we've finally found them."

Charlotte steps in and grabs the phone from me before I can say another word. "Hi, Mom."

"Oh, hi honey. How are you?"

"Good. At Damien's, as I told you I would be."

"I didn't interrupt anything, did I?" she says with a wink. "You know I'd always preach using protection, but an accidental pregnancy wouldn't be the worst thing to happen to you now, dear. You're not getting any younger."

Charlotte clenches her jaw as I feel my heart rate pick up speed. *There will be no accidental pregnancies anywhere near us, thank you very much.*

"Mom, please don't discuss my sex life with me."

Mrs. M. holds her hands up in the air. She must be propping the phone up against something if both of her hands are free. "I'm just saying. Time's ticking, honey."

"How can I help you, Mom?" Charlotte asks, changing the topic, thank God. I can't imagine having someone pressure you to have a kid, let alone your mom. My mom knows I'm not ready to settle down, but my dad? Hell, if he caught wind that Charlotte was looking to procreate, he'd convince me to knock someone up ASAP just to beat her.

Yeah, did you catch that? Oh, just wait until I let you in on just how my dad plays a role in all of my history with Charlotte.

"I wanted to make sure you stopped by the dress shop this week for your fitting."

"Yes, Mom. And I ordered the dress."

"Good. You're going to look beautiful standing up next to us at the ceremony in Hawaii. Now just watch what you're eating between now and then so we don't have to do any last-minute alterations," she says sweetly, but I catch the underlying message underneath. Jesus, is this really what Charlotte is putting up with?

"I wouldn't dare," Charlotte mocks.

I grab the phone back from Charlotte. She tries to fight me for it, but I twist around her and begin to walk away. "Charlotte is going to be the most beautiful woman there, Mrs. M., no matter what she's wearing or what she eats. If you're not careful, she may even show you up." Charlotte's jaw drops open with a slight smile on her lips. "Now, I hate to cut this call short, but I was just about to make Charlotte my dessert, so we best be going."

"What are you making?" her mom asks.

"No, you misunderstood. Charlotte *is* dessert." I smile proudly. "Talk to you soon, Mrs. M." Dropping the phone down, I end the call and then look up to find Charlotte still staring agape at me.

"I cannot believe you just said that to my mom."

"Well, she has a lot of nerve saying shit like that to you." I hand her the phone back and then retreat back to my recliner. But then I notice the plates are still sitting on the coffee table. "Are you done eating?"

Charlotte sighs. "I probably should be. Heaven forbid I can't fit into my dress."

I lift up both plates and head for the kitchen, placing them on the counter, and then turn back to Charlotte, gently gripping her chin in my hand. Her eyes lift and seek mine out, and the minuscule space between us suddenly feels stifling. "Your mother is wrong, Charlotte, okay? Your body is fucking perfect, and you don't need to have kids tomorrow in order to appease her, all right?"

Her eyes bounce back and forth between mine, full of questions. But her response lands on two words. "Thank you."

"For?"

"For sticking up for me."

I drop my fingers from her chin. "Hell, there's a first time for everything, am I right?"

She huffs out a laugh. "Yeah, I guess so. At least if she called tonight, she probably won't bother me for the rest of the weekend. She always loves to call me Sunday morning before I attend brunch with the girls."

"The ladies who brunch, huh?"

She smiles. "Yup. We go to Frankie's every Sunday, and she always manages to ruin one of my favorite parts of the week with her nagging beforehand."

"So why do you answer the phone?"

"Because if I don't she'll just keep calling." Charlotte sighs and I take this opportunity to shift gears.

"So let's finish this conversation. Not to rush you out or anything, but if I don't get at least six hours of sleep, I'm a zombie the next day."

Charlotte follows me back into the living room and we take our seats again. "Oh my God, right? I swear I used to be able to survive on three hours and a few cups of coffee. Now, getting a crappy night's sleep feels like surviving a hangover."

"The perks of getting older," I joke.

"Turning thirty has done cruel and unusual things to my body."

I try to block out the images of Charlotte's body from my mind with her comment, but I fail miserably. "Do you realize that we've known each other for over twenty years?"

"Yes," she says. "I was thinking about that when I ran into you at the restaurant when I was with the girls."

"Speaking of which, should we say that's how we reconnected since it did happen, and that way we don't have to remember another lie?" I suggest.

"Yeah, that makes sense."

"Cool. Now I think we should know what we were both up to between high school and college. I mean, for purely selfish reasons, I want to know just how much trouble you got yourself into without worrying about beating me at everything." I smirk as Charlotte narrows her eyes at me.

"Sorry to disappoint you, but I was primarily focused on school."

"I call bullshit. Those girls you call your friends? They had to have played a part in you making some piss poor decisions. I mean, I know for a fact I woke up naked a few times in college and had no idea what happened the night before thanks to my buddies."

"Why does that not surprise me?" She rolls her eyes. "But sorry to break it to you, my college life was fairly timid. I studied hard and got an internship at *Revision*, then worked my way up to where I'm at now."

"Fine. Don't give me all the dirt just yet. But I know you had fun. It just shows that you're human, Charlotte. I always thought you were part robot growing up. You made everything you did look so easy."

"Ha! Easy for you to say. You're the one who never had to study and would still do better on tests than me."

My face falls and then I'm clearing my throat. It's true. I barely had to study, but the pressure to beat her wasn't just coming from me. She doesn't need to know all of the details about that yet though. "I actually had to study our senior year for once, especially for Calculus. There was no way I was going to pass that class without a little effort."

Charlotte's eyes go wide. "Wow." And then her grin catches on one side. "Tell me something you're not good at, Damien."

"Like?"

She shrugs. "Anything. I feel like I always painted you out to be this guy who could do anything flawlessly. But now I know that everything I thought I knew can't all be true."

I inhale deeply, pondering my answer. "I can't cook."

She shakes her head. "No, you already told me that. Something else."

I stare up at the ceiling in thought. And then decide maybe this is a good time to bare part of my truth to her. "You're not the only one with a parent that's hard to please."

She rears back in her seat, her smile diminishing with each passing second. "What?"

"Yeah." I brush my hand through my hair. "So don't beat yourself up over your mom, because if you knew how much pressure my dad put on me, you might be grateful your mom is as easy as she is."

"Damien…"

A notification pings from my phone, interrupting our conversation. "Shit. Sorry." I leap from my chair and grab my phone, seeing a reminder about my early morning meeting. And that's when I glance at the time on the screen. "Shit. It's almost nine."

"Really?" She stands and then makes her way over to me, grabbing her phone from her purse. "Yikes. Well, I'd better be going."

"Yeah. But we didn't make our list."

She places a hand on her hip, staring at the ceiling. Then she lowers her head and stares me down. "One, no kissing with tongue. A brush on the lips is only necessary if the situation warrants it. Deal?"

Fuck. Does that mean she might actually let me kiss her? *Why are you suddenly filled with excitement, Damien?*

I play it cool. "Okay."

"Two, do not touch my ass."

I smile, I can't fucking help it. "Alright." *You didn't say anything about staring at it though.*

"And three, if either of us feels like this is getting out of hand, we put a stop to it."

"Really?"

"Yeah. I don't want to create problems for you or me, and even though I know things are bound to get complicated, I don't want anyone to get hurt."

I nod, knowing that I already feel like I'm in too deep, but there's no going back now. "Deal."

"Then let's shake on it," she says, holding her hand out to me. I intercept her hand and give it a little squeeze while wondering what her hand would feel like squeezing my cock instead.

It's shitty thoughts like that that will make this harder to get through if you don't knock it off, Damien.

"I know this may come as a surprise, but I actually had a really good time, Charlotte."

"Me too." She smiles, her eyes bright and lighter than I've ever seen them, hinting at the subtle ring of yellow around her irises in the sea of chocolate brown I could stare at for a few minutes longer than necessary. "It was nice to get out of my apartment at night for a change."

"What do you mean?"

"I don't know. I was beginning to feel like Jennifer Lopez in *The Wedding Planner*…"

"Never saw it."

"Oh my God." She rolls her eyes. "Well, there's this scene where she comes home from work, changes her clothes, cooks her own dinner, and sits in front of the television watching her favorite shows. She has this routine where everything has to be in the perfect place and in the same order." She shrugs and then stares down at the floor. "I guess I just feel like that's what life has been like lately."

"I can see that. Things get pretty mundane around here too."

"Well, nothing like a fake relationship and childhood enemies reconnecting to break you out of a funk, am I right?" she jokes.

And that makes me laugh. "Right. Well, get home safe, and I'll pick you up tomorrow around seven. Just text me your address."

Suddenly, she seems nervous as she walks to my door and I follow her. "Okay." Just as she reaches for the knob, her purse slides off her shoulder and falls to the floor, the contents spilling everywhere. "Shit."

"Here, let me help you," I say as we both bend down and avoid bumping heads just barely. Lipstick, keys, and hair clips cover the floor—but it's the Dove chocolates that catch my eye. "You carry chocolate around in your purse?"

"Uh, yes. Is that a problem?"

"No. It's just…don't they melt? That seems messy."

"Sometimes," she explains as we both keep picking up items. "But I have to have some on hand at all times. Chocolate makes everything better."

"Really?"

"Oh yeah. Bad day? Eat a chocolate. Annoying driver on the road? Eat a chocolate. And of course, when your period won't let up, I have to have chocolates on hand. They improve my mood instantly." As she says this, she lifts the foil off one and plops it in her mouth.

"Is there writing on that?" I ask as we both stand.

"Yes. This is my favorite part actually. Each wrapper has a message inside. Some are more inspirational than others, but they can sometimes turn my entire day around."

I take the foil from her and read the message inside. *"Don't settle for a spark. Light a fire instead."*

Our eyes lock and I wonder if she's thinking what I am. Charlotte and I have always felt like two raging fires battling for bragging rights of who could burn faster and hotter. Maybe that's what's always been missing with every other woman, why no other girl has ever got my motor running—because Charlotte has always made it rev the fastest.

"This is brilliant advertising," I say, handing the wrapper back to her.

"Yes, it is." She flattens out the foil and then places it gently in her purse. "And Dove is one of our clients for the magazine, so I always have an endless supply." She straightens up again, clutching her purse under her arm. "Alright, I'm really leaving this time."

"Have a good night," I say as I open the door and watch her walk through the opening.

"Bye, Damien," she says with a wave, and then she walks down the hallway toward the elevator, leaving me standing there with an unfamiliar warmth and desire resting in my chest. But I shake it off, close my door, and head for bed, knowing that tomorrow is what I need to focus on.

This dinner can make or break this ruse. I just hope that Charlotte brings her A-game, and doesn't wear something too distracting. The last thing I need is to be tempted by her even more than I already am.

Fuck, I'm in over my head. And that's not somewhere I'm used to being.

Chapter 7

Charlotte

"So what are you wearing?" Penelope asks as I put on the final coat of my mascara. My phone is lying on the bathroom counter while I have her on speakerphone as I do my makeup.

"A little black dress. I figured I couldn't go wrong with that."

"Okay…but are we talking something you would wear to work, a funeral, or something you would wear to the club?"

I stick the wand back in the tube. "A little bit in the middle, I guess. It has spaghetti straps and a small cut in the front to give me some cleavage, but it's not too short or revealing."

"Okay. That sounds appropriate. I was gonna say, don't go into this thing dressed like a nun. A guy like Damien wouldn't be with a girl who hides everything her momma gave her, you know what I mean?"

Snorting, I reach for my curling iron and pick up a piece of hair that's lost some of its life. "Newsflash, my momma didn't give me these curves. You've seen her. She works out six days a week and counts calories like a psycho. No, my curves come from years of emotional eating and an addiction to chips."

"Girl, you are gorgeous, and there are women who would kill for your curves. I don't know why you let your mother get you down about it."

I sigh. "I know. I don't know either. I guess deep down every person secretly seeks out approval from their parents, and when we fall short in areas they deem important, it makes us feel less than." I think back to instances in my childhood that spark a heaviness in my chest. "My mom was always talking about how she needed to lose weight, or was counting calories, or would beat herself up for having a slice of cake or a scoop of ice cream. I used to think that that was how it was supposed to be, that having that kind of relationship with food is just what you had to battle being a woman. And in college especially, I struggled as I started to put on weight. That spiral is not a place I ever want to end up again."

"I remember that. That night when you passed out on the way to that party is something I'll never forget," Penelope says quietly, thinking about the very instance that was prevalent in my mind. "We'd only known each other for one semester at the time, but I was freaking terrified, Charlotte."

"I know. I hadn't eaten for two days because I'd seen my mom a few days before that, and she made a comment about my weight, Pen. I let it get to me. It took talking to a counselor at school and meeting with a dietician for months for me to get past that, and I still catch myself struggling from time to time."

"I remember, Charlotte, which is why I wish you could see what I see about you. You are headstrong and dedicated, hardworking and loyal. You set your mind to something, and you accomplish it. None of those qualities has to do with your pant size, waist size, or your love life."

"Thank you," I whisper, fighting back the tears threatening to ruin my makeup.

"I mean it. And I know you're going along with this thing for Damien and to appease your mom, but if she can't be proud of the woman you are on the inside, then maybe it's time to put some hard boundaries in place with mother-dearest."

Sniffling, I reach for a tissue to dab under my eyes. "I agree. I just need to make it past Hawaii, and then things are gonna be different."

"You know I'm here for you no matter what," she adds. "And I know there is a man out there that will be lucky to have you as his wife one day. And even if you never get married, my offer to ruffle feathers at the retirement center or nursing home later in life still stands."

I laugh through my tears. "I'm down."

"But you need to talk to your mom at some point and tell her what her bullshit does to you. She may think she's being helpful, but she has no clue the chaos her words create in your mind."

"I know. You're right." So much easier said than done though.

"Good. Now fluff your hair, put on your sexy dress, and help your nemesis kiss ass at his work dinner."

"Ha. You know what's funny? We actually had a normal conversation last night."

"Well, I assumed everything went well since I didn't get a phone call to bail you out of jail."

"Yeah...he ordered us dinner and after we got through our initial little banter, it was...fun." I shrug, checking my hair for more pieces that need a touch-up.

Penelope goes silent and then I hear her tapping something through the phone. "I'm sorry. I didn't hear that. Can you say that again?"

"Oh, Jesus, Pen. Don't make this a bigger deal than it needs to be." I reach for the curling iron again and fix one more strand of hair.

"Forgive me, but you just said you had fun with a man I'm pretty sure you've had dreams about murdering." Little does she know that's not the only dream I've had about Damien lately.

Last night after I got home from his apartment, I tossed and turned in bed for an hour as I replayed our conversation and the things I learned about him. And when he took me by the chin and told me that my mom was wrong after the Facetime conversation—well, let's just say my imagination took that scene further and there was kissing involved.

Yeah, kissing and a lot of P in V action.

"You're not wrong, but we're trying to get along now. We'll see how long it lasts."

"Just make sure to use protection, Charlotte. I'm too young to be the fun aunt just yet."

All I can do is shake my head. "Thank you for your pearls of wisdom and selfish investment in my love life, Pen. Now, if I don't get off the phone soon and get dressed, Damien is going to show up and I'll still be in my robe."

Penelope hollers. "That might not be a bad thing, girl."

"Jesus. I have to go. I love you."

"Love you too, lady. Good luck tonight."

"Thank you." I end the call and then give my hair one more spritz of hairspray, fluffing it up for extra volume. I'll tell you one thing my mother did give me—good hair genes.

Once I slip into my dress and put on a dainty silver necklace, the buzzer for my apartment rings, alerting me that Damien is here. As he requested, I texted him my address so he could pick me up for this dinner, and surprisingly he's right on time.

Nerves run through me as I run my hands down the front of my dress, wondering why my palms sweat so bad. It's embarrassing really, but I can't be the only woman that has this issue, right?

I answer the door, inhaling deeply before I pull it open and come face to face with Damien. His eyes go wide and then he mutters some-thing behind his hand. "Fuck."

"Uh, hello to you too."

Shaking off the look of intensity and wonder on his face, he clears his throat and then straightens his spine. "I'm sorry. Hello. You look…" I watch his eyes dance up and down my body, leaving goose-bumps in their wake.

"I hope the end of that thought is good."

His throat bobs up and down as he swallows and then shoves his hands in his pockets. "It is. You look perfect."

I can feel the heat traveling across my cheeks. "A compliment from Damien Shaw?"

That comment finally has him smirking. "Don't get used to it. Although, if we survive this dinner tonight, you might become my new favorite person."

"From rival enemy to favorite person...that's quite the step up in your world."

"Well, things can change pretty quickly in life—something I've learned throughout the years."

"I feel like you're trying to sound like you've gained some wisdom, but all you've done is remind me that you're old now," I tease.

"Hey, you're not too far behind me, woman."

"You'll always be older than me though which helps me sleep better at night."

Damien shakes his head, smiling the entire time. "Okay then. Are you ready to go?"

"Yes. Just let me grab my purse really quickly. You can come in if you want," I call over my shoulder as I walk into the living room to grab my purse from the couch.

"Nice place, by the way," he says as his eyes scope out my apartment. This two bedroom, two bathroom apartment was a huge step up from the studio I was living in for years. With an updated kitchen featuring white and gray granite and cupboards, a nice sized living room that fits a dark grey sectional couch that I had to have when I saw it, and my love for art displayed proudly on the walls, it feels more and more like home with each passing day. Of course, I'd love to live in a house one day with a husband and kids, but I try not to dwell on that.

"Thank you."

"I love this building."

"So do I. I just moved here last year, actually, after my promotion." Reaching for my purse, I spin around just in time to see Damien's eyes glued on my ass. "Excuse me?"

"What?" He tries not to look guilty but fails miserably.

"I saw that."

"Saw what?"

"You were staring at my ass."

"Okay…"

"Well…that's just…"

"It's not like I was touching it. Remember, that's against the rules."

"So staring at it is okay?"

He shrugs. "You have a nice ass, Charlotte. Sue me for appreciating it."

I stand there, ruffled by his nonchalance, but part of me is reeling with the knowledge that he was checking me out. Or, perhaps, he's just a man and that's how his brain works. Believe me, it wouldn't be the first time I caught a man staring at my backside. I have a lot going on back there. I can't help that. But that doesn't mean it's okay for a man to blatantly eye-fuck you or make vulgar comments about your body. I bet men don't have to deal with that kind of treatment nearly as often as women do.

And I'm not saying there aren't women catcalling men and making comments about their bodies, but I also feel like there's a societal double standard that men can openly do that and we aren't supposed to take offense to it.

"I think we should leave," I say, not wanting to get in a fight before we have to pretend to like each other.

"Yeah, we need to get going if we're going to be on time."

Stepping around him, I wait for him to exit my apartment and then walk side by side with him to the elevator. The ride down is quiet until we exit the lobby of my building and he finally speaks.

"This way. I'm parked down a side street."

"I'm surprised you found a spot at all at this hour."

"Me too."

When we arrive at Damien's car, he unlocks the door and opens it for me. At least he has some manners. "Thank you." I watch him round the hood of the car to his door and get situated inside before we take off down the road. "Okay, so what am I getting into tonight?"

Damien casually grips the steering wheel with one hand, resting the other on the stick shift as he makes his way to the freeway. "In all honesty, I'm not so sure. This is the first time I've ever been invited to one of these things."

"That's right. Do you know who will be there then?"

"So, Dave obviously and his wife, Erin. The CFO of the company Hank Thompson and his wife, Deidra. I'm guessing the other members of the board, which there are too many to name at this moment. Then, maybe a few of the other creative marketing managers that are working on this account."

I nod in understanding. "Well, here's to hoping we can pull this off."

"Here's hoping." Damien holds up two crossed fingers, and then we both get quiet, staying that way for the rest of the drive.

As we drive through the hills of Los Angeles, I think back to the last time I went out with a man and not the girls. I obviously don't consider this night out with Damien a date per se, but it's the closest thing I've had to one in months, so I'm going to make the best of it.

"We're here," Damien announces, pulling into a circle driveway of a two-story house that must be worth three to five million dollars.

"So this is how the other half lives?"

Damien chuckles. "I guess so."

After Damien parks the car, he walks around to open my door for me. "Thank you."

"Have to treat my woman right." He winks, but his claim to me, even as a joke, has a spark of something igniting in my body. And that definitely shouldn't be happening.

"Is it okay to hold your hand?" he asks as we walk up the five small steps leading to the front door. The front porch is decorated with potted flowers, a welcome mat, and a small pineapple statue situated in the corner by the door. *Huh. That's an interesting piece of décor.*

But I focus back on Damien. "Why are you asking?"

Turning to face me when we come to the top step, he shrugs but smiles. "You didn't outline that in the rules last night."

"Oh. Well, I guess that's not horrible." I watch as Damien reaches out and takes my hand in his, intertwining our fingers before twisting to ring the doorbell. And now my heart is lodged so deeply in my throat, I feel like I can't breathe.

The move is so simple, something every couple does at some point, but the reality that *Damien* is holding my hand makes my mind and body start to unravel. Funny how such an innocent move is making me think not so innocent thoughts.

But there's only a few seconds for me to gain my footing before a man I recognize from Damien's office earlier this week answers the door. "Damien. Charlotte. I'm glad you found the place."

"We did. Thanks for inviting us, Dave." Damien reaches out to shake his hand, and then guides me behind him through the door.

"I'm happy to have you here, Damien. This is such a surprising turn of events, but I'm glad that we can welcome you to the other side of the office."

"And what side would that be?"

Dave chuckles. "The side where the women are always right."

My giggle comes out louder than I intend, but I follow Damien's lead behind Dave into a large open concept kitchen and living room where several couples are already mingling.

"Everyone, this is Damien and Charlotte!" Dave announces. "Damien has recently entered a committed relationship, so this is their first time here."

"Welcome!" A few cheery hellos ring out, but my eyes are flitting across the room trying to identify the owners.

"Can I get you two something to drink?" A short blonde with perfectly curled hair and equally perfect makeup comes up to us. "I'm Erin, Dave's wife, by the way. We have wine, beer, whiskey, vodka…"

"I'll have a glass of white wine, please."

"A beer would be great," Damien echoes.

"Be right back then," Erin says and then Dave ushers us over to the couches.

"Come on you two. It's time to sit in the hot seat," Dave teases as we sit on the dark gray couch. "I need to know how the hell Damien landed a woman like you, Charlotte." Dave's eyes bounce up and down my body, and I can't help but feel uneasy while I sit there. But I try to brush it off.

"Oh, it was pure luck," I joke.

"On the contrary, Dave. I've been laying the groundwork for years with this one," he says, leaning back and putting his arm on the back of the couch, resting his hand on my shoulder. And somehow, his arm around me makes me feel safe. "Charlotte and I grew up together in South Carolina, but both moved out here for college. We hadn't seen each other in over twelve years, and then happened to run into each other out of the blue at a restaurant." He turns to me and smiles. "Thank goodness I happened to choose that place that day, huh, sweet pea?" He winks, and I'm instantly ready for battle.

"Oh, I love this," Erin says, walking over and handing us our drinks. "So is this a second chance kind of romance?" she asks as she takes a seat in the chair beside us.

"Ha, not exactly." I take a sip of my wine. "Believe it or not, Damien and I weren't exactly friends before."

"Oh?"

"Yeah, Charlotte and I were kind of enemies. But now we're lovers, huh, babe?"

I don't think I can clench my jaw any tighter. "Guess it turns out I'm attracted to that asshole vibe."

Dave throws his head back in laughter. "She's got your number, doesn't she, Damien?"

"Yeah. It's crazy what a little maturity and time away from each other can help you realize." His eyes lock on mine and the energy between us shifts. "I wasn't looking for a relationship, but seeing Charlotte again made me realize that perhaps the reason I hadn't found someone yet is because I kept comparing them to her."

My face falls from his words. But then I remember, this is all fake. He's playing a role, so there's no way his words could be true…right?

"Sometimes the right person is right under your nose," Erin says through a smile. "Isn't that right, babe?" she asks, turning to her husband.

"Erin was the teacher's assistant for one of my classes while I was working on my master's degree. Apparently, I wasn't very good at picking up on her hints that she was into me."

Erin rolls her eyes. "The man was practically blind. But eventually, he opened his eyes." She winks at him.

"Like all good men do." Dave takes a sip from his tumbler and then clears his throat. "Well, gentlemen—what do you say we move onto the patio to talk shop while the ladies gossip and get to know each other a little more before dinner?"

"I like your way of thinking, Dave," one of the older gentlemen announces and then Damien is suddenly springing from the couch.

"Are you gonna be okay?" he whispers as he leans down toward me.

"I guess."

"Behave yourself, alright?" he smirks playfully.

"I can't make any promises. Mischief is just too much fun."

Damien's eyes light up. "I think we're causing enough mischief by just being here, so let's not add to it, shall we?"

I roll my eyes dramatically. "Fine."

"Thanks." He plants a chaste kiss on my cheek, leaving his warmth against my skin and a flurry of electricity from his beard, and then he stands and follows his boss and co-workers out of the room while the spot on my cheeks where his lips just were tingles as he walks away.

"Charlotte!" Erin calls to me with a wave. "Come over here in the kitchen."

Smoothing down my dress, I stand from the couch and with my wine in hand, join the other women standing around the island. "Thank you again for having us."

"Nonsense. It's nice to see some new blood at these things," she says nonchalantly, but I feel all of the other women's eyes on me.

A platter of crackers and cheese sits right before me, so to keep my hands busy and my mouth from running, I reach for a slice of cheddar and a cracker, form a sandwich, and take a small bite.

"So what is it that you do?" One of the women asks me.

I finish chewing and then answer them. "I'm the Senior Advertising Editor for *Revision Magazine*."

Their eyes go wide and a few mouths drop open. "You're kidding?"

"Nope," I state proudly. "I've been there since I graduated from college and worked my way up. I got lucky too that the old editor chose to retire, and I was ready for the position. Most women have to wait until they're almost forty to secure a job like that."

Erin sighs wistfully, clutching her glass as my eyes drift down to her bracelet that is covered in tiny pineapple charms. Guess the woman really likes pineapples. "I remember those days, when I lived for my job."

"I do love it, but I want more too."

"Oh, I'm sure. I just mean, I used to work at the firm with Dave, actually. But then once we had kids, I chose to quit to stay home and raise them."

"That's a hard choice to make. My goal is to continue working once I have kids. I know it won't be easy, but I love my job. I don't think I could walk away."

Erin nods. "It was hard. My life changed completely overnight, and suddenly I was in charge of raising tiny humans and keeping them alive. They're sixteen and eighteen now, so it's different. But by the time I thought about going back to work, I had been out of the industry for so long, I wasn't fresh anymore. I felt like I didn't have anything to offer."

"I can imagine."

"But you found other ways to keep yourself entertained, didn't you?" One of the other women snickers with a teasing grin on her face.

"Well, I mean...there's only so many bake sales and PTA meetings a wife and mother can attend before she feels like she's going to scream," Erin replies with a smile on her face. "Plus, it gives me an excuse to throw these little parties for everyone."

I feel like there's a conversation going on between the girls that I'm not entirely privy to. But I take a sip of my wine as I simply observe.

"So, Charlotte, are you and Damien headed down the aisle soon?" Erin asks, shifting the attention back to me.

I almost spit out the gulp of wine I just took down. Swiping a few drops from my mouth, I swallow roughly and then clear my throat. "Oh, uh, I don't know. We've just started dating. I mean, he was the boy who dared me to ride the Tilt A Whirl in a park back home and bet that he wouldn't puke before I did. And I lost, big time." The girls laugh. "We were so young the last time we were in contact. And even though we know each other from before, there's still a lot we don't know about one another now. I mean, I feel like I learn something new about him whenever we spend time together." *Not a lie, Charlotte. Good job!*

Another woman chimes in who I believe is Deidra, Hank Thompson's wife. "Oh, that doesn't stop, honey. Even after twenty years, I still learn things about Hank. And just when you think you have the man dialed in, he'll ask you to check his balls for him because he thinks he has an ingrown hair and he can't reach it."

Yup, I'm going to die from choking on my saliva tonight. Coughing roughly, I stare down at the island as I compose myself. Once I do, I struggle to find something to say.

"Why on earth would he ask you that?" Erin asks her friend.

"Oh, he was just getting ready for tonight, you know?"

A lightbulb must go off in Erin's mind because she nods in understanding. "Shaving his balls?" Her friend nods right back at her.

As I bounce my eyes across the group of women, I notice they're all wearing a bracelet just like Erin's—silver with small pineapple charms dangling from it.

And then it hits me.

Oh My God! I've read about this in a romance novel that Noelle shoved in my face. Pineapples are a universal symbol for swingers, and I suddenly realize that Damien and I got ourselves into way more mischief than either of us bargained for tonight.

Trying to keep my composure, but shaking from my revelation, I manage to squeak a few words out. "Uh, can you point me in the direction of the restroom, please? This wine is just running right through me," I say through a nervous laugh.

"Oh, absolutely." Erin guides me through the kitchen with her arm around my waist, resting her hand on my lower back. "It's right down this hallway, third door on your right."

"Thank you."

"You're welcome, Charlotte. And just so you know, I think you're absolutely stunning. And Damien is such a handsome man. It's so nice to welcome a new couple into the group, and I think you two will fit right in with us." With a wink, she spins on her heels and heads back into the kitchen as I scurry to the table by the front door where I left my purse, grab my phone, and then race down the hallway to the bathroom, locking myself inside. Now all of the undertones in their compliments suddenly make sense.

I pull up Damien's number, press call, and wait for him to answer. But it rings a few times and then just goes to his voicemail.

"Dammit. Pick up!" I whisper shout, trying not to be loud but panicking.

I press call again, and this time he actually picks up. "Charlotte?"

"Damien," I hiss into the phone. "We have a problem."

"Where are you?"

"I'm in the bathroom."

"Is everything okay?"

"No, everything is not okay, Damien. Do you have any idea what your boss invited you to this evening?"

He pauses, clearly confused. "Uh, a dinner so I could get in with my superiors—which was going really well until this phone call interrupted it."

"Well, I hate to break it to you, Damien, but that's not the only reason we're here."

"It's not? Fuck, Charlotte, what is going on?" I can sense the irritation in his voice, so I decide to go with the cold, hard truth.

"Dave, his wife, and their friends—they're swingers, Damien."

Silence fills the line until I hear muffled laughter. "Charlotte…are you stoned?"

"What? No!" I huff out a breath in frustration. "Damien, I'm serious."

"Okay, I'll bite. What makes you think that?"

"First of all, there was a pineapple on the front porch. Then, Erin and her friends are all wearing bracelets with pineapples on them."

"What? What do pineapples have anything to do with this?"

"Are you living under a rock? Pineapples are the universal symbol for swingers!"

"Wow. The fact that you know this is alarming."

"It's part of my job to be in touch with social norms and trends."

"Knowing about other people's sex lives is not something you should be concerned about."

"It is if I'm going to be asked to participate," I counter. "I'm telling you, Damien, you should have heard the conversation Erin and Deidra were having. Deidra's husband apparently shaved his balls for tonight."

Damien goes quiet, but then he sounds like he's finally believing me. "That is something I could have lived my entire life without knowing, but okay, say you're right. That doesn't mean we have to participate. Hate to break it to you, but I'm not one that likes to share my women, fake girlfriend or not."

Relief comes out in a harsh exhale, but that doesn't solve the problem entirely. "I agree."

"And I really hate you right now because all I'm thinking about is Hank's balls."

"I'm unfortunately in the same boat. So how do we get out of this?"

"Relax, Charlotte. I'll think of something."

"Somehow that doesn't make me feel better."

Damien laughs again. "Just trust me."

"Damien, I've never trusted you in my life."

"Well, there's a first time for everything, Charlotte. And you're just going to have to have faith in me."

"You owe me after this."

"What? Why?"

"Because nowhere in our agreement did you mention that I would have to fight off swingers during this dinner."

Damien is laughing at me again. "Hell, sweet pea, I didn't know you'd have to either. But if I'm betting on anyone to win, it's you."

Somehow his back-handed compliment makes me smile. "Good. Okay, I've been in here for a while. I should probably go out there."

"We could always just say you got the runs and that's why we have to leave…"

"Fuck you, Damien. I'm not using diarrhea as an excuse to get out of this. Think of something else."

"Yes, honey," he quips, and then the line goes silent. I stare down at my phone in my hand. *Did that dickhead just hang up on me?*

Staring at myself in the mirror, I don't know whether to be mortified or confident that a bunch of married people want to have sex with me. And hey, I'm not one to judge. There are plenty of people out there that do things in their relationships that I may never understand, but that doesn't mean it's something I'm interested in nor that I need to know about it.

However, fake relationship or not, there will be no swinging going on with Damien and me.

Apparently, I didn't start drinking early enough in the evening for this.

"This dinner was delicious," Damien announces after wiping his mouth with his napkin and tossing it onto his empty plate. I wish I had more of an appetite because the food *was* delicious, but in the back of my mind, I kept thinking about what was going to happen after dinner.

"Thank you, Damien. It's always nice to hear that."

"I love your cooking, honey," Dave interjects, and part of me can't help but wonder if his lack of compliments toward her is why she seeks out validation by sleeping with her husband's friends in front of him.

Dear Lord, Charlotte. You are not Dr. Phil, and it is not your job to understand what is going on here.

"Yes, Erin. It was delicious, but I'm afraid I ate too many hors d'oeuvres and couldn't possibly eat another bite," I say as I push my plate away. When I returned from the bathroom, I kept stuffing my face with food to keep myself from blurting out that I wouldn't be having sex with any of them. It was a difficult task, and now I'm afraid that I might actually get the runs from all of the weird things I consumed.

"Well, there's still dessert to look forward to," Erin announces as she licks her lips and eyes me from her spot on the table.

I reach below the table and squeeze Damien's thigh as he chuckles beside me. I'm not sure if he actually believes me or not, but he's definitely finding my uneasiness hilarious.

"So sorry, you guys, but we really have to run," Damien says, winking over at me. The death glare I give him in return has him biting his lip to stifle his laughter.

"So soon?"

"Yeah, Charlotte has the runs." My mouth falls open, but then Damien corrects himself. "I mean, Charlotte has to run in the morning. Training for that 10K, right babe?" The desire to grab my fork and stab it into his thigh is overwhelming.

"A 10K? That's ambitious, Charlotte," Erin replies.

"Oh, thank you. It wasn't something I agreed to at first, but Damien convinced me to do it. Just like I convinced him to shave his balls."

Damien chokes on his drink as I pat him playfully on the back. "What?"

"I meant, chase his balls. He's been volunteering at the recreation center by his place, which is where I signed up for the run, and he's been helping with the soccer clinic on Saturday mornings. Lots of ball chasing going on."

Damien narrows his eyes at me. "Oh yeah. It's a blast."

"Well, perhaps we'll just have to do this some other time so you guys can stay for all of the festivities," Dave suggests as he stands from his spot at the table and the rest of us follow suit.

"That sounds great," Damien agrees. "I'll let you know our schedule."

"We are very busy in the next few months though…remember, my parents' wedding anniversary trip, honey," I say through clenched teeth as Damien wraps his arm around my waist.

"Oh, an anniversary trip? Where to?" Erin asks.

"Hawaii. My parents are celebrating thirty years of marriage by renewing their vows. It's a big weeklong celebration."

The girls awe. "That sounds amazing. We should do something like that, Dave."

"Yes, Dear." He winks over at Damien and me, but my skin continues crawling the longer that we stay here.

Eager to leave, I get the ball rolling again. "Well, thank you again for a lovely evening."

"It was our pleasure, Charlotte. And Damien," Dave says, turning to him, "don't let me down with this account."

"That's the goal, sir. I appreciate the opportunity to talk to you outside of work, though. It's good to know you have faith in me."

"Have a great rest of your evening, you two. I know we will definitely miss you." Erin waves as we turn to leave.

Choking down bile, I smile and let Damien lead me by the hand to the door. And once it's shut behind us, I feel like I can finally breathe. "Oh my God."

Damien laughs as he fishes his keys out of his pocket. "I really think you're overexaggerating, Charlotte."

"Fine. Don't believe me. But my gut was telling me something was going on that we were not completely aware of, and I've learned over the years to listen to that womanly intuition. She rarely steers me wrong," I say as I point back to the house we just walked out of.

Damien follows my hand, and when we both look up at the window, we see Erin holding a giant pink dildo in her hand as she shuts the drapes. Damien spins back to face me, both of our eyes wide.

"See?"

"Holy fuck!"

"That could have been put in your ass, Damien! I'll take that apology any time now, thank you."

He stands there, still shocked by what he saw. "I don't know if I'll ever be able to look Dave in the eyes again."

Patting him on the shoulder, I lead him down the steps to his car. "I think it's safe to say neither of us will ever be the same after this."

"Well, despite a rather disturbing evening, I actually had a good time," Damien says as he walks me to my door. I told him I could get up to my apartment on my own, but he insisted.

"Speak for yourself," I mutter as I dig my keys out of my purse.

"Oh, come on, Charlotte—it wasn't that bad. And I do feel like this definitely helped me schmooze a bit for this promotion I'll be up for."

Sighing, I turn away from my apartment door and lean my back up against it. "That's good. I'm happy for you. And I guess it was…entertaining," I say through a smile.

"Definitely."

"And it was nice to eat a meal that wasn't from a restaurant."

"And?" he asks as if there's something else I'm supposed to be acknowledging right now.

"And?"

He rolls his eyes. "And your companion wasn't so bad now, was he?" He lifts his hand and trails a finger down the length of my arm, leaving goosebumps along my skin.

And there's something about that touch that has me reeling with familiarity. This isn't the first time Damien has touched me, but this is the first time that I'm questioning if it's happened before.

"Yeah, my date wasn't so bad."

"Boyfriend," he corrects me with a finger in the air. "But in all honesty, Char, I really appreciate you agreeing to do this." Staring down at the ground now, he shakes his head. "I still can't believe that you did, sometimes."

The vulnerability he's showing me has my defenses sliding down rapidly. "I can't believe it either."

His eyes lift and catch mine, and then he's taking a step closer to me. "This is crazy, right?"

"What's crazy?" The pounding of my heart from his proximity sends me back further into my door.

"You. Me. Being…friends." Another step closer.

"Well, *friend* is a really strong word."

He smirks, the lift of his lips forcing my eyes to drop down to the sight. "Come on. You know you have to be feeling what I'm feeling, right?" His hand lands on my bicep this time, the warmth of his palm moving up and down my skin.

I swallow hard. There's no way Damien has sensed my attraction toward him. I've been so careful to hide my glances, made sure to daydream in private, and wear pasties to cover up my hard nipples when he's around… "What are you feeling?"

His gaze narrows. "I don't know…relief? Excitement? Like life just got interesting for once?"

"Oh. Yeah, I guess." *Life got a lot more interesting once you came back around, for sure.* "Why relief though?"

He extracts his hand from my arm and runs it through his hair. "Because the energy it took to fight you on everything, hate you when I didn't want to—that was fucking exhausting."

I exhale loudly. "Wow." Wait—he didn't *want* to hate me?

"And now, being near you doesn't feel energy-sucking anymore. It just feels…" I feel like I'm waiting on pins and needles for him to finish, but the ping of a text message notification interrupts his words and breaks our heated stare.

"I'm sorry." Rummaging through my purse while my body temperature rages like an inferno, I see a text from Penelope asking how tonight went. Oh boy, is she going to love this story. "It's just Penelope."

Damien nods and takes a step back, giving me space that I'm not sure I want anymore. *What the hell is happening?* "No problem. I should get going anyway." He hooks his thumb over his shoulder. "Uh, thanks again, Char. I'll call you later."

"Yeah. Okay. Bye, Damien." I watch him walk down the hall, taking one last mental picture of his ass, and then I'm shaking off the thought and unlocking my door.

My brain can only handle so much chaos at once, and I think tonight I hit my capacity. Between the swingers and Damien's shift in how he looked at me, the way in which he touched me and claimed me in front of his co-workers—well, my brain is either going to turn to mush, or I'm going to need therapy to deal with everything I'm feeling. Let's be honest though—It'll probably end up being a little bit of both.

Chapter 8

Charlotte

"Swingers?" All of the girls' eyes are on me as I recount the dinner Friday night. It's Sunday, which means our brunch is in full swing—no pun intended.

"I wish I were kidding. And Damien didn't believe me until we saw his boss's wife holding a pink dildo through the window." I cast my gaze over to Amelia. "I think it might have been one of the models you suggest to clients, Amelia."

She shrugs. "It's a top-of-the-line product. Many couples are purchasing them nowadays."

"Are Dave and his wife your clients?"

Amelia mimics zipping her lips and throwing away a key. "Doctor-patient confidentiality." My jaw drops open and Noelle and Penelope laugh.

"Oh, this is too good. Only something like this would happen to you, Charlotte," Penelope snickers.

"Right?"

"But besides nearly becoming a swinger, how was the rest of the evening?"

"Oh, it was…okay, I guess."

Noelle arches her brow at me. "Just okay? Did Damien do something?"

"What? No. He was actually quite the gentleman."

"Oh, so things went well between the two of you?"

I squint across the table at her. "What are you getting at?"

Penelope lays it all out. "She's asking if you two boned or not."

"I was going for a more indirect approach, Pen," Noelle chastises. "But I guess since she said it out loud, then yes. Any physical developments?"

Slouching back in my chair, I shake my head at my friends. "No, ladies. There was no boning, no kissing…nothing."

Amelia smiles. "You sound disappointed about that."

"Uh, no. I'm not. I just…"

"What?"

"I don't know. Damien is confusing me. I'm trying to place boundaries, I even gave him a list of rules like Amelia suggested. But then he says something or holds my hand or wraps his arm around me, and my body forgets that he used to make my life a living hell."

Noelle chimes in first. "Charlotte, that was twelve years ago. It's okay if you're feeling differently about him now…"

"Is it? Because last time I checked, this entire thing is supposed to be fake. And if he's doing those things as part of the role he's playing, that makes my reaction to them even worse. He gets in with his boss, I get my mom off my back, and then everything goes back to normal. That was the deal."

"I hate to break it to you, babe, but nothing about this is normal," Penelope says around a mouthful of her omelet.

My head falls into my hands. "You guys, I feel like a hot mess right now." And then I lift my head up again. "This isn't me. I'm normally the put-together one—kicking ass and taking names, excelling in my career, and walking around with my head held high. But now, I feel so…"

"Off-kilter?" Noelle asks.

"Yes. And unbalanced."

"You know life is like spinning a plate on a tiny stick," Amelia chimes in. "Think about it. As the plate spins, it naturally tips to one side and then realigns and tips toward a different spot as you try to balance it out. Every aspect of your life is in one spot on that plate, and it's natural to feel like some aspects are well-balanced while others are barely staying afloat."

"Damn, you must be worth every penny as a therapist," Penelope acknowledges.

Amelia smiles proudly. "Well, often the people that come to see me feel like their sex lives are the part threatening to make the plate slip off the stick and shatter to the ground. But my point is, no one says you have to feel stable in every aspect of your life at every moment. In fact, it's the moments in which we feel like we're about to drop the plate that we grow, that our lives change, and we become better versions of ourselves."

Tears threaten to spill over. "Amelia…"

"Think of this obstacle in your life as a learning experience, Charlotte. Granted, I don't necessarily think the decision to invest in a fake relationship is something most people do, but if you use this time as a way to truly figure out what you want and how to handle your relationship with your mother once and for all, then perhaps this will all be worth it."

"Damn, woman. You've even made me speechless, which is not an easy task," Penelope quips.

Noelle pulls Amelia in for a side hug. "Our friend is so freaking wise."

"Thank you, Amelia. I needed that."

Amelia winks across the table at me. "Of course. What are friends for?"

"Wisdom and people to go drinking with," Penelope says, raising her mimosa for a toast. We clink our glasses together and then each take a sip of the bubbly liquid. God, I love these women. They are the other three voices I know I can trust when the one inside is talking herself in circles. "Speaking of drinking, that club event is this Friday and you bitches are coming with me."

"What club is it?"

"Loft 24 in Ventura. They just did a remodel and are basically throwing a grand reopening."

"God, aren't we too old to be going to the clubs?" Noelle whines.

"Um, no. We are only thirty, some of us thirty-one," Penelope replies with a flick of her gaze back at Noelle. "And we can do whatever the hell we want."

"As long as I'm in bed before midnight, I'm there," Noelle answers back.

"It might be fun to go out dancing, you guys. When's the last time we did that?" The four of us look around the table. "See, we can't even remember? And I certainly could use a drink or two and a night of dancing until I can't feel my feet."

"Exactly." Penelope tips her glass in my direction. "We can make a circle around each other and fight off any men that glance in our direction. Just let off some steam and have fun"

"I concur, especially because I am not looking to pick up a man from the club. Those are not the men you marry. Those are the men that you fumble around in the dark with afterward, hope to God he knows how to use his penis or how to find a clitoris, and then regret sleeping with the next day." Noelle fills up her glass with more champagne.

"Speaking from experience?" I ask playfully.

"Duh. And I am past that point in my life, you guys. I need a real man, someone who wants the same things as me and who knows how to please a woman. I don't understand why that's so hard to find." She sighs in defeat.

"You need to stop looking for him," Penelope says.

"What?"

"Haven't you ever heard the saying that things will happen when you least expect them to?"

"Yeah…"

"Well, perhaps if you stop focusing on finding your husband, he'll pop up right in front of you. Looking for love is a surefire way to end up disappointed, which you always seem to be nowadays, no offense. So maybe you should let love find you, Noelle. I refuse to believe that you'll be alone forever. Your heart is too pure." Penelope smiles across the table at our friend and stuns us all into silence. Usually, her words are full of sarcasm, pessimism, and vulgarity—but maybe she knew that Noelle needed to hear some words of encouragement today.

Noelle sits there dazed by this revelation, and I'm not gonna lie, Penelope's words strike a chord with me too. The last thing I wanted was to see Damien again, and then all of a sudden, he appeared. Could it be that the timing of all of this wasn't coincidental? And if so, what am I going to learn from it?

"Helen?" I call out to my assistant as I shuffle folders across my desk. "Where is the file for the year-end projections?"

"I gave it to you this morning," she yells back through my open office door.

"Are you sure? I can't seem to find it."

I hear footsteps coming toward me and look up from my desk just in time to see Trina, the editor in chief and my *boss*, walking into my office. "Charlotte."

"Trina," I greet her cheerily, even though unannounced visits from her are never a good thing. "How can I help you?"

"Oh, I was just in the vicinity and thought I'd stop by, see how things are going with securing the advertising for the rest of the year."

"Oh. Well, it's going. We landed Mercedes, the Honest Company, and Target."

"Fantastic. But we need something new as well, Charlotte. We need to keep up on what's hot and trending."

"Well, word on the street is that Remedy is launching a new campaign, and I think they might be a good fit."

"The new women's health line?"

"Yes. They're taking a stance on taking care of a woman's needs from her period to her mental and physical health. It's quite the project." I take a deep breath. "I don't know how much longer it will be until they have something solid, but I'd like to keep a spot open for them just in case." Suddenly, the memory of Damien and Jeffrey playing around with tampons comes back to me. I wonder if the account he's working on is Remedy? It would make sense, and I instantly make a mental note to ask him about it.

She arches a brow at me. "I think that's wise. But please have something solid as a backup just in case. I'd hate to lose out on other big clients because we were holding out for them." She eyes me up and down skeptically. "And if that happens, I will not be happy."

"Of course." I gulp down the rock in my throat just as a knock on my door pulls both of our attention to the unexpected visitor.

"Knock, knock." Damien peeks his head into the room, grinning from ear to ear. And then when he enters completely, I see him holding a bouquet of sunflowers and a brown paper bag from The Chop Shop. Given any other circumstances, this might seem sweet, but what the hell is he doing in my office right now?

"Damien? What are you doing here?"

"Well, it was my turn to bring you lunch, sweet pea," he says, pleased with using that term of endearment again because he knows I hate it.

"Oh. Well…"

"And who is this?" Trina asks, blatantly checking out Damien in front of me. A spike of jealousy radiates in my chest, and before I know what I'm doing, I'm weaving our lie even further into my life.

"This is my boyfriend, Damien Shaw. Damien, this is Trina, my boss." I walk over to where Damien stands and wrap my arm around his waist, getting a feel for his abs under his shirt—and dear lord, how many abs does this man have? *Eight is the maximum number, right?*

Damien reaches out to shake her hand after he shuffles the items he's holding in one hand, and she reciprocates. "Nice to meet you."

"Likewise." Her eyes drop down his body again. "I wasn't aware that Charlotte was dating anyone."

"Oh, have you been keeping me a secret, sweet pea?"

"Apparently not well enough," I mutter between clenched teeth, but I don't think either of them hear it. Or they simply ignore me.

"Well, most of us in this position don't have time for dating, so it always surprises me when one of us can find time to juggle both," Trina replies cheekily.

"Oh, believe me. I feel like I'm juggling all of the balls right now," I say, instantly slapping myself in the head in my mind.

Damien snickers. "Yes, and I know that Charlotte would work through lunch if I didn't bring her something to eat, so—here I am." He holds up the bag of food again proudly.

Part of me is grateful to him for bringing me lunch, but the other part of me is cursing him for showing up like this unannounced. "Okay then. Well, I guess it's time for me to eat."

"Yes, of course." Trina turns back to Damien. "Nice to meet you. I'm sure we'll be seeing more of you around here."

"You can count on it."

"Keep up the good work, Charlotte. And make sure you have a backup to your backup." With a stern look, she exits my office and I run after her to shut the door.

Spinning around to take in Damien now, I'm met with a devilish smirk and his body encased in a solid black suit. *Fuck, he looks good.* "What are you doing here?"

"I brought you lunch," he says dryly. "And flowers."

"Why?"

"Because that's what boyfriends do."

"Not fake boyfriends," I counter, pushing off the door and walking back over to my desk, trying to rein in my frustration.

"Well, forgive me for being thoughtful." He sets the flowers and bag down on my desk, now irritated with me as well.

"I appreciate it, but you meeting my boss was never part of this plan."

"Is it a problem that I did?"

"Yes," I say, exasperated. "I didn't want this little ruse to affect *my* work life. It was supposed to benefit *yours*, but I wanted mine to be left out of it."

"Well, screw me for trying to be nice, Char. I'll let you get back to work." He begins to walk away, but now I feel like an ass.

"Damien, wait." Walking over to him with his back still turned to me, I cautiously put my hand on his shoulder where he's standing right in front of the door. "I'm sorry." He turns around slowly. "But seriously…why are you here?"

His brow furrows as he stares down at me, and all I can see is confusion in his light blue eyes. His square jaw lined with short facial hair is tense and his lips are pursed. He's truly quite handsome and I hate that I'm finally noticing that about him. "I guess I just wanted to see you."

His answer steals the breath from my lungs. "What?"

"It's been a few days and I don't know…" He shrugs. "You were on my mind so I decided to stop by with lunch and flowers." He nods toward my desk. "You still like sunflowers, right?"

"Oh. Yeah, I do." I look over to the flowers and then back to him.

"I remember you had a backpack covered with them in school, so I figured they were a safe choice. And the salad from The Chop Shop is the Greek one with no onion." His face softens as I feel my heart do the same. "I figured that was a safe order too since it had feta cheese."

"Wow. You were listening to me?"

Damien huffs out a laugh. "Did you think I wasn't?"

"I don't know," I reply with a shrug of my shoulders. "I guess I'm just impressed."

"I can be very impressive," he says with a bounce of his eyebrows.

"And there you go, having to ruin a good moment." I turn around to head to my desk and pick up the flowers, smelling them for good measure. The scent brings back memories from home, where my parents used to have sunflowers planted along the fence line of our property. I loved those flowers—drawing them, painting them, and yes, I even had a backpack and journal covered in them. It's part of the reason I have a tattoo of one now too.

"Thank you," I say once more as I spin to face him.

"You're welcome." And then he's clearing his throat. "So, uh…are you busy Friday night?"

"What?"

"I mean, I was wondering if you maybe wanted to hang out or something?" Perhaps I'm reading him all wrong, but suddenly Damien seems…nervous.

"Hang out?"

"Yeah, you know, like friends do sometimes."

"Oh. Well, that would be great…" His smile becomes blinding. "But I actually have plans Friday night with the girls." And then it falls.

"Ah. No problem." With his head hung low, he turns for the door again.

"I'm sorry. It's just this club grand reopening that Penelope has to go to for work, and she's making us all go. I'm free Saturday though," I counter.

"I'm busy all day." He runs a hand through his hair and turns as if he wants to escape. "Look, it's no big deal."

"Damien…"

"It's okay, Charlotte," he says over his shoulder. "I understand. Have a good time. And enjoy your lunch." And then he's gone, leaving me standing alone in my office with a dull ache in my chest that I'm not sure what to do with. I'm not sure how long I'm standing there either, feeling defeated and thoroughly confused, but a voice startles me back to reality.

"Who in the ever-loving Christ was that?" Helen comes around the opening of the door, eyes wide and smacking her gum.

"Damien."

"Dear Lord, honey. I didn't know they make them like that anymore. Either I'm too damn old or I've been married too long to remember what a man that could fuck you up against a wall looks like."

"Helen!" With my hand over my heart, I stare slack jawed at my assistant. "I don't think I've ever heard you speak like that."

"Oh, Charlotte. This old bird may be slow when it comes to moving around these days, but the kitty that rests between my legs is still feral like a jungle cat."

"I…I don't even know what to say to you right now." I guess a handsome man can turn any woman into a siren.

"So, who is he?" she asks, taking a sip from her water bottle.

"He is...my boyfriend," I choke out.

"Oh, lucky girl!"

"Yeah. It's…complicated though."

"Why?"

With a sigh, I turn back to my desk and start opening the brown paper bag. "We've known each other for a long time, and now things are…"

"Messy," she finishes for me.

"Yes. And confusing."

"Well, just remember that love isn't supposed to be confusing. It's just supposed to feel right."

Love. Yeah, there's no love happening between Damien and me. And bless her heart, but I can't ever say that to Helen. I'll just have to remember to break the news to her gently when Damien and I end this little charade in a month or so.

"But I'll tell you this—the way that man was looking when he walked in here with that bag was anything but confused."

"What?" I glance back at her.

"He's got it bad for you, sweetheart. So stop questioning everything and just see where this man can take you. And it looks like he could take you to bed and show you a damn good time."

Shaking my head, I hold back my smile. "Get back to work, Helen."

"Yes, boss," she chuckles through her words as I sit down at my desk and open the salad that Damien brought me, reeling with the way he looked when he left.

Was he really that disappointed that I couldn't see him Friday night? And why was he even asking in the first place? It's not like spending time together would help him or me in that case, and the more I wonder about this, the more confused I begin to feel.

Just brush this to the side, Charlotte. You need to focus. Your job is what matters at this moment, not the feelings of your fake boyfriend.

Fake. Boyfriend. Right?

Then why does this gesture from him not seem so fake after all?

Chapter 9

Damien

"Are you even listening to me, man?" Jeffrey asks as he leans closer to me in the booth. The guy convinced me to go out tonight instead of staying in, and now I'm regretting that decision. Although I guess being here is better than sulking at home, something I'm not proud to admit.

I can't believe that when I fucking showed up at her office like that with lunch and flowers, she got mad at me about it.

"Yeah, I'm listening," I reply before taking a sip of my whiskey and coke. I'm not much of a hard alcohol drinker, but tonight called for something stronger than beer. My confidence is bruised, my head is a foggy fucking mess, and the last thing I want to do is think about what Charlotte and I would be doing tonight if she had been available to hang out. Or wanted to.

I don't know what the fuck I was thinking, asking her out, but for some reason I just wanted to spend more time with her. Bantering with her, listening to her laugh, making her smile, and seeing the look in her eyes when I tell her that her mom's an idiot for the things she says to her—it's making me feel some type of way that I'm completely unfamiliar with. My gut and my brain are like the devil and the angel, sitting on each of my shoulders. Both are competing to convince me of what I should do in my situation.

My gut is the angel in this situation, urging me to spend more time with her, get to know her, find out everything that makes her tick. I'm justifying it so that when we're in Hawaii, her parents will be more likely to believe that we're a real couple. But I also have this weird feeling that's making me think that it's more because I *want* to be around her. She gets me, can hold her own against my level of sarcasm, and she's nice to talk to. The last thing she cares about is how many calories she's eaten that day or how many followers on Instagram she has.

But most importantly, she's familiar. She reminds me of home, a simpler time, and a life that seems like another century ago.

But the devil is my brain and the man in red on the other side—he's feeding the feud between us, reminding me that Charlotte Montgomery is not to be trusted, that this deal we struck was risky at best, and I'm better off keeping my distance, abiding by her rules, and letting this thing run its course so I can go back to living my life the way it was before she popped back in, except for hopefully with a nice, shiny promotion and raise.

But the devil? Yeah, he really wants me to fuck her too.

And that's the problem. Charlotte has temptation written all over her—from her curves to her big, brown eyes and long brown hair, to her sass that has me wanting to smash my lips to hers just to crush every rebuttal she fires off against me.

"Then what did I just say?" Jeffrey asks with way too much indignation.

"You were complaining about the fact that you haven't been laid in six months."

"It was five, thank you very much," he corrects me. "Why make it sound worse than it really is?"

"You're making it sound worse, Jeffrey. Stop fucking complaining about it, get out of this booth, and go put in some work. Find a woman, talk to her, buy her a drink, and lay the groundwork so hopefully, she'll let you take her home later and you can end your five-month drought."

"Easy for you to say, Damien. Women fucking flock to you." He lifts his glass to his lips and then stares down at it, looking defeated. Jeffrey isn't a bad looking guy—with dirty blonde hair, green eyes, and a nice smile—but he's lacking confidence. That's the key component women look for. Not cockiness—confidence. And yes, there is a difference.

"You need to be more confident, man. You're a decent looking guy, but you cower too much. Go up to a woman, be honest that you think she's attractive and you would like to talk to her. You'd be surprised how far that will get you."

"And if she says she's not interested?"

"Then you thank her for being honest and move on." I take another sip of my drink. "It's really that simple."

"So why aren't you out there making moves tonight since you have the art of picking up women narrowed down to a science?"

"In case you've forgotten, I have a girlfriend now."

Jeffrey smirks. "A fake girlfriend, if I recall."

"Yes, but she's real to everyone else. And if anyone we know was to see me with a woman that is not her, it would not bode well for either of us." That's the explanation I'm giving Jeffrey, and it does have merit. But honestly, no other woman here has sparked my interest, which is yet another issue that I'm having with Charlotte. She's the only woman I've been thinking about lately, especially in the shower. And fuck, she does not disappoint in my imagination.

"Good point." Jeffery stands and then buttons up his coat again. "Okay, well, here goes nothing."

"Unbutton your jacket. We're not at work. And undo the top two buttons on your shirt," I say, pointing to my own that I unfastened before we arrived. My light blue shirt is also rolled up to my elbows, showing off my forearms. I don't know what it is, but ladies go nuts for forearms. Not that I'm looking for that attention tonight, but old habits die hard

"You're not trying to get me to strip for you, are you?" he asks me.

"Fuck, no. I'm trying to help you." I stand, help him situate himself, and then smack him on the ass. "Now go get 'em, tiger."

"I never played football in high school, so that was my first ass slap, and I can't say that I hated it."

"Just go." I pinch the bridge of my nose and say a little prayer to the man upstairs for Jeffrey's benefit. But when I lift my head to see where he ran off to, the last person I expected to see here tonight is on the dance floor, swinging her hips in a gold sequin dress that looks like the gold foil on the end of a champagne bottle you have to rip off before you can pop the cork.

And I have never wanted to pop her fucking cork more.

Charlotte is dancing with a drink in her hand, swaying her body to the music blaring from the speakers. Her friends—the same ones I saw with her at dinner the other night—are circled around themselves, laughing and moving their bodies to the beat.

But Charlotte steals the show, her hair down and wild from her movements, her body fucking delectable in her dress, and her smile bright and free—like she's been transported to another world tonight as she dances her troubles away.

And for a moment, I wonder if I'm part of those troubles.

I knew I caught her off guard when I surprised her earlier this week, and for someone like Charlotte—put together, type A, and a bit of a perfectionist—I'm sure the lack of her control at that moment only spurred on her frustration with me.

But that fire I saw in her eyes, the same one I got pleasure from igniting when we were younger—it was muted somehow, probably subdued by the disappointment I exhibited in front of her when she told me she was busy. I tried to hide it, brush it off like it was nothing. But now that I see her here, I know she was telling the truth. It wasn't a lie she used to get out of seeing me, and it seems she's having a really good fucking time.

Realizing that my drink is empty, I head for the bar, trying to keep my line of sight away from her, but failing miserably. She's captivating me, and as I wait for the bartender to make my drink, I realize I'm not the only one. Several men, all around my age probably, are eye-fucking the shit out of Charlotte and her friends. I can't very well blame them. All four of those women are stunning, each in their own unique way.

Penelope has a Cindy Crawford look to her, height and all, but you can tell she has a few notches of crazy lurking under her smile. Amelia has wild, curly blonde hair and glasses that give her that librarian look that any red-blooded male would be into. And Noelle has the classic, girl-next-door look going for her, with light brown hair and green eyes and a petite little body.

But Charlotte—she's curvy, naturally beautiful with her dark features, and has that sass that gets my engine revving. She stands out in a crowd of gorgeous women because she has that little something extra that is too enticing to ignore. And it's not just her appearance that gets me going, it's her mind. The girl has always been intelligent, even though I know I could match her in that department. But her tenacity, that edge she has that drives her determination and goal-oriented mind is what keeps reeling me in.

And now I know she has a vulnerable side too, a part of her she never let me see before since that would have been like her showing me her weakness back when we used to compete over everything. Knowing she struggles with appeasing her mom was like a breath of relief because I've been dealing with the same shit with my dad for as long as I can remember.

And Charlotte was always a huge part of that.

When the bartender slides my drink to me, I thank him, tell him to put it on my tab, and then turn back around just in time to see one of the guys who was standing next to me approaching Charlotte and her friends. I can almost feel my hackles raise as I watch him slither through the crowd and come up behind Charlotte, planting his hand on her hip. She looks over her shoulder nervously, gives him a tight-lipped smile, and then turns back to her friends with wide eyes, a gaze that says, 'help me.'

Every instinct in my body is telling me to go over there, but then the devil appears and holds me back, reminding me that Charlotte is a grown woman and can handle herself.

But then he whispers in my ear, *"But she is supposed to be yours now, right?"*

Fuck. I don't own her. But she clearly isn't asking for this attention. So does that mean that I should do something? Say something? I mean, we are a fake couple, and for the same reasons I told Jeffrey, I should go over there to keep up appearances. Heaven forbid someone we know says something to one of our colleagues, or worse, our parents. You never know who has eyes, ears, or a camera phone recording something in this day and age.

I know I'm getting a little far-fetched with the possibilities right now, but as I watch this guy clearly *not* take the hint that she's *not* interested, I decide my plan of action. Tossing back my drink, welcoming the burn that courses down my throat, I slam my empty glass on the bar and then march over to where they're standing, parting the circle the girls have created and pulling Charlotte into me.

"There you are, sweet pea."

Charlotte's eyes bug out, but she quickly puts her hand on my chest and gets closer to me, pressing her entire body against mine. And fuck, does she feel good. "You're here?"

"Sorry I'm late." I lean down and kiss her on the cheek, just an inch from the corner of her mouth, and I can smell the alcohol on her breath mixed with her sweet scent. But before I become far too enraptured in her, I lift my head and make eye contact with the man who was dancing with her. "The woman's taken," I declare.

He scowls at me, but then puts his hands in the air in surrender. "Sorry, man."

"Next time, why not ask a woman if she wants to dance with you rather than not giving her a choice, huh?"

"Why don't you mind your own business?" he counters, lengthening his spine.

"The moment you touched my girlfriend, you made it my business. Now I suggest you leave."

"Or what?"

I take a step toward him, puffing out my chest. "Believe me, you really don't want to know the answer to that question."

"Look man, I'm going. Calm the fuck down." He takes a step back, but his gaze is still alight with wanting to challenge me on this.

"Not quite far enough for me," I say. "Keep moving."

He waves me off and finally stalks away as my heart rate skyrockets from the adrenaline coursing through me.

"Damien?"

I look down at Charlotte, her eyes still wide, but she's clutching onto me like a lifeline. And fuck, it feels good, like she's afraid to let go of me.

"Hey, Char."

"What are you doing here? Are you stalking me again?"

"I'm beginning to think that you like when I show up unannounced." I hear giggles behind me, but I keep my eyes locked on Charlotte.

"You clearly don't know how to sense sarcasm and irritation then." She runs her hand from my shoulder down my arm and tries to back away, but I pull her closer to me. "What are you doing?"

"We still have an audience," I say, tossing my head in the direction where the asshole that was just over here is standing, glaring at me from above his drink. He either doesn't believe me that I'm her boyfriend, or he's truly pissed that I claimed the woman he was after. Either way, I'm fine with it.

Suddenly the beat of the music registers, and so I move my hips and urge Charlotte to do the same. A remix of *Shivers* by Ed Sheeran blasts through the speakers, so I take this opportunity to put on a show for our audience, and as an excuse to keep touching her.

Charlotte's face relaxes and then she begins moving with me, spinning around to give me her back. And the way her ass feels pressed up against my crotch is something I can't convince my dick to ignore.

"How did you know I would be here?" she asks me as she leans her head against my shoulder. I wrap my arm around her waist to keep her pressed up against me.

"I didn't."

"I told you I was going out with the girls tonight."

"Yes, but you didn't say where." She eyes me skeptically. "I swear, Charlotte. Us crossing paths tonight was purely coincidental." As the song keeps playing, Charlotte moves one of her arms up, wrapping it around my neck and swirling her hips against my dick. "I'm beginning to think you don't hate me as much as you want me to believe."

"I'm beginning to think that I don't know what to think about you anymore," she counters.

"Ditto, sweet pea."

She spins around to face me, but still keeps her hips pressed into mine. And I know she can feel how hard I am through my slacks and her dress. Dancing is basically like sex with clothes on—well, at least the type of dancing that we're doing. And feeling Charlotte's body this close to mine is making me want to cross every line that's ever existed between us.

"What are we doing, Damien?"

"We're dancing."

"You know what I mean."

"No, I'm not sure that I do."

"You. Me," she says, her face contorting with confusion. "Things are getting too fuzzy between us."

"Fuzzy isn't necessarily a bad thing."

"It is when I'm trying to make the right decision."

"Haven't you ever found that some of the best decisions you've made in your life are the ones you aren't sure you should be making in the first place? The ones that hold a certain amount of risk and danger, the ones that make you feel alive…" I trail my fingers down her arm and watch her skin pebble right before my eyes.

And I fucking love that I have that effect on her.

But then I feel her pulling away. "No." It's one word, but it smashes the smile off my face. "I…I have to go." She releases her arm from around my neck and takes a step back.

"Charlotte."

"Thanks for getting that guy away from me, Damien. But I need…I need to go to the bathroom." She starts to turn away from me and my heart seizes in my chest as I watch her move, increasing the space between us with each passing second.

But before I can think, before I can ponder all of the consequences of my actions, I just react.

Reaching for her arm before she gets too far away, I grab hold of her wrist and yank her back toward me, spinning her into my chest. She gasps, staring up at me in wonder.

And then I smash my lips to hers.

Sweet and sour, the taste of whatever she was drinking is on the edge of her mouth, incomparable to the way her moan travels through her throat and up against my lips, spurring me on even further.

I'm expecting her to push me away, to slap me or shove me back. But before she gets the chance, I stick my tongue out, licking against the seam of her lips, begging for her to let me all the way in.

And much to my surprise and pure fucking joy, she does.

Kissing Charlotte instantly consumes me, the heat of our hands grasping at one another, the silkiness of her hair as I thread my hands through it at the base of her head, holding her in place while I work her mouth with my own—it's unlike any kiss I've ever had.

Desire floods my groin, hunger builds in my gut, and intense need overrules my mind as I hungrily kiss and nip at her lips.

But I want more, and I don't need an audience for how desperate I'm about to become.

Breaking our kiss, I grab her hand and pull her behind me through the crowded dance floor, the heavy bass booming like the beat of my heart right now.

"Damien?" she asks, trying to keep up with me. But I don't answer her.

My eyes keep moving across the club, looking for an alcove or private room that we can dip into. And that's when I run into Hayes Weston, an old buddy of mine from college.

"Damien Shaw? Is that you?" He stops me in my tracks, slapping a hand on my shoulder. I feel Charlotte collide with my back and then peer her head around me.

"Hayes Weston. What's up, my man?"

"Nothing. Just celebrating the grand reopening."

"This is one of your clubs, isn't it?"

"Yup," he states proudly. "So what have you been up to?"

Dreading small talk right now, but knowing that maybe this moment to cool down is necessary, I answer him. "Working for Goldstein Advertising. And this is my girlfriend, Charlotte," I say, pulling her into my side.

"Wow. Nice."

"You're married now, aren't you?"

"Yup. And we have a baby on the way."

"Congrats, man."

"Thank you."

"Say, there wouldn't happen to be a room around here, or little alcove we could duck into for a few minutes, is there? My girlfriend and I—well, we need to have an important conversation."

Hayes's eyebrows lift as he laughs. "Oh. An important conversation, you say?"

"Damien…" Charlotte grates out beside me.

"Very important," I confirm while squeezing her hand in mine.

With a knowing smirk, he flicks his head to the side, prompting us to follow him, and with a slip of a key in the lock of a nearby door,

Hayes pushes the door open and reveals a small room that is full of chairs and spare furniture. "This should work."

"Perfect. Thanks, man."

"No problem. I hope you guys settle whatever it is that you need to discuss," he teases, and with a wink, closes the door behind us. "Just make sure to lock it back up when you're done," he shouts through the door, knocking on it for good measure. And then all that remains in the room is Charlotte and me, our chests both heaving from exertion and need.

"Damien! What the fuck was that?"

"That was me making a choice for you."

"How do you know what choice I was debating?"

"Because I can see it all over your face every time you're near me," I declare. "Fuck, Charlotte." I stalk toward her again, pinning her up against the door. I reach for her hands and hold them above her head as she presses her hips forward, colliding with my cock again. "Tell me you don't want me."

Her eyes bounce back and forth between mine. But she doesn't say anything, and all I can hear is my pulse in my ears.

"Tell me you don't want this, and I'll let you go. I'll make good on our arrangement, I won't even try to be friends with you beyond what we agreed to." Her breathing becomes more shallow. "But I don't think that's what you want. And I sure as fuck know it's not what I want."

"Let go of my hands," she whispers with an edge of irritation, and I reluctantly oblige. I don't want her to feel like I'm keeping her here against her will. But then she slowly reaches up, wraps her hand around my neck, and pulls me down to her.

And I'm fucking gone.

"Charlotte," I mumble against her lips.

"Damien, shut the fuck up and kiss me," she replies, so I listen dutifully. I reach down and lift her up underneath her thighs, pinning her to the door again, lining up my cock with the juncture between her thighs. But the tight material of her dress makes it difficult to press all the way up against her. So holding her with one hand, I use the other to push her dress up over her ass to her hips so the only thing covering her from the waist down is a black lace thong.

"Fuck."

As I stare at the sight between her legs, she lifts my chin and captures my lips with hers again, pulling me forward so now I can rub my cock right against her clit, and the moan she lets out in response spurs me on.

"This means nothing," she says between nips of our lips. "It's just kissing. And maybe an orgasm or two."

"Sure," I say without thinking. Because let's be honest, all of my blood is otherwise occupied at the moment, and my brain is malfunctioning at an alarming rate as I realize I'm fucking making out with Charlotte Montgomery right now.

"Oh God, yes." She tips her head back against the door, exposing her neck to me, so I take advantage of her delicate skin on display and kiss and nibble my way up to her ear. I can feel her shudder in my arms, so I take time to lick her sensitive flesh there as I continue to rub myself against her pussy.

"Damien," she moans as I lift my head to take her in. Her eyes are squeezed shut, her mouth is open, gasping for air, and she looks so fucking stunning that all I want to do is make her feel good everywhere.

Hastily, I wrap my arms around her and carry her over to a chair on the other side of the room, taking a seat and pulling her with me so she's straddling my legs. With force, I pull her hips in tightly to mine and thrust up from beneath her as she gasps again.

"Do you want me to make you come, Charlotte?"

She stares down at me—eyes and hair wild, her dress still around her hips, her mouth agape until she darts her tongue out and licks her lips. "Yes."

With a low growl, I grab her head and smash my lips to hers again, kissing her like I can't get enough. And that's exactly how I feel.

The woman is addicting and I've just had my first taste of her.

Trailing my fingers up her thigh, I listen for her moans of pleasure, the small whimpers she makes as we continue to kiss and I search out the wet heat between her legs with my hand. And as I rub the knuckle of my index finger over the lace covering her pussy, sheer wetness hits my skin.

"This is for me, isn't it?" She moans, so I break my mouth far enough away from hers that she can't reach my lips again. "Answer me." But she just narrows her eyes at me, so I reach behind her head, gently grab a fistful of her hair, and pull her head back just slightly— enough to command her attention and gain my control. "Tell me you're wet for me, Charlotte, and I'll make you come so fucking hard."

"Yes…" she finally mewls.

"Yes, what?"

"Yes, I'm wet for you."

"Fucking right you are." I let go of her hair and bring her mouth back to mine as I slide her thong to the side and press my finger to her clit.

"Fuck," she moans.

"God, you are so fucking sexy like this, Charlotte." I twist my wrist to get better control over my hand and she lifts up slightly on my lap, granting me better access. As I drag my finger up and down her slit, putting a little extra pressure on her clit, she grows wetter, practically dripping for me. And I can feel her tense up more as she waits for my next move, so I slowly slide one finger inside of her and let out a growl of my own as I feel her slick walls squeeze around my finger.

"Damien…"

"Does that feel good, Char?" With my eyes trained on hers, I find a slow pace and continue to push in and out of her, adding another finger that only seems to make her grow even wilder.

"Yes."

"How about this?" I curl my fingers forward, finding that spot deep inside of her that I know will make her come so fucking hard on my hand.

"Oh, God."

"That's it…" I find her mouth again, and continue working her over, moving gently but hard enough that I can give her the friction that I know she needs. The sound of her wetness can be heard over the music blaring outside the door, and it makes my dick grow even harder. And then I know what I really want to do to set her off. "Stand up."

"What?" she asks, completely caught off-guard by my request. "I was about to come, Damien."

"I know. But I'm going to make it better for you. Now stand up."

With confusion in her eyes, she slowly slides off me, and I rise, adjusting my erection in my slacks before guiding her to the seat I was just in. "Spread your thighs."

I watch her swallow and then do as she's told. As I kneel before her, I grasp the strings of her thong, pulling it down her legs as she moves them closer together so I can slide the material down. And once it's gone, I push her thighs open again for me. "Now where was I?"

With my eyes locked on hers, I move my head toward her pussy, getting a front-row seat to the arousal I played a part in and inhaling her scent before I lean forward and swipe my tongue through her slit.

And the sound she makes as she tips her head back was worth every moment leading up to this.

"Watch me," I command, waiting for her eyes to meet mine again before pushing two fingers back inside of her and then flicking her clit with my tongue, gently drawing circles before I pick up the pace and suck her clit between my lips.

"Fuck, Damien."

"You taste so fucking good, Charlotte."

"I'm close."

"Take your time, babe," I say as I bask in the moment of having my head between her thighs. This is definitely not a situation I ever thought I'd be in with Charlotte, but damn, I am not complaining right now.

I continue to curl my fingers against her G-spot, slowly swirl my tongue around her clit before sucking it hard, and repeat the process until I feel her grip my head, tug at my hair, and then scream, "Oh, fuck!"

Charlotte's cries of ecstasy spur me on as I work her through her orgasm, her entire body shaking as she tightens her thighs around my head. And I keep moving my fingers and tongue until I feel her start to relax, indicating I should stop.

When I lean back on my heels, I see she's slouched down in the chair, her eyes are closed, and she's struggling to breathe.

"Are you okay?" I ask, which has her eyes flying open.

Brushing her hair from her face, her entire demeanor changes from satisfied woman to spastic basket case. "Um. Yes. That was…thank you." She stands, lifts her thong from the floor, pulling it in place before shimmying her dress back down her hips and searching the room for something, which I have no idea what that would be.

"You're welcome. Now we should…"

"I have to go, Damien." She runs right past me for the door and just like before, I reach out to stop her.

"Charlotte, no. We need to talk."

"No, we don't." She shrugs me off as my hand drops to my side. "I told you, this was just about orgasms, remember?"

"I faintly remember that mid-make-out session, but seriously, I think we should talk about what just happened."

"Then I'll call you tomorrow," she says on a fake smile before opening the door and running off, leaving me with a raging hard-on and a pile of unanswered questions.

But at least I know the answer to one now—Charlotte definitely wanted what just happened, which means at least I know I'm not the only one that wanted to cross the line.

Now I just need her to admit it.

Saturday morning came and went with no phone call from Charlotte, and by four o'clock in the afternoon after I took care of a few errands, went to the gym, and took a shower, I decided to call her. However, not surprisingly at this point, she didn't pick up.

Frustrated beyond belief with this woman, I settle into my couch Sunday morning with my cup of tea, full of honey and lemon since my throat feels a little dry, clicking on the television to find something to watch. And normally, I'd have no problem finding a show to binge, rewatch an old favorite movie to pass the time, or hell, even do a puzzle. Yes, I like puzzles.

But now that Charlotte is around, none of that sounds as entertaining as being around her, whether she secretly hates me still or not.

After the way you made her come the other night, I doubt she hates you.

Fuck. The woman looked like a goddess when she screamed while my head was buried in between her legs. I swear, I can still taste her on my tongue, and apparently, my dick remembers too as he twitches at the memory.

Sighing in frustration, I reach for my phone again to see no missed calls or messages, but it is only ten in the morning. I'm not sure what time Charlotte wakes up on the weekends, but she's got to be up by now.

I decide to shoot her a text, break the ice and see if I can finally get a response from her.

Me: Hey.

Short. Simple. Open for interpretation.

Well done, Damien.

But then I stare at the screen for an unhealthy amount of time as I wait for a response and never get one. I'm about to throw my phone across the room when a lightbulb clicks on in my mind.

Brunch. Fuck, of course.

Charlotte is at brunch this morning with the girls at Frankie's. I remember her talking about it the night she came over for dinner. They meet every Sunday.

And suddenly, I know exactly how to get Charlotte to talk to me— with three new accomplices hopefully on my side.

As I walk up the sidewalk, I shake my hands and blow out a breath. I don't know why I'm nervous. This could go perfectly right or terribly wrong, which would make any red-blooded male anxious, I suppose. But I know that if I don't ambush Charlotte like this, she's going to keep avoiding me.

When I arrive at the entrance to Frankie's Diner, I see the place is packed, so there's no other option but to go inside to scope her out. I open the door and step through, greeted with the nostalgic look that most diners from the 1950s have—teal booths, black and white checkered flooring, chrome details, and pops of red here and there. But as my eyes scope out the place, realizing I've never been here, I instantly smile when I see Charlotte and her friends seated at a table in the back of the restaurant, entranced in a conversation.

Well, guess who's here to crank things up a notch? This guy.

Walking toward them, all I have is a view of the back of Charlotte's head. But her friend Amelia notices me, indicated by the way her eyes bug out of her head as I close in on their table. And when I arrive, standing right behind Charlotte, everyone's eyes move to me except for hers.

"Good morning, ladies." Charlotte tenses visibly before my eyes before slowly twisting in her seat to look up at me. "Charlotte."

"Uh, Damien?"

"Is that a question, like you're not sure that it's me? Or are you just surprised that I'm here?"

"Oh, I don't think she forgot who you are, not after Friday night," Penelope interjects as Charlotte chokes on air.

I gently pat her back while grabbing an empty seat from a nearby table and pulling it up to join them. "Were you talking about me, sweet pea?" I ask as I take my seat.

"No, but we were just revisiting your claim to her in the club the other night," Noelle answers. "It was quite the show. And Charlotte didn't seem to mind your tongue down her throat one little bit."

"Ah. Well, I can't have men going around thinking they can touch my girlfriend like that."

"Fake girlfriend," Charlotte finally manages to croak out as she reaches for her mimosa and takes a sip to quench her dry throat. When she's finished, she directs her gaze to me, ignoring her friends. "What are you doing here, Damien?"

"Well, I came to see you since it seems you've forgotten how to return a text message or phone call."

"You've been ghosting him?" Amelia asks, fully concerned. "Charlotte…" She shakes her head in disappointment at her friend.

"I know, Amelia, right? I mean, I save her from that idiot, give her a kiss that I know she's still thinking about 'cause I definitely am, and then we fool around in a storage room and she runs away, telling me she's going to call me, but never does." I shrug, but inside I'm fucking cackling at the look on Charlotte's face right now as I divulge vague details from our night to her friends. I'll save the specifics for myself. "What's a guy supposed to do?"

"What happened in the storage room?" Penelope asks, leaning across the table as she waits for me to respond.

"Well…"

"Nothing," Charlotte spits out, slapping her hand on my thigh.

"Oh, it wasn't nothing, ladies," I say out of the corner of my mouth, and they all giggle.

"Good for you two," Noelle adds.

"I have a question," Amelia chimes in again with her hand in the air.

"Yes, Amelia."

"Damien, we all know that this thing between you and Charlotte started out as a deal so you could both get ahead in work and she could pacify her mother, but I think we all want to know, especially after Friday night…" She looks around the table. "What the hell is going on with you two?"

"Yes. Charlotte is all over the place and won't give us clear answers," Noelle says.

Charlotte's head spins toward her friend. "Noelle!"

"I mean, I've been betting since the beginning that you two were bound to end up fucking at some point, but Charlotte assures me it's not like that," Penelope declares.

"Really?"

"Alright, that is enough." Charlotte stands and grabs my hand. "Damien, let's talk outside."

"Wait." Noelle stands as Amelia and Penelope join her. "All jokes aside, you guys…Damien," she says, turning to me. "You'd better not hurt our friend. Whatever is going on between the two of you, figure it out and be sure about your intentions. Charlotte is a catch, and she doesn't deserve to be strung along or played around with, no matter how much we love giving her shit." I nod in understanding. "And rest assured, if you do hurt her, we will hunt you down, slice off your balls and penis, turn them into ground meat, and then feed it to you."

My stomach churns as I dance my sight across all three of the other women who I thought for sure were on my team just a moment ago. But then I realize, they'll always be team Charlotte, and that's how it should be. Women supporting women. Fuck, I wish more women would understand that.

"I understand, ladies. And believe me, I want to know what's going on here just as much as you do. I just need Charlotte to talk to me."

"Outside. Now." I wave goodbye to the girls as Charlotte drags me by the hand to the front entrance and then around the corner to a narrow alley between the restaurant and the next building over. "Damien? What the actual fuck?"

"Well, hello to you too."

"No. Don't try to be all coy with me." She shakes a finger at me. "Why the hell are you here?"

"Why am I here? Because you never called like you said you would, and you won't answer my calls and texts. What the fuck was I supposed to do, Charlotte?"

"God, what do you want, Damien?"

"I want to talk to you…about what happened the other night."

"Fine. Let's talk," she says, crossing her arms over her chest.

"Why did you run away?" I ask, not wasting any more time.

"Because I had just come on your tongue and I ditched my friends and needed to get back to them."

"Was your orgasm not satisfactory enough?"

"No. It was freaking amazing, Damien. But that's what we agreed to before it happened—that it was just an orgasm."

"Well, what if I want more?" I take a step toward her as her back hits the wall behind her.

"Why are you doing this, Damien?" Her eyes close and she takes a deep breath.

I run a finger down her cheek and then tug on her bottom lip with my thumb. Fuck if I know what the hell I'm doing, but all I know is that needing to have more of Charlotte feels a lot like the need to breathe right now. "Why are you fighting it, Char?"

Her eyes pop open. "Because it's us, and it's complicated."

"It doesn't have to be. We're already in a fake relationship, so why not enjoy the benefits of it?"

"What do you mean?"

"I mean orgasms, sweet pea, and lots of them. And maybe…a date, or two?" Perhaps if I make it seem like not that big of a deal, she'll agree. I just want to see her, talk to her, be around her as much as I can right now. And I don't exactly know why, but I don't need all of the answers at this moment. I just need her to say yes.

"Orgasms and dates?"

"Pleasure and food, babe. That's all I want." She stares up at me. "Give me a chance."

"Why?"

I sigh, but then opt for honesty. "Because for some reason, having you back in my life has brightened my days, Char. And I don't want that brightness to dull just yet."

She looks up at me with awe in her eyes before she reels it in and continues to act annoyed. "Fine."

"Fine?" I ask just to be clear.

"I guess a few orgasms and free meals wouldn't be the worst thing to happen to me."

My smile is instantaneous. "Sounds like a win-win to me." I dip my head down and press my lips to hers, sealing the deal. And surprisingly, she doesn't shove me away. On the contrary, Charlotte wraps her arms around my neck and draws me closer to her.

Her words are saying one thing, but her body, well, her body is telling me a completely different story. She wants me. It's clear as day. And I know that Charlotte is stubborn, but she is definitely throwing down a challenge that I want to rise to.

As our mouths move across each other's, a wave of relief comes over me. She's willing to let me in a little bit more, and I don't want her to change her mind.

"Would you be mad if I stole you away from your friends so I could make you come again?" I mumble against her lips, desperate to keep roaming my hands all over her body.

But she chuckles, pushing me away. "Sorry. That's a hard no. Nothing interrupts brunch—hence why I was so pissed to see you here."

"Hey, I'm just glad that I remembered when you told me about this little meet-up. Otherwise, I would have shown up at your office again."

"You definitely surprised me," she says, and I can't help but feel like there's a double meaning to her words.

"You've surprised the hell out of me too, Char." I press a kiss to her forehead, and then one to the tip of her nose. "I'll call you about dinner this week, and you'd better pick up."

"Okay," she relents. "Just…don't make me regret this, Damien."

"When has anyone ever regretted orgasms or food, Char?"

She smiles and then begins to walk away from me. "Enjoy the rest of your day."

"You too, sweet pea."

With a roll of her eyes, she walks back into the restaurant, and I fight the urge to do a celebratory fist pump. Charlotte Montgomery is going to let me give her orgasms and food, and maybe in return, she'll give me a bigger glimpse of her too. Let the planning begin.

Chapter 10

Charlotte

I can hardly contain my smile as I walk back to the diner to join the girls. I shouldn't be happy that Damien showed up and crashed our brunch, but his actions spoke volumes. Our run-in at the club rattled me, causing me to run away from him the second I had the chance. I was pissed at myself for letting things get that far and giving in to him. But when Damien pinned my hands above my head and made me realize that he wanted me as much as I wanted him, that control I've been fighting to maintain snapped.

And then he controlled *me*—with his mouth, with his tongue between my legs—and being bossed around by Damien Shaw lit my entire body on fire.

He gave me one of the best orgasms I've ever had in my life, hands down. And now apparently he wants to give me more.

I know that slipping into this new phase of our fake relationship comes with risks, but it was Damien's words that had me believing this won't be as disastrous as I might think.

"Because for some reason, having you back in my life has been the brightest part of my day, Char. And I don't want that brightness to dull just yet."

What was I supposed to say to that? Especially when every time we're near each other, I'm beginning to feel the same way. The annoyance that I've always felt towards him morphed into lust and then yearning really fast—almost too fast—which I know is something I should be wary of. But then again, getting to spend more time with him before Hawaii can't make things any worse, right? Especially if there are orgasms involved. Lord knows a woman can never have too many of those.

I finally get my smile under control as I walk through the entrance of the diner and back toward our table, the girls' eyes on me the second they see me coming. Nonchalantly, I take my seat again and reach for my mimosa, taking a sip and then smacking my lips together before placing my glass back on the table. I then return to my meal, feeling their eyes on me the entire time as they wait for me to say something.

But why say anything when I know they'll start firing off with questions in just a few seconds?

Three, two, one...

"Um, Charlotte?" Noelle asks timidly.

"What's up?"

"Is there something you want to tell us?"

I look up from my plate at her. "Is there something you want to know?"

Noelle looks over at Amelia and Penelope with a wide-eyed gaze, prompting them to say something. And Penelope takes the bait.

"What do you want me to ask, Noelle? Obviously, they weren't out there fucking because she came back way too quickly. And if they were, and that's as long as Damien can last, then that's just sad for our friend."

Noelle sighs, shaking her head. "*Not* what I was wondering."

"Then just ask, Noelle," I reply, slightly annoyed but knowing that my friends truly do mean well.

"What happened, Char? We're dying to know."

Leaning back in my chair, I grab my glass of champagne again. "Damien wants to take me on a date."

Noelle squeals while Amelia's smile grows brighter. But Penelope? Penelope just smirks. "Is that so?"

"Yes. And he wants to give me more orgasms as well," I quip, waiting for their reactions. The truth is, I had every intention of telling my friends about our storage closet encounter during brunch because I definitely needed to process it out loud, but they were being impatient and then Damien ambushed me.

"What!" Noelle shouts. "When did he give you the first one?"

"At the club," I reply.

"Oh, this just got so much more interesting," Penelope says as she takes a drink of her mimosa. "Please, go on."

So I do—I recount what happened after we kissed, and Damien led me off the dance floor. When I went back to the girls that night, I told them I went to the bathroom, but now they know that was a lie.

Noelle starts to fan herself with a menu, Amelia looks very happy for me, and Penelope just grins from ear to ear.

"Jesus, that sounds hot," Noelle says while smiling and shaking her head.

"It was. But of course, I ran away before we could talk, which is why he showed up here."

"So now he wants to take you out and make you come again," Penelope summarizes. "Sounds like the perfect man. He basically wants to give you what every woman wants."

Noelle holds up a finger. "No. What women truly want is to be able to eat and drink without getting fat."

"I'll second that notion," Amelia adds.

"Do you think I made a mistake by agreeing to this?" I ask, feeling a little more anxious after that conversation with Damien, but in a good way.

Amelia responds first. "I mean, I don't want to derail this development, but you're the one that seemed to be undecided about how you feel about him, Charlotte, at least up until he showed up here."

"Yeah, that's the thing though, Amelia. He did show up and was adamant about wanting this," Noelle interrupts. "They say if a man truly wants you, he'll let you know. I'd say crashing your brunch with your girlfriends to get you to talk to him sends a pretty strong message about how he feels."

"The man definitely had balls doing that," Penelope agrees.

"That's true. So you think I should go for it?" I ask, biting my lip, looking into the eyes of the people I trust more than anything.

Amelia and Noelle shrug, but Penelope nods confidently. "We're talking orgasms and free food, girl. You'd be a fool to say no."

"Ugh, Sonya. I missed you," I say as I sit up from my massage table in my office. My girl has returned and she worked my back and sciatic hard, but my muscles are thankful.

"I'm so sorry about a few weeks ago. My mother slipped and fell and fractured her hip. It's been a long two weeks, but now that she's more settled and my father doesn't look so stressed anymore about taking care of her, I'm glad to be back to work. I can only handle so much of my parents, you know?"

"Uh, I know all too well what you mean. Your replacement was great though."

She eyes me skeptically. "Um, you know, we didn't send someone over here that day, Charlotte. Helen tried to explain this to me too, but I'm telling you the truth."

I grip the sheet around me tighter. "Please tell me you're joking."

"I wish I were."

"Then who the hell massaged me that day?"

She shrugs, worry in her eyes. "I honestly don't know."

Curiosity infiltrating my mind, I think about how I can find out more information about who was in the building that day. Maybe we can look up the camera footage, or I can ask the front receptionist about it. "Well, there has to be a logical explanation for it. I'm sure I'll figure it out soon."

"I hope so. So, I'll see you next week?"

"Absolutely. Thanks again." I watch Sonya close the door behind her and then I stand from the table and proceed to get dressed again. Sometimes I feel high-maintenance having someone come to the office to massage me, but I know I'm not the only one that does, so I remind myself that I work hard and deserve some self-care. Besides, Sonya is a freelance massage therapist, so I'm putting money in her pocket and getting my physical ailments taken care of—it's a win-win for both of us.

After I'm dressed, I take a seat back at my desk and get to work, answering emails and checking the messages that I missed while I was getting massaged. I put on the soundtrack to *The Greatest Showman*, singing the show tunes out loud to myself. As a drama student back in the day, there's nothing I love more than a phenomenal musical—*The Greatest Showman* is one of my favorites. The soundtrack is just incredible.

I'm so entranced in what I'm doing that I barely register my door opening until the person that comes through speaks.

"How's it going, sweet pea?" Glancing up from my computer, I see Damien walk through the door and shut it behind him. "Are you listening to *The Greatest Showman* soundtrack?"

I press pause on my computer, halting the music, and then smile back at him. "Yes, I was. Is that a problem?"

"Nope. Just makes me think that all these years apart didn't change as much about you as I thought."

"What do you mean?"

"I mean the girl who loved musicals that I grew up with is still inside of there," he says, his eyes gleaming with appreciation and contentment as he stares at me.

"I guess a part of her is still in here." I point to my chest, but then remember that his visit here is unexpected. "What are you doing here, Damien?" I ask, even though with the way my heart rate increases, I'd say my body is happy to see him. He's wearing a light gray suit and sky blue shirt which brings out the color of his eyes. And my God, that smile, it's mischievous and hints of promises that I'm dying to know the stakes of.

"I came to see my girlfriend," he says.

"And why is that?"

"Well, I have something to give her. And then I have a question to ask her. Which would you like first?"

"A present or a question?" I ask, leaning back in my chair, smirking in his direction. The confident gleam in his eyes twinkles from the sunlight coming through the windows, and he stands there with his hands in his pockets, pushing his jacket open as he waits for me to reply.

"Yup."

"I think I'll take my present first, please."

And that makes his grin go wider. "I was hoping you'd say that."

Damien walks toward my desk, rounding the solid wood before leaning down over me, resting his hands on the armrests of my chair. "Hey, you," he says before slowly lowering his lips to mine, pressing against my mouth softly.

"Hi."

"I need you to stand up, please."

"Okay…" I do as I'm told, rising from my chair once Damien stands up again, granting me the room to do so. But then he closes the distance between us, slides a hand up the back of my neck into my hair, grabs a fistful of it, and smashes his lips to mine before I can take another breath.

With power and finesse, Damien kisses me intently, backing me up against my desk as he leans down and runs his other hand over my ass cheek. "I'm hoping since I'm allowed to give you orgasms now, that the rule about touching your ass is off the table."

"You should have asked first, but yes."

"Thank fuck." He removes his other hand from my hair before putting his mouth back on mine, bending down and grabbing the biggest handfuls of my ass as he can. "This ass, Charlotte. You have no idea how much I love it."

"There's plenty back there," I mumble against his lips before tangling my tongue with his, really enjoying my gift. A little make-out session in the middle of the day would inflate anyone's mood, I hope.

"I don't know if I was too fixated on hating you back then, but I'm kicking myself for never noticing how delectable this is." He gives my ass a little smack. "And now it's time for your present." He lifts me up and plants me on the edge of my desk before taking a seat in my chair.

"What—what are you doing?"

"I'm giving you an orgasm, babe. Like I promised."

I twist around to look at my closed office door but then nerves fire off at rapid speed. "In my office? Are you insane?"

He shrugs innocently, tearing off his suit jacket, even though he is anything but innocent in this moment. "Maybe a little. But I'm dying to taste you again. Besides, are you telling me you've never had a fantasy about a man eating you out on your desk like I'm about to do?"

Um, duh. But that's why it's called a fantasy. "Um, no."

Damien doesn't buy it, indicated by the grin he flashes me. "You're a liar."

"Damien," I plead, looking around my office again. "This is my job, my place of employment. Anyone could walk in at any moment."

"No, they won't. Helen is guarding the door and I locked it when I came in."

"Helen knows you're in here?"

"Yup. And she encouraged me to make you relax a little. So, how many orgasms am I delivering today? Two? Three?"

"Three?" I shriek before reaching up and covering my mouth. But then I lower my voice to a whisper. "Damien, you're insane."

"How about we make this a competition?"

"What?" I ask nervously as I feel his hands grace the sides of my thighs, pushing my dress up to my hips. He keeps moving the fabric up until my bare ass is sitting on the wood.

"I bet I can make you come more than you can make me."

I scoff. "Um, that's not a fair competition, Damien. Men can't have multiple orgasms like women can. I'd lose by default."

His smile is devilish. "Exactly. So I win, but you're the true winner, Char. I'm offering you as many orgasms as I'm capable of," he grates out, his voice thick with lust. I feel his thumb glide over the silk of my underwear right over my slit, making me arch my back in response. "So why are you saying no?"

"I guess you're right," I moan out, closing my eyes as I brace my weight on my arms behind me and feel him hook his thumbs in the band of my underwear, pulling them down and off my legs.

"Of course I am. Can I get that in writing?" he jokes.

"No."

"Fair enough. I'll just make sure you never forget the time I was right."

I reach forward and grip the back of his head as he moves forward, the anticipation killing me. I remember how phenomenal Damien is with his mouth from the other night. Now, four days later, my body obviously didn't forget either, indicated by how wet I already am and he hasn't even touched me yet.

"Pull on my hair, Char. Let me know how much you like this."

"Damien…shut up and get to work," I say as I pull his head forward and his tongue makes contact with my clit. "Oh, yes…" Suddenly my reservations about doing this at work have flown out the window completely.

Damien growls and then I brace myself for the onslaught of pleasure he brings to my body at lightning speed. Struggling for air, I close my eyes and focus on the feeling of Damien's tongue—short flicks, long strokes, kisses to the inside of my thigh before he licks me from bottom to top and then repeats the process. His mouth covers me, feasts on my pussy, and sucks my clit so deep between his lips that I don't know how long I'm going to last.

"Fuck, Char."

"It's so good, Damien." I'm trying to keep my noises down, but it's hard when the man before me is giving me the best oral of my life— better than the club because he knows my body more this time, and he's not afraid to listen to what I tell him. "Harder." He sucks me harder. "Fingers, please," I ask as he slides two deep inside of me, filling me up and giving me that pressure and friction that I need in order to reach my climax.

With the hook of his fingers forward, he strokes my G-spot as I feel my pussy flood his fingers, and with a few more strokes of his tongue, I reach the edge and fall over.

"Oh, shit!" I shout before Damien reaches up with his free hand and covers my mouth. I fall back on my desk, breathing through my nose as the tremors make my body quake and I moan against his palm before my body starts to relax. He slowly lifts his hand from my mouth, allowing me to take in a full breath of oxygen, and then he keeps sliding his fingers in and out of my core.

"That's one."

I lift my head up from the desk, looking down at him still between my legs, his lips and short beard glistening with my arousal. "Damien, there's no way I can come again."

"I promised you multiples, Char, so we have to have at least one more." I feel him press a finger against my asshole and then suddenly I feel my eyes go wide.

"What are you doing?"

"Up for a little anal play?"

"Um…"

Confession time. I've never let a man back there before. I've toyed around with things myself out of curiosity because, why not? You don't know if you like something until you try it, right? But letting a man back there—I'm not so sure I'm ready for that. Although, Damien seems to be reading my body pretty well already. Perhaps he's the perfect man to give that experience to.

"Okay…"

"You sure? We don't have to. It was just a suggestion…"

"No." I cut him off as I feel him rub against my G-spot again with his fingertips, making my body come to life again. "I want you to."

"Fuck, Char." He stands, leans over me, and plants his lips on mine, allowing me to taste myself before he pulls away too quickly. "You trusting me is such a fucking turn-on."

Oh, sweet baby Jesus. Those words hit me in the center of my chest.

Trust. That's a big step for Damien and me.

"Be gentle."

"I promise I'll make you feel good," he says as he sits back down and removes his hand from me. Sliding his pinky finger into his mouth, I watch his lips wrap around the digit before he pops it out, drops his eyes to my exposed flesh in front of him, and then I feel him slide it into my wet pussy as well gathering more lubricant before he presses against the place where no man has gone before.

Jesus, I sound like a voice-over for a space movie right now.

"Relax, Char. I just want you to feel good, babe." Taking a deep breath, I wait for the push I know will happen, and when it does, the feeling hits me in a slow wave.

"Oh…"

"Fuck, this is so hot." Damien pushes in his finger and then retracts it just enough to make this forbidden experience entirely too pleasurable, and then I feel his other two fingers slide back into my core at the same time, and I gasp at the intrusion.

"Oh my God…"

"Jesus, Charlotte." His head moves down again and then his tongue toys with my clit and I'm writhing on my desk. I'm so full, exquisitely full and my senses are overwhelmed. There's so much going on that I don't have much time to process it all before I feel my body building back up to another orgasm.

No man has ever given me more than one. Any multiples I've ever experienced have been from my hands and toys alone.

But Damien—he's taking me to a whole new world right now, one that is opening my eyes and heart up to possibilities.

Comfort. Pleasure. Freedom.

It's what I feel with him, what he gives me, and it's allowing me to enjoy this experience when I normally wouldn't have let this happen at all.

But I'm letting it happen with him.

"Damien…"

"I can feel you getting close, Char. Let go, sweetheart. Give it to me," he says as he goes back to work—flicking his tongue over my clit, sucking it between his lips, moving his fingers in and out of my pussy and asshole at the same time.

And then I'm gone—I detonate, releasing fluid all over my desk, his hand, and his fingers in a silent scream that ends in an exhale and moan that I've never made before.

"Holy shit."

"Fuck, that was hot. You squirted, Charlotte."

"What?" I lean up on my elbows and forearms, noticing the pool of liquid beneath me. "Oh my God." Clenching my thighs together, I instantly feel mortified.

"Don't be embarrassed, babe. That is so fucking sexy. And especially because I know that I did that to you." Damien's face shows nothing but lust and pride across his features as he reaches for some tissue and cleans up the mess between my legs after he pries them back open. He then grabs a few more and wipes me clean before sliding my underwear back up my legs and helping me stand from my desk.

On wobbly legs, I look up at him and then kiss him with appreciation and something else—something I don't think I want to admit just yet.

Never in a million years did I think I'd be kissing Damien Shaw, let alone letting the man stick a finger in my ass and eat me out on my desk—but here I am.

I feel alive though, like I've stepped through a door that exposed something I've been missing with other men, something that my past relationships never developed into or were lacking—an element of need.

Dropping to my knees, I reach for the buckle on his pants, and then Damien sucks in a breath.

"Charlotte, what are you doing?"

"Returning the favor."

"You don't have to…"

"I want to, Damien," I say as I release the clasp on his belt, undo the button, and pull down his zipper.

"I'm not going to last, Charlotte. I barely held back just doing that to you."

"I don't care." I'm zealous as I pull his boxer briefs down and expose his cock to me. And holy shit, what a cock it is. "Damien," I gasp.

"What Char?"

"You're…big."

"Bigger than most, babe. But not gigantic."

I reach up and stroke him, noticing pre-cum dripping from his tip. "Bigger than any I've had."

"Fuck, that's making me harder, Charlotte."

I look up at him, finding his eyes locked on me, and while he's watching, I run my tongue along the underside of his length before taking the tip of him in my mouth.

"Jesus, I'm going to come." Damien looks like he's in pain watching me suck him back as far as I can, licking around his head, before repeating the process. "Seriously, Charlotte. This is going to be embarrassing."

"I don't care. Come down my throat," I say, shocking even myself, but I'm already growing wet again as I work him over with my mouth.

I feel Damien's hand move to the back of my head as he gently urges me forward and then I feel the first hot spurt of his come on my tongue.

I've never swallowed during a blowjob before, so I'm not sure what to expect, but for Damien, I will take every last drop. The man came into my office with the intent to please me, so I'm going to do the same for him. Even more than that, *I want to*.

"Fuck. God. Shit." Damien curses and gasps as he spills his orgasm into my mouth and I wait until he's done before releasing him and then swallowing it all down.

Okay, that wasn't too bad.

"Jesus Christ," he exhales before falling back into my chair while I'm still on my knees. I take that moment to admire how undone he looks and the small patch of trimmed pubic hair around his cock. *Fuck, why is that so sexy?* "You sucked the life out of me, woman."

"Well, you made my legs feel like jelly, so I think we're even."

"Nope." He shakes his head. "I gave you two orgasms, so I win." Standing from the chair, he tucks himself back into his slacks and then helps me off the floor. "Fuck, this was the best idea ever," he mumbles before pressing his lips to mine, kissing me with much more sincerity than the carnal moments we just shared.

"Not a bad break in the day at all."

"Shit." He glances down at his wristwatch. "I gotta go. That took longer than I thought."

"Wait. What was your question?"

He smiles and then reaches up with both hands and cups the sides of my face. "Will you go to dinner with me on Friday?"

And I can't help but smile. "Okay. You do owe me food anyway."

"That I do. I'll pick you up at six."

"Sounds good. And thank you…"

"For?"

"The orgasms," I say, feeling the blush of my cheeks come to life.

"The pleasure was mine, Char." With a kiss on the tip of my nose, he turns for the door, unlocks it, and then winks at me over his shoulder before leaving.

"Sweet Jesus," I whisper, falling back into my chair, closing my eyes, and reliving the past twenty minutes.

"I am so jealous right now," Helen says, alerting me to her standing in the door of my office.

"Oh, God." I bury my head in my hands, giggling behind them with embarrassment. "I'm sorry if I was loud."

"Oh, I had my earbuds in, but by the way that man was smiling when he left, I'm guessing your visit went well?"

Biting on my lip, I nod. "Um, you could say that."

Helen does a little shimmy and then starts to walk away. "Enjoy those moments, Char. Those are the ones you look back on later in life and know you truly were living—spontaneously and in the moment."

"Yeah," I simply reply, knowing that there aren't many others I can remember that made me feel that good. And maybe that's something I should keep in mind.

"Where are we going?" I ask in the passenger seat of Damien's car. It's Friday night and he just picked us up for our date like we arranged. My eyes take in the city zooming past us as we drive along the freeway and he holds my hand in his.

Our date.

I'm on a freaking date with Damien Shaw. And the man has given me three of the best orgasms of my life so far in the past week. I'd say the smile on my face is one I'm wearing proudly at this moment, even though there's trepidation still over what all of this means.

"Have you ever been to The High Rooftop Lounge?" he asks, glancing over at me quickly before focusing back on the road.

"Oh! No, but I've been dying to go."

"Well, then I'm glad I made our reservations there for tonight. We're getting dinner with a view, Char." He lifts my hand that he's holding and kisses the back of it, eliciting tingles all over my skin.

On the way to the restaurant/bar, we catch up on the rest of our week. Damien tells me about how Dave was trying to invite us to another dinner, but he told him we had plans for the next few weekends. I tell him about dinner with the girls on Wednesday, in which Noelle told us about her latest online dating fiasco.

And then Damien brings up what happened in my office on Tuesday. "Have you been thinking about Tuesday as much as I have?" he asks suggestively, glancing in my direction as we arrive at the bar.

I decide to tease him a little bit. "What happened on Tuesday?" I tap my finger to my chin in thought. "I don't remember anything eventful on Tuesday."

Leaning over the center console, he grins at me. "If you need a reminder, I'd be more than happy to oblige."

So I get a little closer, leaving just enough room between us that our lips don't touch, but I still get a strong whiff of his scent—that masculine cleanliness that I can't seem to get enough of. "You might just have to do that. Three days without an orgasm has my mind kind of fuzzy."

Damien grabs my head and pulls me closer, his lips brushing against mine as he speaks. "Be careful what you ask for, Char." And then he kisses me chastely, leaving me wanting so much more than what he gave me.

He releases me and exits the car, coming around to open my door for me and helping me out with his outstretched hand. As I stand, I take him in once more. I already ogled him when he picked me up, but

Damien looks so sexy in dark wash jeans, a simple olive green shirt, and brown sneakers.

He told me to dress warmly since once the sun goes down, the rooftop gets cold from the breeze coming off the ocean. So I also chose a pair of jeans which I coordinated with wedges, a flowy pink top that hangs off my shoulders, and I brought a cream-colored sweater just in case.

With my hand in his, he leads me to the front of the restaurant, where the hostess checks us in and then leads us to the rooftop. When we climb the last few stairs, and I see the view of the ocean in front of me and all of Los Angeles in any direction behind us, my mouth drops open in awe. "Wow."

"This way. We have a table over here for you two." Damien follows the hostess while I trail behind him to a small couch facing the railing around the space, looking out over the city around us. Two tall planters sit behind the couch and an umbrella that isn't open stands next to one side. Propane heaters are spaced out all around the rooftop, close enough to keep us warm once the sun goes down. "Here you go."

"Thank you," I reply as we sit down and she hands us menus. "Your server will be by shortly and if you get cold, all you have to do is ask for a blanket. We have a clean one available for all of our guests."

"Awesome." Damien turns to me and puts his arm around my shoulders as we stare off into the distance. "Damn. This is some view."

"Right?" I spin my head around, looking behind us too.

"Sunset over the ocean," he says, looking over at me now. "Doesn't get much better than that."

"I agree." I debate pressing my lips to his gently, but then a server comes by asking us for our drink order. Damien orders a beer and I order a glass of white wine, and we watch the sunset before us as we wait for our drinks.

Oranges, yellows, and pinks paint the sky in between clouds that look like brush strokes on a canvas. The waves of the ocean crash onto the shore below, and palm trees sticking up into the sky flow freely in the soft breeze.

"This is stunning."

"Yeah, pretty fucking spectacular," Damien replies when I realize he's looking at me now and not the view. Our waiter comes by with our drinks and then Damien proposes a toast. "To old friends and new beginnings."

"We were never friends, Damien," I tease.

"I don't know. I think deep down we were. We just never let ourselves get close enough to explore it." We clink our glasses together and then return our stare to the sunset.

"Do you think we would have been more back then?" I ask, avoiding his gaze. But then I regret asking that question immediately. Nothing about how and who we used to be even compares to this moment right now.

Damien thinks about his answer before he replies. "No," he says soundly and part of me cringes at how easily the answer came to him. "We were young, driven by the wrong circumstances and aspirations." And then he turns to me. "But this, where we are right now? This is where I want to be, okay?"

The rest of his answer makes me feel resolute again. "Okay." With a press of his lips to mine, I get lost in his touch, almost spilling my wine on my jeans. "Whoops." I laugh as Damien follows suit and grabs both of our drinks and sets them on the table in front of us.

"Let's figure out what we're going to eat, and then we can do some more kissing in a minute."

"Okay." I lean my head on his shoulder as we share a menu and pick out what we're going to eat—the act feeling so normal and comfortable, for a second it almost feels real. But maybe that's because it's beginning to feel that way and the giddy girl inside of me is enjoying this way too much—while the woman in my head is begging me to proceed with caution.

"So, I've been meaning to ask you, but thought I'd save it for tonight," Damien says while wiping his mouth with a napkin.

"Okay…"

"Do you always listen to *The Greatest Showman* soundtrack while you're working?" He smiles around the last bit of his food.

I roll my eyes but smile back at him. "I knew you were going to give me shit about that."

"You've got to admit, it's kind of endearing."

"Oh really? How so?"

"Well, you're a grown-ass woman and you listen to show tunes while you work. It's cute."

"Have you even seen the movie?"

Damien licks his lips before replying. "Yes, I have."

"Then you should know how phenomenal the soundtrack is."

He leans closer to me grazing his nose against mine. "I have a confession to make then."

"Okay…"

"I sort of listen to the soundtrack when I work too."

"What?" I shout, leaning back in my seat and then adjusting my legs underneath the blanket over us. Once the sun went down, I wasted no time asking for the complimentary blanket. It did get cold rather quickly. "You were just giving me shit about it and you do the same thing?"

Damien throws his head back in laughter. "I know, but that's why I had to bring it up. I wanted you to know that we share that little quirk. Apparently, we're more alike than we realized."

"Well, I already know we're both extremely competitive and hard-working—but an admiration for that movie is definitely something I wasn't banking on."

"I bet I know the songs better than you," he challenges, arching his brow at me again.

"Oh, Jesus. Turning this into a competition now, are we?"

"Would you expect anything less from me, Char?"

All I can do is shake my head at him. "Nope. Not at all."

"It's kind of nice knowing a little bit about me, isn't it?"

"I mean, yes. But I feel like there's still a part of you that is a stranger," I answer honestly, brushing my hair from my face.

"I feel the same about you. But I tell you what, that makes this more fun, I think."

"Why?"

"Because that means we still have things to learn about each other."

"Okay, so what do you want to know?" I ask, taking this opportunity for us to discover more about each other. Twelve years is a long time to change.

Damien rubs his hands together. "I want a crazy story from you while you were in college."

"Oh, God. You already asked me this and I told you that there's nothing to tell." Correction, there aren't any stories that I want Damien to know.

"Nope. I don't believe you." He points a finger at my chest and then draws it up over my exposed collarbone, making a path for the electric current his touch evokes to follow. "You owe me a story and then I'll give you one in return."

"Tit for tat?"

"I mean, if you wanna show me your tits, I wouldn't object to that."

Rolling my eyes, I take another sip of my wine. "Oh, brother. Fine, you want a story? Here's one." I search the Rolodex of my memory and land on one that I think will appease him. And even though I'm acting annoyed, I can't remember the last time I had this much fun on a date—or with Damien, for that matter. And all I keep thinking about is how I don't want this night to end.

Chapter 11

Damien

"Fine. You already know I went to UCLA…"

"Don't rub salt in the wound, woman." Remembering how Charlotte got into my dream school and I got into hers only reminds me of how juvenile we acted about trivial shit like that. But I'd still like her to believe that it bothers me, which it only does for a fraction of a second before I focus back on her lips and how fucking beautiful she looks curled up in her sweater under the blanket over both of our legs.

She laughs, bringing my attention back to her story. "Well, I never joined a sorority. However, I met Penelope, Amelia, and Noelle my freshman year in our English class and we became inseparable. Penelope was the wild child of the group and she did join a sisterhood, so she got us to do all kinds of shit."

"Like…"

"Well, off the top of my head, we went to an ABC party…"

"Anything but clothes," I reply in understanding.

"Yup. And I was in a dress made out of Saran wrap, which seemed like a good idea at the time. But then the cops broke up the party and the four of us had to hop a fence because we were all underage and didn't want to get caught. Try climbing a chain-link fence in plastic wrap."

"I don't think I want to," I chuckle as she keeps talking.

"Naturally, my dress got caught on the metal and tore open, leaving me in nothing but pasties and a thong as I ran down an alleyway back to the dorms. It was mortifying."

I throw my head back, laughing at the image of those four girls running down a back street in L.A. "Fuck, that's great, Char. Little Miss Perfect running down the street practically naked."

"Glad I can make you laugh at my expense." She lifts her drink to her lips and I lock my eyes on the sight. "Now it's your turn."

"Okay, I made a promise and now it's time to deliver."

"Yup, and you'd better make it good, Damien."

I think back over the years when partying was like a second job. I always gave my classes the attention they deserved, but at the age of twenty, I did some really fucked up and stupid shit, shit that my parents and grandparents can never know about. "Okay, I've got one."

She rubs her hands together. "I'm ready."

"Well, unlike you, I did join a fraternity, and part of being in the brotherhood meant never backing down from a dare. And you know me, Charlotte, I love a challenge." Her eyes narrow as I say the words, but then she nods for me to continue. "So, there was an amateur drag queen show at one of the local bars by the university, and a bunch of my brothers dared me to enter." Charlotte's eyes widen. "Now let me say, I have nothing but the utmost respect for the LGBTQ community, and what we did was all in good fun. In fact, the owner of the bar was adamant that we all participate if we wanted. But you know me, I wanted to take it seriously. I wasn't going to half-ass that shit. So, I had a few of the sorority girls hook me up with makeup, bought a wig, borrowed some heels and a tight dress, and pranced on that stage like the diva I was. I freaking rocked the hell out of my performance."

Charlotte nearly spits her wine out, catching herself before she does. "Please, God, tell me there are pictures and videos of this."

"Of course." I reach for my phone from my pocket but pause before I show her. "What am I going to get in return though?"

"What do you mean?"

"Well, I only got a story from you. No photos. I don't think it's fair that you get a story and pictures from me."

Charlotte squints in my direction. "I'm sorry that I was too busy running down the street practically naked to snap a picture so I had something to show you ten years after the fact."

"You're telling me even Penelope didn't take advantage of that situation for some blackmail?" Penelope seems like the cutthroat one of the group.

"No. We were running so we wouldn't get arrested. And Penelope would never blackmail me. Hoes before bros, Damien."

I laugh and then relent to her argument. "Fine. Whatever, I'm sure I'll have to cop to this one day or another." I search through my photos and then turn the phone toward Charlotte once I've located the damning evidence.

"Oh. My. God." She loses it, cackling loudly while holding her stomach, drawing attention from the people around us. But I don't care. Just watching her be free, making her laugh and smile—it's those images that make my time with her so addicting. I never got a chance to see this side of her before when we were growing up.

There was no joking around, trading stories, or orgasms for that matter. No, it was just animosity and underlying hate.

But this—this place where we are right now—I'd never trade this for anything. And that has me feeling more content than I have in a long ass time.

"This is the greatest show," I sing out loud as I move some papers around on my desk, listening to the soundtrack play out through the speakers on my computer. After our date Friday night, I knew it was time for a relisten.

The truth is, it had been a while since I'd listened to the songs from the movie. But after hearing Charlotte do so and then sharing with her that I did the same sometimes, we scrolled through our favorite songs on the way home from the restaurant after we finished our meal and stayed until almost closing time.

It was the best date I've been on, ever, and I can't fucking wait to do it again.

"Oh! This is the greatest show!" Jeffrey bellows as he comes through the door to my office, arms stretched out on both sides. "Fuck! I love this movie!"

I reach for the mouse on my computer and press pause on the song before turning around to face him, pointing a stern finger in his direction. "Tell anyone I was listening to this and you're dead."

Jeffrey's smile falls. "Why? There's nothing wrong with that."

"I know. It's just…something I like to keep to myself, alright?" Yeah, definitely something I wouldn't share with other people. Charlotte was obviously the exception.

And she's becoming the exception in more ways than one.

"Whatever, dude. It's cool. So, have you thought about the Remedy account more? I was thinking we should sit down and run through some ideas, come up with a plan. Time is ticking, my friend." He taps his finger on his wrist where there is no watch.

"Oh. Uh, not really. I've been kind of busy." I look away from him, knowing I'm slacking on this account, the account that I went after in the first place.

"Busy with Charlotte?" he prods.

"Um, yeah. We've been hanging out a bit."

"Just a bit?"

I turn to face him as he eyes me with a knowing gaze. "Fine. We've been hanging out as much as she'll allow, okay?" I run a hand through my hair. "And it's my idea. Fuck."

"What's going on?"

Scrubbing my hands down my face, I admit what I am finally accepting. "Jeffrey, I'm into my fake girlfriend."

His eyes go wide. "Noooooo…"

I nod. "Yup."

"Fuck, Damien. What are you thinking, man? Isn't this the girl that hates you and vice versa?"

"I'm thinking that the woman intrigues me and I fucking love talking to her. She's not the same girl I remember while we were growing up. Or maybe she is, but I was too blinded by our rivalry to see who she really was. And now…I just want to be around her as much as possible."

"Holy shit. And does she feel the same way?"

I think back to our date, to the conversations we had and the orgasm I gave her under the blanket on our laps. She curled into my side, slid her jeans down off her hips, and I made her come on my fingers as we stared up at the stars. Then we drove home and sang the songs to that fucking movie throughout the entire drive. Who the fuck does those things?

People that are in a real relationship.

"I mean, I think she does. Hell, there's been kissing and touching, lots of touching. And I took her on a real date Friday night."

Jeffrey smiles, his face softening as he registers my inner turmoil. "Dude…"

"I know. So I'm sorry that I'm slacking. I am. I just…"

"Hey, it's okay. I get it. If I had a girl like Charlotte giving me attention, I'd be acting the same fucking way." He takes a deep breath but then grows serious again. "But we have to remember why this all started in the first place, Damien—the Remedy account. We have to land it. If we go into that pitch with a half-ass attempt, Dave will have our necks and then we look like fucking wankers. You want that?"

"Wankers? Are you British now?"

"No, it was just the word that came to mind at the time." He shrugs.

"Okay. Noted. But I hear you, man. And you're right. This week we buckle down. I promise we will get to work."

"It's a plan. And the next time you see Charlotte, try to pick her brain about her period."

I wince at his suggestion. "I don't know. I don't see how there's an easy way to broach that subject with her. I can't just ask her out of the blue. It needs to seem organic."

He rubs his chin in thought. "Yeah, I think you're right. But she's our best bet of getting an accurate glance at what women look for when it comes to that, you know?"

"I'll see what I can get out of her."

"That's all I ask. Okay, let me grab my notepad and I'll be right back. Shall I order some lunch so we can work through it?"

I glance at my phone, debating if it's worth canceling my lunch plans with Charlotte. It's the Tuesday after our date and I was really looking forward to seeing her. But Jeffrey is right—we need to work on this pitch. It has to be perfect and nothing short of brilliant. And if I don't put forth some effort toward it, this lie will have been for nothing.

"Yeah, sounds good. I just need to make a call really quick."

"Okay. I'll be right back." I watch him leave and then bring up Charlotte's number and hit the green call button.

She answers after the third ring. "Hello?"

"Hey, beautiful."

"Hi," she replies, giddiness in her voice. "What's up?"

"Listen, I hate to do this to you, but I'm going to have to cancel our lunch plans. This account I'm working on needs my attention and Jeffrey wants to work through lunch."

"Oh. That's okay, I understand." I can hear the disappointment in her voice, but she also sounds like she's trying to hide it.

"Are you sure?"

"Yes, Damien. I understand that sometimes work needs to come first. No worries. We'll get together soon."

"How about tonight?"

"I can't tonight. I have a yoga class with Amelia."

"Tomorrow?"

"Wednesdays we do our weekly dinner."

"Thursday?" I ask, hoping she isn't just making up excuses to blow me off because she's upset.

"I can do Thursday night."

A sigh of relief escapes my lips. "Great. Thursday night. My place. I'll order from Tony's and we can catch up. Maybe watch a movie?"

"Only if I get to pick," she counters, a hint of a smile in her voice.

"You got it. Sorry again, Char."

"It's okay, Damien. Call me later if you want."

"I will. Bye, babe."

"Bye."

When she hangs up, my chest feels heavy and a part of me yearns to call her back, tell her I was joking and that I'll be at her office in fifteen minutes.

But the responsible part of me—the part that wants this promotion more than anything—knows that this is the right thing to do. There's more than one reason why this promotion will make my life easier, and I'll need to face it soon enough.

And as much as it kills me, I need to remember why Charlotte is back in my life in the first place. It will make this all a lot easier when this is over.

But the deeper you get into this, the less you want it to end, isn't that right, Damien?

"Hey, Dad." I prop my phone up on the counter as I finish cleaning a few dishes I left in the sink. It's Thursday night and Charlotte will be here soon, but I've been avoiding his calls all week, so there's no time like the present to get this conversation over with.

"Damien. Long time, no talk, son."

Yeah, for a very good reason. "Well, I've been busy."

"Yeah, I heard—hanging out with Charlotte Montgomery, huh?"

I close my eyes, exhaling in frustration. I knew it was only a matter of time before I got this phone call. "We've reconnected, yes…"

"Reconnected? That seems a lot more casual than what her mom said the other night at dinner."

"And what did Savannah say?" I prod, wanting to hear what he knows before I give him too much information.

"That you two are dating."

"Okay…" I say, waiting for the outburst.

"What the hell are you thinking?" *And there it is.*

"You make it sound like this is a problem?"

"It's not a problem, per se. But Charlotte is…" Here it comes. "Well, she's not the type of woman you need."

Pinching the bridge of my nose, I dry my hands on the dish towel right beside me. "And just what type of woman do I need, Dad?"

"A woman who knows her place, who will remember that the man is the head of the household. Charlotte always had too much grit for my liking, and given her job now, I'm pretty sure she makes more money than you, doesn't she? I just don't understand why you would want to date her?"

And there it is—the glaring reminder that my father's chauvinistic views of the male/female dynamic are way too outdated, and therefore women like Charlotte are threatening to his manhood.

You see, the competition between Charlotte and me? It wasn't perpetuated solely because we're both competitive people. Sure, it was fun for me to ruffle her feathers and beat her when it counted, but most of our competition was driven by my father's need for me to be better than her.

Because our parents are best friends, all I ever heard was how smart Charlotte was, how good she was at soccer, how hardworking she was, and how successful she was going to be. And every time he could, my dad would tell me that I should be doing more than she is. As a man who carried the last name Shaw, I should be on top in all aspects of my life. A woman shouldn't be showing me up—ever.

Call it crazy, because that's exactly what it is, but my dad was the one who wanted me to beat her at everything, to give him bragging rights about his kid. And for the longest time, I played into it. His praise made me feel ten feet tall, and when praise came from other people too, it validated who I was and my namesake.

By the time I was a senior, I was done. I didn't want to worry about Charlotte anymore. I wanted to worry about *me*—what I wanted for my future, my life beyond high school, and my career. If my father had it his way, I would have stayed in South Carolina for college and gone to work for him in real estate after graduation. I probably would be rolling in dough right about now, but that career aspiration didn't interest me in the slightest.

I wanted to work in advertising, and applying to school in California was a way for me to get as far away from him as possible. Sure, part of me applied to Charlotte's dream school because I had to for my father's wishes, but also because I wanted to see if I would get in too. Ironically, things didn't work out the way either of us wanted them to, but in a way, they did. Getting into USC allowed me to escape my father's wrath and his outdated view on the world—that I should marry a woman who would stay home and raise my kids, inherit the family business, and be just as blissfully happy as he and my mom appear, even though I wonder if they truly are.

Watching my parents' marriage from within gave me a glimpse of one way life could look in the future. And it works for them, but I know I'm meant for something different. The truth is, my mother's demeanor always made me think she regretted playing the part she did in their life. I always wondered if she wanted more for herself, especially after I started seeing my father's controlling ways, which made me wonder if he was controlling her too.

Anyway, I remember running into Charlotte one night at the park back home, and we said some not-so-nice things to each other. I was seething from the argument with my father earlier when I told him I'd be going to college in California. To say he was upset would be an understatement. But for the first time, I felt like I had some kind of control over what I was going to do in my life, the decisions that I was making felt like my own and not driven by someone else's wishes.

Our entire childhood though—the competition, nasty words, and drive to outdo the other—it was all caused by my dad pushing his superiority onto me. And now, knowing that with each day that passes

I want to keep doing whatever it is that we're doing, eventually, I'm going to have to tell her. I just don't know how.

"It's not your job to understand it," I say, going back to our conversation and standing up to him as best as I can through the phone.

"Yeah, but you know this won't last, right? Her mother says she's married to her job. Is that what you want? A woman that puts her career first?"

"Look, I can't talk about this right now. I'm expecting company," I say as I glance at the clock on the microwave. "Was there a point to this call?"

My father sighs. "I guess I just wanted to check up on you. Your mother talks to you all the time, but it feels like we never talk, so..." *Yeah, because every time we get on the phone, this is what happens.*

"Well, life is good. Work is good. I'm actually up for a promotion." And hopefully securing it will get him off my back a little, show him this direction I chose for my life wasn't a waste.

"As you should be. You know I was worried you were throwing away your potential on this advertising route, but at least you seem to be doing okay. Although, you could have been running things already if you had stayed home and worked for me." *Fuck, why can't he just be proud of me? Why does it have to always feel like it's not enough?* "Anyone with the last name Shaw should be on top."

"Yup, doing okay. I guess I'll see you and mom in Hawaii in a few weeks, right?"

"Oh, yeah. That trip should be a good time. It's been years since we've been, although Cal and Savannah aren't staying at my favorite resort, but whatever. It isn't my party."

I close my eyes and take a deep breath. He's so fucking judgmental. "I'm sure everything will be fine and we'll all have a good time. I'll see you then, Dad."

"Looking forward to it, son." He ends the call and all I can do is stare down at the phone, wondering how in the hell I'm going to get him to see things from my side for a change, especially when it comes to Charlotte.

I wonder how I even got to this place—thirty and still feeling cut by my father's words, still fighting the chains I feel around my wrists with being who I want to be and making my parents proud at the same time. My mother, bless her soul, always makes me feel loved. She listens, offers advice when I need it, and I never feel like I ever have to be anyone other than who I am with her.

But my dad—I feel like there's only so much more I can take from him until I'm about to crack. It had been a while since he'd made me feel this way, but I knew once he found out about Charlotte and me, his temper and disappointment would come back with a vengeance.

I wonder if I should talk to Charlotte about it, especially since I know she deals with similar shit with her mom. It's almost like all these years we were battling the same demons but took out our frustration on each other instead. Time apart gave me the space to live my life without her and my parents around, but now it's all coming to a head—and part of me is grateful that I at least have her on my side this time.

Like my mind conjured her presence, I hear the buzzer for my apartment ring out, so I go over to the button to let her up. And when I hear her knock on my door a few moments later, I waste no time opening it up so I can see her gorgeous face.

In a grey skirt and black blouse, Charlotte stands there in heels with her purse and one other bag slung over her shoulder and her hair fastened back in a low bun. It appears she came straight from work, and the urge I have to strip her out of her clothes becomes relentless.

"Hi," she says breathlessly as if she were running here, but she still has an enthusiastic smile on her face.

"Hey. Do you need some water?" I ask her as she walks through my door and sets her purse and bag on the floor.

"Yes, please. That would be great."

"Did you run here or something?" Making my way to my kitchen, I reach for a glass and begin filling it up from the dispenser on the fridge while I watch her.

"No, but I was walking pretty fast. I didn't want to be late." She takes the glass from me as I hold it out to her. "Thank you."

"You're welcome, Char. But there was no need to rush. Although, I am really fucking happy to see you."

She smiles after she drinks half of the liquid, placing the glass down on the counter, and then closes the distance between us, reaching up to wrap her arms around my shoulders as my hands find her waist. "I'm happy to see you too."

Taking that as an invitation, I lean down to kiss her, and she meets me halfway. Just having her here in my arms, with our lips pressed together, takes away some of the anxiety I'm feeling after the phone call with my dad.

Charlotte moans as I reach down and grab her ass, pulling her closer so she can feel what she's doing to me. But as our tongues tangle, I remember that the food will be here any moment, so this can't go much further just yet.

"The food will be here soon," I mumble against her lips.

"Oh, good. I'm starving." I release her reluctantly, and then she goes back over to her bags. "Do you mind if I change? I brought some extra clothes."

"Of course. You know where the bathroom is."

She nods and then walks down the hallway just as the food arrives. I arrange the tacos, rice, and beans on two plates and then bring them over to the table along with a bag of chips and a container of salsa. Charlotte comes out from the bathroom in black yoga pants, a white tank top, and her hair removed from her bun, curling slightly at the ends but free and flowing.

Fuck, she's beautiful.

"That smells good."

"I hope you don't mind Mexican. I was craving the tacos from Miguel's."

"Oh, yes. I love that place. Apparently, you and I like a lot of the same food," she says as she takes a seat at my table.

"Looks like we have more in common than we thought."

As we eat, we catch up on our week, and I apologize for canceling our lunch plans again.

"Did you end up getting some work done?" she asks, dipping a chip into the salsa and then popping it in her mouth.

"We did. Jeffrey and I have a solid start on our pitch, so now it's about coming up with the details."

"I love small details in a commercial or story. I feel like they give the viewer or readers breadcrumbs to follow so when they get to the end, every part of the story makes sense."

I look up at the ceiling in thought. "I like that. Breadcrumbs…" I drift off, making a mental note to keep that idea for later when I see Jeffrey in the morning.

"Oh my God, I'm stuffed." Charlotte leans back in her chair, rubbing her belly. "That was so good, though. Thank you."

"You're welcome. Ready to watch that movie?"

That question has her smiling. "Yes. And I know just the one." She goes over to her bag and pulls out *The Greatest Showman* on Blu-ray.

Smiling from ear to ear, I watch her walk toward me, shaking the movie container in her hand. "How did I know you were going to suggest that?"

She walks toward my television and bends over to put the disc in the player, giving me a perfect view of her ass. "Well, I thought it was only fitting that we watch it together after last weekend."

"Sounds like a plan to me."

We settle into the couch and start the movie, singing along to the songs as they play—well, Charlotte sings. I mostly just hum along and enjoy the sound of her voice. The girl could always carry a tune.

At one point, Charlotte lies down across the couch with her head propped up on a pillow on my lap. The movie is playing and we've both been enraptured by it, so when she speaks, she startles me.

"Did you ever think we'd be here, Damien?" she asks, twisting so she's looking up at me, flat on her back now.

"Where?"

"Here. In your apartment, watching a movie together?"

"If someone asked me five years ago if this is where I'd be at this moment, I'd have accused them of being senile."

She giggles. "Same."

"But now that I'm here..." I inhale deeply. "It feels like a part of my life was missing. It's weird, but having you back in my life, in this new way, just feels right."

"Me too, Damien..." she breathes, but then clears her throat. "Where do you see yourself in five years from now?"

"Hopefully married, a couple of kids...happy."

"I want that too."

I think she's going to say more, but she doesn't; she turns back to the movie and readjusts herself on her side. And in that moment I feel content again, like maybe I could have those things with Charlotte...

I stroke my hand along her hip, down her thigh, and then back up her side and along her arm until I'm stroking the side of her face with the tips of my fingers.

"Damien..." I watch her skin pebble, her thighs rub together as her body starts reacting to my touch. So I repeat the process, loving how my hands are making her squirm. "What are you doing?"

"Nothing," I tease, moving my hand around to her chest, circling my finger around her nipple this time. It's at that moment that I realize I've yet to see her chest. Between the massage I gave her and the handful of times we've fooled around so far, I've only seen her naked from the waist down.

"That doesn't feel like nothing." She turns onto her back again. "We're supposed to be watching a movie."

"How many times have you seen this movie, Char?"

"Too many to count," she moans as I circle her nipple again and then draw a line up to her collarbone and neck that's exposed from the cut of her tank top.

"Exactly. So stop acting like you're not enjoying what I'm doing."

"What *are* you doing?"

"Feeling you up. Turning you on. Getting ready to give you a few more orgasms tonight since it's part of our deal."

She smirks, her lips parting slightly as I keep running my hands all over her body. But then I reach up to her face and pull her bottom lip down with my thumb, remembering what those lips looked like wrapped around my cock.

Charlotte darts her tongue out to lick my thumb and then reaches up to grab my wrist, bringing my thumb further into her mouth, where she sucks on it while keeping her eyes trained on mine.

"Keep doing that, Charlotte, and you're not going to like what happens next."

She releases my thumb with a pop. "On the contrary—I believe I'm going to *love* what happens next." She takes my hand and shoves it under the neckline of her tank, right toward her bra, sliding my hand under the cup. And when my fingers graze her nipple, she arches up, granting me better access.

Using my thumb and forefinger, I twist her nipple, drawing a moan from her lips. "Fuck, Char."

"I want you, Damien," she whispers.

"I'm right here…"

She shakes her head, reaching up to play with my lips this time. "No, I want you. All of you. Right now."

I freeze in my movements and try to digest what she's saying to me. Does Charlotte want to sleep together? Like, for real?

"Are you saying…" I start, but she removes my hand from her shirt, moves to sit up and straddles my lap.

"Do you want me?"

"Fuck, of course I do, Charlotte."

She reaches for the hem of her shirt and rips it over her head, tossing it somewhere to the floor. Her breasts are covered in a white cotton bra that is surprisingly sexy given how simple it is. But I don't give a fuck what she's wearing—it doesn't change how badly I want to feel her wrapped around me. "Then fuck me, Damien."

"Jesus, are you sure?" I ask, running my hands up and down her sides, relishing in the softness of her skin and how sweet she smells.

"I wouldn't be telling you I want this if I wasn't serious, Damien." She grabs my chin, forcing me to look into her eyes. "I know I was hesitant about this at first, okay?"

"Uh huh," I reply, my lips squished together.

"But I'm dying to feel you inside of me. We're already this far over the line—might as well go all the way. We'd be reaping the benefits of our fake relationship, like you said."

I'd be lying if I said I didn't want that too, but the deeper I get pulled into her orbit, the more I feel like I won't be able to come back out. But do I even want that?

I do, but I also don't want her regretting what happens between us either. Charlotte definitely seems more invested in our fake relationship now, but she's still a flight risk. I know this woman—she's going to convince herself of something that will send her running for the hills, questioning everything, and making me chase after her again.

She releases my mouth as she waits for me to speak. But on instinct, I reach up and start to massage her shoulders as I think about how I want to respond.

I don't want her to think I'm denying her, that I don't want her because I really fucking do. I just don't know if tonight is the right time.

"Charlotte, I want you too, babe. I do, but…"

She closes her eyes and moans, throwing her head back as I work her shoulders. "God that feels good." And then she begins to rock herself over my length.

"Fuck, Charlotte. What are you doing?"

Her head falls forward again as she keeps moving and I keep rubbing my thumbs down the side of her neck. "I'm just doing what feels right."

"You're trying to make me come in my pants, aren't you?" I ask breathlessly, fighting the urge to flip her over and pound into her so fucking hard.

"Do you think that I can? Or is this yet another competition you want to win?"

"Oh, come on, Char. You know I love a challenge."

And the second after the words leave my lips, Charlotte freezes with my hands still on her shoulders, her eyes wide and her mouth agape. "Oh my God, it was you," she whispers before launching herself off my lap.

"What?"

"The massage!" she shouts, holding her hands up over her mouth now. "I can't believe I didn't put it all together before."

Fuck. Shit. Fuck. "Look, Charlotte. I can explain…"

"How? How do you explain how you ended up rubbing me down before we ever crossed paths with one another?" And then another lightbulb goes off, her eyes indicating so. "Jeffrey! You told me your name was Jeffrey."

"It was the first name that popped into my head!"

"Jesus." She spins away from me, over to her purse and starts shoving her clothes into her other bag that spilled out, but her shirt is still on the floor over by the couch. "I'm a moron."

"No, you're not," I say, walking over to her and grabbing her arm. "Please, Charlotte. Just let me explain."

She twists to face me, shrugging me off. "Is that why you wanted me to agree to this thing? Because you saw my naked body and wanted to know if you could see the rest? If I would be desperate enough to sleep with you? Was I just another challenge to you?"

"I didn't see your entire body, Charlotte," I correct her. "If you recall, you were face down the entire time."

With a narrow gaze at me, she goes silent before she reaches back and frees the clasp on her bra, slipping it down her arms and then throwing it to the floor. "There. Now you've seen it all."

Jesus. Her tits are magnificent, but I don't feel like this is the time to mention that. "Charlotte…"

"Oh, wait. That's not everything, right?" And then she shoves her yoga pants and underwear down to the floor, kicking them to the side as well. "There, Damien. Now you've seen it all. Happy now?"

"Fucking A, Charlotte. Will you calm down?" I'm going insane trying to get her to listen to me, but it's hard to tell my dick that now's not the time for him to pop up to play.

Charlotte's body is entirely bare, standing there before me with so much hate in her eyes. But there's lust there too, and I know I fucking feel it because it's taking everything in my body not to reach out and spank her ass for putting us in this situation.

"Don't tell me to calm down. I was practically throwing myself at you and you were coming up with reasons to push me away. So which is it?" she asks. "Do you want me or not?"

"Of course I fucking want you, but not like this. Not until you understand how this all happened!" I throw my hands in the air, pulling on my hair on the way back down.

"Fine. Explain it to me," she says, crossing her arms over her chest as she taps her foot, butt-ass naked in front of me.

I'm trying to convince my brain to keep thinking even though all of my blood is traveling south right now, making this task very difficult. But I'll be damned if she leaves after this.

"Fine. The day I saw you at The Chop Shop is when I realized you might be able to help me out with the lie I told. So, I went to your office the next day to speak to you—say hello, lay some groundwork before I asked you for a favor. But when I walked into your office, you were already under the sheet on the massage table. You thought I was there to give you a massage, and the last thing I wanted was for you to look up and see me and freak the fuck out, especially since it had been twelve years since we'd seen each other and you were basically naked at the time." She continues to glare at me, but doesn't say anything so I continue.

"And you said you were in a hurry, so what was I supposed to do? Walk away? Tell you who I was and make the situation worse?" Her face starts to soften. "So yeah, I gave you a fucking massage. And you know what, I'd do it again. And asking you to do this for me had nothing to do with what I saw under that sheet, Charlotte. In fact, after I left your office and realized how much I fucking enjoyed touching you, I *should* have left you alone. But I couldn't. Yes, your ass is magnificent, and I would love nothing more than to worship your entire fucking body for hours…" I take a step closer to her as her arms drop by her sides now. "But none of that has to do with how I truly feel about you, with how talking to you and having you back in my life has made me feel…" I pull her closer to me. "So I'm sorry. I should have said something, but I can't regret where it's gotten us. Not now." She stands there for a moment, her eyes bouncing back and forth between mine before she pushes me off her and starts to walk away. "Where are you going?"

"This was a mistake," she says as she moves across the room, picking up pieces of her clothing while trying to put them back on at the same time. "I can't believe I went along with this…"

"Charlotte, I know I fucked up, okay? But please don't leave."

She spins around to face me, her eyes wide with shock. "Why shouldn't I?"

"Because I don't want you to."

"Damien…this never should have happened. God, I'm an idiot thinking that this was…that we were…"

I stride over to her, gripping the back of her neck with one hand while cupping the side of her face with another. She's still naked, but I'm trying not to think about that right now. "Why not?"

"Because it's you! And me! We hate each other and this was just supposed to be platonic and momentary. It never should have gotten this far!"

"Lust can sometimes feel a lot like hate, Charlotte."

She scoffs, closing her eyes but then turns her face away from me.

I can't let her leave, not after the past few weeks, not after watching her submit to me and feeling her wrapped around my fingers and digging herself into my life. I have no idea what the fuck this means moving forward, but all I know is that at this moment, I don't want to let her go.

I can't let her go.

"You and I…this thing we're doing…it's not just a few orgasms to me."

"What?"

"I like you, Charlotte."

Her face looks like she's seen a ghost, white and full of disbelief. "You *like* me?"

"Fuck yeah, I do. I can't stop thinking about you, I can't stop wanting you." I reach up and tug on my hair. "I know it's fucking nuts, and I know I should have told you about the massage a long time ago, but the more we hung out, the more I just wanted you near, to spend time with you."

"I like you too, Damien," she says and an exhale of relief leaves my lips. "But this scares me. And you lied to me."

"It scares me too, Char. And I was going to tell you, I promise. But fuck, what if this is right? What if it was meant to be this way our entire lives?"

"I find that hard to believe," she counters.

"I do too. But I also find it hard to believe that we spent twelve years living in the same city and never crossed paths until now. There has to be a reason. We both needed to live our lives away from each other before maybe finding our way back to one another." I pull her into my arms. "Just give this a chance…please?"

"Damien," she breathes out before pressing her lips to mine and melting in my arms. And I hold her up, support her weight as I tangle my tongue with hers. "I'm still mad at you."

"I'm mad at me too, babe. But I'm begging you—let me in, Char. Just let me in, please."

"I already have." A tear runs down her cheek, and my heart feels like it can beat again. "I already have." Before I can say another word, Charlotte lunges at me, pressing her mouth to mine and sweeping her tongue out to meet my own.

"Charlotte…"

"Stop fucking talking, Damien. Shut up and fuck me, please, before I change my mind."

And with a sigh of relief, I make good work of following directions. "This isn't over."

"It is if you want to worship my body," she replies, fisting my hair in her hand behind my head.

Grabbing two handfuls of her ass, I lift her up and take her down the hallway of my apartment toward my room. When we arrive at my bed, I lay her down on my comforter and then stand up, staring down at her magnificent curves while I take off my clothes.

"You want me to fuck you, Charlotte?"

"That's what I said."

"You want hard and fast or slow and sweet, babe?"

"Fuck me until I can't walk, Damien," she says, reaching up to play with her nipples as she drops her legs open and shows me her pussy.

Tossing my shirt to the side and then popping the button on my jeans, I shove them down my legs with my boxer briefs as well and then reach down to stroke myself as she glances down at my cock.

"You want my cock, Char?"

She licks her lips. "Yes…"

"I wanna make sure you're ready for me first, babe. Get on your hands and knees." With a gleam of delight in her eyes, she maneuvers herself on my bed, granting me the perfect view of her ass as she perches it in the air. "Fuck, you look perfect like this."

"Please touch me, Damien," she says over her shoulder, lowering her head to the mattress. I get down on my knees so my face lines up with her pussy.

With one long stroke from her clit to her core, I relish in the moan she gives me. So I repeat the process, flicking her clit and eating her out until I can hardly stand it anymore. I slide my fingers inside of her, drenching my hand in her arousal. She's soaked, more than ready for me, but I have to make her come first before I fuck her.

Thrusting my fingers deep inside of her, I reach for her front wall and stroke her softly, building up her release.

"Oh God…"

"You close, Char?" I ask against her pussy, diving back in to suck on her clit.

"Uh huh."

I keep going, working my fingers in tandem with my tongue until she's writhing and then screaming out through her orgasm.

I hold her in place, my hands on her hips as she rides out the waves and I continue to flick her nub while her body shakes with aftershocks. And then she collapses on the bed, but I flip her over before she gets too comfortable. "There's one."

"You are so ridiculously good at that," she says on a shaky breath.

"I aim to please, babe," I say before standing up fully.

She smiles and then gets up on her knees, reaching for my neck to pull me down to her lips. And as we kiss, my dick grows achingly impatient.

"God, Charlotte. You're so fucking incredible. How could you think that I wouldn't want you?"

"You scare me, Damien. All of this scares me," she answers, leaning back slightly but peering up into my eyes.

I take her hand and place it over my rapidly beating heart. "You scare me too, Char. But *not* being here right now with you scares me even more."

She pulls me back to her lips and our tongues collide as I run my hands over her ribcage, down to her hips, and then around to her ass again. "Fuck, this ass," I growl out, and her giggle makes my dick twitch. "I want to claim it. I want it to be mine."

"It can be. I've never done that with anyone."

I look back down at her as a rock lodges itself in my throat. "Jesus. I don't think I can handle that tonight, but we are definitely going to revisit this conversation later." Pressing a chaste kiss to her lips, I release her from my grip and walk over to my nightstand, opening the drawer to take out a condom and then ripping the package open, covering myself as I go back over to her. "Lie down on your back."

She nods, getting in place before I kneel on the bed and hover over her. We're parallel to the headboard, and the moonlight outside is coming through the window and curtains, bathing Charlotte in shadows that accentuate everything I love about her body—her round and full breasts, her soft stomach and wide hips, and her smile. The same soft smile she's giving me in anticipation of what comes next.

I reach down and position myself at her entrance, looking back up for clarification from Charlotte that she's ready. And with a nod of her head, I push forward, stretching her open and sliding inside of her as far as I can before I rear back and push forward farther this time.

"Yes," she moans, arching her back while reaching up to cup my face in her hands.

"Fuck, Charlotte. You feel incredible."

"More, Damien." I slide in further, pushing down until I bottom out and inhale a sigh of relief. I can't believe I'm inside of her right now.

"Jesus, woman."

"Move, Damien. Please."

Pulling out, I thrust forward, memorizing the feeling of how tight her pussy is gripping me, how wet she is for me, and the noises she's making as I find a pace we like and start fucking her as I promised.

I lose track of time as I keep sliding in and out of her while she digs her nails into my back. And from how hard she's gripping me, I'm sure she's going to leave marks.

But I don't care. I want Charlotte to mark me, to claim me like I'm claiming her right now. I can't remember the last time I felt so over-come with need for someone—in fact, I don't know if I've ever felt this way at all.

I lean over her and find her lips, kissing her as I piston my hips, making sure to press forward as far as I can on each drive because she lets out a moan of pleasure every time I do. And then I feel her tight-ening around me, her breathing growing ragged, so I reach down between us and start to circle her clit.

"Oh, God, Damien…yes, right there…" And with a few more deep thrusts, she falls apart as I fuck her through her release, drawing out every last tremor.

"You're so fucking hot when you come and scream my name," I say in her ear, licking her neck and biting her gently as I continue to slide in and out, slowly and luxuriously, as her body twitches and she cries out like she can't take anymore. "Get on your knees again, Char." I help her up and watch her move around before she shakes her ass in my face and presses up against me. Without hesitation, I smack her white skin, watching it turn pink before my eyes.

"Oh shit," she moans, resting her forehead on the bed.

So I do it again on the other cheek. "You like that, babe?"

"God, yes. Damien…" she pleads as I drop another strike of my palm against her skin.

"Fuck, Charlotte." I line myself up to her entrance and drive forward once more, looking down to watch my dick disappear inside of her before repeating the process all over again. "I can't believe I'm buried inside of you right now." Concentrating on lasting as long as I can, I pump my hips and soak up the sounds of our bodies connecting as Charlotte lets out a breathy moan.

"Right there…" she cries, gripping the comforter beneath her as I squeeze her hips for more leverage. "Fuck me harder, Damien. Deeper."

Using all of the energy I can muster, I slam my hips into her ass, watching her body tighten and struggle against my brute force. But her cries of pleasure tell me she loves it.

Fuck. I love it too. Sex with Charlotte Montgomery is annihilating every fantasy I've ever had about this. The real thing is so much better.

I stick my thumb in my mouth, wetting my digit before pressing it up against her asshole, waiting for her reaction.

With a glance over her shoulder, she bites her bottom lip. "Do it."

Without any hesitation, I press my thumb inside of her as I continue to fuck her, and her sounds grow louder. Pumping my hips like my life depends on it, I make sure to give her the depth she wants, the pressure she needs, and when I feel her start to clamp around me, I know she's about to come undone—and so am I.

"Oh God, I'm gonna come, Damien!" Her cries follow in an instant as I fuck her through her release again, waiting until she's over the precipice before finally emptying my release into the condom.

As I feel the last drop leave my body, I fold myself over her back, kissing her gently between her shoulder blades and finding the base of her neck, moaning against her skin. Struggling for air and words, I slide out of her slowly then collapse to the mattress beside her. "Holy shit."

Charlotte's eyes remain closed, but her breathing is heavy. "I second that."

As we lie there for a minute and I replay every second back, I feel Charlotte move toward me, resting her head on my chest and draping an arm across my stomach. It takes a few more moments before she speaks. "I'm still mad at you," she whispers as I glance down at her and see her staring up at me.

"I'm mad at me too."

"But I meant what I said…"

"What?"

"I like you too, Damien. Just please…" she trails off as I twist on my side to face her.

"Please what, Char?" I reach up and brush her hair from her face so I can watch her eyes sparkle in the light coming through the window.

"Please don't lie to me again. And no more secrets."

"I promise."

Chapter 12

Charlotte

My eyes flicker open as the light coming through the window alerts me that it's morning. With a groan, I try to stretch my limbs but hit another body in the bed.

Damien.

As if I've lost all control over my lips, they lift in a smile as I roll onto my side and tuck my hands under my head to watch him sleep.

Last night was…*incredible*, but shocking to say the least. I knew in coming over here that I wanted to test the waters, see how far we could take our physical relationship. Every physical interaction we'd had up until then was priming my body for the much needed sex I wanted. But when I put all the clues together about my mystery massage, I panicked.

My reaction that day to the way he touched me would still filter in and out of my mind at times—the way my skin zinged, the way my muscles softened under his fingers, and the electricity I felt buzzing between my legs from his touch.

I thought I was crazy, that I was turned on by some stranger, facing mortification if Jeffrey ever returned.

Well, apparently *Jeffrey* was Damien all along.

I wonder if the real Jeffrey knows he was a ploy in Damien's scheme?

However, after he explained how it all happened, I understood his predicament. And as much as it pains for me to admit this, I'm glad it wasn't some stranger. Knowing that it was Damien only solidifies how he's made me feel all along.

Christ, this is getting way too complicated.

Lying here next to him feels like living an entirely different life, one where I didn't once hate the man in front of me. Despite us knowing each other and growing up together, I feel like the man lying next to me is an entirely different person than the boy I grew up with.

Lately, I've laughed with him more than I can remember with anyone else, except my friends. I love arguing with him and giving each other shit, our sarcastic banter from before only strengthening with our age. And my God, does the man know how to make me come, our physical connection unlike any other I've experienced with another man.

Just thinking about our sexcapades last night has me rubbing my thighs together. We went at it two more times before finally passing out, and each time only got hotter.

"Don't settle for a spark. Light a fire instead."

The message on my Dove chocolate wrapper from a few weeks ago travels to the forefront of my mind.

As women, we've been trained to look for "the spark", that connection that happens between two people when intellectual and physical chemistry collide.

But this thing between Damien and me is definitely more intense than a spark.

I can't help but wonder—and the potential answer is what scares me—if Damien and I are a raging inferno that will eventually be contained and put out?

Or can our fire turn into a more meaningful connection, too?

My eyes travel across his face, soaking up his manly features. The young boy I once knew has clearly transformed, and I have to say, he's manly in all the right ways—a scruff-lined jaw that forms a beard I never knew I was a fan of until now, short chest hair across his pecs, defined abs that contain a happy trail that leads down to trimmed pubic hair, and a cock that they should model dildos after. Seriously, the fact that Damien's cock is perfect only makes me think his cockiness wasn't a front. He obviously knew what he was packing all these years, even though he probably didn't know how to use it for a while.

Timidly, I reach out to trace the lines of his face, from his jawline to his lips, tugging on the bottom one just slightly. I run my nails through his chest hair, over his shoulders and muscular arms, and then over his abs—those gloriously tight and cut mountains of muscle that flexed every time he thrust into me last night.

It was magnificent, exceptional in every way sex is supposed to be—but the fact that it was Damien making me feel that way is still making me question what this is.

I like him. And he likes me too.

Our confessions remained like the elephant in the room all night as we took out almost a month of sexual frustration on each other, and let's be honest, probably some old hate wounds too.

And now that the sun has risen on the day after, I'm not sure where we go from here.

"Why are you awake?" he mumbles with his eyes still closed as I keep dragging my nails across his stomach.

"The sun woke me up."

One of his eyes pops open, and he smiles at me, his eyes crinkling at the corners when he does. "I can't believe you're in my bed." He reaches out and strokes the side of my face with one finger. "How'd you sleep?"

"Like a rock. You wore me out." Flashes of last night make my body warm up again, but I'm also deliciously sore and need to get to work.

"Same, Char. What time is it, by the way?" Groaning, I twist around to glance at the alarm clock on his nightstand but feel his fingers on my shoulder blade as I do, closing my eyes as I feel him trace my sunflower tattoo. "I love that you have this here." His lips hover over the flower as he pulls me closer to him by my hip. "Whenever I see sunflowers, I think of you."

"Really?"

"Yes. And when I saw this while I was massaging you, memories of you in high school flooded my mind. It was like being transported back in time."

"I know the feeling," I say, feeling my body heat up from his touch again. But then I pop open my eyes and sheer terror slams into my chest when I see the time on his alarm clock. "Shit! It's almost eight!"

Damien launches out of bed. "What?"

Both of us catapult from the mattress, searching out our clothes and panicking as we run around each other. "Jesus. I'm never going to make it to work on time."

"Me either. But I have to go in today. I'll just call Helen on the way in, tell her something came up, and I'll be an hour late or so." I speed walk down the hallway, picking up my discarded clothing along the way and trying to dress myself at the same time.

"Jeffrey can stall for me," he says behind me, buttoning his shirt. "Damn, this is not how I wanted to spend this morning."

"What?"

He walks over to me, his arms shaking from the adrenaline, but he reaches up to cup the sides of my face, freezing me in place. "I wanted to lie in bed with you. Worship this body some more." With a soft press of his lips against mine, he pulls away just as quickly. "Have dinner with me tonight."

"Okay," I whisper before he kisses me once more and butterflies take flight in my stomach. I feel like I'm drowning in a cloud of sex and the unexpected, but there's no breaking through the haze.

"I'll pick you up at six-thirty." I nod in agreement as we part and I finish gathering my things. When we're finally fully clothed, I meet him at the door. "See you tonight."

"Okay. Bye, Damien."

"Bye, sweet pea," he says with a lilt to his voice before kissing me with just a small slip of his tongue. And then he smacks my ass before opening the door for me.

With a small wave, I hustle down the corridor and hightail it to the elevator, texting Helen as I make my way to the street.

There are two things I am grateful for at this moment, good assistants and good sex—and not necessarily in that order.

"Your mom is on line two," Helen announces as she pops her head in through my door.

"Ugh. She called my office?"

"Yup. And why do you think that is?"

"Because I wouldn't pick up her calls on my cell phone." I glance at the screen again. "She's called three times in the last hour."

"Maybe it's an emergency?" she suggests.

"I doubt it. She would also text if it were." Sighing, I slide my chair across the carpet and move to pick up the phone on my desk. "If I'm not off this call in fifteen minutes, I need you to pop in here again with some excuse as to why I need to get off the phone."

She salutes me. "You got it, boss."

Picking up the receiver, I brace myself for what this phone call entails. "Hello, Mom."

"Charlotte! There you are. You are just the hardest person to get a hold of sometimes, I swear."

"Well, I'm working right now, Mom. I can't just answer the phone whenever you call, you know."

"I know, but this is important. I need to know what time you and Damien want your breakfast delivered in the morning during your stay in Hawaii."

I can feel my face drop. This is my mother's idea of something that she can't wait to talk to me about until after five o'clock. "Um, I don't know, Mom. Eight is fine."

"Are you sure? Wouldn't you rather eat right when you wake up? I hear it's better for your metabolism if you eat earlier in the day."

"That's fine," I say, shuffling some papers around while pretending to listen to her at the same time.

"I need a time, Charlotte."

"I honestly don't care, Mom. Seven is fine."

"Okay, okay. I'll put you in for seven." I can hear her scribble something down on a piece of paper, the scratch of the pen echoing through the line. "All right, and then I had another question for you."

"Yes?" I say as I try to read the contract in front of me.

"How would you feel about Damien walking you down the aisle during the ceremony?"

I drop my pen on my desk. "What? Why?"

"Well, because now that you two are a couple, I thought it would be sweet if you didn't have to walk by yourself. Besides, we've known

Damien for practically his entire life, so it would be meaningful to us if he did this as well."

My heart pounds violently at the thought of him doing this—out of anxiousness and a little excitement. "Well, I guess I could ask him." I wonder how he'll react to that? Is asking him to walk me down the aisle too much?

"I think it would be perfect, and it would answer the question of whether you're still single or not." And there it is—the real reason she wants him to do it.

"Oh, heaven forbid there should be any speculation about that," I admonish.

"Charlotte, you finally have someone, and that should be celebrated. Plus, it will give you practice for when you two get married."

I nearly choke on my saliva. "Uh, Damien and I are not getting married, Mom."

"Well, not now. But I imagine soon, right? I mean, no one is getting any younger, and it's not like you two don't know each other already. That little fact in itself would cut down on the length of time you needed to date."

Jesus Christ, this conversation just took a turn that I wasn't expecting. "Listen, Mom. Things are still new, and the last thing I need is for you to put any pressure on him, or me, okay?" Especially since this won't be lasting beyond Hawaii—because that was the plan, right?

Well, it was until I slept with him last night, and now my brain is wondering if my vagina is getting a little too attached to all of the orgasms he's given me. Plus, having a warm body next to me last night wasn't awful either.

"I'm not. I'm just saying…"

"Mom, I love you, but I really can't talk about this right now. I have a meeting in ten minutes and I need to make sure I'm prepared."

"Okay, okay. I'll book your breakfast delivery time, but please talk to Damien about walking with you." And then she squeals. "I am just so excited to see you next week, honey. This trip is going to be so much fun, especially now that I know you have someone to share it with."

Sighing, I stare out the window when I realize I feel the same way. It is kind of nice knowing I'll have someone else to share in my misery and perhaps enjoy the scenery and some relaxation with too.

You're getting too attached, Charlotte. Your vagina is drunk on Damien's dick. Remember, he's just scratching a physical itch you had. You're getting in too deep. But then again, you both confessed that you like each other last night, so what does that mean in regards to this situation now?

"We're looking forward to it. I'll talk to you soon, Mom."

"Love you, Charlotte. And make sure you increase your cardio for the next week," she says before hanging up.

Extra cardio, huh? I think I can figure out a way to make that happen.

After a long day at the office—where it was difficult to concentrate because I kept reliving every moment from last night—five o'clock finally comes around, and my entire body is buzzing with the thought of seeing Damien again.

I rush home, change my clothes, restyle my hair, and start a load of laundry before he's hitting the buzzer for my apartment. When I open the door to see him standing there in a plain black t-shirt, grey shorts, and a megawatt smile on his face, my heart does backflips.

"Hey."

"Hi," he replies before stepping through my door, closing it after him, and then spinning me around so my back lands up against it. Before I can get a word in, his lips are on mine and my body ignites once more for this man.

Our hands roam over one another, grasping for leverage as our mouths say the words we don't have to—*I missed you today*.

Breathlessly, we part, and I peer up into his light blue eyes. "Well, that was quite the hello."

"I've been thinking about that all day."

"Do you wanna just stay in tonight?" I ask as I cup his dick through his shorts, reveling in how hard he already is and how I can almost feel him inside of me again just standing here.

He groans and then weaves his fingers through the hand I was just touching him with. "Don't tempt me. Believe me, we will be fucking later, but tonight I want to take you somewhere, and I think you'll love it."

"Really?"

He reaches for my door, opening it and then leading me through as I grab my purse from the table by the door. "I know it." And with a cocky grin, he takes my hand in his as I follow him out of my building and to his car, eager to see how well Damien thinks he knows me— because I'm beginning to realize that I never really knew *him* at all.

We drive for about fifteen minutes until we pull up to a brick building that has a sign on the front that says, "The York".

"What is this place?"

Damien parks the car and turns to face me in his seat. "It's a craft brewery and restaurant, and tonight, they're hosting a trivia night in the private event space in the back."

"A trivia night?"

"Yup. And we're gonna win." Opening his door, he rounds the hood of his car and then opens my door for me.

Taking his hand, I let him help me up. "You seem awfully confi-dent about that."

Damien shuts my door, locks the car, and then leads me toward the front door of the building. "I am. You and I are two of the most competitive people I know, Char. We have to be unbeatable as a team."

I laugh at his thinking. "Just because we're competitive, doesn't mean we're going to know the answers to all of these questions, Damien. And I'm pretty sure they make you hand over your phones for things like this so you can't Google answers."

"Well, we're definitely not going to win with an attitude like that, sweet pea. Now, turn on your positive thinking, and let's go win some prizes."

When we enter the restaurant, my eyes drift over the space. Exposed brick walls covered in chalkboards displaying the beers on tap catch my eye first, and then I turn to my right and see a bar with glass shelves covered in bottles of liquor and televisions hanging above the mirror behind the alcohol. Dark leather booths and chairs line the walls, and matching stools perch under the expansive bar.

"This way," Damien says, leading me toward the back of the building where I see another chalkboard sign outside of an open doorway that says *Trivia Night* in hot pink writing.

I take a deep breath as Damien smiles back at me over his shoulder and squeezes my hand in his. Guess it's time to see if the person I've always competed against is a better teammate than an opponent.

"Who was the first bachelorette on the popular ABC franchise show?" The MC asks over the sound system in the room as Damien and I huddle together in our booth. And he instantly turns to face me, looking at me for the answer.

"What? You don't know the answer to that question?"

"Forgive me for not watching that ridiculous show where people fall in love after four dates and then get engaged only to call it off three months later," he replies sarcastically.

"Well, I mean, you're not wrong. But I feel like I'm carrying our team right now." I scribble down the name Trista Sutter on our paper and then drop the pencil on the table.

"Hey, I've answered all of the sports questions, haven't I?"

"Not all of them. I knew a few things."

Damien rolls his eyes. "Okay."

I shove him from the side just as the MC reads the next question. "On the show Friends, how many times has Ross been divorced?"

Damien turns to me. "Two."

"Nope, it's three."

"What? No, it's two—Emily and Rachel."

"What about Carol?" I counter, and his face falls.

"Fuck. You're right."

I cup my hand around my ear. "I'm sorry. What was that?"

"Nothing." He takes a sip of his beer, avoiding my eyes even though there's a smile on his lips.

"Oh, no. That was something. I believe you told me I was right."

Leaning over toward me now, he brushes his nose with mine, and my skin tingles from the contact. "Don't get used to it. But it's good to know that *my* partner is pulling *her* weight."

"I'll be pulling something else in a few minutes if you don't stop arguing with me."

He chuckles. "You can pull my dick or balls, babe. Doesn't matter to me. A gentle tug goes a long way."

The MC calls out another question as we stare at each other. "What is the name of Chip and Joanna Gaines's lifestyle brand?"

"Magnolia," Damien answers with his eyes still locked on mine.

"Oh, dear. How did you know that?"

"Lots of HGTV, babe." He takes a sip of his beer.

"You watch HGTV?"

He nods. "I feel like once you turn thirty or feel too old to go out every night anymore, you go from watching mindless reality television to home improvement shows. I can sit there and watch episodes of Fixer Upper for hours and have no idea what time it is when I finally decide to look at the clock." I laugh in agreement. "And I will never understand how some of these people have the budgets they do. He's a lion tamer, she writes raunchy romance novels in her spare time, but their budget is like 1.2 million dollars."

I snort. "You're not wrong. But also, you're right. It is Magnolia." I scribble down the answer on our form.

"Looks like I'm not the only one that can be right tonight."

Shaking my head at him, I question why he looks so sexy in the low light above us as the MC fires off the last question. "Last question! What can be broken, but is never held?"

"Oh, is this one of those trick questions, huh?" I ask as I think for a moment, tapping my chin with my finger.

"A promise," Damien answers simply as I turn to him.

"Are you sure?"

He nods. "Yup. My mother used to say that to me all the time to remind me that you can hurt people emotionally more than you ever can physically."

His comment has my face scrunching up in thought. "What do you mean?"

Damien opens his mouth to reply, but then one of the servers comes around to gather our answer sheets. I hand her the paper as Damien drains the last of his beer. "Let's just say, I know a thing or two about people breaking promises."

"How so?"

He stares at me before replying, "Well, for instance, I broke one that I made to you."

My heart rate starts to pick up. "What? When?"

"Alright, we have a winner, ladies and gentlemen!" The MC announces, cutting Damien off just as he reaches below the table and squeezes my thigh, resting his palm there. "In third place are Becca and Robby." A round of applause rings out. "In second place are Liz and Shawn." Another round of applause. "And in first, the winners of the fifty-dollar gift card to The York and bragging rights are…" He pauses for effect. "Damien and Charlotte!"

"Fuck yeah!" Damien pumps his fist in the air and then turns to me and kisses me hard, kickstarting my heart. "See? We do make a good team, Char."

I smile at him, running my nails through his soft beard. "Yeah. I guess we do."

"There's one more place I wanted to take you tonight," he says once we get in the car after the trivia game. The smile on his face when we won almost made every fight we've had leading up to this night worth it. But it's also making me more anxious about when this ends.

"Okay."

A few minutes later, we arrive in a parking lot surrounded by darkness. But then when I look out of my window, I see it. "Oh my gosh."

"Come on." I wait for Damien to get me from my side of the car, and then with my hand in his, he leads me over to the Griffith Park Merry-Go-Round. "It's not as extravagant as the one back home, but this one has more history than that one does."

My eyes travel over the ride, taking in the painted horses, intricate carving details in the top, and the bright bulb lights shining out into the darkness.

"Damien, this is…" Emotion clogs my throat as we make our way to the ticket booth to purchase tickets. Damien pays and I don't argue otherwise, mostly because I'm still in shock. My stomach is a mess with nerves and sentiment as we get in line and wait our turn. "I can't believe you brought me here."

Cupping the side of my face, he stares down at me. "The last time we were at a carousel, I was certain I'd never see you again. And I thought that's what I wanted. You made me promise that I would forget you existed and for the most part, Charlotte, I did. I moved out here, put you out of my mind, and focused on my goals, on making something of myself. But the second I saw you again, it made me face the truth."

"Which is?"

"That I broke that promise. I did think about you. I wondered what you were doing, if you accomplished your dreams, and if you ever thought about me too. And then when I saw you again, this rush of memories mixed with feelings I couldn't name flooded my mind and body. It's crazy that all these years later we found each other again, but in an entirely different way. I know that this is supposed to be fake, but…"

"I get it," I reply, cutting him off. "I feel that way too."

Oh God, I'm falling for him. This wasn't supposed to happen, but I think he's falling for me too.

With a press of his lips to mine, Damien doesn't speak another word and then removes something from the back of his jeans. "I got this for you." He holds out a notebook to me with sunflowers all over the white surface. But before I can say anything, the employee working the ride ushers us forward so we can get on.

We find a sleigh bench to sit in and as we wait for the ride to begin, I stare at the notebook in my lap, running my fingers over the top.

"Do you like it?"

The corner of my mouth lifts up. "Yes, I do. Thank you for this."

"It reminded me of the one you were writing in that night."

"It is very similar."

"I have no idea what you wrote in those damn notebooks, but I just remember you always having one."

I huff out a laugh and then decide to bare a little of the truth. "Well, most of the entries had to do with you, actually."

"Really?" He smiles, pleased with learning this information. I feel him wrapping his arm around my shoulders, drawing me closer. So I lean my head on his shoulder as I feel the merry-go-round jerk and then start to slowly spin.

"Don't get all excited, Damien. They weren't words of me professing my love for you. On the contrary, they were more like wishes that you would step on a Lego or drop your phone in the toilet, types of thoughts. You gotta remember, I wasn't exactly your biggest fan."

"Sounds reasonable," he replies through a laugh. "Can I read them sometime?"

"Ha. No."

"Why not?"

"Because those thoughts were private," I say as the ride begins to spin a little faster and the world around us becomes one big blur. "And I don't want to live in the past anymore."

"So what are you going to write in this one?" He points to the notebook in my lap as the lights above us bounce off the surface.

Sliding my fingers across it again, I ponder that thought. "I don't know. I'm still trying to process this gesture."

He grabs my chin gently with two fingers, turning my face toward him. "I'm sorry."

"For?"

His brow furrows and his lips purse. "For every mean thing I ever said, for every petty competition and instance where I tried to make you feel bad to make myself feel better, for not actually getting to know you back then instead of thinking I knew who you were."

"Wow. Did I just get an apology from Damien Shaw?" I tease him as he smiles down at me, glancing at my lips and then looking back up to my eyes.

"You did. And you should know I don't hand those out easily."

"Well, thank you." I lean forward and press my lips to his softly, leading to a gentle kiss appropriate in front of the small children around us.

And it's not intense or desperate—no, it's laced with something else, something I don't think I want to admit just yet.

My fake boyfriend isn't acting so fake anymore, and these feelings running through me aren't fake either.

Suddenly, my mother's conversation comes back to me, her suggestion that Damien and I would be engaged soon, which I know is preposterous because this arrangement we agreed to has a deadline. But now, so many lines are blurred, so many feelings are prevalent, and the idea that this could be more isn't so far-fetched anymore.

"This ride is making me dizzy," I say when we part, even though I don't think it's the ride. I think it's just Damien and everything he's making me feel.

But then he leans his forehead on mine and says, "Yeah, I think this ride we're on is making me dizzy too."

"Good morning," I say cheerily as I take my seat at our table at Frankie's, where my three best friends are waiting for me. I'm a little late, but that's because Damien wouldn't let me out of bed this morning without giving me another orgasm, even though he gave me three the night before.

"You sound well rested," Noelle says.

"No, she sounds well *fucked*," Penelope interjects as I turn to face her.

"What?"

She eyes me up and down. "Oh, girl, it's written all over your body. You're relaxed, your skin is glowing, and there was an extra little pep in your step as you walked into this place. I take it Damien has been keeping you with your ass and legs in the air for the past few days, huh?"

I slump back in my chair as I stare at her. "How the hell do you do that?"

She just shrugs. "It's a gift. Plus, we haven't heard from you since Wednesday, and I know you were supposed to see him Thursday, so I'm guessing you've been busy fucking all weekend." Then she leans closer with a gleam in her eyes. "Tell me I'm wrong."

I reach for my mimosa that someone already poured for me, taking a sip and then admitting what I already knew I was going to tell them today anyway. "Damien and I had sex."

Penelope laughs before sitting back in her chair. "Took you long enough."

"Charlotte!" Noelle exclaims, but not in a chastising way, more like she's in excited shock.

"What? It's just sex. Orgasms and food—that's what we agreed to," I claim as I take another sip of my drink, trying to convince myself that that's all this is too—which I now know, after our date Friday night, is a bald-faced lie.

"Well, by the look on your face, I assume Damien is a worthwhile sexual partner?" Amelia asks before taking a sip of her coffee.

Licking my lips, I debate how much I should reveal. But then I remember these girls are my best friends and deserve to know that there are men out there who do know what the hell they're doing in bed—and I just happened to find one of them. "He's incredible."

Penelope snickers. "All of that hate had to translate to insane sexual chemistry."

"Ah!" Noelle squeals before clinking her glass in mine. "I'm so freaking happy for you!"

"Really?"

She nods. "Yes, because the last guy that I was with kept playing with my belly button, trying to get me to come. I swear, he thought it was my clit."

I nearly choke on my drink. "Are you serious?"

"I wish I wasn't, but yes, I am. However, it sounds like Damien won't be disappointing you for the time being, so I'm telling myself to be happy for you in the hopes that one day I'll find a man who will fuck me, feed me, and tell me I'm pretty too."

I sigh. "He does all of those things, which should make me feel more at ease than I do right now."

"Uh oh," Penelope chimes in from beside me. "Sounds like someone is catching feelings."

"Ugh." I shake my head, closing my eyes as I rub my forehead. "This wasn't supposed to happen. I mean, I hated this guy, you guys. There was a black hole in my soul reserved for devious thoughts regarding him and him only."

"You used the past tense of hate," Amelia points out. "So it sounds like you don't hate him so much anymore?"

"He took me to a carousel Friday night," I state, even though they don't know the significance of his gesture. But it's all I've been able to think about.

"What?" Noelle asks. "A carousel?"

"Yeah. There was one back home that I used to go to at night all the time to get out of my house and away from my mother's incessant nagging. It was my favorite place to be. The old security guard would let me in at night as long as I brought him a Snickers bar." The girls chuckle. "I would sit on the bench and write in my journal, and one night, Damien saw me there."

"When was this?" Amelia asks.

"One month before we graduated. And naturally, he said something to piss me off, we exchanged some words, and then I told him to promise never to think of me again."

"So why did he bring you to this one the other night?" Noelle questions.

"I don't know. He apologized for how he treated me back then and told me that he broke that promise—that he did wonder about me. Honestly, you guys, the entire night left me in a daydream of what a life would be like with him, the man he is now. I…"

"You're falling for him," Noelle finishes.

Swallowing down the lump in my throat, I nod my head. "I am. And it's terrifying."

Amelia speaks up next. "Charlotte, I hate to break this to you, but you have intimacy issues, honey."

"What?"

She reaches across the table and places her hand on mine. "Part of the reason you've never had a relationship last very long is because you don't let men in all the way. You don't allow yourself to be vulnerable. And I think it has a lot to do with your relationship with your mom. Hell, it took a while for you to do that with us." I stare at her perplexed as she continues. "But now, Damien is breaking through the walls you've erected that tell you your vulnerability isn't worth it. And for once, I'm urging you to listen to what your gut is telling you."

"My gut?"

"Yes, your womanly intuition, that voice in your head that is telling you what your heart can't put into words."

"I like him," I say. "That's what it's saying. He makes me feel comfortable in my own skin, secure in who I am. It's like…"

"He doesn't make you question who you are or if you're enough," Noelle finishes for me.

"Yes," I whisper, feeling the sting of tears in my eyes.

"Then enjoy the ride, Charlotte. Believe that this is real, and just see where your heart takes you," Amelia finishes with a smile.

"And in the meantime, enjoy some stellar sex," Penelope adds as I roll my eyes but feel my cheeks blush as well.

"I'm telling you, I don't think I've ever come this hard in my life, you guys."

"Hear, hear!" Penelope exclaims as we all laugh and clink our glasses together. "I just hope I don't end up sharing a wall with you in Hawaii. Otherwise I might have to find a handsome stranger to fuck to drown the two of you out. No way am I going on vacation just to listen to someone else have sex. That sounds like pure torture to me."

"I'm making no promises of how quiet I can be." Smiling around the rim of my glass, I take a sip and then place my order with Frankie once he comes around to check on us. "But I don't think I've ever been on a vacation with someone to have sex with, so I'm going to take full advantage."

Chapter 13

Damien

"Oh, God yes. Right there." Charlotte's hands are in her hair as she lifts her hips up and down while she rides my cock. I watch her breasts bounce, her mouth part, and listen to her breathy moans as I feel her grow tighter around me.

Thrusting up from underneath her, I piston my hips to go as deep as I can while I enjoy the show—and fuck, what a show it is.

Her hands have gathered her long brown hair, holding it in place on her head, her eyes are closed, but her body is undulating in a rhythm that has me holding off my orgasm until she gets hers.

"I'm gonna come," she announces, moving faster as she clamps down on my dick and explodes, her screams echoing into my room.

I reach up and pinch her nipples while she rides out her release, earning me a shriek that has her coming harder and longer than I think we both anticipated. And even though I probably could have come alongside her, I'm not ready to stop fucking her.

It's all I can really think about anymore.

Once she comes down from her high, I flip us over so she's now beneath me as I continue to slide in and out of her wet heat. She's fucking drenched but feels so good wrapped around my cock that I wonder how I thought any sex was good until I had sex with Charlotte.

Her eyes are still closed as she struggles to breathe and moans every time I slide out and back in.

"Look at me, Charlotte," I command while hovering over her. She turns her face slightly, and then her eyes pop open, holding me captive as I stare down at her. I reach up and toy with her bottom lip, pulling it down before sliding my thumb into her mouth. "You are so fucking sexy, babe."

"Hmmmm," she moans around my thumb.

"You have no idea what you're doing to me, how hard you're making my dick right now."

"Uh huh," she mumbles.

"I wanna feel you come around my cock again." She nods, sucking on my thumb even harder. "I want you to look at me as we come apart." I pull my thumb from her mouth and then stroke the side of her face, slowing down my speed as something shifts in my chest. "Are you with me?"

"Yes…"

Running my hand down her side and then under her ass, I lift her up slightly, changing the angle as I keep hitting her with smooth strokes. And then I find her clit, the entire juncture between her thighs covered in her arousal as I rub her gently, coaxing another orgasm from her.

"Damien…"

"God, I love it when you say my name," I whisper in her ear as I feel her breathing grow ragged again. And then I find her eyes with my own as I build us up and over the edge. "Fuck," I groan as I feel that tingle form at the base of my spine and rest my forehead on hers. "Are you close?"

"Yes, keep going."

So I do. I keep up the pace, holding her stare until she gasps and then comes apart, giving me permission to do the same. My entire body shudders as I come and feel her grip my dick with her pussy, and my back with her hands. My orgasm is one of the most powerful I've ever had and keeps me frozen in place until I feel Charlotte relax underneath me.

Groaning, I roll off her but pull her into my arms. "Fuck, Charlotte."

"Hmmm," she hums as she hooks her leg over mine.

"I can't feel my legs," I mumble and then feel her chuckle against my chest.

"Same."

"You are so incredible," I say against her forehead before pressing a soft kiss there.

"You're not so bad yourself," she replies, pushing up on her elbow to meet my eyes. "I need to use the bathroom."

I watch her rise from the bed and saunter into my bathroom, fully naked, enjoying the view of her ass as she walks away from me. While she's in there, I toss the condom in the trash and then pull on a pair of boxer briefs before lying back down in bed.

Once she's done, she returns and finds her underwear, pulling them up her legs, and then grabs one of my t-shirts and pulls that over her head as well.

"Come back to bed."

"You're sure you don't mind having me here?" she asks nervously, fiddling with the hem of my shirt as she stands next to the bed. Watching her entire demeanor shift after we just had intense sex has me wanting to hold her and assure her of how I feel.

"I *want* you here, Char."

With a smile, she joins me under the covers before I pull her back into my chest, her back to my front.

We lie there in comfortable silence until I barely hear her say, "Goodnight, Damien."

And I reply with, "Goodnight, sweet pea."

"S hit." I hear Charlotte's voice that breaks me out of a dead sleep. "Charlotte?" Rubbing the fuzziness from my eyes, I search the room for her but she's nowhere to be found. The light in the bathroom catches my eyes, but then they're drawn to the sight on the sheets next to me and that's when I see it—blood, and quite a bit of it.

"Fuck." I launch out of bed, staring down at the crimson puddle on my white sheets as my heart begins to race. And then it hits me. "Charlotte?" I shout, rushing toward the bathroom. "Are you okay?"

"Yes. I'm okay. Oh my God, Damien…I'm so sorry about your sheets!"

"You're bleeding? What happened? Do I need to take you to the hospital?"

"What? No. I just—" she pauses as I hear the toilet flush and then she emerges from the bathroom, her face flushed with embarrassment and tears in her eyes. "I started my period." Covering her face, she rushes past me, pulling my shirt down her legs and out to my living room, reaching for her purse.

"Charlotte…"

"God, this is so embarrassing. And I knew it was coming." She shakes her head as her wild hair moves with her. "I should have been prepared, worn a pad to bed or something." She rummages through her purse and pulls out a tampon—something I'm familiar with now after

Jeffrey bought the whole damn aisle from the store—and runs past me again back to the bathroom, locking herself inside.

"Charlotte!" I call after her but remain frozen in the same spot, in nothing but my boxer briefs. Running a hand through my hair, I debate what the hell I'm supposed to do right now. I mean, I rarely let a woman stay the night to begin with, but I've never encountered this situation before, that's for sure.

I look down at my underwear and notice a small spot of blood on the side. I figure while Charlotte is handling her business, I might as well start cleaning up.

I return to my room and strip my bed of the sheets and change my underwear while I hear Charlotte call out to me from inside the bathroom. "Damien? Do you mind if I take a shower?"

"Of course not. Go ahead." I stare down at the sheets in my hands before deciding to ask Charlotte what I should do. "Hey, Char?"

"Yeah?" she says through the door before the water turns on.

"Are you okay? Can I get you anything?"

She's silent for a beat before finally saying, "No. I'm good. I'm just sorry I ruined your sheets."

"They're just sheets, Char."

She doesn't say anything in return, and then I hear the shower door open and close, so I take the sheets to my laundry basket, getting ready to place them inside before finally just deciding to throw them away. Blood and white fabric don't exactly mix.

Feeling restless and anxious, I wait for Charlotte to finish in the shower, sitting on the edge of my bed while I try to decide what to do for her. I know she's embarrassed, and I'm not going to lie, this entire situation is making me uneasy too. But the bottom line is, I just want to make sure she's okay and she knows I'm not mad.

When she finally emerges from the bathroom wrapped in a towel with her wet hair down around her face, she takes my breath away—

not just because she's so fucking beautiful, but because she looks so vulnerable right now.

"Can you grab my bag for me, please? I'm just going to put on my clothes from last night."

"Okay." I do as she asks, returning to my room in record time.

"Thank you." She shuts herself back in the bathroom to dress, and then when she comes out, she walks right past me without saying another word.

I follow her back out into the living room, reaching for her hand to stop her from leaving without talking to me. "Where are you going?"

"Home."

"Why?"

She spins toward me. "Because I need to lie in my own bed, Damien. The first day of my cycle is rough and I've already ruined your sheets. I don't want to ruin anything else."

Gripping her chin, I stare down into her eyes. "They're just sheets, Charlotte. It's not that big of a deal, okay? You didn't ruin anything."

"Well, I'm still sorry. I'll buy you new ones."

"Don't you dare." She looks away from me. "Are you sure I can't get you anything?"

She shakes her head. "No, I just want to be alone. I already have cramps, and if I don't get home soon to take some painkillers and put my heating pad on, I'm going to be miserable for the rest of the day. Luckily it's Saturday so I can relax." She places a small kiss on my lips. "Thank you for last night, but I'm sorry I ruined this morning."

"You didn't. Please don't freak out about this. It's…it's not that big of a deal. It's natural."

She huffs out a laugh. "Yeah, I guess." And then she reaches for the door and shuts it behind her, never glancing back once.

Standing there in confusion, an overwhelming need to care for her comes over me. I know she's used to handling everything on her own, and honestly, I don't know how much I can help with this aspect of her life.

But I sure as fuck want to try.

"Okay. What did she have in her hand this morning?" I mutter to myself while scouring the aisle of feminine products, feeling instantly overwhelmed. This is how Jeffrey must have felt when he bought all this shit, and now I feel bad for giving him a hard time.

How does a woman make a decision? And what's with all of the different sizes and brands. Isn't a tampon just a tampon? And a vagina a vagina? Are there super vaginas and light vaginas? Is that a thing? I'm so fucking confused.

The woman working at Target must have taken sympathy on me because she walks over from the shelf she was restocking and places her hand on my shoulder. "You look lost."

I huff out a laugh. "Yeah, a little bit."

"Who are you shopping for?"

"My girlfriend," I say without hesitation because the more I use that word, the more I like the way it sounds.

"Aw. Okay, well does she use tampons or pads?"

"Both, I think?" I vaguely remember Charlotte saying something about a pad this morning before she ran out of my apartment.

"She didn't tell you what to buy?"

"She doesn't know I'm here. I was trying to surprise her."

Her smile builds. "Alright. And how old is she?"

"Thirty."

"Is this the first day of her period, or is she toward the end?"

"She started this morning. I'm trying to surprise her and bring her the things she needs since this is all new territory for me, but staring at these shelves? Well, it's just a reminder that I'm way outside of my comfort zone here."

She nods through her laugh. "Any man is when it comes to this. Bless your heart for trying to help. That means more than anything you bring her." She reaches for a box of tampons and a package of pads. "I recommend these, but honestly, it doesn't matter what you bring her supply-wise. I would think of the things that make her happy and comfortable because that will mean more to her than these." She places the items in the basket I'm carrying in my hands.

"What do you need when it's your time of the month, if you don't mind me asking?"

"Well, it's been years since I've had to deal with this issue, but a woman never forgets what it's like. I always liked chocolate, potato chips, and watching a good romantic comedy, while I had my heating pad on my stomach."

I stare at her, shocked. "Forgive me, but you look far too young to have gone through menopause."

"You're right. I didn't. I had a partial hysterectomy when I was thirty-seven because I had endometriosis. It would get so bad that my periods sometimes put me in the hospital."

"Wow," I say as my heart pounds violently. "Seriously?"

She nods. "Yup. There are a lot of women who live with it but never get any relief. Mine was bad, so my doctor took my uterus." And then she starts laughing nervously. "Oh dear, I'm sorry. I'm giving you a lot of information about me right now that you probably could have lived without knowing." She turns away from me, pink tinting her cheeks.

"No, I asked. And I don't mind. I actually find it fascinating." I can't believe women have to deal with this stuff, even to the point of needing surgery. "It's just a period. Men need to get over it, huh?"

"Your girlfriend is lucky to have you," she says through a laugh, squeezing my bicep while smiling up at me.

"Well, that's still to be determined," I mutter. "So, tell me again what you think I should buy for her besides the necessities, of course. I need to make her feel better and I'm not sure how."

Her smile stretches wide. "I've got you, boy. Follow me."

"Damien?" Charlotte says through the speaker outside of her building.

"Hey, Char. Let me up."

"What are you doing here?"

"I brought you a few things, and I just want to check on you..." Silence fills the line, and for a moment I wonder if she'll turn me away. I know she was upset when she left my apartment earlier, but I don't want to leave things like this—not after the week we had together.

Since our date last Friday, we've spent every other night together having dinner and sex, but last night I insisted she stay the night at my place. If I hadn't, she wouldn't have been so embarrassed when her period came in the middle of the night—which I didn't even know could happen. Apparently, I have a lot to learn when it comes to what women manage in that aspect of their lives, and I hope Charlotte can give me some more insight. That was one of the goals of this agreement in the first place.

The buzzer signals that she's letting me in, so with my hands full of bags, I reach for the door and then head for the elevator up to her place.

I softly knock on the door and wait for her to answer, and when she does, my heart slows at the sight. Her hair is up in a messy ponytail, she's wearing baggy black sweats that look incredibly comfortable, and a dark gray spaghetti strap tank top. But her face is sullen, laced with pain and exhaustion that I've never seen on her before.

"Hey, babe."

"Damien," she says as she squints in my direction while crossing her arms over her chest. "What are you doing here?"

"I brought supplies," I say proudly while holding up the bags in my hands.

"Supplies?"

"Yup. Period supplies." Walking through her door, I head straight to her kitchen and place the bags on the counter.

"Damien, I have stuff. You didn't need to do this," she says as she follows me.

I look back at her over my shoulder. "I know I didn't need to, but I wanted to…okay?"

Her face instantly softens and then I see moisture building in her eyes. "I can't believe you did this after this morning."

Abandoning my bags that I was ridiculously excited to open for her, I close the distance between us and pull her into my chest. A sigh of relief escapes my lips when she wraps her arms around my waist. "I told you, it's not a big deal."

"I appreciate you saying that, but still, I was mortified. I was sure you would want some space from me."

"What?" I tip her chin up so I can stare down into her eyes. "Why on earth would you think that? You got your period, Charlotte. There's nothing about that that would make me want to stop seeing you."

She laughs through a few tears. "I know it sounds silly, but I mean, I'm a thirty-year-old woman. It's been years since I started in the middle of the night. That happened more when I was younger, but then it happened with you, and…"

"Honestly, my mind didn't even drift toward your period. The moment I saw the blood, I thought there was something seriously wrong, not to minimize your period, that is." I raise my hand in the air in a fist. "Girl power and all that."

Shaking her head at me, she presses up on her tiptoes and then plants a kiss on my lips. "Thank you for making me laugh. So what did you bring me?"

The rush of pride I felt when I got here returns as I take her by the hand back over to the bags. "Well, let me paint you a picture. I was standing in the aisle at Target where all of the tampons are, debating on what to purchase," I explain as I wave my hand across the air. "And thankfully, one of the employees took pity on me and came over to help me. But it was something she said to me that struck a chord."

"And what did she say?"

"She said that managing your period doesn't have to do so much with the products you use. It's all of the other things you need to help make it bearable." I reach into the bags and start pulling out items. "For instance, your favorite meal or something you've been craving," I say as I pull out a fresh plate of spaghetti and meatballs and the antipasto salad from Tony's that I know she loves. "And of course, you need chocolate," I continue as I pull out a package of Dove Chocolates and a tub of Ben & Jerry's Double Fudge Brownie. "Then she also suggested salt, so I grabbed these." I place the bag of Lay's Classic potato chips on the counter. "And ibuprofen and heat patches to help with cramps." Holding up the bottle proudly and the box of patches, I watch Charlotte's face for any reaction.

"You got me all of this?"

"Well, yeah," I say matter-of-factly. "And for entertainment, this." I pull out a DVD that has four different rom-coms on it from the early 2000s that all feature Matthew McConaughey.

"A Matthew McConaughey smorgasbord?"

"Hell yeah. I love that guy, so how bad can these movies be?"

Charlotte fights to contain her smile. "This is by far, one of the sweetest things anyone has ever done for me, Damien."

I pull her into my arms again, resting my forehead on hers and breathing her in. She smells like my soap from when she showered at my place earlier, and her body is warm to the touch. "I care about you, Charlotte, and I couldn't stand the way you left. Obviously, sex is off the table tonight, but that's not the only reason I want to hang out with you. I just want to be…*with you*."

She peers up at me before sighing. "I want to be with you too."

After we grab our plates of food and pop the DVD in—settling on *How to Lose a Guy in Ten Days* first—Charlotte and I eat side by side in comfortable silence. We pause the movie once we finish with dinner, and we're ready to move on to dessert. She decides to share the ice cream with me, and then as the movie continues playing I revel in unwrapping Dove chocolates and feeding them to her as she rests her head on my lap.

"Thank you for this again," she says, staring up at me, chewing her chocolate.

"You're welcome. Thanks for letting me crash your night." She rearranges the heating pad on her stomach as she lies there.

"Does the heat really help?"

"Yeah. Between that and the ibuprofen, it makes the first day or two bearable. Luckily I started over the weekend this month, so I can lounge like this."

"So what happens if it's not the weekend when it comes?" I ask, genuinely interested. Before Charlotte and this Remedy account, the last thing I wanted to talk about was periods. But this is part of her life, and as real as it gets when it comes to understanding what women go through, so my mind is reeling as I take in as much information as possible.

"Well, if it's a weekday, I pop some ibuprofen, stick one of those heat patches on my stomach, and keep doing my job."

"You don't take time off?"

She laughs. "No. It's not like they give us period days as part of our sick leave, which I fully believe should be a thing, by the way."

"Wow."

"Yup. And if I leak through something like my clothes at work, I'm kind of shit out of luck. This morning I was lucky I had clothes to change into, but that's not always the case."

"Does that happen a lot? You…leaking?"

She shrugs. "It depends. The first few days my flow is heavy, so it might happen. And it's a pain in the butt to deal with when the world just continues to spin around you."

"I can't imagine," I say as I stroke her face, pushing her hair back so I can see all of her deep brown eyes.

"At least I won't be on my period in Hawaii. That's a plus."

"God, I couldn't imagine having to deal with that while on vacation."

"Yeah, it sucks, but it's part of being a woman. And we're just expected to smile and act normal every month when it happens while our insides are literally ripping themselves to shreds. Men like to make comments that if a woman is in a bad mood, it must be that time of the month. Meanwhile, we're on the verge of crying or screaming or simultaneously doing both some days because our bodies are pumping copious amounts of hormones through our veins, and we're powerless to stop it."

"I see that now. You don't really have much control over it, do you?"

"Nope. Not when it starts, not when it ends, nor how painful it can be."

"The woman who helped me at Target said she had a hysterectomy because hers were so bad."

"Yup. I've heard of that."

"I guess this morning just gave me a different glimpse of what it's like being a woman," I say softly, staring down at her.

"Yeah?"

"Uh-huh. And now lying with you here—I know there's nothing physically I can do to help you, but part of me feels like you're more fragile right now, and all that makes me want to do is hold you."

Her bottom lips trembles. "That would be nice."

We rearrange ourselves on the couch so I'm spooning her from behind while the movie continues to play, nearing the end.

"Is this okay?" I whisper in her ear, placing my hand on her tender stomach and nuzzling my nose against the back of her neck.

She pushes her ass back into me, and even though I know there's nothing more that will happen, it still makes me hard. "Yes."

"Good."

"Damien…"

"Yeah, babe?"

"I need to ask you something."

"Okay."

"My mother wanted me to ask you if you would walk me down the aisle during their ceremony. You don't have to, but…"

"I'd love to," I say, cutting her off and holding her tighter.

"Really?"

"Hell yeah. Although, if I do, I won't be able to stare at your ass as you walk down the aisle, so maybe that's not the best idea now that I think about it…"

She elbows me in the ribs. "Pervert."

"When it comes to your body, I'll wear that badge loud and proud."

She grows silent again as we continue to lie there. "Damien?"

"Yeah, Char?"

"You're the best fake boyfriend I've ever had."

Her words make me smile. "I told you I was going to be."

"I have an idea," I say to Jeffrey Monday morning after he hands me my cup of tea, my adrenaline and mind racing after my weekend with Charlotte.

"You do?"

"Yup. I think it's what we need for this pitch, but we need to get as much done as possible before I leave this week."

"Fuck. You're going to Hawaii already? How did that happen?"

"Yeah, we leave Wednesday morning."

Surprisingly, I'm more nervous about this pitch now than that trip because, after this weekend, things with Charlotte and me feel like they're on solid ground. I've never felt this way about a woman before, never felt the desire to know about her day or think of ways I could make it better. And the crazy thing is, she was always in my life. I guess I just never let myself see her that way because I was too busy finding ways to beat her and make my father proud.

But now our relationship as adults is so far removed from how it was when we were kids, I feel like that was an entirely different life. The woman I've reconnected with in the last month is someone that I crave, someone who makes me feel needed, someone who I'm proud to be with, even if it is under unorthodox circumstances.

"So are you wanting to scrap everything we've come up with so far?" Jeffrey asks, reaching for the file we've been using to keep ideas while turning on his laptop.

"Not exactly, but I think we need to attack it from a different angle. I want to get as much work done before I leave so I'm not stressing about it when I return. The pitch is next week, and we're going to win this account, Jeffrey," I say, clenching my fist in the air. "I can feel it."

"I like your confidence, I do, my friend. But we're definitely pushing our deadline."

"I know. And I know that's partially my fault. I've been preoccupied with Charlotte."

"How are things going by the way?" he asks as he takes a seat in the chair opposite my desk, his laptop resting in his lap.

My lips instantly lift into a smile. "Fuck, dude. She's…" I trail off, shaking my head and reminiscing about holding her Saturday night on her couch. I never thought something as simple as cuddling would make me feel manly. But it did. Holding her, keeping her warm, feeling as if I was easing her pain, this rush of need ran through me, and it made me realize that I don't want this to be fake anymore. I want this to be real.

"Man, I can see it all over your face."

"Yeah. It's crazy, but I want her…for real."

"Have you told her that?"

"Not yet. I planned on doing it in Hawaii. I figured the setting was more romantic. We'll be surrounded by our families, who think we're together anyway, so before we leave, I want to make sure that we really are a couple." I thought about this all day yesterday and still came to the same conclusion—I want Charlotte to be mine, for us to build a future together.

"Does she feel the same way?"

I think back to the past five weeks and how far we've come—from her threatening to poison me, to her telling me I'm the best fake boyfriend she's ever had. "I think so."

"Is there anything you think might stand in the way of this going the way you want it? I mean, making it real will cover our asses when it comes to Dave ever finding out, but other than that…"

"Well, I'm not sure how my dad is going to react to seeing us together."

"Your dad?"

I slouch back in my chair, heaving out a sigh. "Yeah. I don't think I told you this, but part of the reason why Charlotte and I hated each other growing up was because of my dad. He's the one that always told me I needed to be better than her, and by trying to beat her at everything, I made her hate me too."

"What the fuck?"

"Believe me, it sounds as fucked up as it is. He actually called me last week to berate me about 'dating' her and the fact that I'm not the freaking CEO of Goldstein Advertising yet."

Jeffrey shakes his head. "Man. My parents are just glad I'm not living in their house anymore like my brother."

"Well, the standard I've always been held to was far more than that, no offense."

"None taken. But if he says shit like that, tell him off. I mean, you're a man now, Damien. Your father shouldn't be acting like that towards you anymore."

"I know. But trying to reason with him is like trying to argue with a brick wall. And I'm afraid he's going to say something to Charlotte and fuck everything up. Living all the way across the country from him has made avoiding him so much easier."

"Jesus. Dude, I would not want to be in your shoes, that's for sure."

"Ha. Thanks." I take a deep breath and then sit up in my chair just as there's a knock on the door.

"Hello, gentlemen," Dave announces as he walks into my office. "How's it going?"

"Working our asses off," Jeffrey replies with a hint of pride in his voice as he holds his pinky out and takes a sip from his coffee.

"Looks like it," Dave snickers. "I just wanted to come by and make sure you have something ready for next week for the Remedy account."

"I actually came up with a new idea this weekend that we're going to incorporate into what we already have," I say.

"Excellent. I hope it's better than what the girls have because Elizabeth just gave me a little glimpse of what they're working on and… it's gold," he says confidently.

"Don't worry, Dave. We won't let you down," Jeffrey chimes in. "Dream team over here, remember?" he says, waving his pen between me and him.

"Normally, yes. But when it comes to something like this, I'm a little skeptical, gentlemen. This pitch needs to be perfect. The board is breathing down my neck, and my wife keeps telling me how important it is to give positive female representation. Society is much different these days than it was back in the eighties and nineties. Did you know before 1985, you couldn't use the word 'period' in an ad for feminine products?"

"No shit."

He nods. "Yup. So I want this to be groundbreaking, limit-pushing, but something a woman would look at and say, 'Thank you!'"

"I get it, Dave. I promise we'll give you something worthwhile."

He holds his hands up in the air as he approaches the door again. "That's all I'm asking. And hey, Damien?"

"Yeah?"

"Enjoy your trip this weekend. Just make sure you're ready to go when you get back."

"I will."

"And tell Charlotte that Erin says hello. She still wants you two to come over again for dinner."

My insides cringe at his suggestion. I don't judge, but knowing about Dave's extracurricular activities outside of the office is something I've fought to ignore every day of my life since finding out. "I'll let her know."

"Get back to it, guys." And then he's gone, closing the door behind him.

Jeffrey turns back to me. "Why do you look like you're about to throw up?"

I shake off my nausea. "Trust me, you don't want to know." A shiver runs through me as I adjust myself in my chair. "Okay, enough about that. Let's get to work."

Jeffrey nods. "Yes. Let's make Dave regret ever doubting us. Let's make those girls wonder if we don't really deal with periods on our own. Let's make…"

I hold my hand up, cutting him off. "Jeffrey, I beg of you…just shut up and let's get to work."

He salutes me from across my desk. "Aye, aye, captain. Let's get to it."

After a hectic few days in which I didn't get a chance to see Charlotte, I was more than eager to see her smiling face this morning while picking her up for our early morning flight to Hawaii. And now that we're safely onboard the plane and survived takeoff, in which I thought Charlotte might break my hand from how hard she was squeezing it, I turn to her to strike up a conversation.

"So how were the past few days?"

She twists to face me, leaning her head against her seat. "Busy.

Stressful. It seems no matter how hard I tried to prepare for this vacation, the responsibilities at work just kept piling up. I got as much done as I could before leaving the office yesterday, but I know I'll be returning to madness when we get back next week."

"I'm sorry. I know what you mean. I left a small list of things for Jeffrey to get done for our pitch while I'm gone, and normally I can rely on him. But I'm nervous that something is going to happen to mess this all up."

"Oh, that's right. The pitch is next week, huh? The account that is the entire reason for this fake relationship to begin with," she teases.

"Yup. And I feel confident, but I'm also nervous. This account is a big deal for our firm, and after seeking out the opportunity at a shot to pitch, I hope Jeffrey and I don't make fools of ourselves."

"Well, just harness that cockiness I know you possess, even if you're feeling unsure. Anyone in the room will pick up on your nerves if you show them."

"My cockiness, huh? Remember what I told you, Char. There's a difference between confidence and cockiness." I lean in closer to her. "And you know I have the cockiness covered now," I say, glancing down at her lips and then back up.

"I do, do I?"

"Do I need to remind you? We could always join the mile-high club on this flight," I say suggestively.

She smirks and then leans in closer to me. "That's not happening."

I shrug. "No problem. I'll just remind you when we get to our room." She laughs and then blows out a harsh breath. "So are you nervous about this week?"

"I'd be lying if I said no. I know that having you as a buffer will help, but I also know my mother. Did I tell you that she asked me last week when we would be getting married?"

I nearly choke on my saliva. "What? No."

"Yeah. Now that we're 'dating'," she says, using quotes on her fingers, "she's putting pressure on the next step. I swear, nothing is good enough for her. If I had grown up in the 1800s, she would have had me married off and birthing my first child before I turned eighteen. It's like…"

My mind is still focused on the idea of marriage while Charlotte continues to vent about her mom.

Could I see myself marrying Charlotte? Her walking toward me in a white dress, waking up next to her every day, having babies with her, and building a life with her?

Suddenly visions of all of those things pop up in my mind and my heart lurches. I don't hate it. In fact, the thought makes me really fucking happy.

I already knew that I wanted to make our relationship real and have that discussion while we're on this trip. And even though marriage is something I don't want to rush into, I know that it's something I eventually want—and now I realize I want it with her.

God, I'm in love with Charlotte Montgomery.

The girl who caused so much strife between me and my father is now the person I want with me every second of every day. She makes me feel worthy, useful, masculine, and proud. She gives me purpose and makes me laugh, bringing light to the lackluster life I was leading before.

I had my fun, enjoyed a lack of responsibilities and dedication to one woman for any extended period of time—but now I want to give her *all* of my time.

And I want her to be mine.

As I listen to her talk more about her mom, hear her struggle with her inner turmoil and how to deal with her mother, my reflexes kick in. Without warning, I cut her off with my lips, thrusting my tongue in her mouth and catching her gasp of surprise before she moans and kisses me right back with just as much ferocity. I grip the back of her head and hold her lips to mine as I silence her frustrations, drown out her doubt, and claim her in front of the people around us.

Kissing her wakes my body up, reminding me that it's been almost a week since we've been intimate since she was on her period. And the anticipation of reconnecting that way is making my dick stand at attention as I move my tongue across hers and drown out all of the noise around us, except for the sounds of pleasure coming from her.

We must be making a scene or a discernible amount of noise because a throat clearing behind us interrupts our moment. When we part, Charlotte's cheeks are flushed, and I glance back to the woman sitting behind us with a small boy in the seat next to her.

"Sorry," I mutter before turning to face the front of the plane in my seat as Charlotte giggles beside me.

"Did we just make out in front of a little kid?" she whispers.

"Apparently so. But whatever. One day when he finds a pretty girl and wants to kiss her, he'll remember this moment and think, 'if she's making that much noise, I must be doing it right.'"

Charlotte playfully smacks me. "Damien!"

I lean in closer to her again. "Don't worry though. That was nothing compared to the noises you'll be making when I get you alone later."

A throat clears behind us again, and the woman has wide eyes this time as she glares at me. Charlotte sinks low in her seat, and I reach for her hand, intertwining our fingers, and holding on to her for the rest of the flight as we watch the movie provided on the small screens in the back of the seats on the plane.

Everything is going to work out. I'm going to win this Remedy account. I'm going to tell my father off if he makes one peep about my job or life. And I'm going to admit my feelings to Charlotte.

Let our week in Hawaii commence.

Chapter 14

Charlotte

"There they are!" My mother squeals as soon as we exit the van from the airport. She and my dad are standing right in front of the entrance to the hotel, along with Damien's parents, a few of their other friends from back home, and my Aunt Gigi, who I am so freaking happy to see it almost brings tears to my eyes.

"Mom." I watch as she runs toward me, her dark hair bouncing with each of her strides.

She pulls me into a hug. "God, I've missed you, honey," she says as she squeezes me, and then rears back before studying my face. "You've started using night cream, right?"

My stomach drops once those words leave her lips. Jesus, I've been in front of her for less than sixty seconds and she's already starting.

Before I can say anything in response though, my mother continues. "Looks like Damien has been taking good care of my girl, though," she says, releasing me and then pulling Damien in for a hug.

"I'm trying. She can be a little difficult though, as I'm sure you know." He winks over at me as my jaw drops open.

"Oh, I'm aware. How was your flight?" my mother asks.

"Not too bad. A little turbulence, but nothing unbearable." Damien pulls me into him just as his dad and mom walk up to us. "Dad."

"Son. Good to see you." He reaches out to shake his father's hand, dropping it after only a few seconds.

"It's been a while, hasn't it?"

"Well, when you move clear across the country, that's what happens," his father chides as I turn to catch Damien's expression on his face.

The carefree and playful man that kept me company on our flight has grown cold and standoffish in an instant. But then he forces out a smile and turns to his mother. "Hi, Mom."

"Oh, honey. I've missed you." They share a hug in which he holds her for far longer than he shook his father's hand, and my heart melts a little at the sight. Over the past month he's told me about how close he and his mom are, and I'm not going to lie, it's made me fall for him even more.

Damien releases her and then reaches for me again. "I know we have a lot of catching up to do, but we'd really like to get checked into our room first."

My mother takes a step back. "Oh yes, of course. We have reservations at six for dinner at the Beachside Grill for everyone. You two have to come."

"We'll be there." With my hand in his, we bid our parents farewell for the time being and then head for the receptionist counter to check in.

"Thank you for cutting that short," I tell him as he hands the employee his credit card for incidentals.

"I figured we have plenty of time for our parents to pry later, but right now, all I can think about is getting you naked and finishing what we started on the plane," he says, smirking over at me.

"Did you think you'd be getting lucky this entire trip just because we're staying in the same room?" I tease him, a coy smile on my lips.

"Oh, sweet pea, you're the one who's getting lucky because you get to stay with me."

My body ignites with need as I wait for the receptionist to check us in. And once the keys are in our hands, Damien pulls me behind him with our suitcases in tow to our room.

Each couple has their own suite with an ocean view. Palm trees dot the shore, providing pops of green against the turquoise water, all visible through the sliding glass doors that open to our own private patio. Our room is on the first floor, so we also have a small gate that leads directly to the sand, giving us beach access at our feet.

"The view is incredible," I say as we walk into the room decorated in dark greens and white fabric, and I deposit my suitcase in the corner before walking toward the windows.

"Yeah, it is." Damien comes up behind me, pressing up against my back as he wraps his hands around my waist and drops a kiss to the base of my neck, moving around to my collarbone and nipping lightly with his lips.

"Damien," I moan as I reach behind me and grip his head as he continues to kiss my skin.

"I need you, Charlotte. I've missed this body. I want to feel you wrapped around me."

Spinning in his arms, I find his lips and capture them with mine, weaving my hands around his neck and dragging my nails through the short hair on the back of his head. I've missed him too. This week has been long. As much as I've been dreading many elements of this trip, the one thing I was looking forward to is being alone with him again after several days apart and almost a week without sex.

Damien reaches down and lifts my shirt from my body, unclasping my bra next as we continue to kiss and reconnect physically. And something hits me almost instantly—this feels different. I don't feel the desperation and raw need coming off him. I feel tenderness and reverence instead.

"I missed you," he mumbles against my lips.

"I missed you too."

"Come here." He leads me to the bed, where I lay down and he strips my leggings and underwear from my body, leaving me naked on the bed to watch him undress above me.

When he bares his torso to me, I hum in approval at the sight of his cut physique, his trim waist, and then his hard cock that he reveals as soon as he pushes his shorts down. A possessive gleam transforms in his eyes as he stares down at me on the bed, stroking himself as he does.

And then he leans over me, reconnecting our lips as his hand drifts between my legs and tests my wetness.

"I love that you're ready for me already, Charlotte."

"I've been thinking about this on the plane for the past five hours."

He chuckles. "Me too, babe." Sliding one finger inside of me, I gasp at the intrusion and then drown in the feeling of his touch as he warms me up even further.

"Damien, please."

"Please what?" he asks, peering down at me, locking his gaze with mine as our eyes stay focused on each other while he touches me.

"I need your cock."

"Fuck, I love when you talk like that." He presses a chaste kiss to my lips and then pushes up from the bed, going to his suitcase to locate a condom, tearing it open, and putting it on before resuming his position on top of me.

And then he kisses me tenderly as he enters me, forcing my body to melt into the bed and him as we lose ourselves in each other, coming apart at the same time twenty minutes later.

"So what's on the agenda for the weekend?" Damien asks as we walk hand in hand along the sand. After we had sex, we took a shower together and Damien watched television while I got ready for dinner. But before we face everyone, Damien suggested that we take a walk and explore the resort a bit. We walked around the grounds, taking note of where the gym, pools, and restaurants are, as well as the room where my parents' reception will be held in a few days.

And now, as we step gently in the white sand, I stare at the man holding my hand in his so naturally that I struggle with the overwhelming feelings rushing through me. He's wearing a white linen shirt, khaki shorts, and brown leather flip-flops. When I saw his outfit, I instantly gave him shit for looking like a tourist. But in all honesty, he looked so damn handsome that I contemplated pushing him down on the bed and having my way with him again.

"Well, tomorrow is the girls' spa day, which I'm bummed my friends will miss."

"The girls don't get in until late tomorrow, right?"

"Yeah. They'll be here around eight."

"And they're staying just for the weekend?"

"Yeah, they'll be leaving Tuesday with us." He nods.

"But then Saturday is when the boys will be golfing and the women will be exploring around town a bit. Then Sunday is the ceremony, and Monday will probably just be a pool day and a nice dinner before we leave Tuesday."

"Okay. Sounds manageable."

I huff out a laugh. "It sounds manageable, but there are far too many opportunities for my mom to make me want to jump into the ocean and never return."

Damien stops me in our steps. "Hey. I know she can drive you crazy, but remember that ultimately you're the one that gets to choose how you live your life. I, for one, am in awe of everything you've accomplished, how driven and confident you are," he says, lightly gripping my chin.

"Thank you." My eyes sting with the threat of tears and my heart lurches toward him. The way Damien makes me feel about myself is unlike any other relationship I've had with a man. With him, I am confident and secure. He makes me feel safe and beautiful.

He makes me feel loved.

And I think I'm falling in love with him too…

"It's those qualities of yours, along with your ass, that make me want—"

"Oh, look who we found!" My mother squeals, cutting off Damien's thoughts. We both twist around to see her and my father walking up to us.

"Oh. Hey, Mom."

"Are you two on your way to dinner?"

Damien snaps back into his role. "Yeah, we are. Just wanted to take in some of the scenery and enjoy the sun setting before going inside."

"Well, you're in luck. We actually got a table on the patio so we can watch the sunset as we eat." My mother claps her hands in approval and then she shakes her head in awe. "Gosh, you two just make the most beautiful couple. I need a picture." She starts digging through her purse for her phone.

"No, Mom. That's really not necessary…"

She waves me off. "Nonsense. These are moments you're going to want to look back on and remember." Opening up her camera, she urges us to move closer together.

Damien pulls me into his chest, wrapping his arms around me from behind and encasing me in his warmth. And it feels so good, like we really are a couple and this isn't just some ploy to make my mother happy.

Maybe this can be real if you just talk to him, Charlotte.

"God, I can just see the grandbabies now." She takes a few shots. "Can't you just see how beautiful their children will be, Cal?" she asks over her shoulder, glancing at my father.

"Savannah, let them be," he says so quietly that my mother completely ignores it. But I can see the smile on my father's face before he flashes me a wink.

"Are you done, Mom?"

"Yes." She flicks her finger over the screen. "Gosh, I am going to have to frame this one. Look at you two," she says before turning the phone toward us. And the picture of Damien and I has my heart bursting.

We do look good together. We do look happy. We do look like we could be in love.

I mean, I think I am. But does Damien feel the same way?

"That is a good picture, Mom. Can you send it to me, please?"

"Already done." She shoves her phone back in her purse and then reaches for my hand, pulling me toward the restaurant. "Now come on. It's time to eat, and I want to know how much longer you're going to wait to make me a grandmother."

I peer back over my shoulder at Damien, who's talking to my

father, pleading with him to help me. But all he does is grin in my direction and shoot me a wink, leaving me to my mother's chatter about what season is best for a wedding.

When we arrive at the restaurant, I escape my mother's hold long enough to give my Aunt Gigi a proper hug.

"God, I've missed you, Aunt Gigi," I say in her ear as I squeeze her as hard as I can.

"Charlotte, it has been far too long." When she releases me, I take in my mother's sister, who has always been one of my favorite people in the world.

Aunt Gigi was around a lot when I was younger, but then she moved to Texas when I was ten. She always sent me birthday cards with money every year, and I made sure to keep in contact with her about any significant changes in my life, but it has been months since we last spoke and years since I've seen her.

Where my mother has always been extremely focused on her looks and social status, Aunt Gigi is the type of woman who lives her life for herself. She never married and instead established herself as a commercial real estate agent, opening up her own firm in Texas and dominating a male-dominated field. She's loud, opinionated, and who I want to be when I grow up—because honestly, do you ever really feel like a grown-up, even when you're technically an adult?

"You are such a stunning young woman," she says. "California seems to agree with you."

"It does. I'm very happy there."

"Damien seems to agree with you too," she says, arching her brow.

I turn to find him across the room, speaking with another couple of our parents' friends. "Yeah, he's…okay."

Aunt Gigi laughs. "Just okay? If he's just okay, then he's not doing it right."

"Aunt Gigi!" I admonish.

"Charlotte, life is too short to do work you don't love and have bad sex. Trust me, girl. You can have both."

I can feel the heat creeping up my cheeks. "Well, luckily I have both right now." *Yes, but for how much longer, Charlotte? As soon as this trip is over, there's no need for you and Damien to keep pretending to be together anymore…*

But are we really still pretending?

"That's my girl. And how is that fancy job of yours?"

"I love it. It's stressful sometimes and a lot of work, but it makes me happy, for sure."

"I'm happy for you. And how are you feeling about all of this?" she asks, waving her hand through the air.

"I mean, my parents deserve it. You don't hear of too many people celebrating a thirtieth wedding anniversary anymore."

"True, true."

"And you know how Mom loves to be the center of attention," I suggest.

"Yes, I'm aware…"

"There you are, Charlotte!" My mother rushes up to us, cutting off our conversation.

"What's up, Mom?"

"I want you to come talk to Cheryl. She's the wedding coordinator for the hotel that we've been working with."

"Okay…but why do I need to talk to her?"

"Well, just in case you and Damien want to get married here, then you'll already know who she is."

My shoulders drop. "Mom, that's not necessary."

"Nonsense. You can never over plan." She takes my hand and whisks me away from my aunt as I glance back at her and notice a furrow in her brow.

After listening to my mom and Cheryl drone on and on about

wedding options that don't mean anything to me right now, the hostess takes our group out to our table, where Damien takes a seat beside me, looking far more irritated than he did when we arrived.

"Hey. Are you okay?" I ask him, placing my hand on his thigh.

"Yeah. I'm fine," he says curtly.

"Are you sure?"

He clears his throat and rests his arm around the back of my chair. "I'm fine, Charlotte." The tight-lipped smile he gives me before rubbing my shoulder reassuringly says otherwise. I don't have time to question him further before my father clinks his champagne glass gently with a butter knife, pulling everyone's attention to where he stands at the head of the table.

"Before we eat tonight, I just want to thank everyone for joining us for this celebration. Savannah and I know how blessed we are to have shared thirty years of our lives together, but we are even more blessed with the people that have been by our sides through this journey. Our family and friends, and our beautiful daughter, Charlotte," he says, tears clouding his eyes. "You all bring richness to our lives and we can't thank you enough." I stifle my own tears as he gathers himself. "To the weekend. May our time here together be filled with more memories that will last us the next thirty years."

Everyone murmurs in agreement and clinks their glasses together. And just when I think it's time to relax and eat, my mother mouths across the table to me, "You're next."

I fight the urge to roll my eyes, and instead glance back at Damien, his jaw clenched tightly. Something must have happened in the last thirty minutes while we were apart, but apparently, he doesn't want to talk about it. Part of me wants to press him, but the other part knows that this is neither the time nor place to do so.

I grab my champagne and take a sip, casting my gaze over our table, taking in everyone that made this trip—multiple couples that have been friends with my parents for years, my aunt and my dad's brothers, and of course Damien and me. But when my eyes land on Damien's father, I'm met with a glare that has me rearing back in my seat. Twisting my head to the left and then the right, I try to find something or someone else that would deserve that stare. But after realizing there's no one in the vicinity, I settle back on him, wondering what the hell happened that would warrant that reaction from him. Before I can wonder about it further, the waiter comes by to take everyone's order, commencing our meal and allowing me to enjoy the rest of our first night in Hawaii, despite a feeling of unease takes root deep in my gut.

"This is the perfect start to a vacation," my mother says as all of the women invited gather around in the waiting area of the spa, wearing robes and sipping on glasses of champagne. "Getting pampered always makes me feel more relaxed for the rest of the trip."

"I agree. And I slept on my shoulder wrong last night, so hopefully that massage therapist can loosen me back up," Aunt Gigi replies, circling her arm and gripping her shoulder as her robe threatens to open. Gigi has a voluptuous body, but I'm not sure we all need a show like that this early in the morning. "I requested a male, so hopefully he can manhandle me a bit."

I stifle my laugh while thinking about the last massage I got from a man who turned out to be Damien. He definitely gave me some much-needed pressure, and then ended up manhandling me in other ways later on down the road—like last night. When we got back to our room after dinner, Damien didn't even say one word to me before he pushed me up against the door, lifted me in his arms, and fucked me against the wall, holding his hand over my mouth as I screamed through my orgasm. And then we passed out in bed after a long day of traveling.

It felt so normal, so easy, like we should be doing this all the time.

And the more normal relationship things we do, the more I want that. But something definitely happened with him last night, and my gut is telling me not to let it go.

"Cal doesn't like for other men to touch me, so I have a female massage therapist," my mother interjects, which surprises me.

"Really? Dad has a problem with that?"

"Yes. I learned the hard way, long ago, that your father has boundaries when it comes to our marriage, and that is one that I respect. I'm sure Damien would feel the same way if another man was touching you while you had no clothes on."

Would he? "I'm not sure."

"Trust me. It's a caveman instinct. They don't want any other man touching or seeing their woman that exposed." A bunch of the other women nod in agreement. "Speaking of exposed, I'm doing something for Cal that I've never done before today."

"What it is?" Cheryl, one of my mom's friends asks.

"I'm getting waxed," my mother whispers as a bunch of the women chuckle and some wince.

"What?" I ask as my stomach plummets with this information.

My mother turns to me with a smile on her face. "What? I've never done it and thought it would be fun for our anniversary…you know, spice things up. I've never been completely bald down there, but I heard it's quite pleasurable."

My eardrums are bursting into flames as I take in this information. "Mom, I beg of you, please stop talking."

She laughs. "Charlotte, you're old enough to realize that your parents have sex, hun."

"Oh, I'm not naïve. I just don't want to hear about it."

Damien's mom, Brenda, speaks up at this moment. "Well, I've

always been bald down there. Got it lasered off years ago when the bush was no longer popular. And Derek loves it."

"I'm gonna throw up," I say dramatically as my Aunt Gigi laughs at me. "This is information I do not need to know."

"Well, don't you have a wax appointment today?" my mother asks.

"Yes, but that's none of your business." I tighten my robe around my body, suddenly feeling glaringly naked underneath and traumatized by this conversation.

"Doing those things for your man keeps things exciting, Charlotte," my mother declares. "I'm sure Damien will appreciate it, and you don't want to go ruining the first real relationship you've had in years. You're finally close to being a married woman, so don't jeopardize it. Sometimes a little pain is necessary to keep your man happy."

I bite my lip to keep myself from responding in the way I truly want to, which is much harder than it sounds.

Aunt Gigi comes up beside me, wrapping her arm around my shoulder. "Come on, Savannah...don't scar your daughter for life."

"I'm not. It's just a little bit of girl talk," she jokes as everyone shares a laugh and I contemplate faking a marriage as well to get her off my back.

Aunt Gigi squeezes my arm just as an army of spa employees comes in to take each member of our party to their respective rooms for pampering. But Gigi keeps me back and tells our girls that we need a minute. Pulling me to the side, out of earshot, she soothingly rubs my arm. "Are you okay?"

"Yes. Why wouldn't I be?"

"Because of what your mom just said to you."

"Oh, you mean how I'll never get married if I don't tend to my pubic hair?" I tease. "Don't worry, Aunt Gigi, I'm used to those types of comments by now."

"You shouldn't be used to them, Charlotte."

My brow furrows. "Well, that's just how Mom is."

She shakes her head. "No, that's how *our* mom was. And right now, listening to my sister say the things she said to you in front of all of her friends? It was like seeing my mother reincarnated right before my eyes."

My face falls. "What?"

"Our mother was the exact same way, Charlotte," she continues. "Always reminding us to mind our place and find a husband by a certain age so we wouldn't end up alone. Keep in mind, that was a long time ago when the world was very different, but the memories and feelings her words are sparking are all still the same."

I stand there, flabbergasted. "You're telling me that your mom did the same thing to you?"

"Yup. And guess who told her off and didn't speak to her for years until she got very sick?"

I vaguely remember when my grandmother fell ill, diagnosed with cancer when I was about four. I don't have many memories of her, so I can't connect the similarity between her and my mother. But Aunt Gigi would know.

"How long did you go without speaking?"

"Ten years," she replies. "But even on her deathbed, my mother told me how I wasted my life by never marrying, never finding a man, and having children. And there are days that I regret waiting until that moment to tell her off, because maybe if I'd done it sooner, we could have had a relationship for the last part of her life."

I swallow down the emotion in my throat. "You told her off on her deathbed?"

"Yup. I didn't want to live with that regret, and now I'm telling you that you don't have to either." She grabs both of my shoulders, standing square in front of me. "I'm begging you, Charlotte—don't wait. Tell her now how she makes you feel, get her to see that her words have an effect on you."

"I mean…"

"They do, honey. I can see it in your eyes, in the clench of your jaw when she makes those comments. Hell, whenever she and I speak, all she says to me is how she's worried that you'll end up like me." She rolls her eyes and then places her hands on her hips. "But between you and me, there are far worse people to end up like."

A chuckle escapes my lips as my brain struggles to process this information. But instead of thinking, I just blurt out the first thought that comes to mind.

"My relationship with Damien is fake."

Her face drops. "What?"

Nodding, I clear my throat. "We made a deal. He needed me to be his fake girlfriend for this work thing, and I thought that maybe bringing him as my boyfriend would get my mom off my back about my single status. But God was I wrong, Aunt Gigi. It's only gotten worse. Every conversation or comment since then has been about when we're getting married or having kids. She just won't stop."

My aunt studies me with a perplexed look on her face, leaving my confession to travel in the air between us as if I set it free by rubbing a lamp. "Well, either you and Damien are the best actors I know, or your fake relationship isn't so fake anymore, sweetheart."

I sigh in admittance. "I'm falling for him, which makes her comments even worse because he and I haven't even talked about what happens after this is all over, and the last thing I want is for him to freak out. But then part of me wants to end it just to spite my mother and not give her the satisfaction of knowing I fell in love with someone trying to appease her."

She laughs. "Let me tell you this. Don't give up a man you care about because of her. Your issues with your mom are an entirely different thing, Charlotte. But you need to talk to Damien about how you're feeling if that's what you want."

I look around me, locating the nearest chair before sinking down into it and letting out a loud breath. "You just blew my mind right now."

"Good to know I'm still full of surprises, but it seems you're full of a few of your own." Walking toward me, I see her face soften. "Look, I'm not trying to tell you how to live your life, honey, because you know damn well that I love the way I live mine. But life is too short to be unhappy, to put up with toxic people just because they're family. Boundaries are healthy, and your mother is wrecking any and all of them that need to be put up."

"I just don't get it, Aunt Gigi. I have no problem standing up for myself in any other area of my life. But with her? I just…" I trail off, looking to the side of the room.

"She's your mom. I get it, Char."

"Did you regret speaking up to your mom?"

"Yes and no. I regret the time we missed together, but I also know that I was happier not listening to her degrade my life every time we were together. It was a double-edged sword. However, I know our mother was much more stubborn than your mom is, so maybe she'll be more willing to listen." She shrugs. "You'll just never know if you don't say anything."

Standing from the chair, I bob my head up and down in agreement. "Thank you, Aunt Gigi…for saying something."

"Anytime, Charlotte. And you know I'm here for you always. I'm only just a phone call away." Hugging me from the side, she leads me back to the main part of the waiting room where our massage therapists are waiting, leaning down to whisper in my ear as we walk. "But just so you know, in my experience, a man doesn't really care what kind of hair situation you have going on down there. As long as there's a hole to stick his dick in, he's happy."

"Oh God, no more pubic hair talk, please."

Gigi throws her head back in laughter. "Sorry, had to get my two cents in too."

"Well, I will gladly give everybody their pennies back to erase that conversation from my brain."

"Oh, come on, Char. What's a family get-together without a little emotional and mental scarring?"

After hours of massaging, waxing, plucking, and painting, I stumble back to my room feeling like Jello from head to toe. My body is smooth, relaxed, and pliable, but my mind? My mind is still reeling from my aunt's confession.

However, when I slide the keycard into the slot to unlock the door, I'm greeted with a shirtless Damien, his wet hair slicked back, his tan skin shining in the sunlight coming through the windows, and his smile blinding as he watches me walk toward him.

"How was your day of pampering?" he asks.

"Good. It was good, and also…weird."

"Weird how?" I stare off into space as I relive the conversation from earlier, shuddering when it gets to be too much. "Are you okay, Char?"

"No. No, I'm not." I shake my head. "I just learned way too much about my parent's sex life and our mothers' pubic hair."

Damien stares blankly at me. "Please, for the love of God, don't tell me anything else or I'm going to chop my ears off. My mother and pubic hair should never be used in the same sentence."

"Right?" I chuckle. "But it wasn't just that. My aunt said something to me about my mom that has my brain spinning."

His hands find my hips, pulling me into his hard chest. "Really? What was it?"

"It was…" Suddenly the smell of the ocean hits me. "Wait. Did you go swimming?"

"Surfing, actually."

"Surfing? How come I didn't know you surf?"

"Because I didn't tell you." He shrugs. "I'm not very good at it, so I don't really like telling people. But it's fun and a great workout and I just kind of wanted to be alone, so…"

Running my hands up his arms, I wrap them around his neck. "Did you just reveal something to me that you're not very good at?"

His eyes narrow. "Maybe."

"Hmmm. Seems you're human after all."

"I swear it's the only thing I'm moderately bad at."

"I can think of plenty of things you excel at, so we'll just let this one slide."

He arches a brow. "Really? Like what?" he asks, gripping my ass as he pulls me closer and thrusts his already hard erection into me.

"Definitely that. But unfortunately, I need to wait a while before we partake in that particular activity."

"Why?"

"Because I just got waxed and that area is very sensitive right now."

His eyes light with mischief. "Is that so?"

"Damien, I'm serious," I say while attempting to push him back, but he holds me tighter.

"What if I could help with the swelling and give you an orgasm at the same time?"

"What are you talking about?"

He leads me over to the bed. "Get naked, lie down, and I'll be right back." With a chaste kiss to my lips, he grabs his key card and the ice bucket and disappears swiftly. Confused but humming with arousal, I follow his orders and get naked on the bed, waiting for him to return.

The sound of the door unlocking tells me he's back, and when he shuts the door behind him and sees me lying there, a wicked grin falls over his lips. "Good girl."

"Damien. What are you planning?"

"Don't worry, Char. Sometimes doing things we've never done before is the best part of living." He brings the ice bucket to the nightstand, setting it down before reaching in to grab a cube, which he brings over to the juncture between my legs. I know my skin is still red from the waxing, but Damien doesn't seem to mind, which turns me on even more.

The way he looks at me–like he appreciates every inch of my skin and curve on my body–gives me a confidence I don't think I've ever experienced with another man. It's part of what makes falling for him so easy—a man that I swore would never even kiss me, and now I can't fathom living without his touch and his kiss.

The icy structure hits my skin and makes me gasp out loud. "It's cold."

"Usually ice is, babe."

"Don't make me kick you before we ever get to the good part."

Damien chuckles. "You'd only be denying yourself, Char." Readjusting himself on the bed, he continues to drag the ice along my tender skin as he leans down and places his lips on mine. His kiss is tender, but the mix of his lips heating me up from the inside and the cold ice running over my hot skin is making all of my senses come alive.

He trails his mouth from my lips to my neck as he moves the ice cube further between my legs, dragging it over my slit as he licks the skin along my collarbone and then down to my breasts, circling my nipple as he slides the ice along my clit.

And the sensation—it's equal parts pain and pleasure that make my entire body shudder.

I close my eyes, focus on my breathing and the hum of electricity coursing through me until I hear the sound of the ice shifting in the bucket and the absence of Damien's mouth from my nipple. When I peer my eyes open, I see him reach for more ice, but this time he places the cube in his mouth and then descends on my body.

His cold tongue licks a circle around both of my nipples, hardening them into tiny peaks that elicit goosebumps over my skin, and then he moves down my stomach, licking me with his cold mouth and pausing over my slit.

"Does the ice feel good?" he mumbles around the cube in his mouth.

"Yes..."

"Good."

He lowers his head between my legs and then licks me from my entrance to my clit, the icy temperature of his tongue bringing a new realm of pleasure to me. Then he slides his tongue inside of me, and I lose it.

"Damien..." I clutch the back of his head and writhe against his mouth as he eats me out, licking me intensely and holding me to him.

My internal temperature spikes a few more degrees as the coldness of his tongue touches my clit and he flicks that button perfectly.

"God, yes."

"I could do this all day, Charlotte."

"Don't stop," I command as I pull on the short strands of his hair and hold him in place. I feel his arm move to the side as he grabs another piece of ice and pops it in his mouth, starting the process all over again.

He kisses my mound, dragging his tongue along my sensitive skin, giving my pussy a chance to relax but making me frustrated as I feel my orgasm lying in wait.

"Damien, please…"

"Please, what?"

"Please make me come, damn it!"

He chuckles. "God, I love it when you beg." With a smirk up at me, he moves back down to where I want him and works me up again, building my orgasm like a crescendo. And then I explode, moaning incoherently as I come and wait for the waves to subside, which feels like an eternity before I can feel my body start to relax.

Damien kisses his way up my body until he arrives at my lips, where he presses his own to mine, allowing me to taste myself on his tongue.

"Did that help with the swelling?"

I smile up at him. "Maybe a little. But what about your swelling?" I say, reaching between us to cup him through his board shorts.

"I mean, if you want to return the favor, I wouldn't be opposed to that," he says while staring down at me.

With a renewed bolt of arousal, I push him off me and then climb on top of him, pulling the string on his board shorts to release his cock. And before he can say anything, I take him in my mouth, releasing *his* swelling and making me forget all about the chaos of this morning as I immerse myself in him—in us.

Chapter 15

Charlotte

"Ah!" I power walk across the hotel lobby, screeching like a wild bird as my three best friends appear in front of me and I pull each one of them into my arms for a hug. "You're here!"

"We made it. Barely," Penelope says as she takes off her sunglasses and rolls her eyes. "I had a child behind me on the plane that kept kicking my seat. If I didn't respect the sacrifice his mother made for him to be alive, I would have pulled his oxygen mask down from the ceiling and used it on him like a muzzle."

Noelle smacks her. "He wasn't that bad."

"Easy for you to say. You were too engrossed in a book with your earplugs in to notice."

"New author?" I ask Noelle.

"Yes. And a very promising one at that. I haven't had a book capture me like this one in a long time. I'll tell you about it later."

Amelia walks up behind them with a nervous smile on her face. "Hey, Amelia. You okay?"

"Oh, yes. I'm fine," she stutters, which instantly has me questioning why she's acting so weird.

"Something happened to our little Amelia Be Delia, but she insists everything is fine. Perhaps you can get her to speak up once we get some alcohol in her system," Penelope explains.

I shift my sight over to her and notice she's definitely not acting like herself. "Okay, well, let's get you checked in first, and I know you all must be hungry."

"Starving and in need of alcohol," Penelope replies as I lead them over to the concierge's desk to receive their keys.

After the girls go to their rooms and get settled in, we all meet down in one of the restaurants for a late dinner. Damien is catching up with one of our other friends from back home tonight since he knew the girls would be arriving, and I'd want to spend time with them.

That's one thing I appreciate about him that other boyfriends have had a problem with in the past—he understands how important the girls are to me. I don't feel like I have to justify my decision to see them like I've had to with other men. It's refreshing, and yet another reason that has me contemplating the future of our relationship.

"So, how have things been going so far?" Noelle asks after we place our orders and receive our first round of drinks.

"Um, interesting. My mother has been up to her usual shenanigans, and I've just been trying to let her comments roll off my back, although it's getting harder and harder to do when she keeps bringing Damien into the mix. The poor guy—he probably thinks my mother is going to try marrying us in our sleep."

"Well, has he told you that it bothers him?"

I shake my head. "No. He's actually been really great. It's crazy, but having him here makes me feel like I can handle all of this better, like I'm not handling it alone for once. In fact, he did something last weekend that really surprised me."

"What did he do?" Noelle asks.

"Well, I had something happen to me that never has before. I…I started my period in my sleep…"

"You've never started in your sleep?" Penelope asks incredulously.

"No, I have, but not while I was staying the night at a guy's place." They all cringe.

"Oh, God. How embarrassing," Noelle interjects.

Penelope chimes in too. "I mean, yes, that's unfortunate, but periods are a part of life. Please tell me he didn't freak out."

"No, I was the one who freaked out. I ruined his sheets and locked myself in the bathroom to shower. And then when I emerged, I ran off."

"So what did Damien do?"

I smile, thinking back on how understanding he was. "Well, he assured me it wasn't that big of a deal. But then I left in a hurry and it kind of left things awkward between us. I was sure he'd want some space, that maybe what happened was a little too real for our fake relationship. But then he showed up later that afternoon with tampons, my favorite meal from Tony's, ice cream and Dove chocolates, and Matthew McConaughey rom-com movies."

"Oh my God," Noelle squeals, clutching her hands together under her chin. "That is totally something that one of the men in my books would do."

"Yeah, it sounds too good to be true," Penelope teases.

"I thought the same thing. But he was so sweet and just held me and fed me chocolates while we watched movies." I sigh, slinking back into my chair as I take another sip of my drink. "I'm so screwed."

Amelia finally speaks up. "You finally experienced some intimacy with him," she says. "And how did it make you feel?"

"Uh-oh, she's going into therapist mode," Penelope chides under her breath.

"Stop it," Noelle shoots across the table at Penelope before directing her eyes back to me. "Answer the question, Char."

I take a deep breath. "It made me feel like I want this to be real. I was lying there with him in my old sweats, no makeup and hair thrown up, and he stared at me like I was the most beautiful thing on the planet. He's nothing like I thought he would be, but I'm so scared that I'm the only one that feels this deeply. And last night, he shut down during dinner with everyone, like he became someone else for a little while—silent, retreating, barely saying two words to me. I wonder if all of the pressure of playing this part is getting to him."

"His actions dictate that you're not the only one with feelings," Amelia replies. "But you need to talk to him about it, Char."

"I know, but part of me just wants to wait until this weekend is over, when we can breathe a little. Besides, my aunt said something to me yesterday that still has my head spinning."

"What did she say?" Amelia asks.

"She said that the way my mother is with me is the same way their mother was with them—constantly making underhanded comments about their life choices and love lives, pressuring them to get married and watch their figures so they could snag a man. I never knew this and I feel like it explains so much."

Amelia nods. "It does. But just because that's how your mother was raised does not mean that she has to perpetuate that cycle."

"Spoken like a true therapist," Penelope interjects before turning toward me. "Look, I know you don't want to make a big scene because it's your parents' anniversary and all that, but you need to stand up for yourself, Char. Your mother has beaten you up from the inside out long enough. And as your friend, I'm tired of seeing you put up with it, and it's getting harder to keep listening to it."

"Well, I'm sorry if it's irritating for you, but this entire thing is complicated, Penelope," I retort, my defenses growing as I instantly feel the need to defend myself to her.

"Hey, I'm sure she didn't mean it like that, Char," Noelle interrupts.

"No, I did," Penelope counters, holding a hand up to our friend. "This bullshit has gone on long enough. And it's obvious that you have feelings for Damien, so you need to man up and tell the man what you want before you chicken out about that too."

Standing from my chair, I stare down at one of my best friends, confused, angry, and hurt; hurt that she really feels this way and waited until this moment to tell me how she feels. "You know, just because you don't have a relationship with your mother doesn't mean you get to pass judgment on mine, Penelope," I say. "And secondly, when's the last time you actually let a guy in longer than it took for him to give you an orgasm?" She narrows her eyes at me. "Exactly. In fact, I know you avoid commitment because you're too fucking scared to let people in. You don't even let your parents into your life. So, don't judge me for how I'm dealing with mine." I look over at Noelle and Amelia, whose eyes are wide and are bouncing back and forth between Penelope and me. "Sorry, girls, but I think I'm done for tonight." I say before draining the rest of my drink and walking away.

"Charlotte! Come back," Noelle calls after me, but the last thing I want is to go back over there.

My pulse is racing as I leave the restaurant and walk along the first path I find, trying to get as far away from my friends as possible at this moment, with no clue as to where this path is going to lead me.

And the irony is, that's how I feel about multiple facets of my life right now—my relationship with my mother, my relationship with Damien, and now my relationship with my friends.

I have no idea what happens next, and that feeling is far too unsettling for a girl who's always known what she wants, that is until I let other people's voices and opinions invade my thoughts.

Well, no more. I'm going to get through this weekend, and then I'm going to make some decisions. I just wish I knew that my friends would be there for me from the possible fallout—and that's the scariest part of all—I don't know that they will.

I stride toward the beach, kicking off my flip flops when I hit the sand, carrying them in my hands as I move closer to the water. When I find a spot that seems suitable, I take a seat and pull my knees into my chest, shaking from the anger and sadness the conversation with Penelope ignited.

"Hey." I look up over my shoulder to find Amelia standing behind me. "Mind if I sit?"

Turning back to stare out over the water, I shrug. "I guess."

She takes a seat in a similar position and sighs. "Penelope and you will get past this."

"I don't know, Amelia. She was pretty clear about how she feels… and it hurts."

"Well, like you said, she has her own issues she hasn't dealt with and is most likely projecting them on you. We all have things we like to brush under the rug." Her words seem to have a double meaning.

I turn to her. "What's going on? The girls said you aren't yourself right now."

A heavy sigh leaves her lips again. "I sort of ran into a problem with my new office this week."

"Oh shit." I reach up to rub her shoulder, knowing that she's been so thrilled about her new office for her practice. She's been holding her sessions out of her house since she started counseling, but next week is when she'll finally have her own space to keep building her business. "What's going on? I thought everything was good to go when we return from here…"

She scoffs. "Well, it was going well, swimmingly, really. But last night I met the guy who bought the other empty space in the complex as my office now."

"And?"

"And he's a divorce attorney."

I can feel my eyes go wide. "Oh, shit."

"Yeah. How on earth am I supposed to keep couples focused on repairing their marriages when just around the corner will be a reminder of the other solution to their problems?"

I rub her shoulder, trying to provide her some comfort. "Maybe it won't be as bad as you think it is. Maybe you'll barely see him. Maybe you two could team up and he might actually help you with clients. He might be working with a couple and recommend they seek counseling before going through with their divorce," I suggest optimistically.

"Ha. As much as I love you for trying to convince me of that, based on our first encounter, I'm going to say that chances of that happening are a big, fat no. He basically told me that I've already made him richer because my clients are going to walk right across the complex to him when they realize that what I do is pointless."

My mouth drops open. "Oh, Jesus."

"All I want to do is help people, Charlotte. It's important to me given what I went through growing up."

"You do help people, Amelia. This guy being there isn't going to change that."

She sighs. "You know what the worst part about him is?"

"What?"

"He's hot as hell." She stares off in the distance, probably fantasizing about him as we speak.

All I can do though is laugh. "Wow. So you really do have yourself a little problem to deal with back home, don't you?"

She nods. "See, Char? We all have things in our lives that cause us to make decisions we're not necessarily proud of, or to react to situations that we don't know how to deal with, even me, the therapist." She points a finger to her chest.

"Well, if it makes you feel any better, you're a sex therapist, so as long as you didn't sleep with him, I think you get a free pass here."

She flashes me a small smile. "Yeah, there is no sex going on with Ethan, nor will there ever be, so that logic works for me."

I rest my head on her shoulder. "Thanks for coming to check on me."

"Of course. Everything will be okay."

"I'm just really mad at her right now."

"That's valid. But when you're done being mad, make sure you two talk. Tell her how she made you feel. It will make you feel better and help you process why you got angry with one another."

"Man, what do other people, who don't have therapists as friends, do in crises like these?"

"Live the same way you do. Just because I'm a therapist doesn't mean everyone listens to me."

That makes me laugh. "Well, I think they should."

"I do too. But hey…I get paid either way."

"You need to talk to her," Noelle whispers in my ear as we walk through one of the shops in town the next day. My mother and her friends are milling about as well, but Penelope is avoiding me just like I'm avoiding her.

"I'm not saying anything to her right now. She was very honest about how she feels, and so was I in return. I'm still pissed about it, Noelle. And until I can calm down a bit, I think it's best we don't speak at the moment." Amelia's advice comes back to me, but this morning I woke up still angry, so I think space is the best option for us right now.

"But we're all on vacation, we're supposed to be having fun, and now…"

"I'm still having fun," I say through a fake smile, holding up a t-shirt that says, 'I got lei'd in Hawaii.' "At least I can wear this t-shirt with pride after this."

"Damien is delivering on the sex on vacation aspect, then?"

"God yes. It's the only thing keeping me sane right now. When I got back to our room last night, I mauled him and took out my aggression on his dick."

"Using sex as a way to deal with your feelings, I'm not sure Amelia would approve."

"I'm not searching for her approval, or Penelope's. I know that the way I'm handling this entire situation isn't healthy, all right? I mean, for heaven's sake, I agreed to let my childhood nemesis be my fake boyfriend. Nothing about this is sane. But all I needed was my friends to listen and support me as I figured this shit show out, and Penelope apparently can't do that anymore and waited until she arrived in Hawaii to tell me that." I put the shirt back on the rack and keep moving through the store as Noelle follows.

"I agree that the timing wasn't the best, but I beg of you, don't let this ruin the entire trip. We're only here for a few days. There has to be a way for you two to make up."

"I will when she apologizes," I reply stubbornly, just as my mother comes up to me holding a floor-length maxi dress.

"Charlotte! Look at how beautiful this is." The purple dress has bright pink hibiscus flowers on it and spaghetti straps that lead to a modestly low-cut neckline. It's definitely something I would wear.

"Oh, that is pretty," Noelle agrees with a smile on her face.

"I really like it, Mom. What size is that?"

"It's a small. You should try it on."

"Oh, I'm probably going to need a medium. Do they have it in a medium?"

Her face scrunches as she looks down at the dress and then back to me. "I don't know. I grabbed a small because that's what I wear," she laughs. "And I remember there was a time when you wore a small too."

My shoulders fall as she looks back at the dress. "Well, now I wear a medium, and sometimes a large, depending on the brand."

My mother turns on that sweet southern charm in the snap of her fingers. "Good to know. I'll just go check if they have it in a bigger size then." Her eyes travel up and down my body, assessing my figure. "You know, if you dropped about ten pounds, I bet you could fit into the small. Maybe you could buy this one as a goal to fit into it."

I bite my lip and shake my head, holding back the lava I feel boiling inside of me, threatening to erupt. But Noelle replies for me before I can.

"You know, Charlotte was just telling me she has so many dresses at home that another one is the last thing she needs. So why don't you just put that back, Savannah."

My mother's eyebrows shoot up. "Oh, well I just thought she'd like it. Perhaps I'll just buy it for myself then." She spins on her heels and walks away from us as Noelle rubs her hand on my arm.

"Are you okay?"

"I'm fine," I say through clenched teeth and then turn to look at other knickknacks in the store.

"Charlotte…"

"Just drop it, Noelle."

With shaky hands, I exit the store and take out my phone, looking for someone to talk to, something to distract me from my inner turmoil.

And when I land on Damien's name in my text messaging app, I begin to type out a few words to the one person I know doesn't care what size clothing I wear.

Me: Hey. Hope you're having fun.

I cringe after I hit send, wondering why I said that instead of what I really feel—*I miss you. I wish you were with me right now. I could really use a hug from you at this moment.*

I see the text send and get delivered. After a few moments with no response, I can tell he hasn't read it yet. He's probably busy with the guys on their golfing excursion today. Shoving my phone back in my purse, I stare out along the street I'm on, wondering how on earth I got here and why, after what just happened with my mother, I know Penelope was right.

But I'll be damned if I mention that epiphany right now.

Only three more days—three more days of holding my tongue and pretending like everything is okay.

But when is enough, enough?

Chapter 16

Damien

"Your swing is sloppy."

I clench my teeth together as I watch the ball sail through the air and land farther away from the hole than my father's ball did, but not by much. "Still within putting distance though."

"Yeah, but I definitely have the advantage." He smirks as he slaps me on the shoulder and moves toward the golf cart. I follow him over and deposit my club back in the holder before we both take our seats, and I start driving to the spot where our balls landed. "You know, if you would have come work for me, you'd have more time to work on your game."

"Well, golf was never my favorite pastime anyway, Dad."

This is the third time he's brought up my job since we started golfing and each occurrence only serves to remind me why I moved three thousand miles away from him and could have never survived working for him.

"You used to be so much better at it though, Damien. It's like you're slacking."

"I was good at it because you made me play, Dad. Now I'm too busy at work and doing other things to worry about golf."

"You're working too hard then. If you were the boss, you'd have more time to play."

I huff out a laugh. "Maybe that's how it works for you, but if I get this promotion, that won't be the case."

He scoffs. "I can't believe you're still working your way up in that company, Damien. For how long you've been there—"

"I should be running the show by now," I finish for him. "Maybe I don't want to be the boss, have you ever thought about that?"

"Well, if anyone asks, I told them you're in charge anyway, so just play along."

Rolling my eyes, I'm grateful for when we arrive where our balls landed, eager to keep this game moving so these conversations can stop as well.

The first night when we arrived in Hawaii, my father pulled me aside before dinner and told me he couldn't believe I was actually dating Charlotte, that seeing us together made his insides turn. Part of him wished I was lying and that Charlotte's mom was just exaggerating the news that we were dating.

But when I told him it was real, he shook his head at me and assured me it wouldn't last.

The truth is, he'd love nothing more than to know it was fake, but I don't want to give him that satisfaction, and I'm still hoping this fake relationship will end up real when I talk to Charlotte.

"She's not the woman for you," he said.

"Well, what you think doesn't matter."

"It should. I'm your father. My opinion should mean more to you than anyone else's."

Little does he know that it's taken years for me to learn that his opinion doesn't matter. Being happy for the first time in my life helped me realize that listening to him, telling me what *he* wanted for me while I was growing up prevented me from figuring out what *I* truly wanted for my life.

By the time we were done talking, I was so on edge that when I sat down next to Charlotte at dinner, I knew she noticed the change in my demeanor. I didn't want to worry her about it given how on edge I knew she was about her mom—which is an entirely different animal we're dealing with—so I told her I was fine and brushed it under the rug.

But then yesterday, he commented on Charlotte's body in her bikini when we went swimming after lunch before the girls arrived from the airport.

"Looks to me like Charlotte is too busy working at that ridiculous magazine to fit in a few workouts here or there."

"What?"

He eyed her up and down in her suit, which I happened to think was a sexy-as-hell black one-piece with cutouts on the back and sides that showed glimpses of her tan skin. It was all I could do to let her leave our room after she put it on and showed me.

"She's overweight, especially for her height. A few hours at the gym should be a priority for her as a woman who's not very tall."

"Funny, I happen to think her curves are sexy as hell," I countered.

"To each their own, I suppose. But just remember, if she has children, she'll only gain more weight and then fight to lose it. Thank God your mother did, but not all women care enough to do that for their husbands."

"Jesus, Dad. We need to get you a muzzle. Do you hear yourself?"

He threw his hands in the air. "What? I'm just speaking the truth.

And I'd hate to see you wind up with a woman who has no problem letting herself go."

I walked away from him at that point because if I stood there any longer, I was afraid I was going to punch him, and that's the last thing I needed while trying to survive this trip.

But making comments about my job is his favorite way to remind me that I have failed to live up to his expectations as his son.

"You know, I made five million last quarter," he says as he reaches for his club and prepares to sink his ball in the hole, completing this hole under par.

"Good for you, Dad."

"You could have been making that kind of money if you had stayed home."

"Well, money isn't everything in life," I say as he goes to line up his shot. And apparently, my comment struck a chord with him because he misses. I smile with pleasure.

"It's not too late, son. You could move back home, and I'd bring you on at the firm in a heartbeat. You can stop living in that small apartment, have a real job making real money, and meet a petite southern girl that would worship the ground you walk on."

"Sounds like your life, Dad."

He grins, bigger than I've ever seen him. "And what's wrong with that? You should be proud of your old man."

"And you should be proud of me for not perpetuating your chauvinistic ideals for another generation of Shaw men."

"Watch your tone with me, boy," he says with a heated stare as he takes a few steps toward me, getting in my face and seething, his pupils dilated and his eyes growing darker.

"Or what?"

"Everything okay here?" Cal Montgomery, Charlotte's dad, steps up toward us as a few other golf carts pull up to the hole as well. I guess the rest of the party has caught up to us finally, and just in the nick of time.

My father's demeanor instantly changes, his death stare from before transforming into a slimy smile to hide the fact that he was about to get physical with his son.

Wouldn't be the first time, unfortunately.

"Oh, just a father and son disagreeing over a few things. No biggie." He flicks his eyes over to me and then back to Cal. "Nice of you boys to finally catch up."

"Well, we're just enjoying the day, taking our time," Henry, one of the men here for the ceremony, interjects.

"Time is money, Henry. But the slower you go, the better chance I have to win now, isn't that right?"

The men chuckle as Cal casts a look over to me. "That competitive spirit is alive and well, I see. Is Damien giving you a run for your money?" he asks.

And I take this as my opportunity to get a jab in at my dad. "Well, I learned how to compete from the best, isn't that right, Dad? It would only be right for me to prove that sometimes, the path less traveled leads to greater success."

"Is that your way of saying you're going to beat me, Son? You realize you're about twenty more feet away from the hole than I was."

"Doesn't matter," I say with a shrug as I grab my club from my bag. "Winning isn't everything, Dad. And I happen to like being the underdog. It makes the win that much sweeter when I clench it."

After surviving a long day in the sun and coming in a respectable second place to Cal—who ended up coming back from behind and beating us all—the men gathered at one of the bars for drinks and cigars as a toast to the night before the ceremony.

I haven't seen Charlotte all day since the girls were out exploring the island, and part of me wishes we could just take off to another resort and enjoy the rest of this trip alone. It would be far more enjoyable than making small talk with a bunch of old white men who are so far removed from normal society that it makes me even more grateful that I moved away from that environment.

"What are you drinking?" My father comes up to me, holding a glass of bourbon, probably. That was always his drink of preference.

"Just a beer."

"Beer? That's not a real man's drink. Let me get you a bourbon, Son."

"No thanks. I'm good. I don't want to feel like shit tomorrow, Dad." Tomorrow's ceremony needs to go off without a hitch, and I want to have my wits about me so that it does. We're almost home free, and nothing needs to wreck that.

He shrugs and then takes a drink. "Suit yourself. I figured you'd want to celebrate beating your old man today."

"Ah…is your ego bruised?"

He scoffs. "Hardly. Our little tiff got in my head is all. Didn't take you for one to use psychological warfare, but it definitely helped you out today. Although I'm sure you perfected that with Charlotte as a kid, so I guess I should be impressed."

"Wow. Okay, Dad." I drain the rest of my beer and then proceed toward the bar for a refill.

"How about a rematch?" he asks as he comes up beside me.

"I'm not playing golf in the dark with you just so you can feel better about yourself."

"Not golf." He looks around the bar. "How about darts? You know I can kick your ass in darts."

"Oh, really? Well then, sign me up," I reply sarcastically as the bartender slides me my beer.

"Too afraid to lose?" he asks, slurring his words a little.

I turn to face him head-on. "No, I just have no need to compete against you to prove a point."

"Man up, Damien," he bellows, drawing attention to us as he grows angrier. This is usually how our fights would start when I was younger. And when he's been drinking, I know he has no problem putting his hands on me to prove who the alpha male is.

Well, I'm not the same boy I was back then, and I'm also not about to engage in this dance with him tonight, especially in front of all of these people.

"Sorry to disappoint you, Dad, but I'm not gonna man up for anything. But you should have another drink. Clearly those are bringing out the best in you." I tip my glass against his and then walk away, leaving him there seething because I didn't play into his game—and damn, does that feel good.

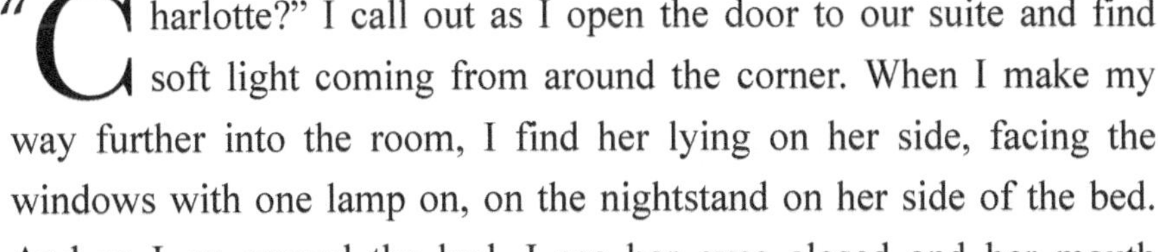

"Charlotte?" I call out as I open the door to our suite and find soft light coming from around the corner. When I make my way further into the room, I find her lying on her side, facing the windows with one lamp on, on the nightstand on her side of the bed. And as I go around the bed, I see her eyes closed and her mouth slightly parted, those luscious lips of hers calling to me.

Without hesitating, I lean down and press my lips to her forehead and then to her mouth, causing her to stir and blink her eyes open slowly as she stares up at me. "Damien?"

"Hey, Char."

She props herself up and then looks around the room. "What time is it?"

"A little after nine. What time did you get back?"

"About an hour ago. I laid down for just a minute to let my feet rest and must have passed out."

Pushing her hair from her face, I sit on the edge of the bed and stare down at her. "Did you have a good day?"

"Ha. No."

"You wanna talk about it?"

Her eyes bounce back and forth between mine before she says, "Not really. I don't want to talk right now."

I arch a brow at her. "What do you want to do?"

She reaches for my shirt, pushing the fabric up to reveal my stomach to her, and then she leans forward to press her lips to my abs. "I want you to fuck me."

My dick stirs from her words, but I know something must be really bothering her since she's avoiding talking about it. "Are you sure you're okay?"

"I'm fine," she says between kisses, pushing my shirt up higher so she can access my chest, circling her tongue around my nipple. "I just want you."

And those four words, they're like music to my ears.

Knowing that being with her right now would help soothe my soul after my day as well, I oblige her request, stripping her bare as I do the same, and making her forget her day right alongside mine, reaching our release together before passing out in each other's arms.

The next morning I wake up with Charlotte wrapped up in my arms, the scent of her skin hitting my nostrils as I take in a deep breath. "Good morning." Pressing a kiss to her shoulder, I wait for her to stir and press her ass back into me.

God, I love her ass.

"Good morning," she says sleepily. "What time is it?"

"A little before seven."

"Our breakfast will be here soon." She spins to face me, her face pure and absolutely gorgeous after she just wakes up.

God, I want to wake up to her like this for the rest of my life.

"My breakfast is right here," I say before reaching down between her legs and running my finger across her slit. And damn, she's already fucking ready for me. "Good dream last night?"

"Maybe." She smirks and then gasps as I push a finger inside of her. "Damien…"

"What Char?"

"Make me come," she commands as she widens her legs and gives me full access to her.

"I'll gladly deliver on that part of our deal," I say as I latch my lips onto one of her nipples and suck the nub gently before burying my face between her legs and bringing her to orgasm in record time.

Once she's physically sated and resituated in my arms, a knock on the door interrupts us. I answer it once I slip a pair of shorts on, collect our breakfast, and then fall back in bed, where I press Charlotte about last night. "So, you wanna tell me what happened yesterday?"

She sighs as she drags her nails through my chest hair. "Well, I kind of got in a fight with Penelope Friday night when the girls got here, and then yesterday things were just awkward while we were seeing the sights."

"What happened?"

She sucks in her lips as she gathers her thoughts. "We both said some things that were a little harsh."

"Okay…"

"I hate fighting with her, or any of my friends for that matter, but I just feel like so many things are spiraling out of control right now and she tried telling me what she thinks I should do, but her honesty… stung a bit."

"So you stung her back?"

"Yeah."

"Well, I'm sure you both are feeling bad about it. Maybe you should just talk it out."

"I know. I want to, but I have to get ready with my mom and aunt this morning, which is stressful enough."

I pull her closer to me. "You'll figure it out. You girls are too close and have been friends for too long to let something like this come between you."

She closes her eyes and rests her head on my chest. "I hope so."

After Charlotte insists on returning my earlier favor with a blowjob to rival the one she gave me in her office, we say our goodbyes as she grabs her dress and heads for the bridal suite, where the girls will be getting ready. Thus, leaving me alone for the remainder of the morning.

The ceremony isn't until four, so I figure I'd get in a good gym session beforehand and then maybe call Jeffrey to make sure nothing is falling apart back home.

I'm happy to find the hotel's gym empty when I arrive, so I take my time with some cardio before doing a weight-lifting routine that I know will help burn off some calories and pent-up aggression.

I'm in the middle of a barbell squat when my father's voice pulls my attention away from my breathing.

"Only three-hundred pounds? You've gotten weak, Son," he says as I watch him walk into the room in the mirror in front of me.

"You look better than I thought you would this morning," I reply as I finish my rep and set the bar back on the racks.

"What's that supposed to mean?"

"Bourbon doesn't usually agree with you. Good to know you've built up your tolerance." I walk around him, grabbing my water bottle from the floor as I go to the sanitizing station, grabbing a towel and spray to clean off all of the equipment I just used. Now that my dad's here, I'm definitely not sticking around.

"Well, a real man can handle any kind of booze, Damien. And where did you wander off to last night? Back to your room to your girlfriend?"

"Where else would I have gone, Dad?"

He shakes his head at me. "I just never thought I'd see the day that my son was pussy-whipped."

"Excuse me?"

"That girl has you throwing your life away. No pussy is that good, Son."

"Is that what you said about Mom? Was she just the safe choice and that's why you married her?"

"You leave your mother out of this," he says, coming toward me now.

"I think it's only fair I question your relationship choices since you're questioning mine."

"You wouldn't be here if I hadn't chosen your mother, and you'd be wise to remember that."

"Good to know that she was worthy enough for you to procreate with, and I'm the lucky sperm that was fortunate enough to be your son and the object of your unhealthy affection."

"You've gotten pretty bold in the time since we've seen each other. Good to know you still have some balls." He eyes me up and down before raising his chin to me. "I just don't want to see you end up unhappy, with a woman who isn't going to be the type of partner you need."

"I find it ironic that you don't find your best friends' daughter worthy enough for your son," I argue. "Do Cal and Savannah know that you feel this way about her?"

"That's irrelevant."

I smile smugly. "No, I don't think it is. Perhaps they might find this information interesting after over twenty years of friendship."

"I don't like the tone you're taking with me right now, Damien," he warns. "You need to remember who you're speaking to."

"Oh, I'll never forget the way my father speaks to me, Dad. And *you'd* be wise to remember that." I throw the towel in the basket for dirty towels and then head for the door. "See you at the ceremony."

Chapter 17

Charlotte

"Oh, honey. You look so beautiful." My mother stands from her chair where the stylist was just finishing her hair and walks over to me, studying my face. I'm not gonna lie, I love the way the makeup artist did my makeup, and the low bun hairdo the hairstylist did for me looks great too. I feel beautiful.

"Thanks, Mom."

But then her brows draw together, and she reaches up to push a finger between my eyes. "Have you considered Botox yet, Charlotte?"

"What?"

She holds up her hands. "I'm just saying. You have a few lines between your eyebrows that you could stop before they get worse with a little injection, sweetheart," she says with a wink. "Think about it."

Aunt Gigi comes up beside me as my mother walks to the other side of the bridal suite. "Don't do it, Char. Botox will have your face frozen in place, looking like the Wicked Witch of the West."

"I'm going to scream," I say under my breath. "She's ridiculous."

"Just wait until after the ceremony to do so, because if you ruin that, you'll never hear the end of it from your mother." She shoots me an amused look and then pats me on the back. "Come on, let's get our dresses on. This is almost over."

My mother, my aunt, and I are the only ones in the bridal suite. Since I'm the daughter of the bride and groom, the role of bridesmaid falls to me. And my aunt is here with us to get ready since she's family. It's been a long morning of primping and listening to details about the ceremony, things my mother has already told me about several times by now. My aunt and I shared many discreet eye rolls, but this day is important to my mother, and regardless of my conflict with her right now, I truly am happy for my parents. Any long-lasting love should be celebrated.

Thirty minutes before the ceremony, a knock on the door of the suite pulls me in that direction. But when I answer it and find Damien on the other side, my entire body jolts when I see him.

He looks so handsome in his dark gray suit and tie, a light pink to match the shade of my dress. My mother must have coordinated that without me knowing. His hair is combed back and gelled in place, his beard neatly trimmed and his narrow waist highlighted by the fit of his jacket which perfectly contrasts the crisp white of his shirt.

God, he's so handsome, and seeing him right now is making me even more aware that everyone believes this is as real as it feels.

I'm no longer faking it with this man. I'm wanting to keep him forever.

"Damn, Charlotte. You look gorgeous, babe," he says as he leans in through the doorway to kiss my lips and then retracts, eyeing me up and down.

The pink dress that my mother picked out for me has a corset bodice that feels a lot like a girdle. I'm not gonna lie, it's a bit hard to breathe in it, but it does help accentuate my waist and leads into a mermaid-style fit of pink silk, with the base of the dress complete with a light, shimmery organza formed into ruffles that look like roses. It's fancier than my prom dress from high school, which doesn't surprise me. My mother has never been one to blend in, and she doesn't like for me to do that either.

"Thank you. You look very handsome yourself," I say as I reach up and straighten his tie; the gesture feels so normal, like something we do all the time.

"I can't wait to strip you out of this dress later," he whispers in my ear, his warm breath making my skin pebble with anticipation.

"I'm counting on that."

"Damien?" I turn around to find my mother in her dress, the lace overlay standing out against the champagne color underneath. Her dress is also form-fitting, yet elegant and eye-catching. She looks stunning.

"Savannah, you look amazing."

"Aw, thank you. That means a lot coming from my future son-in-law."

"Mom!"

Damien laughs but pulls me toward him. "With any luck, huh?" *Jesus, he plays his part so perfectly.*

"Oh, Charlotte would be a fool not to marry you. Besides, it's not like she's had many other opportunities," she says with a wave of her hand and internally, the lava starts to boil again.

Damien clears his throat. "Well, the wedding coordinator told me to come and get you girls so we can get this show on the road."

"Oh, it's time!" My mother claps her hands. "Thank you again for walking Charlotte down the aisle, Damien. It will be such good prac-tice for when it's your turn." She winks again and then moves into the other room to gather her bouquet.

I twist to face Damien. "I'm so sorry. You know how she is—"

He cuts me off with his lips. "Stop apologizing for her," he says when we part. "Come on." He takes my hand and pulls me out of the door. "Let's just get this over with so we can lock ourselves away from everyone tomorrow, pretend like we're here alone, and then we can leave on Tuesday and get back to our lives."

Resting my head on his shoulder as we walk, I sigh in contentment. "That sounds wonderful."

"Then it's a plan."

At four o'clock sharp, the ceremony begins and my nerves are on high alert.

"You okay?" Damien asks as the music starts while waiting for the coordinator to give us the signal to start walking.

"Yeah, I'm fine."

"Don't worry, Charlotte. You look amazing. I'm lucky to be walking you down the aisle right now."

I peer up at him as he stands by my side, my arm weaved through his. "Damien…thank you for doing this."

"Hey, you're not the only one who benefited from our arrangement, remember?"

"I know, but I feel like you've done more for me than I have for you."

He shakes his head. "No, Char. You have no idea how much you've helped me. In fact, there's something I want to talk to you about later…" A reverent smile spreads across his lips.

My heart jumps with anxiousness. "Okay…"

"Alright, you two," Cheryl says, pulling us from our conversation. "It's time." She waves us forward, and Damien pulls me with him as I put one foot in front of the other, exiting the building we're in and walking out onto the patio where the guests are waiting in rows of white wooden chairs. An archway decorated with magenta hibiscus flowers and white lilies stands at the end of the aisle, where my father is standing proudly, tears forming in his eyes.

"I love you," I mouth to my father as I fight back my own emotions while Damien leads me to the end of the white silk aisle sprinkled with flower petals and kisses me on the cheek before letting go of me.

"My job is over," he says with a wink as he releases me and walks back to his seat.

But I don't want your job to be over...

Swallowing down the sadness that overcomes me, I take my spot near the officiant and watch as my mother appears in the doorway I just walked out of.

I quickly glance at the rows of guests, finding their attention fixated on my mother, until I land on a pair of eyes staring back at me.

Penelope flashes me a sad smile before mouthing, "I'm sorry."

And relief floods my chest. "I'm sorry too," I mouth back to her as my mother arrives at the arch. The officiant begins speaking so I turn my attention back to my parents and stand there like the proud daughter that I am while wondering if I'll ever get my happily ever after too.

"Come here, bitch," Penelope calls to me from the few feet away that she stands. The reception is in full swing, so I can finally converse with the other guests and take in some much-needed alcohol after spending the last hour taking pictures, pretending to be perfectly happy while inside, I'm completely off-kilter.

Pulling her into a hug, I squeeze her tightly. "I'm sorry, Pen."

"Me too, Char. I know your relationship with your mom is complicated and so is this thing with Damien. I just hate seeing you so indecisive. I know who you are and what you deserve, and I just wish you'd finally fight for that."

"I'm trying, Pen. And I'm sorry for what I said about you and men. I know you've been hurt and that was unfair of me to point out how you choose to handle those relationships now."

She rolls her eyes. "You're right though. We all have our own shit to deal with in our own way. But I love you and the last thing I want you to think is that I don't support you." She grabs me by the shoulders. "I do."

"I know. Just let me figure this out, okay?"

She nods. "Okay. You look freaking hot by the way," she says as she eyes me up and down. "And your ass looks amazing in that dress."

"That it does." Damien comes up behind me, laying claim to my rear-end with his hand as he pulls me into his side.

"Damien. You treating my girl right?" Penelope teases.

"As good as a fake boyfriend can," he says as my heart twists with more indecision. This is the second time today he's mentioned something about our fake relationship, which has me wondering if he's trying to remind me of the terms. Perhaps all of the comments my mother has been making about marriage and babies are finally getting to him. "Forgive me, Penelope, but I came over here to steal Charlotte away for a second."

"I guess you can have her, but you'd better be prepared to keep her," Penelope replies with a sneaky smile on her face.

"What's up, Damien?"

"Come dance with me, Charlotte." He grabs my hand and leads me toward the dance floor as a slow song starts playing over the speakers.

When we reach the corner of the dancefloor, he pulls me into his chest and rests his hands on my hips and his forehead on mine.

"Are you and Penelope okay now?" he asks as we start to move side to side.

"Yeah. We talked a bit just before you came over actually."

"Good. You seem a little more at ease."

"Yeah, I guess. But my entire body just feels wound tight right now."

He smirks down at me with a mischievous glint in his eyes. "I know of a way to help you relax."

Chuckling, I pull his lips closer to mine. "That sounds amazing, but it was a feat to get me into this dress, and it doesn't exactly allow for easy access."

"Sounds like a challenge to me. And you know I never back down from a challenge."

"There you two are!" I spin around to see my mother and Damien's mom speed walking across the room toward us.

"Oh God, what does she want now," I mutter under my breath.

"Damien, I really want a picture of you with your father and me," Brenda says. "Can I borrow you for a second?"

My mother has to add her suggestion, of course. "Well, shouldn't Charlotte be in the picture too since they're practically engaged at this point?"

Brenda's eyebrows perk up. "Oh, yes! That would be lovely. It will be a great memory to have down the road."

"Oh, no…that's not necessary," I say, trying to avoid any more lies to look back on through copious amounts of photo evidence.

"Yeah, I don't think that's necessary." Twisting to the side, I see Damien's dad approach us with a menacing look on his face.

"Either Charlotte is in the picture, or I'm not," Damien counters, and suddenly the tension between everyone increases tenfold. The two men have a silent stare down as everyone waits to see who will speak first.

Brenda's face transforms from worried to a fake smile in a flash. "Perfect. Well, let's do this then."

Feeling unwanted and awkward as hell, I follow Damien and his parents over to the wall that the photographer directs us to. We gather close together and then pose for a few shots as I feel Damien tense beside me. His face is stoic, but I can tell he's pissed by what just happened.

When we're done, Damien goes to lead me away, but his father reaches out and grabs Damien's arm before we get too far. "Damien, a word, please."

"I don't have anything to say to you."

"We need to talk and you will listen to what I have to say, young man."

Damien narrows his eyes at his dad, but then turns to me for a second. "I'll be right back, Char." With a press of his lips to my cheek, he leaves, following his father through an archway that leads to a hallway just outside the room the reception is being held in.

"Oh my God, Charlotte! Those pictures are going to be so lovely," my mother says, coming up to me once more. "You and Damien will be joining our families together, and your father and I couldn't be more thrilled."

"Mom…" I try to cut in as my pulse spikes, and I worry about what's going on between Damien and his dad.

"You two need to start talking about wedding plans so we can get to planning and booking a venue. You know most places book out at least a year in advance, but I think we could find something sooner or call in a favor if needed. And then babies," she croons, faking tears. "Remember, it takes nine months to bake one of those little bundles of joy, ten technically."

"Mom…" But she just keeps talking as my adrenaline roars through my body.

"And you need to think about when you will be due. If you get married in the spring, you could have a baby by next Christmas. It would be the perfect present for me and your father, besides you getting married of course. I'm just so happy that you and Damien are together now. It's really helped relieve the stress I carry about your future, wondering if you're going to end up all alone like my sister," she says before rolling her eyes. "But it looks like I don't have to worry anymore, and neither do you. Damien is a great guy, although he doesn't make as much money as I'd like for your husband to make, but you're lucky to have reconnected with him at this point in your life. Who knows how much longer you would have been single if you two hadn't crossed paths again—"

"Oh my God! Just stop!" I shout, drawing the attention of everyone in the room over the volume of the music, but my mind can't take any more of this. The lava is hot, and my soul is ready to erupt.

"What?"

"Jesus, do you hear yourself?" I say, throwing my hands up in the air. "You just had an entire conversation with yourself about *MY* life, and when I should get married and start having children. I hope to God you don't say stuff like this to other women." The rubber band keeping my mouth shut has finally snapped, and now I have no control over what is coming out of my mouth. "What if a woman wants kids but is struggling with fertility? What if another decided that kids aren't for her? But more than that, when a woman decides whether or not to have children is none of your goddamn business!"

My mother acts shocked and appalled that I'm raising my voice to her, but I don't care. "Charlotte, please lower your voice," she says as her eyes scan the room and then land back on me. "I just don't want you to waste any more time. You're not getting any younger, dear."

"Oh, believe me, I know! You know why? Because you use every available moment to tell me so!"

My mom starts looking around the room again where I'm sure numerous people are gathering around to witness my blowup.

But I seriously don't fucking care anymore. *I am done.*

"I just want you to be happy, Charlotte."

"Happy? You want me to be *happy*? Then stop telling me how to live my goddamn life! And forgive me, Mom, but the last thing you seem is happy because all you care about is what my relationship status will mean for *you*."

"Well forgive me for wanting to celebrate the fact that you're no longer single. A thirty-year-old woman and you haven't married yet? That's not how you do things, Charlotte," she admonishes.

And then I spew the truth. "Well you can stop celebrating, Mom, because guess what? This is all a lie!"

"What?" she gasps as other people around us do the same.

"Damien and I..."

But my thoughts are cut off as I hear a deep voice on the other side of the wall drown me out. "Listen up, you little shit. You might think you're being the martyr here, doing things your own way and disappointing me at every turn, but the boy I raised was a winner, not someone who comes in second place and settles in his life, especially with *that* girl. I always made sure you were reminding her of who the superior person was, beating her at any and everything because that's how it should be, and I won't apologize for that. But when it comes down to it, this life you lead will lose its luster. You'll wake up one day and regret the choices you've made and want to come back home and live the life you were *meant* to live. You'll realize that girl is not right for you, that she will never be the woman you need. She's too much—too independent, too driven, and too heavy for her frame. She'll fight you at every turn, and that's the last thing you want as a man—a woman who thinks she's your equal when you should always be superior to your partner. And when you do realize that, I'll be there for you because that's what fathers do."

My breath catches in my lungs as I begin to walk toward the shouting match between Damien and his father.

"Charlotte, where are you going?" My mother calls from behind me as I take a few steps closer to the wall that separates me from Damien and his father. And then I hear Damien speak up.

"No, fathers support their children's decisions, even if it isn't what they want for them. *Good* fathers would just want their children to be happy, even if that means living a life that was different than the one they envisioned for them. And *great* fathers would realize when their son finally understood how toxic their parent is and is done listening to them." There's a break in Damien's speech. "And I don't *think* Charlotte is the right person for me either," he says. "I know…"

A crack the size of the Great Wall of China fissures in my heart from his words. "Fuck this," I shout, barreling into the hallway where Damien and his dad are, my heart pounding frantically inside of my chest with anger. "Don't worry, Mr. Shaw, I'm not going to ruin Damien's life."

A shocked Damien turns around to find me standing right behind him. "Charlotte? What are you doing?"

"It's kind of hard to do that when our relationship isn't real." Gasps can be heard across the room. I turn my head to see my mother surrounded by a bunch of her friends, all staring in our direction.

But you know what? The truth is already out there, so I might as well lay it all out.

Let the verbal diarrhea commence.

"That's right, Mom. I convinced Damien to be my fake boyfriend just so I wouldn't have to deal with your incessant nagging about me still being single. But you know what? Even with a boyfriend, it wasn't good enough for you. Then it became about when we were getting engaged, or how soon we planned on having kids." I throw my hands up in the air. "And when it wasn't about that, it was my weight, needing to book a Botox appointment soon, or wearing clothing more flattering for my body or in the same size you wear. Well, guess what? I'll wear whatever I fucking want to because I'm a grown-ass woman, and I'm tired of trying to get you to see that!"

Damien's dad snickers. "Well, isn't this rich?"

Seething, I turn back to him. "And you," I say, pointing a finger in his direction. "*Fuck you*! Fuck you and your chauvinistic ideas of a woman's place. Fuck you and the way you speak to your son. And fuck you for thinking I'm too much! How's this for too much?" I scream. "Telling you off in front of everyone you know so they can see what an ass you are! Telling you that you can kiss my fat ass since apparently, I'm carrying too much weight for my body that doesn't need your approval anyway. And telling you that your blatant display of arrogance just goes to show exactly why I *am* superior to you—because I would never allow a man to treat me that way."

"Tell 'em, Char!" Penelope shouts across the room, pulling my attention to the corner where she, Noelle, and Amelia are standing. Penelope wears a proud smile, Noelle is standing there with bugged-out eyes and a slack jaw, and Amelia is chewing on her nails as they watch my eruption continue.

"Listen here you little bitch," Damien's father snaps as he charges toward me, pulling my attention back to him. But before I can back up a step, Damien swings his arm and punches his dad in the face. Another round of gasps echoes around the room, easy to detect since the DJ has stopped playing music at this point.

I clasp my hands over my mouth as I watch Damien shake out his hand and his father fall to the floor, clutching his hands around his nose.

And then it hits me.

I reached my breaking point, and I did it during my parents' thirtieth wedding anniversary party.

Holy shit.

As reality smacks me in the face, I see my father walking slowly toward me. "Charlotte…"

With tears building in my eyes, I take a few steps back and then turn to my father. "I'm sorry, Dad." Feeling my emotional breakdown on the horizon, I pivot in my heels and take off down the hallway toward the door, anger and regret flooding my chest.

"Don't apologize, Charlotte!" Penelope screams. "Women need to stop fucking apologizing for everything!"

"Hear, hear!" Another voice shouts, but I keep moving.

"Charlotte!" Damien calls after me as I shove open the doors, racing down sidewalks lined with palm trees while coming up with a plan as I briskly run to our room.

I pull my keycard from the side of my dress, tucked safely next to my boobs (where I've found is a great place to keep things safe that I don't want to lose) and open the door to our suite, running toward my suitcase and throwing my things inside as I frantically move around the room.

After only a few minutes, I hear the door open, and an out-of-breath Damien appears in front of me. "Jesus Charlotte, are you okay? What are you doing?"

"I'm leaving," I say as I move into the bathroom and gather my makeup and hair straightener.

"Where are you gonna go? Our flight isn't until Tuesday."

I walk back to my suitcase and throw the items in before reaching for my shoes on the floor. "I haven't thought that far ahead. I just know that I can't stay here."

"Okay, then I'll go with you," he says, pulling my eyes to him as I freeze in place.

"What? Why would you do that?"

"I'm not going to leave you alone right now."

"Damien, you're not my boyfriend, and now everyone knows it. There's no need to pretend anymore. Besides, you made it pretty clear with your dad how you feel about me."

His face falls. "And how exactly do I feel about you?"

"It's okay, Damien. You were really good at pretending. Hell, you even had me believing this was real for a moment, but here's the thing," I say, glancing up at him to see anger written across his features. "I'm not the right girl for you, right? I'm too much and will always be too much."

"God, you're the most stubborn woman I've ever met, Charlotte!" he shouts, startling me. "You can't even see what is right in front of you!"

"I know what I see! I see a cluster fuck, Damien! That is my life right now! I just told off my mom and your father in front of everyone we know. And you just punched your father in the face!"

"Well, he fucking deserved it!"

"And this thing between us? It was always temporary. That's what we agreed to." I zip up my suitcase and start pulling it toward the door as the walls I tore down start to resurrect.

"We also agreed to orgasms and food, which you had no problem collecting on when it helped you avoid your problems, huh?" I falter in my steps from his words. "I thought you were going to let me in, Charlotte. I thought you had. Have the last six weeks meant nothing to you?" He holds out his hands at his sides, his face pained and angry.

I shake my head, fighting back more tears. "I can't do this right now, Damien. I can't fight anymore."

"Then you're not the girl I remember you being. You used to fight me on everything."

"I just don't have any more fight left in me right now," I whisper, turning back toward the door until another thought reappears. "One more thing though," I say as I spin around real fast. "Were you ever going to tell me about your dad?"

He clenches his jaw as he glares back at me. "Why do you even care at this point?"

"Why do I care?" I scream. "Because our entire childhood was a product of his need for you to beat me. That's why we hated each other? Because your dad couldn't handle the idea of a woman beating his son? And you played along with it?"

"You're not the only one with a parent who's hard to please remember, Charlotte?" he replies, and his words from the first night in his apartment ring a bell.

But it's too late. Too much has happened, and I'm ready to be done with this all. I'm ready to get back to my life and job, and those things don't involve him *or* my mother anymore.

"Yeah, but this is different. You lied to me after you promised that you wouldn't again. You kept this secret while we were… This is…"

"This is bullshit and you know it. You're running away right now instead of facing your problems." He points a finger at me. "We could talk this out like adults, but you're cowering instead of owning up to your actions and giving us a chance."

"Well, it's what I did twelve years ago—ran away from all of my problems at home—so maybe it's just what I know." With tears streaming down my cheeks, I pull open the door and take one quick glance back to find Damien standing there, his face unreadable as I wait for him to say something.

But he doesn't—and if that isn't a clear indication of where he stands, then I don't know what is.

Chapter 18

Charlotte

I unlock the door to my apartment and breathe a sigh of relief once I finally enter my home. The last two days have been draining and long and not without their frustration.

After I left Damien in our room, I ordered an Uber and took the ride to another resort on the other side of Oahu. My phone would not stop ringing or pinging with notifications, so I eventually texted Noelle, told her I was safe but wanted to be left alone, and then turned my phone off.

And I haven't turned it back on since.

I was able to switch my flight to leave Monday afternoon instead of Tuesday morning with everyone else, and now it's past eleven and I am exhausted.

As I take my suitcase to my room and prepare to sleep to avoid my problems, I figured I should at least let someone know that I'm home. But as I stare down at the black screen on my phone, I think about how blissful it's been with no one bothering me. And the truth of the matter is, I don't want to face the repercussions of my actions just yet. I'm not even sure how to go about solving any of the problems I created; ruining my parents' vow renewal, admitting that mine and Damien's relationship was a lie, and wrecking a trip that was supposed to be a vacation and celebration for everyone. Not to mention, how I left things with Damien.

The look on his face, his words, and the truth he spewed, it's been haunting me for the past twenty-four hours, and I wish I could just forget it too.

Knowing I can't avoid my life forever, but I can at least put it off until the morning, I turn my phone on, ignore all of the notifications that pop up, send Noelle a quick text letting her know that I'm home, and then turn it right back off. Then I head for the shower and leave my suitcase to unpack another time. My eyes are dry and swollen from crying, my heart is aching in my chest, and my head is pounding from the mess I created that keeps spiraling through my mind.

But my bed is calling my name, and that is the only call I will be answering presently.

"Good morning, Helen," I say Tuesday morning as I walk into my office and see my assistant stare up at me like she's seen a ghost.

"Charlotte? What are you doing here?" she asks around a bite of her blueberry muffin, wiping her mouth quickly as she finishes chewing.

"Well, I came home earlier than expected and decided to come back to work instead of wallowing around my apartment."

"Uh oh. That doesn't sound good. Does it have anything to do with the video?"

I freeze as my heart gets hit with jumper cables, speeding up its steady beat. "What video?"

Helen's eyes grow bigger. "Oh, God. You haven't seen it?"

"Seen what?"

Helen grabs her phone and holds it to her chest. "It's nothing."

"What the hell are you talking about, Helen?" I reach for her phone before remembering I have my own. I was so stubborn about refusing to turn my phone back on that I used my actual alarm clock to wake me up this morning instead of the alarm on my phone.

Digging through my purse, I locate my cell and turn it on, waiting for it to wake up before the screen starts flooding with notifications. There are about a hundred missed calls, fifty text messages, and social media notifications up the ass, but nothing from Damien. And my heart deflates with that realization, although I don't really blame him.

I start scrolling through the most recent text messages.

Mom: Charlotte! We need to talk! Call me or your father right now! This isn't a joke. Please call us, sweetie.

Noelle: Are you sure you're okay? We'll be home tomorrow and we'll stop by once we land and get out of the airport.

Penelope: I'm so fucking proud of you! And look, you're an internet sensation. *link

I click on the link that Penelope sent, which leads me to a social media app where people upload random videos all of the time. And then I see my face, my dress, and hear the words I spewed in front of the entire wedding reception.

I gasp, covering my mouth with my free hand as I watch the entire altercation play back right in front of me—me screaming at my mom, me telling off Damien's dad, and Damien punching his dad in the face before I ran off. Watching my outburst immortalized on the internet for anyone to watch has my stomach dropping over and over again.

"Oh. My. God." My entire body is numb and I seriously feel like I'm going to pass out.

And then I look at the views—over three million people have viewed it, and one million people have liked it.

"What the fuck?"

"I take it you didn't know," Helen says shyly, staring up at me from her seat.

"No! How long has this been up?"

"Since yesterday sometime. It's gone viral, honey, and I can only imagine it's a matter of time before the boss rolls in here."

"Oh, she's already here."

I spin around to find Trina standing in the doorway to my front office where Helen's desk is. "Trina, I had no idea…"

She holds up her hand, cutting me off. "I figured as much. I doubt any self-respecting businesswoman would agree to let something like that get plastered all over social media."

"Someone was obviously recording it and uploaded the video."

"Obviously." She rolls her eyes. "But here's the problem, Charlotte, this is bad. Bad for you and bad for the magazine. People know who you are, and clients are going to be running for the hills if we don't spin this the right way or get it taken down."

"I know." My eyes well with tears. I wasn't sure how this entire situation could get any worse, but I never imagined something like this happening. "I'm sorry."

"Hey, I sympathize with you. Luckily, I grew up in a very forward-thinking, female-driven household where we were encouraged to be whatever we wanted to be. My sister is a tattoo artist, and I went into the world of magazine publishing, obviously. But we were never berated for our choices, so I can't imagine what that must be like." A part of me just developed a newfound respect for my boss that she is trying to put herself in my shoes. "However, this is a PR nightmare from a business perspective, so I think it's best that you lie low for a little while."

"Am I fired?"

She scoffs. "Hell no. We just need some time to figure out how to tackle this. Take some time off, handle your stuff, and maybe let that fake boyfriend of yours tend to your wounds."

I huff out a laugh as I wipe my tears. "He and I aren't exactly on speaking terms right now. Things didn't end well before I left Hawaii."

She shakes her head at me, tsking before she says, "That man is way too hot to let go of, Charlotte. And even if it was fake, there was nothing fake about the way he looked at you."

Her reminder of what I messed up stings, but I can't worry about that right now. "I'm so sorry, Trina."

"Stop fucking apologizing, Charlotte," she says, and I think it's the first time I've ever heard her curse. "I know you didn't upload the video. It sucks, but there are always moments in life that we'll never forget, choices we'll make that will shape us. You will never forget this, that's for sure," she says through a laugh. "But be the woman I know you are, take care of your private life, and come back to work next week when the dust has settled."

"Thank you." I reach for a tissue from Helen's desk as Trina leaves the office.

Helen stands and walks over to me. "I'm so sorry, Charlotte."

"I didn't think this could get much worse after what happened there. Boy, was I wrong."

"Not that it's any consolation, but I am damn proud of you for standing up to your mother. If I ever acted that way with my daughters, I hope they'd tell me off too."

Smiling through my tears, I pull her in for a hug. "Thank you."

"Now go. Try to stay off the internet, take a deep breath, and decide where you go from here. That's the only thing you should be worried about right now."

"I'm gonna try."

I leave my office and head out the back exit of the building to avoid reporters that have started to gather outside. Sometime in the last twenty minutes, photographers started swarming the building and the last thing I need is to fuel this fire by going off on a reporter for trying to take my picture or get a comment about the situation.

This has to be a nightmare. I can't possibly be living through this right now.

Damn the age of social media. And damn me and my loud ass mouth. I had to blow up in a public place. I had to curse and scream and act irrationally. And I had to ruin things with Damien.

However, I will say this, I felt exponentially better after getting my frustrations off my chest with my mother, so at least there's a slight silver lining after all.

"Oh, Charlotte," Noelle sighs as I open the door and see my three best friends standing on the other side. My bottom lip instantly starts trembling as the tears that have been streaming on and off since yesterday fight to come out again.

It turns out their flight home got delayed, so by the time they landed at LAX Tuesday night, it was almost midnight. Noelle insisted they could still come by if I needed them to, but the last thing I wanted to ask of them after they traveled all day was to come to my apartment. Instead, we settled for the next day around eleven, the perfectly acceptable time for day drinking to commence.

"I've got four bottles of champagne, one for each of us, and two bottles of orange juice. Will that do?" Penelope asks, holding up two very large reusable grocery bags.

"I have the best friends," I say as I open the door wider to let them all in and then close the door behind them.

"How are you doing?" Amelia asks, wrapping her arm around my shoulders.

"Oh, well, I'm somewhere between feeling like a toilet brush and gum that's stuck to the bottom of someone's shoe."

She grimaces. "Yeah, neither of those sound very promising."

"Nope. Nothing is promising right now, especially now that I'm internet famous," I bark out as I lift one bottle of champagne from the bag and start to unscrew the metal ring around the foil on top.

"Well, if you're famous now, we've got to work on your wardrobe," Penelope teases as she assesses my attire. I'm wearing my fuzzy purple robe, black sweat shorts, and a baggy t-shirt underneath that I'm sure has at least three stains, no bra, and I haven't brushed my hair since yesterday morning when I got ready for work. I'm sure I look phenomenal at the moment.

"She's allowed to look like this right now," Noelle interjects. "She's going through a crisis, and I, for one, don't know that I'd be handling it any better."

Once we all have a mimosa in hand, we settle into my couch and the two oversized chairs in my living room to talk.

"So have you spoken to your mother?" Amelia breaks the ice first.

"Nope." I stare down into my glass, watching the bubbles in the liquid float up from the bottom.

"Your dad?"

"Nope."

"Damien?" she says last and my eyes lift to find hers full of concern.

"No."

"Why not?"

"We…I didn't exactly leave on good terms with him."

"Yeah, we kind of figured since he was a bear the rest of the trip." Penelope sighs.

"Did he say anything to you guys?"

"Not really. Just that he needed to know if we heard from you, so he knew you were okay," Noelle says. "And when I told him you were, he grunted and then stormed off."

"He never called or texted, so…"

"Did you expect him to?"

I shrug. "Not really. We both said some harsh things before I left."

"Sounds like the theme of the evening," Penelope snickers. "But for what it's worth, Charlotte, I was so fucking proud of you."

I suck in my smile. "Thanks."

"No, I'm serious. Not only did you finally snap on your mom, which was gold, by the way," she laughs, "but you also told off Damien's dad, and that was like a feminist move for the ages."

"I just…I couldn't believe the things that he said about me. I overheard him and Damien arguing, and when he said I was too much and not the right woman for Damien, I snapped."

"What did he say exactly?" Noelle asks. "We couldn't hear everything from where we were standing."

My blood starts to boil as I remember everything he said and relay it to my friends.

"Well, besides the fact that he's an ass and completely wrong, I think it says something that you took his disapproval of you to heart," Penelope says.

"What do you mean?"

"Do you honestly think you're not right for Damien?"

I stare down at my lap. "I don't know anything right now," I say, taking the easy way out instead of going down that rabbit hole again.

My entire relationship with him has been flashing back in memories for the past two days. I thought I was in love with him, and then everything changed in the blink of an eye.

"Well, he looked pretty distraught on the video. I kept rewatching it, trying to pick up on more clues of how this started," Noelle says with a shrug.

"Of course you guys watched it." I take a long drink of my champagne as my buzz starts to develop.

"Hell yeah, we did. Our best friend got her sixty seconds of fame and we wanted to make sure that you were portrayed accurately." She leans forward in her seat. "You looked fabulous in your dress, by the way."

"Ha. Thanks. Only now I'm just a joke. My boss even asked me to stay home this week until it blows over."

My friends all share a look before Penelope pipes up. "Um, Charlotte, you are not a joke. Have you seen how many views it's gotten?"

"Um, yeah. Three million as of yesterday…"

"Girl, you're up to ten million today."

"What?" I almost drop my glass of champagne, but quickly recover. "Are you serious?"

"Yes." Penelope nods. "And what's even more impressive than that are the comments."

"The comments?"

"You really haven't been looking?"

"Um, no. The last thing I wanted to do was let everybody's ridicule go to my head and make me feel even lower than I already do right now."

Penelope stands from her chair and comes to sit next to me on the couch, opening up her phone and clicking on the video in question. "Look at what people are saying. You're not just famous because you blew up at a wedding. You're famous because people related to you."

I take the phone from her hands and start reading through the comments.

"I thought fake relationships only existed in romance novels!"

"I sympathize with this so much! My mother keeps pressuring me to find a husband, but I'm not just settling for some guy to make her happy."

"This just goes to show how much pressure there is on women to have it all. But whose timeline are we on? Our own, that's fucking who's!"

"You go, girl! Tell your momma what a hoe she is!"

"Female power! Keep being too much, because we need more women like you who aren't afraid to stand up for yourself!"

"Oh my God." I keep scrolling, reading more and more words from women saying that they understand what I'm saying, how I should be proud of being 'too much', and cheering me on as I cuss out Damien's dad.

"Don't get me wrong, there are some trolls on there who have nothing better to do than try to tear people down, but overall Charlotte, your story is real, it's something people can relate to, and that means something."

I slink back in my chair. "This is crazy, but it's kind of nice to know I'm not the only person who deals with this shit. And I know it wasn't the best time to explode, but I just couldn't take it anymore, you guys."

"You were bound to blow up," Amelia says. "That's what happens when you hold in feelings of frustration and anger. If you don't process them, they will come out at the most inopportune time."

"Well, I'd say I picked a doozy." I stare down at my glass as a new wave of emotion passes through me. "I thought I was a strong woman, you guys. I prided myself on being confident in who I am and what I want and feeling like I could handle anything. But dealing with my mother brings out the worst in me, and after all of this? I don't feel very strong anymore."

Amelia cuts me off. "Being a strong woman doesn't mean that you're not allowed to be human, Charlotte. Being strong doesn't mean that you're not allowed to have moments of weakness or make mistakes. Being strong means admitting when you made them and working to correct them. It means knowing when you've had enough and setting boundaries to maintain your inner peace so you can live your life the way you want to. Being strong means having people around you to pick you up when you've fallen—because it happens to everyone—and knowing you can lean on them when your plate goes crashing to the floor."

"You and your plate again," Penelope teases, which actually brings a smile to my face.

"No one is strong all of the time, and more often than not, the people that try to pretend to be strong every second of every day are the ones who are battling internal demons that no one else can see."

"You guys knew though. You know what I've been dealing with."

"We do, and that's why we were encouraging you to talk to your mom about it so something like this wouldn't happen," Noelle says.

"I know. But it did, and even though it's shitty, a part of me feels relieved. Although I keep thinking about all of the stuff I should have also said. Do you guys ever do that? Think about things you should have said in an argument after the conversation is already over?"

They all nod. "All the damn time, particularly in the shower," Penelope says.

"Right?" I laugh and then drain my glass.

"So are you going to call your mother?" Amelia asks again.

"Not yet. I need some time. She's been calling nonstop and texting. But her concern is with what people are saying and trying to fix this so it doesn't look so bad. She still doesn't think that she's done anything wrong. I just can't with her right now."

"Then let her wait. And remember, you don't have to apologize to her, Charlotte," Amelia adds. "A parent's love is supposed to be unconditional. It's ingrained from conception. No matter what mistakes their children make, a good parent knows that inherently they will be there for their kids no matter what. But a child's love for their parents doesn't have to be unconditional. Parents have to earn their children's respect and love. Just being someone's mother isn't enough to validate that love and respect. And if they damage that relationship, it's up to them to repair it. Let your mother own her mistakes."

"Thank you," I say through my tears, feeling stronger with every second of being near my friends again.

"Now what about Damien?" Penelope changes the subject.

"Ugh. I can still see the look on his face when I walked out of our suite. But he just let me, you guys. Does that mean that he didn't care?"

"I think it's the opposite," Noelle answers. "I think he cares too much. He knew at that moment that there was no reasoning with you, so he let you go to work through this on your own. He loves you, Charlotte. It was plain as day to anyone who was watching you two."

"I don't know. There were so many instances where I thought the same, but then everything happened, and it just made me question whether any of it was real."

"The only way you're going to know where he stands is if you talk to him."

"He has his pitch on Friday, though, and I'm not sure that I want to jeopardize his mental state when I'm not even sure where mine is right now." And then it hits me. "Oh, fuck."

"What?"

"The video. He's in it too. Do you think his boss has seen it?"

The girls look around at each other before Noelle speaks up. "I mean, with ten million views and both of you clearly identifiable, I think the likelihood is high that at least someone he works with has."

"Shit. I admitted our relationship wasn't real in the video, you guys, the relationship that was Damien's idea in the first place so he could secure this account he's been working so hard to land."

"Yikes."

"God, this just keeps getting worse." I stand from my seat on the couch and rush over to the bottles of champagne, pouring more into my glass.

"Charlotte, I know this probably isn't what you want to hear right now," Noelle says, "but there's nothing you can do about it at this very moment. Everything is still fresh, and until you know exactly what you want to do about Damien, you're better off just letting things be."

She's right. I know she is. I haven't processed the last week of my life yet, and until I do, there's no sense in rushing out trying to be a hero. It could make things worse. Besides, I don't even know if Damien would want to see me right now.

But God do I miss him—his sarcasm, his arms wrapped around me, the way he looked at me like I was perfect to him.

But no one is perfect, and the decisions I've been making recently are lackluster at best.

I just need some time. And hopefully, he'll give me the chance to explain myself once I figure out what I want.

And that's the question I need to answer more than anything— what do I want now?

Chapter 19

Damien

"My entire life all you did was project your vision of what my future looked like on me, and because I didn't want to let you down, I went along with it. I tried to be the best at everything, win everything, do everything, and beat out Charlotte in the process. But it was never enough."

"Damien…"

"But it's my life, it's my future. And I'm happy," I say, hitting myself square in the chest. "For the first time, I'm truly happy. I'm going after a promotion I want and I have a woman in my life that accepts me and allows me to be who I really am, even if it started out as an arrangement for us both to get what we wanted. And I'm sorry if that's not what you want for me, but that's not your decision." I take a deep breath. "I'm in love with her. And now thanks to you, she's gone."

The elevator dings and pulls me back to reality as I replay the last words I said to my father before chasing Charlotte through the court-yard of the hotel in Hawaii. And as if I didn't need another reminder of my actions, Jeffrey gives me a wake-up call as soon as the elevator doors part.

"Dude. I never knew you could throw a punch like that." He slides in front of me as I exit the elevator, back at the office after the trip that ended up being a shit show of epic proportions.

"Fuck, not you too." I step around him and head toward my office as he trails me like a lost puppy.

"Um, hello. You're fucking viral. And nice punch, by the way. Your dad shriveled up like my balls do when I step out of the shower."

"Jesus, Jeffrey. It's too early for ball talk." I unlock my door and head for my desk as I hear Jeffrey shut the door behind me. "And please don't take this the wrong way, man, but the last thing I want to do is talk about what happened in Hawaii."

"I get it, Damien. I do. But here's the thing…Dave knows."

My head pops up as I take in his words. "Fuck."

Jeffrey nods slowly. "Yup. Elizabeth fucking showed him the video. She was more than eager to rat you out."

"Jesus." I pinch the bridge of my nose, cursing the past few days, yet again, and wondering how this is going to ultimately jeopardize everything I've been working toward.

What was supposed to be one of the best nights of my life turned into one of the worst. I had every intention of taking Charlotte down to the beach after the ceremony and laying my heart on the line. I wanted her to know how I truly feel about her—that nothing I feel about her is fake. That deep down, I wonder if all those years ago I was burying feelings for her that I knew I could possess if I had only tried, if I had only had the opportunity to explore them.

But after my dad performed his one-man show and Charlotte overheard, there was no way things were going to go the way I wanted them to.

And laying him out like that? Damn, it felt good. He fucking deserved it, even though my mom was frantic as I walked away from her when I chased after Charlotte. My dad ended up staying in their room until we all left on Tuesday, and let's just say the family dynamic was tense. My parents barely spoke to one another or Charlotte's parents the entire way home. And he didn't say one word to me when I left the plane and headed for baggage claim while my parents stayed in the airport, waiting for their flight back home.

I've since spoken to my mother and apologized to her, but insisted that I didn't regret hitting my dad. She cried, wondering how on earth our relationship ended up this way. But I reminded her that his behavior, his actions, and his words are the root of the problem. I asked her if he's ever laid a hand on her since I know he had no problem doing that with me as a kid, and she assured me that he hadn't. But I honestly don't believe her, and I can hear in her voice that she's not happy. And now I'm worried that he may take out his frustrations on her, and that has me even more furious than I was when I left Hawaii.

And Charlotte. Fuck, I wanted to go after her, but at that moment, my brain stopped me. Deep down, I knew there was nothing I could say that was going to keep her there, so I convinced myself to let her go. And she was right. I did break my promise to her, something that I should have known better than to do. I didn't tell her about my dad when I should have, and for that part I take full responsibility.

I worried about her all night, though, barely sleeping and then walking around on edge the entire next day before I finally asked Noelle if she had heard from her. When I knew she was safe, that gave me a little sliver of relief, but the hole left in my chest that she dug with her words was—and still is—bleeding.

I know she fucking cares about me. I know that our relationship was far more than casual and temporary. And I know that the only way she's going to figure that out is on her own.

Knowing her since we were kids does have its advantages, and her stubborn streak is as strong as they come. I'm also trying to remind myself that she had a critical moment with her mother and that she needs to work through that as well. I worked past things with my father a long time ago, limiting contact and standing up for myself numerous times since then, living my life the way I wanted, regardless of what he thought.

But I imagine that may be different for women and their mothers—that's a relationship I won't pretend to understand the first thing about.

However, I know that I was proud as hell to see Charlotte finally standing up for herself to not only her mom but also to my dad. It only solidified what I already knew—she *is* the woman for me, the type of woman I want standing by my side because she *wants* me there, not because she *needs* me.

And there's nothing more that I want than to be that man for her.

I just don't know how to ask for that when I can't bring myself to call her.

Maybe that stubborn attribute isn't exclusively unique to her.

"Have you spoken to Dave yet?" Jeffrey asks, pulling me back to the present.

"No. But I'm sure it's only a matter of time before he stops by."

"Fuck." Jeffrey slumps down in a chair. "We're screwed. All this hard work was for nothing."

"Not necessarily. And you know what? If it is, then I'll take the fall, Jeffrey. You deserve that promotion. I'm not going to let you suffer for my poor decisions."

A knock on my door pulls both of our heads in that direction.

"I'll get it." Jeffrey sighs and then stands, heading for the door and opening it up to reveal Dave on the other side. "Hey, boss man."

"Gentleman. Mind if I have a word?"

"Of course," I say, welcoming him in as Jeffrey closes the door behind him.

"Actually, I'd like to speak to Damien alone, Jeffrey, if you don't mind." He twists around as Jeffrey stands frozen in place, his eyes bouncing between me and Dave.

"Uh…"

"It's okay, Jeffrey. I got this." I give him a reassuring nod, and then he slowly exits the office, leaving me with the man I need to face before giving me a good luck thumbs up.

"Let's take a seat." Dave gestures to the chairs situated in front of my desk.

"Sure."

As Dave unbuttons his coat and sits in his chair, he lets out a heavy sigh. "I imagine you know why I'm here."

"I think I'm aware."

Dave blows out a whistle. "Seems like your trip turned out to be more than you bargained for."

"You could say that."

"And what Charlotte said on the video? Is it true? She asked you to fake a relationship with her?"

"No, Dave. I approached her first," I admit. "I lied to you in the beginning about having a girlfriend and happened to run into Charlotte on the same day that I came up with the lie—who I actually *do* know from back home. After some careful manipulation, she agreed to the scam because it was ultimately helping her out with her mother."

He nods in understanding. "I was wondering. From what I knew of you prior to Charlotte, it surprised me to hear that you were in a committed relationship."

"I surprised myself by telling the lie," I joke.

Dave shakes his head. "You know, this leaves me in a complicated position, Damien. You lied to get ahead."

"I know. And I understand if you don't want to allow me the opportunity to pitch anymore, but please don't punish Jeffrey for my decisions."

"But he went along with it…"

"I know, but he didn't lie."

Dave stays silent for a few moments, and I have no idea what is going through his mind. But then he says, "Let me ask you something…"

"Okay."

"Did being with Charlotte—in whatever facet you were—change your view on women?"

I answer without hesitation. "Undoubtedly. Not only when it comes to dealing with a menstrual cycle—which is far more complicated than I ever realized—but more than that; it changed the way I valued companionship, in having a partner who felt equal to me, but also, that I felt protective over. Charlotte has been dealing with issues with her mom for years and pressure from society that I know men don't experience in the same way. And watching her battle all that was difficult. I don't know how she balances it all—her career, her friendships, her emotions—and still walks around with a smile on her face…"

"You love her," he says, smiling over at me.

"I do. Fuck, I really fucking do." I lean forward in my chair, bracing my forearms on my knees, struggling to come to grips with how horribly fucked up this all got. "But things didn't end well in Hawaii, and right now, we're not speaking."

"Then I say you learned your lesson." Dave stands, buttoning his coat back up. "Be ready for the pitch tomorrow. I can't wait to see what you came up with."

I look up at him. "Are you serious?"

"Yup. But do me a favor? When the pitch is over, go get your girl.

Tell her what you just told me, and don't let her go again." He nods as he walks toward the door but then turns back around with an afterthought. "You know, Erin and I would really love to have you two over again once you figure everything out."

I sit back in my chair, debating how honest I should be with him. "I appreciate that Dave, but I'm not sure that Charlotte and I are into the same things you and your wife are."

His brow furrows. "What do you mean?"

"Well, Charlotte and I know about your extra-curricular activities, and I'm not one to judge, but that is not something we are open to. I mean, hell, I don't even know if she still wants to be with me at this point."

"I'm sorry, Damien, but I'm confused. What are you talking about?"

"The pineapples," I say, widening my eyes.

"You and Charlotte don't like pineapples?"

"No." I breathe out before finally saying, "Charlotte and I aren't interested in swinging with you and your wife, Dave."

His eyes bug out, and then he leans forward slightly like he's about to fall over from shock. "What? What on earth would make you think that?"

"Uh, you have a pineapple on your front porch, which is like the universal sign of swingers, and your wife was carrying around a pink dildo the second we left your house that night. We saw her through the window." Dave continues to stand there, perplexed. "As I said, I'm not one to judge, but if you like that sort of thing…"

"Oh God, Damien! It's not what you think! First of all, my wife just really likes pineapples. We got that stupid thing in Hawaii when we went a few years ago, and then she sort of just started collecting things with pineapples on it." He tugs on his hair as he runs a hand through it. "Shit. Is that really true?"

"Yeah, that's what Charlotte said."

"Jesus Christ," he mutters.

"Well, what about the dildo that Erin was holding then?"

"Erin started doing these passion parties—that's what she calls them, at least. She sells sex toys to her friends and has to test them out first. I mean, it's fun for me," he says, bouncing his eyebrows, "but I'm sure that's what you saw through the window when you guys left. She uses the front room to show the girls and likes to close the drapes for privacy, naturally. The guys and I just end up playing poker and drinking. We all have a good time and then go home, and everyone enjoys the stuff the girls buy from Erin."

"Holy shit." I slink back in my chair once more. "I am so fucking sorry, Dave."

"Clearly, you got the wrong idea, and I'm sorry too, Damien. I swear, the only woman I have sex with is my wife."

"Good to know."

Uncomfortable silence descends upon my office as I wait to see what I should say next. That conversation just turned incredibly awkward in a hot minute.

"Okay, well, glad we got that squared away," Dave says, shuffling on his feet toward the door. "As I said, make your pitch tomorrow as planned, and then go get your girl."

"Will do. Thanks for being understanding."

"Hey, I'm a man too. I know we do dumb shit all the time. It's how we make up for it that matters."

"Good morning, ladies and gentlemen." I clasp my hands in front of me as I stare out into the sea of faces in the conference room.

Three representatives from Remedy sit to my right, followed by Dave and a few members of the board, and then Elizabeth, Ashley, and Kerissa, who are all scowling in my direction.

I hope they're nervous; after watching their pitch, I know mine and Jeffrey's is better. They relied solely on packaging and marketing tactics instead of emotional appeal, which right now I feel is worth its weight in gold, especially given what I understand about women's emotions now.

"Jeffrey and I are honored to show you what we've created for a marketing campaign for you, specifically for the feminine products you wanted us to focus on. So, without further ado, let's get to the presentation." I nod to Jeffrey to press play on the screen, bringing up the video montage that our graphic arts team helped us create before turning the lights off and returning to his seat.

"Now, without being able to test the products ourselves, we valued reviews of your customers and women close to us as evidence of the reliability of your products and hope that explains some of the dialogue choices in the video."

The girls snicker, but Dave just winks in my direction.

"Our vision is this. The commercial opens up to a man standing in the aisle where every brand of tampon and pad is located in a store, his eyes narrowed as he scans the aisles looking for the brand he came to purchase for his significant other, but he's clearly overwhelmed by the selection in front of him. To his right is a mother standing with her teenage daughter, explaining the different items to her as tears stream down her face. To his left, a woman walks up on a mission, dressed in workout clothing and visibly sweaty after a workout, reaching for a box of Remedy products and throwing them in her cart before walking away. She's clearly busy, doesn't have time to dawdle, and gets what she needs and gets out. He watches the woman leave and then turns back to the mother and daughter duo, the mother trying to console her child who obviously has just crossed over into womanhood, and the man becomes visibly distraught. Another woman strides up to the aisle, dressed in business attire, looking calm and confident as she quickly locates the item she needs and turns to leave, just as she sees the young girl." Jeffrey continues clicking through the slides as I breeze through the script I memorized over the past two days.

"The woman's features soften as she walks over to the girl, crouches down in front of her, and rubs her arm, saying *'Don't worry, sweetheart. I know this seems overwhelming and the end of the world right now. Being a girl is hard. There are so many things we have to worry about and deal with that men will never understand. But as long as you have the right tools to deal with this problem, you'll be able to focus on the things that matter—just remember to be the strong and brilliant woman that you are.'* She hands the girl and her mother a box of pads and says, *'I recommend these. As long as I have Remedy products, I know I'm protected and I can get right back to my life, to doing the things that I want.'* Then she stands and flashes a smile before turning to leave, walking briskly past the man still standing there before saying to him, *'Periods are a part of a woman's life. If you can't handle that, then you're in the wrong aisle.'* And then she walks away."

The Remedy representatives are smiling from ear to ear.

"The man watches her leave, his eyes wide with alarm, but then he pulls his phone from his pocket and places a call. *'I got what you need, babe,'* he says as he reaches for a box of Remedy tampons. *'Now what can I get you that you want.'* And then the commercial ends as he walks away with a smile on his face."

The video ends, and the screen goes black as Jeffrey stands and turns the lights back on. Dave is fucking beaming, a wave of relief and pride washes through me, and Jeffrey claps me on the back before whispering in my ear. "Nice job, man. You crushed it."

"Gentleman, that was fantastic," one of the women from Remedy stands and walks over to us. "I think I speak for the three of us when I say you surprised us and exceeded the expectations of what we could have wanted for this campaign. Your ideas are forward and celebrate female embodiment. Well done." She turns to Dave. "We want them on the account. Send over the paperwork by the end of the day so we can get this going."

The room clears out one by one after we shake hands with our new clients, leaving Dave, Jeffrey, and me alone after the girls give us dirty looks as they pass by.

"Damn, Damien. And Jeffrey. You guys did it." Dave declares proudly, shaking both of our hands. "Seems you did just need to get in touch with your feminine side after all."

"I have to give Damien most of the credit. He came up with that last-minute adjustment that helped bring it full circle," Jeffrey explains, hugging me from the side, borderline inappropriately.

I shake him off. "Thanks, man. But you and the graphics team did a great job bringing it to life."

"I tried to model the business woman after Charlotte as best I could. I think they did a pretty good job matching her ass," he says as I shoot him a death glare. "What? You said…"

"Jeffrey, stop while you're ahead," Dave suggests with a grin on his face. "This is big, guys. Really fucking big for Goldstein. Looks like a promotion is in your future soon." He winks before heading for the door. "I'll be in touch."

When he leaves, Jeffrey and I turn to each other and lock in a manly hug before sharing a handshake. "Fuck yeah, man. We did it."

"We did," I say, but my excitement is short-lived. There's only one other person I want to share this with, and I'm still not sure what to say to her.

"Just call her, Damien."

I shake my head. "I know her, Jeffrey. She'll call me when she's ready."

"But what if she doesn't? What if you never hear from her again?"

His hypothetical suggestion sinks in, but I can't accept it as truth. "I don't think that will happen. I'm trusting my gut on this one. Sometimes we have to have faith in what our heart knows. And I know that Charlotte loves me. She just needs to get to the point where she can admit it."

"Ugh. You've turned into a lovesick sap, and I fucking love it."

I laugh as we head back toward our offices. "I owe you a celebratory lunch, fucker. Meet me in thirty minutes, and we'll go out to celebrate."

"Deal."

I step inside my office, leaning up against the door after I close it and breathing out a sigh of relief. Everything ended up working out the way I wanted it to.

So why do I feel sad and defeated? Why do I feel like this moment that should feel like watching fireworks on the Fourth of July is more like watching rain cascade down a window while being trapped on the other side?

I got the account, got the promotion, and proved that my skills shouldn't be limited to one area in this job. This serves as validation—to both myself and my father—that making this choice for my future, choosing this career, was the best thing I could have done for myself.

But success doesn't feel so monumental without someone to share it with, someone that knows how hard I worked to get here.

Someone like a certain brunette that I can't get out of my mind.

My phone vibrates in my pocket and I dig it out as quickly as I can, hoping to see one name in particular on the screen. But when I see my mother's face staring back at me in her contact picture, my pulse spikes as I answer the call. "Hey, Mom."

"Damien?" she says through tears, her voice broken and her breathing heavy.

"Mom? What's wrong?"

"I'm…I'm at the police station, honey."

Red clouds my vision before panic accompanies it. "What happened?"

"Your father…he…"

"What did he do, Mom?"

"I didn't think he'd do it. I've never seen him like this…" she sobs into the phone and my gut tells me what she won't say.

"Did he hit you?" I grate out. "Did he fucking lay his hands on you, Mom?"

"Yes," she says so quietly, her voice full of shame.

"Are you safe right now?"

"I am. And he's in custody. I ran to the neighbor's and stayed there until the cops arrived. They want me to go to the hospital, but it's not that bad. But I'm scared Damien. I can't go back to that house."

"I'm coming to get you," I say, pushing off the door and heading to my desk to grab my keys and wallet.

"What? No, that's not necessary."

"Bullshit. This stops here, Mom. Either it's him or me," I say, the ultimatum leaving my lips without a second thought. "You don't deserve this, and I'm tired of letting him think he can do whatever the fuck he wants." I pinch the bridge of my nose. "I never should have let you leave with him."

"This is not your fault, Damien. But I'm clear across the country, honey."

"There are these things called airplanes, Mom."

"Damien…"

"No. I'm coming to get you, and you're flying back to California with me. He's never going to touch you again."

The line is silent for what feels like hours before she finally speaks. "Okay."

"Okay." I nod as multiple emotions run through me—anger, sadness, surprise, and more anger. "I'll find the earliest flight, and I'll call you in a bit to let you know when I'll be there. But please go to the hospital, Mom. Get checked out, and then there's evidence for the police report."

"I love you, Damien. You are the best son. I don't deserve you…"

"I love you too, Mom. Stay safe until I get there." Hanging up and feeling like a junkie as adrenaline races through me, I burst from my office door and stop by Jeffrey's office to tell him I can't do lunch anymore. He takes in my frazzled state and immediately understands.

Then I head straight for Dave's office, knocking frantically on the door.

"Damien, you okay?"

"No. Yes. I…I don't know, but I need to go out of town for a few days."

"Well, it's Friday, so will you be back by Monday?"

"I honestly don't know. And I'm so fucking sorry, but it's kind of an emergency. My mom—"

He holds his hand up. "Say no more. I get it. Go. Take care of what you need to and just keep me in the loop on when you think you'll be back."

"Thanks, Dave," I say as I run out of his office and to the elevator, only thinking about how quickly I'm going to be able to get home.

Time seems to be moving faster than I can keep up with, which is ironic considering how the past few days have felt like the longest of my life and now I wish things would just slow down for a minute. But I can't waste another minute.

Hold on, Mom. I'm coming to save you.

Chapter 20

Charlotte

"Okay, you answered the phone. That's a good sign." My Aunt Gigi's voice fills the line as I reach for my coffee cup and refill it from the carafe.

"I almost didn't. But then I saw your name and figured you'd be able to offer me some pearls of wisdom that may snap me out of this pity party I'm throwing for myself."

She laughs. "That is kind of my specialty. But first I wanted to make sure that you're okay."

I sigh, taking my coffee cup back to the couch and plopping down onto the cushion that has a permanent indentation from my ass by now. "I don't know what I am. I'm currently at home since my boss told me to lay low until this video fiasco blows over."

"Smart. But I agree with the statement they released," she says, tapping into her business-like mind frame. "I gotta hand it to them; an editor for a woman's magazine standing up for herself against male superiority and unrealistic societal expectations is good for business."

"Yes, I agreed with what they said too because, well, it's true. I was standing up for myself. I just wish the whole world didn't get to experience my toxic family dynamic firsthand while I was doing so."

"Hell, honey, you know how the world works. You're the hot topic right now, but it will only be a few days before something else comes along, and then you'll be old news."

"God hoping." I take a sip of my coffee. "So why did you really call?"

I hear her let out a breath through the phone. "Seeing you in Hawaii and watching that blow up between you and your mom made me realize I haven't been there for you as much as I should, and I'm trying to change that."

"You're busy, Aunt Gigi. I get it."

"I know, but I want you to know that I will never be too busy for you, Charlotte. You're my favorite niece in the world."

"I'm your only niece," I counter with amusement.

"True, but you're the best one a woman could ask for. I'm so damn proud of you and what you've accomplished, how headstrong and determined you are, and watching you blow up was like the equivalent of a mother watching their child take their first steps." I chuckle. "I never had kids, so I can only assume the comparison is accurate, but I'm telling you that that moment will be a catalyst that will change the course of your life and what you're willing to accept any more. No one, not even your mother, deserves to hold that kind of power over you, to make you feel any type of way for the choices that you've made in your life. You are the one that gets to decide who is in your life and in what capacity, as well as how much energy they get from you. Life is too short to surround yourself with shitty people, and there is only so much of yourself that you should give before you finally realize that what you have to offer will never be enough for some people—and that is okay."

"You should give motivational speeches for a living, Aunt Gigi," I joke through my tears.

"I'm going on the road next year. I'll make sure to send you tickets when I'm in Los Angeles," she teases right back. "I just want you to know that I love you and support you, and I hope you find peace and balance with your mother soon. I do regret not trying to repair the relationship with my mother at least somewhat, but that's my burden to bear. I'd hate for you to have to live with that too."

"I appreciate your advice. I truly do."

"Anytime, kiddo." A voice calls to her in the background. "Uh oh. Duty calls."

"Thank you for calling, Aunt Gigi."

"I promise to call more, Charlotte."

"Me too."

We end the call and then I settle back into the couch, staring at the television. I guess I could watch some movies today between answering emails and staying in the loop at work.

I head over to my television stand and suddenly, the urge to watch *The Greatest Showman* hits me. That story always puts me in a good mood; fighting for your dreams, daring to be different, never giving up even when you make mistakes. That's good shit that may help me figure out what I want to do with my life right now.

As I search for the DVD in question, I come up empty-handed and then start racking my brain for where it could be. And then it hits me— I left it at Damien's apartment.

"Damn it." A sudden wave of sadness rushes through me, but then I settle on the DVD he brought me of Matthew McConaughey rom-coms since it's already in the machine. *The Wedding Planner* starts playing, and as soon as it gets to the scene where Jennifer Lopez is in her apartment eating alone, it hits me—this was my life before Damien came back into it. In fact, I remember telling him about this parallel the night we had dinner in his apartment at the start of this arrangement.

So I guess now I need to decide if this is the life I want to go back to, or do I want to fight for one with him in it?

I think my heart already knows the answer, but my bruised ego is fighting hard to catch up.

It's officially been one week since I've seen Damien, and I'm starting to have withdrawals, craving him like I do with certain food items the week before my period hits. Going back to work yesterday helped distract me, but my mind is still all over the place. I'm sad one moment, then I feel fine the next. Then a spark of anger will build when I think about my mom, and then I'm crying again when I realize that all I want is for Damien to hold me and tell me everything is going to be okay.

He still hasn't called or texted me. I honestly don't know what I was expecting though. And the longer I go without hearing from him, the worse I think this has turned out to be.

But this morning I woke up realizing that while I know I need to work through some things, I want Damien by my side while I do. Without his support, without knowing that I have him to turn to when everything gets to be too much, my life feels empty, like it was before we reconnected, and I don't want to live like that ever again.

I guess watching romantic comedies all weekend helped me realize that I had the man I've been looking for all along, and now I need to fix things to try and get him back.

Spontaneity has never been my forte. But with every second that passes, I have an overwhelming need to see him. So I leave work after asking Helen to cover for me and stop by the coffee shop to get Damien a hot tea before walking over to his office, hoping to at least talk to him for a minute and feel him out.

I realize I've been back to work for one full day and I'm already ditching—employee of the year here.

But this is life or death. Well, more like love or agony, and today I'm choosing *love*.

When I get to the floor for Goldstein Advertising, the receptionist acknowledges me by name, letting me pass with just a friendly wave as she continues a conversation on the phone.

I arrive at Damien's door, taking a deep breath of courage before knocking, and then waiting for him to answer. But several minutes pass without any acknowledgment. So I knock again, wondering if he just didn't hear me.

Growing worried, I look down the hall to one side and see nothing, turn around and come face to face with Dave, Damien's boss.

"Jesus," I say, placing my hand over my rapidly beating heart.

But he just smiles at me, ignoring the fact that he scared the shit out of me, and proceeds to speak. "Hi, Charlotte. What are you doing here?"

"Um, I just wanted to see Damien. I brought him tea," I say proudly while holding up the cup in my hand.

"Well, I hate to tell you this, but Damien is not here."

"What?" My heart starts to pound even more.

"And I'm not sure when he'll be back. He had an emergency and had to go back home for a while."

Suddenly, it feels hard to breathe. *What kind of emergency? He went to South Carolina? And Dave doesn't know how long he'll be gone?*

I knew I shouldn't have waited this long to try to reach out to him. My God, my stomach is swaying as I take in this information.

"Oh, well, okay…"

"Just so you know," he says, "Damien told me it was his idea for you to be his girlfriend."

That has my heart twisting a bit. "He did?"

"Yes, even though I saw the video and heard what you said. But I think it was the best thing you could have done for him, Charlotte. You changed him for the better, and he knows that. So do me a favor and tell him how you feel before it's too late. I almost lost my chance with Erin years ago because I was too stubborn to admit my feelings. But I know what I saw between the two of you is real, and you'd both be fools to let it slip away."

"It was real," I whisper. Every kiss, every conversation, every moment with him was indicative of the type of relationship I've always wondered if I would find.

And I found it with him.

"Then make it real, *for real*," he says, resting his hand on my shoulder. "And another thing, Erin and I aren't swingers."

My stomach drops. "What?"

Dave laughs and takes his hand back. "Damien told me about the misunderstanding, and I talked to Erin. She and I never knew about the pineapple thing."

"Oh, Jesus." I cover my face with my hands. "I'm so sorry."

"Nonsense. It was partially our fault. Now we know." He waves his hand through the air. "Anyway, find a way to make things right with Damien, and we'll call it even." He winks.

"Deal. Thank you, Dave, for being understanding about all of this."
I go to walk away, but he calls after me before I get too far.

"He won the account by the way."

"He did?" I ask, looking back at him.

"Yup. He nailed the Remedy account pitch, and apparently, you were his muse."

Remedy... Remedy...

"Remedy? Damien was pitching to a company that sells tampons and pads?" I remember wondering about this, but never asked him about it.

Dave laughs. "Yup. And he nailed it. You obviously taught him a thing or two about being a woman during your fake relationship."

I laugh at the irony. "I guess I did. But, you know, he's taught me a lot too."

He smiles. "I'm sure he has. So make sure you can keep teaching each other things for years to come, Charlotte."

"I'm gonna try. Thanks again, Dave."

"Hey, what can I say? I *love* love. I think everyone deserves to feel the real thing once in their life. And if you're lucky, you get to help others find it too."

Sitting on my couch, I unwrap another Dove chocolate as I read the message inside. *Everything will be okay in the end. If it's not okay, it's not the end.*

"Oh, everything is definitely *not* okay right now," I mumble to myself as I chew the candy and say a silent prayer to God for the creation of chocolate. But perhaps the wisdom on this piece of foil is correct—this isn't the end quite yet.

After leaving Damien's office today, I felt lighter and heavier somehow, the weight of what happens next hanging over me like a black cloud that just keeps raining down on me even though Dave's words gave me a sliver of hope that the sun would break through those clouds soon. And my mind keeps wondering what happened that had Damien leaving town so suddenly.

I hope he's okay and that he's safe. And I wonder if he's eager—maybe not as eager as me—to get back home.

I grab my phone, debating sending him a text. At least I could break the ice, let him know that I'm thinking about him, let him know that I stopped by his office today to talk to him, but he obviously wasn't there.

Looking at the time, it's just after six here in California, which would make it past nine in South Carolina. I'm sure he's still awake, but is this how I want to reconnect with him? Via text?

As I debate what to do, my phone rings in my hand with a Face-time request from my dad, and my pulse kickstarts while I decide if I want to answer it or not. I haven't spoken to either of my parents since Hawaii, but I guess there's no time like the present to face the music.

"Hello?"

My father's face appears on the screen, the poor lighting high-lighting the wrinkles in his skin as he smiles back at me. "Charlotte."

"Hi, Dad."

"Hi, my girl. God, it's good to hear your voice and see your face."

Tears instantly form in my eyes. "It's good to see you too."

"How have you been?"

"Well, that's kind of a loaded question." He chuckles softly and nods in understanding. "Feeling a little lost and sad. Embarrassed, but relieved. Heartbroken…"

"I think we all are, honey."

Feeling more resolute in where I stand with my mother right now, I speak my truth to my dad, realizing I'm holding a grudge against him because he stood by and watched this happen.

"My relationship with my mother officially crossed the threshold of toxic, and it's not because she doesn't care; it's because she cares too much and has a shitty way of showing it," I voice honestly. "Why didn't you ever say anything to her, Dad? You've heard the things she's said to me, and you never spoke up or defended me."

"I did, sweetie. I warned her, but she assured me everything was fine. I figured the only way she'd listen was if *you* told her enough was enough."

"Well, guess what? I did, and now the entire world knows about it."

"Yes, well, that's unfortunate. But I think this was the wake-up call you both needed. You needed to stand up to her, and she needed to know that she's been wrong this entire time. Just promise me you two will work this out."

"How are we supposed to do that three-thousand miles apart?"

"Well, how about you start right now by just telling her that you still love her because she's your mom?" he says before turning the phone to the side where my mother is sitting, her face red and blotchy from crying.

"Charlotte?" I don't say anything as tears well in my eyes again, and a few slip down my cheeks. "Honey, please say something to me."

"What else do I need to say, Mom?"

"God, I'm so sorry, Charlotte. I didn't realize…"

"No, you did. Dad just said he's been telling you this entire time to back off, but you never stopped."

She sucks in her lips and nods. "No, you're right. He has. I just…"

"Listen, Mom. I love you. I always will, but I am tired of having this type of relationship with you." *God, it feels good to say that.* "And Aunt Gigi told me that you sound just like grandma did, which makes a lot of sense if that's how you grew up. But I don't want to feel that way toward you anymore, so promise me something…"

"Yes, anything…"

"Deal with your issues from your childhood and I'll deal with mine. Then don't call me until you feel that you can talk to me without degrading the choices I've made with my life."

Her lips tremble. "Charlotte…"

"I'm serious, Mom. I need some space from you, and I think we both need to talk to someone professionally. I love you, but I think it's best if we don't speak for a while until we've both had time to process all of this and how we want to move forward." Damn. *Look at me being all mature and shit, saying the things to her that I should have said years ago.*

She nods. "Okay. I can do that."

My father turns the phone back to him. "I think some space will do you both some good, but don't shut each other out forever, Charlotte. I don't want to have my two girls at war with one another. You both mean the world to me and I have faith that we can fix this."

"Maybe we can talk in a month then? Or two? Set a timeline so we have to work on this?" I suggest.

He turns toward my mother and nods. "Yes, that would be good."

"Okay. I love you both, but I'm beat. It's been a long day and I need a shower."

"Alright, Charlotte. We love you. Have a good night."

"Love you too, Dad." I end the call and then put my phone on the coffee table before bursting into tears, curling up in a ball as I realize that I finally had a mature conversation with my mother where I spoke up for myself and it felt so freeing. It sucked, and my heart feels like it's breaking even more right now, but I also know it was the right thing to do. And I can't share it with the one person I want to talk about it with. Not until I make things right with him first.

Staring up at the ceiling, I let my tears cascade down the side of my face, hoping they take some sorrow and confusion with them as they leave my body. Knowing that I'm headed in the right direction finally, I sit up on the couch, and as I look across the room, my eyes land on the notebook that Damien gave me on the carousel that night, and it hits me, that I know exactly how to show him that this was real. I just hope he gives me the chance.

Chapter 21

Damien

"Are you sure you're going to be okay?" I ask my mother as I watch her place her last piece of clothing from her suitcase in the closet in my spare room.

"Yes, Damien. I'm fine. I have my books to read, and I'm expecting a call from the attorney today to move forward with the divorce."

My mother is living in my apartment until further notice, or at least until her divorce from my dad is finalized.

Racing back home to help her out of that situation was one of the most gratifying and terrifying things I've ever done as a man. My mother was trapped in an abusive marriage—emotionally and verbally mostly, but physically as of last week—and I'd be damned if she continued to live that way anymore.

After talking to her more in person, she said my father started spiraling when they returned home from Hawaii. His drinking escalated, he grew angrier and unpredictable. My mom urged him to stop, but he wouldn't listen. And then that morning, when she called me, was his breaking point. He hit her for the first time in their marriage—at least that's what she says. Part of me wonders if he's been physical with her before, but at this point, I'm just glad she made the decision to leave him.

It didn't take much coaxing to get her to agree to move out to California temporarily while she decided what to do, but then she shocked the hell out of me on the plane when after a long bout of silence, she turned to me and said, "I want a divorce."

Honest to God, tears ran from my eyes. Talk about strength—the ability to decide to fight for your life and not let someone else dictate how to live it. My mother's strength is where I must have gotten mine from, but it took her a lot longer to realize that she had it in her all along.

"You can call me after if you need to talk to me, okay? I'll just be at my desk today going through some paperwork and the plans for filming next week."

She spins around and smiles at me, the kind of proud smile only a mother could give. "I still can't believe that my son is responsible for a commercial about tampons and pads."

I laugh, mostly out of joy for my mother smiling at me for the first time in days. "You and me both."

"Have you talked to Charlotte?"

"No."

"You know, you could be the one to call her if you wanted to. There's nothing wrong with a man going after the woman he wants…"

"I know, Mom. But I don't want to chase her. I want to know when she comes to me that it was her decision."

She nods. "I get that. But I also know that every day that you continue to wait for her is another day that you two could be together," she says with an arch of her brow as she turns her back to me and I take in her words.

After making sure she's completely comfortable, I head for work, eager to finalize the details of next week's commercial shoot. This process has been challenging and a lot more work than I realized, but I don't think I've ever taken so much pride in what Jeffrey and I have worked to create.

By lunchtime, my stomach is growling, and if I don't eat soon, my hangry alter ego is going to appear.

"What should we order for lunch?" Jeffrey asks me. "And by the way, I'm really glad you're back. Eating alone in my office was starting to depress me."

"I take it you missed me then?"

"Fuck yeah, I missed you. You are far prettier to look at than the wall across from my desk. And sitting in my office brainstorming about tampons is not a good place to be alone."

"Good to know I'm more attractive than some drywall and paint."

A knock on my door halts our conversation. "Delivery for Damien Shaw," the person announces as he steps into my office holding a rather large box full of bags.

"What is this?" I walk toward him as he sets it down on one of the tables.

"Please sign here." I sign my name on the digital handheld device, even though he straight-up ignored my question. "Enjoy." And then he's off. Well, have a nice day to you too.

"Oh, that smells good," Jeffrey says as he walks over and helps me start to unload the box. "Tony's?"

Shaking my head, I take a mental note of everything in this box— spaghetti and meatballs from Tony's, Dove Chocolates, heat patches, and a DVD with four Kate Hudson rom-coms on it, plus a box of Remedy tampons. "Jesus Christ."

"Oh shit. Is this from Charlotte?"

"It has to be." I search through the box and find a card, rushing to open the envelope as my eyes scan her writing at a furious pace.

Damien,

Congratulations on acing your pitch. I knew you'd win since you always seemed to win when it mattered for as long as I've known you —which has been forever, hasn't it? It's crazy how you can know someone for so long and yet feel as if you never really knew who they were.

The six weeks of being your fake girlfriend were the best six weeks of my life, and it's taken me the last two weeks to realize that. And the night you brought me these items, I knew that what I was feeling was no longer fake.

But since I was the inspiration for your campaign (yes Dave told me), and therefore partially responsible for your success, I was hoping you would give me the opportunity to give you my own pitch for a story that I'm working on—the story about a girl who fell for a boy and now just needs the opportunity to tell him. If you want to know how the story ends, meet me at the Griffith Park Carousel at eight tonight.

*I hope to see you there so we can both get the ending that I think is worth sharing with the world—although it seems they already know about part of our story. *winky face*

Love,

Charlotte

"Damn, she's good," Jeffrey mumbles around a bite of spaghetti. I guess while I was reading her note he already dug into my lunch. "And so is this pasta. My lord, what kind of crack is this?"

Ignoring Jeffrey, I continue smiling down at the note in my hands, feeling a breath of relief wash through me.

I knew she'd come around. I knew she just needed time.

And I know that *this* is now the night in my life that I'm never going to forget.

The day drags on even though I have plenty of things to keep me busy. But by the time I get home and tell my mom what happened, reality starts to sink in.

"You know, I always wondered if you two were really dating," my mother says, sipping on her glass of hot tea. I made a kettle for the two of us as I wait until I need to leave to meet Charlotte.

"I guess we weren't fooling you huh, Mom?"

She shakes her head. "No, not recently. I mean when you were kids."

"Really?"

"Yes. I always watched the way you looked at her. I wondered if you had a little crush, and that's why you two were always at each other's throats. Now I know that it was more your dad's fault, but I still think there were some feelings there."

I smile over at her. "Now that I look back, I think there were too. I was just too distracted to realize." She starts to cry and I rush over to console her. "What's wrong?"

"I'm just so sorry that I didn't see what was happening back then, Damien. I could have spared us so much pain and grief."

"It's okay, Mom. You were being manipulated. It's much easier to see it once you're not surrounded by it anymore."

She hugs me tightly and whispers in my ear. "Go get your girl, Damien, and keep being the man every woman deserves. Lord, knows we need more of them in this world."

While driving to Griffith Park, I keep replaying memories of Charlotte and me, particularly the last one while we were here on our date, as my nerves bounce around in my veins.

I know her note sounded promising, but what if I misread it? What if wishful thinking has me believing that this night is going to end one way while it might end in another?

With determination, though, I park my car and head toward the outcome, whatever that may be. I need to know how this ends so I can move on either way, with or without her.

I purposely arrived a few minutes late to keep Charlotte guessing, tapping into that natural instinct to keep her on her toes and make her sweat a little bit. Old habits die hard.

But the sight of her standing before me in a yellow sundress steals the breath from my lungs, and I know that will never change when it comes to her.

"You're late," she says as I stride up to her standing just outside the gate to the carousel. The sun is setting in the distance, the sky full of pink and orange hues, and only a handful of people are milling about around the park, preparing to leave. But the carousel is empty, and I wonder how she managed that.

"Were you getting worried?"

"A little," she admits as I arrive just a few feet away from her. "Hi," she says timidly, her smile and features soft despite the threatening tone of her earlier comment.

"Hi, gorgeous."

"Thank you for coming."

"Well, I want to know how this story ends. Spaghetti and meatballs are always a great way to convince me to do something, by the way, in case you need that for use in the future."

"Good to know." She smirks. "Care to join me for a ride?" She gestures behind us to the carousel.

"Do we have tickets?"

She pulls two from her bag I see slung on her shoulder. "Purchased and ready."

"Then after you," I say, waving my hand in front of me for her to lead the way. It also gives me a view of her ass that I've missed way too fucking much, so I make sure to take full advantage of the view.

I follow Charlotte around the ride until she locates the bench we sat in last time, and we take a seat next to each other, waiting for the ride to start.

"I'm more nervous than I thought I'd be," she says, rubbing her palms over the front of her dress.

"Nerves are part of the gig. After you do this a couple of times, you get used to it."

But she shakes her head at me. "Well, I only plan on making this type of pitch once in my life, so if you're ready, I'd like to begin."

"I'm all ears."

She clears her throat. "Well, you see? I need to sell this idea to someone, and I figured I would try to speak his language in order to do so."

"Is that right?"

"Are you gonna let me speak?" She narrows her eyes at me playfully, and I return her sass with a smirk.

"I guess. But it better be worth my time."

"I think you'll like it," she says, handing me something from her bag. And as I peer down and see what it is, my breath hitches.

"Is this your journal?"

She nods. "Yes. And if you'll turn to the page that's been earmarked, there's something I'd like for you to read."

I flip to the page of the well-worn book that she marked and notice her elegant handwriting, followed by the date. "This is the day…"

"Yes. The day we last spoke before we left for college and then didn't see each other for twelve years."

"And you want me to read what you wrote?"

"Uh huh. Just please remember, I used to hate you, okay? So take what I said with a grain of salt."

I chuckle and then look down at the page, being transported back in time by her words.

Dear Journal,

I came out here to get some peace and quiet, you know, how I normally do... but of course tonight Damien Shaw had to ruin it. I swear, any time I get a moment when I feel like I can just breathe, Damien is there to ruin it with his ingratiating smile and cocky attitude.

I wonder if he even knows how much I hate him, how much the sight of him makes my blood boil and my hands curl into fists, how I'm sure he gets off on competing against me just because I'm a girl and it feeds his ego when I lose to him.

It's easy to accept defeat when I know that the person who beats me is better than me—but Damien Shaw is not. Nope. He's a kiss ass, a prick with a capital P, and the person I can't wait to leave behind the most in this Godforsaken town, even though I know he's leaving for California too—a decision I'm convinced he made because I did the same. I swear, he's obsessed with me or something.

And tonight, after being bulldozed by my mother again for my choice to go to college in California, I just needed to get away—to remind myself of what life will be like without her opinions hitting me from every direction.

But no...I couldn't even have that. Damien showed up in my park, at my carousel, and during my time.

He probably knows nothing about what it's like to have a parent criticize every move you make. He probably doesn't know what it feels like to never be enough. But one day, I hope he does. I hope he realizes that there are far worse things in life than coming in second place, like being a girl who wants more for her life than just to be someone's wife and a mother, and having a mother who doesn't understand that.

Before he finally left my sanctuary, clearly pissed off about something tonight, I made him promise not to contact me, not to think about me, and pretend like I never existed—because that's what I plan to do about him.

I'm craving a world where Damien Shaw is not lurking around every corner, and I can't wait to see what that's like.

"Damn," I mutter, my heart pounding as I realize just how harsh her words hit.

"I know. When I read it back, it made me cringe. It sounds so immature, so conceited, and not at all how I feel about you now, Damien. Please remember that. Those words were written by a seventeen-year-old girl who was pissed off at the world and her mom, and you were the easy target for a lot of my anger."

"I understand that because I think that was the truth about you for me."

"And now that I know about what you've gone through with your dad, I regret that I ever assumed things were perfect for you. I now know they weren't, and I'm so sorry you've had to deal with that shit too."

I reach out and cup the side of her face. "Thank you."

She takes the old journal from me, the worn corners folding as she closes it and puts it back in her bag before pulling the new one out that I got her just a few weeks ago. "Now it's time for you to read this," she says as she hands me the notebook.

"You wrote in it?"

"I did. But only one entry because there's only one realization I've come to since you gave it to me."

With curiosity flooding my mind, I open the journal to the first page and begin reading, jolted by the first words I read on the page.

Dear Journal,

I'm in love with Damien Shaw.

I know...you're probably asking yourself 'what the fuck?' right now, and I don't blame you. Thinking of the countless times when my words on these pages would curse his name and spew hatred for his existence, it may come as a shock that the man I fell in love with is him.

But it's happened, and it's taken twelve years for me to understand why.

You see, Damien and I aren't that much different. Sure he's far more egotistical than I've ever been, but if his ego is based alone on his sexual skills, then the man can be as cocky as he'd like.

However, deep down, we both craved the same thing growing up—acceptance. While I was battling my mother with her anti-feminist views regarding what it takes for a woman to be happy—and how I wasn't living up to that—Damien was being belittled by his chauvinistic father who never saw the merit in anything he did. There was always a 'but' attached to his achievements, and apparently, he was expected to live up to the standard that I was the measure of according to his father.

We spent our entire childhood competing over who was the best, only to realize after all this time that the only people we are the best for are each other.

Damien not only values my hard work, determination, and drive, he finds it sexy. He loves that I have a job I worked hard to earn and am good at. He also loves my body, has no problem showing me affection, and makes me feel safer than I ever have on my own.

And I love how he fought his dad to pursue the career that he wanted, despite what his father deemed was best. It takes guts to do that, and I'm proud to say that the man I fell in love with chose the best path for himself. He's also ridiculously attractive, smart and hard-working, and challenges me in a way that is addicting and sexy in its own right.

So how did we end up here? In love with one another?

Well, that may take some time to explain. But right now, all I need is to make sure that the man who asked me to be his fake girlfriend might still want me to be his real one.

You see, in true Charlotte Montgomery fashion, I let fear get in my way—fear of telling my mom how she made me feel all these years kept me from having a healthy relationship with her. And now, fear of admitting that I fell in love with my childhood nemesis may cost me the best man I've ever been with.

I want to be brave. I want to be strong. And I want a love that you read about and see in the movies. I want to find the Matthew McConaughey to my Kate Hudson. Hell, even my parents have proven that marriages can stand the test of time, though, I'm still not sure how my father has put up with my mother all these years.

But I feel like Damien is that person for me. He understands me, appreciates me, and deep down, I believe he loves me too.

I just hope it's not too late for us to get our happily ever after.

I hope to be writing again soon with an answer to this question, and Damien beside me.

After all, I didn't settle for a spark. I stoked a fire that had been ignited since we were kids, and by doing so, found the man I'm supposed to be with for the rest of my life.

I shut the journal when I see I've reached the end just as Charlotte moves to speak with moisture in her eyes. "I'm never going to be the perfect woman, employee, daughter, or mother, because lord knows I didn't exactly have the best example to go off of. But I really just want to be a good person, and part of that begins with making things right with you." She looks up at me, and all I see is the soul of the woman who has captured mine. "I'm sorry, Damien, for so much, but mostly for pushing you away when I know all you wanted was to be there for me."

"I don't want you to be perfect, Charlotte. I've always just appreciated you for who you are—tenacious, driven, beautiful, loyal, and strong. You are so fucking strong for putting up with what you have from your mother all of these years."

"You're strong too, Damien. Your dad," she says, shaking her head. "I had no idea what you were dealing with on your side of everything."

"But look at us, Char," I say, cupping her face and drawing my thumb across her cheek to swipe away her tear. "Look at how we thrived despite those obstacles, despite being told we weren't good enough by the people we were supposed to be unconditionally loved by." My eyes latch onto hers, and at this moment, I see my future staring back at me. "God, I love the way you look at me," I say, stroking her cheek still.

"How do I look at you?"

"Like I'm not the boy you once hated, but maybe the man who could be everything you've been looking for."

And then she finally says the words my heart has known for far too long. "I love you, Damien," she breathes out as I feel the weight of the past two weeks lift from my chest. "I love you so fucking much and I'm just so sorry for everything leading up to this moment."

Chapter 22

Charlotte

Damien's lips turn up in the widest smile I've ever seen from him, and instantly I know that this was all worth it. "I love you too, Charlotte." He rests his forehead on mine and exhales. "And don't be sorry, babe. I wouldn't change our story. You're the one for me. It took me twelve years to figure that out, but I know it's true, deep in my gut. I love you more than anything."

Not another second passes before I press my lips to his, savoring his kiss—that I've been missing every day—and the feeling of being enough for him. We may be scarred internally from self-doubt and seeking acceptance from others, but at least I know that Damien will always accept me. He may have been the person I swore I would never think of again, but now he's the man I can't live without—my own enemy turned lover—and I couldn't be happier.

The ride begins to spin slowly as our mouths move over one

another and he pulls me closer, holding me in his arms as I drown in him.

"I missed you so much," I mumble against his mouth.

"I missed you more, but I knew you needed some space."

I shake my head at him. "You act like you know me or something." He laughs. "But you were right."

"I do know you. And even though it was killing me, I had faith that when you figured out what you needed to do, you'd come to me." He lifts his hand and cups the side of my face. "I love you, but you are one stubborn woman. But I also know that a lot happened that you probably needed to work through."

"I wanted to see you last week but you were gone."

He breaks apart from me, staring down into my eyes. "I know. I had to go help my mom. She's actually living with me for a while."

"What happened?" Damien spends the next few rotations of the carousel telling me about how he raced home to help his mom when his dad snapped on her. "I'm so sorry, Damien, but thank God you went back there and she realized what was going on now—the mental and emotional abuse he's been using on both of you."

"I know. He's never touched her until now. And when I saw him, it was all I could do not to punch him again."

"You're such a good man," I tell him as I cup his jaw, rubbing my thumb along his beard.

"It's important to me to be one after what I witnessed from my father."

"I know." I place my hand over his heart. "I know and I see that. No man has ever done the things you did for me. No one has ever made me feel what you make me feel."

"You've allowed me to feel love, Charlotte. There's no better feeling than that, babe." Pressing a kiss to my forehead, he pulls me into his arms again. "What ended up happening with your mom?" he asks. Reliving the past few weeks in regards to that brings us to the end of our ride. "I think it's smart that you take some time apart, and therapy will help. I saw a counselor back in college when I got out here. I didn't want to live feeling like my dad still had control over me, and understanding what happened helped me move forward and draw lines in the sand with him."

"I know I need to work through it."

"Well, I'll be here every step of the way. You're going to have a hard time getting rid of me ever again"

"Ditto." I pull his lips to mine again as a security guard walks past us.

"Time is up, Charlotte."

Damien cuts off our kiss. "You're on a first-name basis with the security guard here?"

"Turns out a Snickers bar is security guard catnip." Damien picks up my bag for me and walks me to my car. "So I guess a reconciliation at your place is out of the question?" I joke.

"Yeah," he says with a pained smile. "Just for a little while until she gets on her feet. She wants to get a job and take care of herself, but I know she's also fragile right now, and I don't want her to feel like she has to leave."

"Understandable. I'm just happy that she has you." I wrap my arms around his neck, pressing my chest against his. "So my place it is, then?"

Damien crowds me against my car, pressing my back into the metal and lining up his body against mine as heat builds in my core. "Do you think you're getting lucky tonight, Charlotte?"

"I mean, orgasms and food were part of the deal," I reply with a shrug of my shoulders and a smirk on my lips.

"You bring the food then, and I'll bring the orgasms."

A moan escapes my lips as I feel his erection press into me. "Will

Dove chocolates suffice?"

"Only if I get to melt them down, spread them all over your nipples, and lick them off."

"Oh! I read about that in one of Noelle's romance novels once. It was hot, *and* there was peppermint in the chocolate."

"Then let's bring all of your fantasies to life, babe. I want to do everything with you, Charlotte."

I pull him closer. "The only fantasy that I care about is the one where I find a man that loves me unconditionally. And thanks to you, Damien, that fantasy is now a reality."

Four Months Later

"This event is insane." Noelle brings her champagne to her lips as her eyes move around the room. Fabrics and decorations in gold and white cover every surface around us, sparkling in the light.

"I know. And now it's making me even more nervous for my speech." Clutching my glass tightly in my hands, I scan the room, looking for the rest of my friends. But then my eyes lock on a man walking toward me, and suddenly my nerves start to dissipate.

Damien strides across the banquet hall while buttoning his jacket, his smile growing wider as he makes his way over to me. His blue eyes stand out against his dark features and full black suit, giving him a James Bond look that is definitely working for him, and my body still reacts as strongly to him as it did six months ago.

"Hi, sweet pea," he says as he kisses me on the cheek. And even though I initially hated the pet name, it reminds me of how far we've come, so I don't fight it anymore.

"Hey, babe. Where's your mom?"

"Oh, she'll be here soon. Theo wanted to pick her up himself and for them to ride together."

Damien's mom recently started dating someone, a man she met through a group she started attending once a week for divorcees in their fifties. My boyfriend acted as the protective man that he is when she first told us, but the happiness radiating off his mom convinced him that this was a good thing. She was moving on, healing through therapy, and starting a new life out here, and that made Damien happy.

His father agreed to move forward with the divorce after Brenda threatened to press charges against him. He didn't want to tarnish his name and reputation any more than was already done, so he's been quite amicable. But Damien and his mom haven't spoken to him much since she left. And everyone is happier that way.

His mom is still living in his apartment though, but Damien spends most of his time at my place anyway, so there's been no rush for her to move. She's been working at Frankie's Diner, making her own money for once in her life, and says she feels more fulfilled waiting tables than she ever did being married to Derek. And even though she doesn't need the money because of alimony, my friends and I make sure to tip her generously on Sunday mornings when we have brunch.

"They are so cute together," Noelle chimes in as we see Brenda and Theo walk through the door, her reaching out to straighten his tie as they walk toward us. "But sadly, it just serves as a reminder that I'm still single. Please tell me I won't be fifty before I find my person. No offense to your mom, Damien, but I can't wait that long."

"There's no way, Noelle. He's out there. You just have to be patient," Damien says, pulling me closer to him. "And remember, keep an open mind. You never know who the love of your life could end up being," he says, staring down at me with reverence in his eyes. "It could be the one person you thought you'd never think of again."

"Never say never, huh, babe?" I press a kiss to his lips and then turn just in time to see Penelope and Amelia gliding over to us. "You made it!"

"Barely. Traffic is a nightmare around the Morgan Hotel because of this event." Penelope kisses my cheek and then Noelle's.

"Amelia? You doing okay?" I reach out to stroke her arm, not sure what state she's in right now. One of my best friends is very fragile at the moment.

"What? Oh yes, I'm fine. Here to celebrate you, Charlotte. This is so exciting." She plasters on a mask of enthusiasm, but I can tell she's conflicted underneath. And I sympathize with her, knowing what it felt like when Damien came back into my life. I can only imagine how it must feel to have the man you fell for deny what you both know.

"Thank you all for being here. We're just missing…"

"I know you were waiting on me for the night to truly begin!" A boisterous laugh comes from behind us as I spin around and see Aunt Gigi standing with her arms spread wide.

"Gah! You made it!" I run up to her, hugging her like my life depends on it.

"Of course! It's not every day that my niece is named a Mover & Shaker in the city of Los Angeles. I wouldn't have missed this for anything, Charlotte."

"Thank you."

Aunt Gigi pulls me aside once she's greeted my friends and Damien. "Have you heard from your mom?"

"Yeah. She sent flowers today and her congratulations. But, things are still strained."

"Just give it time."

Like we agreed, my mother and I didn't speak for almost two months. In that time, we both started seeing a therapist separately and then together for one session every two weeks. Last week, we dove into some pretty heavy topics, but I feel like we're making progress toward healing. Things are far from perfect, but we're moving forward, which is all I can ask for right now.

"We are. She asked if she could come, but I told her no," I say, shaking my head. "I'm just not ready for that yet."

"And you have every right to say no, Charlotte. Remember, boundaries are okay." Squeezing my hand, she leads me back to Damien and my friends. "Seems your man is taking care of you though."

"Damn right I am," Damien replies proudly, clutching my waist. And I smile, knowing how well he took care of me this morning to calm down my nerves. It's amazing what an orgasm can do for anxiety. Perhaps pharmaceutical companies should try marketing that instead of pills?

Just then, a voice comes over the sound system. "Ladies and gentlemen, if you could please take your seats. The event is about to start."

"Anyone need more champagne?" Noelle asks our group. After collecting a count of our hands, she finds a server to deliver a tray full of glasses to our table right in front of the stage before the host of the event starts speaking at the podium.

"Tonight is about celebrating women and men who are making waves in Los Angeles this year, whether that be in their careers or through social media. And hey, some are doing both." The crowd laughs. "The first nominee knows a little about this. Please help me welcome Charlotte Montgomery, Senior Advertising Executive for Revision Magazine, to the stage."

Applause rings out as I stand and brush my hands down the front of my black dress, inhaling oxygen deeply so I don't pass out.

"You got this, babe." Damien winks up at me as I squeeze his shoulder before making my way up to the stage.

"Thank you," I speak into the microphone as the applause dies down. "Honestly, I'm not sure I belong up here. But when the mayor of Los Angeles calls you and says he'd like to honor you for making a difference in the community, you smile and say yes." I look out over the audience, zeroing in on my friends. "The truth is, this year I have learned more about myself than I ever realized. Stepping into your thirties brings a clarity with it that gives you permission to be who you want to be. A very wise friend of mine compared our lives to a spinning plate." I glance at Amelia as she smiles. "As it spins, it naturally teeters toward one way or another as it seeks balance to keep moving. Every direction it tips can be labeled as an aspect of our lives that can feel off-kilter at times, but the key is finding a way to make you feel like you can continue to spin."

"This year I've realized that I can handle anything that comes my way as long as I have a support system behind me—good friends, supportive family, and lucky for me, a man that loves me unconditionally." I stare back at Damien as love floods my chest. "I may have become an internet sensation for snapping on people who doubted me, but in my life and career, I've connected with people who have experienced the same things, and I promise to continue to be a voice for women through Revision Magazine. You are never alone. Being a woman is not easy. We battle opinions and doubts at every turn, but oftentimes, the doubts we're hearing the loudest are coming from within ourselves. However, I want women to realize that there is always someone you can talk to or someone going through the same things as you. And if you let them in, you might just find everything you've been looking for to help keep your plate spinning. Truthfully, I feel like my life has been shaken this year, but for the better. And if I can help inspire people to do the same through the magazine or a viral video on the internet, then I'll consider myself lucky and keep moving forward toward a better me. Thank you."

I step down from the stage, feeling relieved and honored that my story has inspired others, but grateful that at the end of the day, I feel stronger than I ever have because I found the capacity to stand up for what I want and who I am—and there's a freedom in that which has changed my life for the better.

Once the event has finished and I say goodbye to my friends and our family, Damien and I share an Uber back to my apartment with anticipation in the air. His hands danced along my thighs all night as we sat at our table throughout the event, hinting at the promises he inadvertently made to continue our celebration once we were alone.

As soon as the door to my apartment closes, Damien presses me up against the wall. "I'm so fucking proud of you," he says as his lips hover over mine.

"Thank you."

"And I love you. I love the woman that you are, what you stand for, and how strong you've become." He places his hand over my rapidly beating heart. "You are the only woman for me, Charlotte."

"You are the only man for me, Damien. I love you."

No other words are spoken as he locks his lips with mine and leads me back to my room, stripping us of our clothing before we fall into bed.

With no hesitation, Damien slides into me, pulling me flush against his body as we writhe and moan and make love to each other. And just when I don't think I could feel any closer to this man, we reach our release simultaneously, and collapse in each other's arms.

"I need something sweet," I mumble against his chest as we lie in bed under the covers, sated after two very powerful orgasms. Fall has descended upon southern California, so the air coming through the slightly cracked window has a bite to it that requires a heavy blanket at night.

"You didn't eat the cheesecake tonight?"

"No. I wasn't very hungry. But now, I need some chocolate." I move to stand from the bed, but Damien presses me back down.

"Chocolate makes everything better, right?"

Chuckling, I pull his lips to mine. "Right. Glad to know you've been paying attention."

He grins. "I'll get it. You stay here."

"Okay."

Damien walks out of my room naked, and returns in just a few moments with a handful of Dove chocolates. "Will these do?"

I smile knowing that he knows me so well. "Always."

He unwraps the first one and drags it over my lips before gently placing it in my mouth as it melts on my tongue. Getting comfortable in bed again, he props his head up on one of his arms while lying on his side, watching me as I savor my favorite treat and then stick out my tongue for more.

"Still on that two piece rule?"

"I mean, I feel like it helps me enjoy them more. If I devour an entire bag, I don't appreciate the decadence as much."

He shakes his head before unwrapping the second piece and feeding it to me as well. I chew, watching him in the darkness of the room as he smoothes out the foil wrappers and places them on my chest. "I know you'll want to read these before I throw them away."

"I have to. I want to know if I'll get a quote I haven't read yet." I pick up the first one and read the words out loud. "Inhale the future, exhale the past." Taking a deep breath, I hold it in for a few seconds before releasing it slowly. "I feel like I needed that one today."

"That is a good piece of advice." He nods. "What does the other one say?" Flicking his eyes to the foil, I pick it up and gasp as I see the words written on the wrapper—*Will you marry me?*

"Damien? What is this?"

"What does it look like?" He cups the side of my face before pulling a ring from under my pillow. "Thank God this didn't fall behind the headboard." Laughing, he pulls me flush against him, our naked bodies connected from chest to toe.

My entire body begins to shake as I lock eyes with him. "Is this really happening right now?"

"Charlotte, I love you. You are the one person I never knew I could love this much. And being with you for the past six months has been the best part of my life so far, hands down. But now? I want to spend the rest of my life making memories with you, new ones that are our own, that aren't tainted by our past." Tears build in my eyes as the outline of Damien grows fuzzy before I blink them away. "I want to prove I'm the man that deserves you. I want to buy you tampons and pads when you're on your period, but also hold you to help you feel better. I want to support and encourage you in anything you choose to do with your life, and I want to prove that I can give you more orgasms than you can give me." I laugh as I choke back a sob. "I also want to prove that on the other side of trauma, there's healing and love. And I want to create a life with you, have kids with you that have your smile and my wit, and sing the songs to *The Greatest Showman* with you until we take our last breaths." He draws in a shaky breath of his own. "Will you marry me?"

He holds out a princess cut solitaire ring between his fingers, but I don't stare at it too long because the sight of the man in front of me is the most beautiful thing I see right now. He's the only thing that matters in this moment—the man that I thought I hated is now the one I don't ever want to live without. I can't believe that we've ended up here, but the possibilities in front of us are the only things I see now and I want them all with Damien Shaw.

"Yes," I manage to squeak out as he gently places the ring on my finger, and that's when I stare down at it before telling him, "I want all of that with you too. I love you so much."

"I love you more, Charlotte."

"Never," I counter back.

"Never say never, babe. We're proof that what you think you know can always be proven wrong."

THE END

Thank you SO much for reading Never Say Never! If you enjoyed it, please consider leaving a review on Amazon and/or Goodreads!
And would you like a peek into Charlotte and Damien's future? Get an extended epilogue HERE!
And get ready for Amelia and Ethan's story next! Pre-Order it HERE before it comes out this Summer!

Acknowledgments

THIS BOOK.

I stepped away from another story I was writing because this idea popped into my head and my heart started to race. I got excited again at the prospect of creating something unique, fun, and the type of story I want to read, and I'm so glad I listened to my gut.

This book consumed me while writing it. It was like watching my favorite movie and laughing out loud at all of the parts that were funny, cringing at the parts that made my heart hurt, and swooning when the hero and heroine got their happy ending. It was magical, and exactly the type of feeling I was looking for again after finishing the California Billionaires series last summer.

I spent so much of my time growing up watching chick flicks. The early 2000's were filled with some of the best romantic comedies of all time, in my opinion, and when I was thinking of something new I wanted to write, I thought back to those stories that I loved and got inspired.

Today, we live in a world where women have more freedom, more power, and more pressure than ever to have it all. No man will ever understand what it is like to be a woman and manage the social, emotional, physical, and mental expectations that are put on us. And so through this series, I want to explore that. I want to write women that are relatable, that you can see yourself in, that are going through things that you have gone through.

And I hope to entertain and make you proud while I do it.

Charlotte and Damien were special, but their story isn't over. You'll get more of them in the next three books in the series. And if you haven't already, make sure to download that <u>extended epilogue</u> to give yourself a little sneak peek.

To my husband: Thank you for cheering me on and celebrating my success with me as I release each book. Thank you for understanding how much joy this hobby brings me. And thank you for being my real life book husband and giving me my own true love story to brag about.

To Liz: You are my right-hand woman. Thank you for answering every phone call when I get excited about a new idea. Thank you for cheering me on and listening to me vent. I couldn't do this without you.

To Keely: Our friendship means so much to me. This book, and so many others, wouldn't be possible without you cheering me on and your support. It's amazing to me that our friendship grew from reading romance novels, but I wouldn't have it any other way. I love our video chats, and I can't wait to meet you officially this summer at Book Bonanza.

To Kerissa: I am so happy that we connected and you fell in love with my books. Now, you're one of my biggest cheerleaders and I don't know what I would do without you. This book happened because you kept cheering me on behind the scenes. And your voice messages with reactions while reading give me life! Thank you for being a supporter and friend.

To Jeanine: It has been a pleasure working with you as the editor on this book. I look forward to a long, professional working relationship for many future releases.

To Melanie: Thank you for your work and help with this book.

And for your friendship. It's rare to find people you connect with on so many levels, and we do. I am grateful to have you as an author friend, and friend in general.

And to my beta readers (Keely, Kerissa, Carolina, Skye, Erica, and Liz), ARC readers, and every reader (both old and new): Thank you for taking a chance on a self-published author. Thank you for sharing my books with others. Thank you for allowing me to share my creativity with people who love the romance genre as much as I do.

And thank you for supporting a wife and mom who found a hobby that she loves.

About the Author

Harlow James is a wife and mom who fell in love with romance novels, so she decided to write her own.

Her books are the perfect blend of emotional, addictive, and steamy romance. If you love stories with a guaranteed Happily Ever After, then Harlow is your new best friend.

When she's not writing, she can be found working her day job, reading every romance novel she can find time for, laughing with her husband and kids, watching re-runs of FRIENDS, and spending time cooking for her friends and family while drinking White Claws and Margaritas.

facebook.com/HarlowJamesAuthor
instagram.com/harlowjamesauthor

More Books by Harlow James

<u>One Look, A Baseball Romance Standalone</u>

<u>Guilty as Charged</u>

An intense enemies to lovers standalone that will melt your kindle.

<u>McKenzie's Turn to Fall</u>

A holiday romance where a romance author falls for her neighborhood butcher.

<u>The Emerson Falls Series</u>

<u>Tangled (Kane & Olivia)</u>

<u>Enticed (Cooper & Clara)</u>

<u>Captivated (Cash and Piper)</u>

<u>Revived (Luke and Rachel)</u>

<u>Devoted (Brooks and Jess)</u>

<u>The California Billionaires Series</u>

<u>My Unexpected Serenity (Wes and Shayla)</u>

<u>My Unexpected Vow (Hayes and Waverly)</u>

<u>My Unexpected Family (Silas and Chloe)</u>

<u>Lost and Found in Copper Ridge</u>

A holiday romance in which two people book a stay in a cabin for the same amount of time thanks to a serendipitous $5 bill